THE FALL OF THE GIANTS

THE DANCE OF LIGHT: BOOK TWO

Gregory Kontaxis

GK

Translation: Sophia Travlos

Cover Design: Miblart

Interior Illustration: Ömer Burak Önal

Editing: K.E. Andrews

Proofreading: Sue Bavey

PaperBack ISBN: 978-1-7397294-7-9

Ebook ISBN: 978-1-7397294-6-2

Hardcover ISBN: 978-1-7397294-8-6

To my beloved parents

Contents

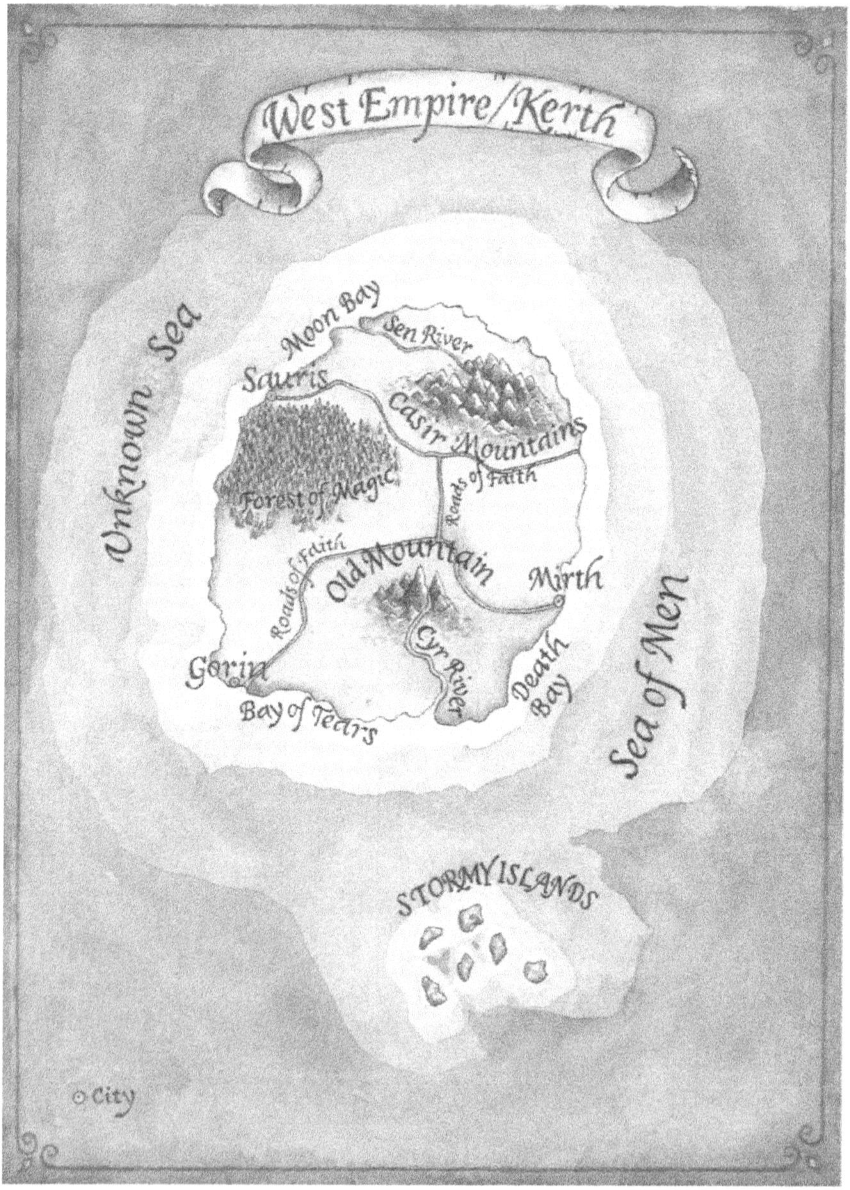

West Empire/Kerth
Unknown Sea
Moon Bay
Sen River
Sauris
Casir Mountains
Forest of Magic
Roads of Faith
Roads of Faith
Old Mountain
Mirth
Roads of Faith
Gorin
Cyr River
Death Bay
Bay of Tears
Sea of Men
STORMY ISLANDS
City

Knightdorn
ICE ISLANDS
Sea of Shadows
Forest of Tears
Eryn Bay
Minor Castle
Ghost River
Tahos
Sea of Men
Cold Sea
Pirate Bay
Mermainthor
Mermaid Path
MYNLANDS AREA
Tyverdawn
Mountains of Darkness
Stormy Bay
TAHRYN AREA
Northern Path
Northern Forest
Three Heads
Path of Shar
Relanger
Long River
OLDLANDS AREA
FELADOR AREA
Aquarine
Iron Mountain
Road of Steel
Vale of Flowers
Yellow River
East Bay
Mercenary River
Road of Elves
BALLAR AREA
Ramerstorm
Vale of Gods
Silver Bay
Goldtown
Lonely Mountain
VYLOR AREA
Mount Elwyn
Joybridge
Cursed River
Road of Elves
Ersemor Forest
Land of Fire
Mountains of the forgotten world
ISISDOR AREA
Lake of Life
Stonegate Castle
Rock Mountains
City of Heavens
Wirskworth
Forked River
ELNOR AREA
South Bay
Elves Mountain
Sea of Sun
Scarlet Sea
Castle
City
Region

List of Regions, Organizations, and Characters

Kingdom of Knightdorn

King: Walter Thorn

Royal Council/Trinity of Death: Anrai, Rolf Breandan (Short Death), Brian the Sadist

Capital: Iovbridge

Emblem of the Kingdom: Seven swords in a laurel wreath on a white field

Emblem of the queen's House: A white tiger on a red field

Regions of the Kingdom of Knightdorn

Isisdor

Governor / Ruler: Walter Thorn

Capital: Iovbridge

Faith: The Unknown God

Emblem of the region: Seven swords in a laurel wreath on a white field

Emblem of the governor's House: A white tiger on a red field

Elmor

Governor / Ruler: Syrella Endor

Capital: Wirskworth

Faith: The God of Souls

Emblem of the region: A snake on a yellow field
Emblem of the governor's House: A snake on a yellow field

Felador
Governor / Ruler: Andrian
Capital: Aquarine / City of Healers
Faith: The God of Wisdom
Emblem of the region: A golden oak tree on a green field
Emblem of the governor's House: None

Oldlands
Governor / Ruler: Ricard Karford
Capital: Kelanger
Faith: The God of the Sun
Emblem of the region: A hammer and an anvil on a brown field
Emblem of the governor's House: An axe on a brown field

Mynlands
Governor / Ruler: Launus Eymor
Capital: Mermainthor
Faith: The God of Youth
Emblem of the region: A mermaid on a violet field
Emblem of the governor's House: A mermaid on a violet field

Gaeldeath
Governor / Ruler: Walter Thorn
Capital: Tyverdawn
Faith: The God of War
Emblem of the region: A white tiger on a red field
Emblem of the governor's House: A white tiger on a red field

Vylor / Black Vale
Governor / Ruler: Liher Hale
Capital: Goldtown
Faith: The Avaricious God
Emblem of the region: A rusty coin on a black field
Emblem of the governor's House: A rusty coin on a black field

Tahryn
Governor / Ruler: Eric Stone
Capital: Tahos
Faith: The God of Rain
Emblem of the region: An old ship, *The Fairy,* on a white field
Emblem of the Governor's House: The tide of the sea on a green field

Ballar
Governor / Ruler: None
Capital: Ramerstorm / White City
Faith: The Goddess of Nature
Emblem of the region: A white hawk on a black field
Emblem of the governor's House: None

Elirehar
Governor / Ruler: None
Capital: City of Heavens / City of Pegasus
Faith: The God of Life / The God of Light
Emblem of the region: A white pegasus on a light blue field
Emblem of the governor's House: None

Regions Independent from the Kingdom of Knightdorn

Ice Islands
Leader: Begon the Brave

Faith: The Goddess of the Sea
Emblem: An iceberg in the sea

Ylinor Castle in the North Beyond the North
Lord of Ylinor: Gereon Thorn
Faith: The God of War
Emblem: A wyvern on a dark green field
Emblem of the Lord's House: A white tiger on a red field

Stonegate
Guardian Commander: Jarin
Faith: None
Emblem: A red-and-black sun, with spears for rays, on a white field
Emblem of the Guardian Commander's House: None.

Western Empire in the Continent of Kerth
Emperor: Odin Mud
Capital: Mirth
Faith: The God of Justice
Emblem: A red sun, with a white field
Emblem of the emperor's House: A shield, covered in blood, on a white field

Characters

Ador – Deceased. Anrai's father.
Adur – A giant.
Ager Barlow – Deceased. Former King of Tahryn.
Aghyr Barlow – Deceased. Former Governor of Tahryn.
Aiora – A giantess.
Alan Ballard – Deceased. Borin Ballard's son.
Alaric – An elf.

Albous Egercoll – Manhon Egercoll's brother.

Aldus Morell – A lord of Gaeldeath.

Aleron – One of the wisest people of the elwyn race.

Alice Asselin – Deceased. Aymer Asselin's daughter and King Thomas Egercoll's wife.

Althalos Baudry – Deceased. Former Grand Master of Isisdor. He is considered the greatest Grand Master to have ever lived.

Alysia – An elf.

Amelia Reis – Deceased. Lady of Elmor and Sigor Endor's wife.

Andrian – High Priest and Governor of Felador.

Annora Egercoll – Manhon Egercoll's sister.

Annys – Walter's tiger.

Anrai – Member of the Trinity of Death. His father was a giant and his mother a human.

Anton Loken – Captain of Ballar.

Aremor – Deceased. Aleron's brother.

Areos – Deceased. A former leader of the centaurs. He helped Manhon Egercoll to curse the Elder Races.

Arianna Erilor – Deceased. John Egercoll's wife.

Arne Egercoll – Manhon Egercoll's brother.

Aron – Stonegate's Guardian.

Arthur Endor – Deceased. Syrella Endor's brother and Velhisya's father.

Avery Elford – Deceased. First King of Mynlands.

Aymer Asselin – Deceased. Former Governor of Oldlands who found murdered in his sleep.

Azelor – The God of Light.

Beatrice Egercoll – Deceased. Thomas Egercoll's sister and Queen Sophie's mother.

Begon the Brave – Leader of the Ice Islands.

Bernal Ballard – Deceased. First King of Ballar.

Bert Dilerion – A lord from Felador. Eleanor's brother.

Berta Loers – Ghost Soldier. She is one of the most trusted soldiers of Walter Thorn.

Borin Ballard – Governor of Ballar.

Brian the Sadist – Member of the Trinity of Death.

Brom Endor – Deceased. Lord of Elmor and Syrella Endor's uncle.

Byron the Sturdy – Deceased. Great warrior of the Ice Islands.

Conrad Miller – A lord of Felador.

Daryn Endark – Lord Counsellor of Elmor.

Devan – Captain of Oldlands.

Doran Brau – Deceased. Peter Brau's son.

Edgar – Deceased. A former High Priest of Elmor.

Edmund – High Priest of Elmor.

Edric Egercoll – Manhon Egercoll's brother.

Edward Endor – Deceased. Former Governor of Elmor and father to Syrella, Sigor and Arthur Endor.

Edward Ewing – Man of Isisdor's City Guard.

Egil – A soldier of Gaeldeath.

Egon – A man of the Sharp Swords.

Eimon Asselin – Lord of Oldlands, Aymer Asselin's son and Alice Asselin's brother.

Eira Egercoll – Manhon Egercoll's sister.

Eleanor Dilerion – A lady of Felador. Bert Dilerion's sister. She is one of the most trusted friends of Elliot.

Ellin – Velhisya's mother.

Elliot Egercoll – A young man hailing from a village burdened by his past. He is the last apprentice to have ever been trained by Althalos.

Emery – Captain of Ballar.

Emil – A soldier of Gaeldeath.

Emil Ballard – Deceased. Borin Ballard's son.

Emma Egercoll – Deceased. Thomas Egercoll's sister, Robert Thorn's wife and Walter Thorn's mother.

Emy – Deceased. Anrai's mother.

Eric Stone – Governor of Tahryn.

Erin – An elwyn.

Erneas – Deceased. Grand Master of Gaeldeath.

Eshina – Deceased. Erin's soulmate.

Euneas Molor – Deceased. Grand Master of Felador.

Euric – A guard of Goldtown.

Favian Egercoll – Deceased. Thomas Egercoll's brother.

Frederic Abbot – Captain of Isisdor.

George Thorn – Deceased. First King of Knightdorn and Walter's grandfather.

Gerald Thorn – Deceased. Uncle to George Thorn and former Lord of Ylinor.

Gereon Thorn – Lord of Ylinor. Robert Thorn's brother and Walter's uncle.

Gervin Gerber – Royal Guard of Isisdor.

Girard – Deceased. Grand Master of Oldlands.

Giren Barlow – Slave. Aghyr Barlow's son.

Gregory Egercoll – Deceased. Thomas Egercoll's brother.

Gregory Mollet – Lord Counsellor of Isisdor.

Grelnor Lengyr – Lord Counsellor of Elmor.

Hann – Deceased. Grand Master of Mynlands.

Henry Delamere – Deceased. Former Governor of Felador and Sophie's father.

Henry Endor – Deceased. Sigor Endor's son.

Hereweald Delamere – Deceased. Former Governor of Felador and Henry Delameres's father.

Hugh – Captain of Isisdor.

Hurwig – Elliot's hawk.

Iren Selin – Deceased. Wife of George Thorn.

Iris Alarie – A lady of Felador.

Ivar – A soldier of Wirskworth.

Jackin Dilerion – Deceased. Eleanor's father.

Jacob Hewdar – Lord of Elmor.

Jahon – General of Elmor.

James Segar – Deceased. Captain of Iovbridge.

Jarin – Guardian Commander of Stonegate.

Jeanne Karford – Cousin of Reynald and Ricard Karford.

John Egercoll – Deceased. Former Governor of Elirehar. Father to Thomas, Favian, Beatrice, Emma and Gregory Egercoll.

John, the Long Arm – Former Bounty Hunter. He holds a special place of trust in Elliot's circle, being one of the people he relies on the most.

Lain Hale – Deceased. Former Governor of Vylor and Liher's older brother.

Launus Eymor – Governor of Mynlands.

Laurana Brau – Lady of Isisdor. Peter Brau's wife.

Laurent Mill – Deceased. Lord of Oldlands. He died when Lain Hale attacked to his castle.

Leghor – Leader of the centaurs.

Leonhard Payne – Healer of Felador.

Leuric – High Priest of Iovbridge.

Liher Hale – Governor of Vylor.

Linaria Endor – Captain of Elmor and Syrella Endor's daughter.

Loren Elford – Deceased. Former Governor of Mynlands.

Lothar Hale – Liher Hale's younger brother.

Magor the Terrible – Former leader of the giants. He is presumed dead.

Manhon Egercoll – King of Elirehar and brother to Thomyn Egercoll. He was one of the seven riders of the pegasi.

Maris Magon – Deceased. Lord of the Knights and Regent of Elirehar. He served as a regent of Elirehar by the time that Thomas Egercoll became king, and he kept his title after Thomas's death.

Maygar Asselin – Deceased. Former King of Oldlands.

Mehryn – Deceased. Grand Master of Elmor.

Mengon Barlow – Deceased. First King of Tahryn.

Merhya Endor – Captain of Elmor and Syrella Endor's daughter.

Merick – Captain of Isisdor.

Morys Bardolf – A lord from Wirskworth.

Myren Endor – First King of Elmor.

Odin Mud – Emperor of Kerth.

Orella – Deceased. Anrai's grandmother

Patrick Degore – Lord Counsellor of Isisdor.

Peter Brau – Lord of the Knights of Isisdor.

Philip Segar – Peter Brau's squire and James Segar's son.

Raff – A captain from the Ice Islands.

Renier Torin – Deceased. Grand Master of Ballar.

Reyna – Deceased, Morys's sister.

Reynald Karford – Guardian Commander of Stonegate.

Ricard Karford – Governor of Oldlands.

Richard Lamont – Captain of Isisdor. George Thorn made him captain when he resolved a siege by Lain Hale against the castle of Laurent Mill.

Righor – A centaur.

Robert Thorn – Deceased. Former Governor of Gaeldeath. Father to Walter Thorn and husband to Emma Egercoll.

Robyn – Captain of Isisdor.

Rolf Breandan – Member of the Trinity of Death. He is known as Short Death.

Ronald – A guard of Aquarine.

Sadon Burns – Most powerful lord of Elmor.

Saron Gray – Lord of Gaeldeath.

Selwyn Brau – Lord of Isisdor and Peter Brau's son.

Selyn – Elliot Egercoll's sister and lady of Elirehar.

Sermor Burns – Deceased. Sadon Burns' only son.

Shilor Penn – Lord Counsellor of Elmor.

Sigor Endor – Deceased. Syrella Endor's older brother.

Sindel Brau – Deceased. Peter Brau's son.

Solor Balkwall – A lord of Felador.

Sophie Delamere – Queen of Knightdorn.

Sygar Reis – Lord Counsellor of Elmor.

Syrella Endor – Governor of Elmor.

Thindor – The last pegasus of the world. He is presumed dead.

Thomas Egercoll – Deceased. Former King of Knightdorn and Alice Asselin's husband.

Thomyn Egercoll – First King of Elirehar. He was one of the seven riders of the pegasi.

Thorold – Grand Master of Elirehar. He is presumed dead.

Velhisya Endor – Syrella Endor's niece. She is the only known being with an elwyn mother and a human father.

Vyresar Tobley – Guard of the City of Heavens.

Walter Thorn – Governor of Gaeldeath and King of Knightdorn. Currently, he controls Isisdor.

Will – Captain of Ballar.

William – A Defender of the Sharp Swords.

William Osgar – Deceased. Lord of the Knights.

Wymond – Deceased. Grand Master of Tahryn.

Zehir – A centaur.

Zhilor – The God of Death.

The Story So Far

Sophie Delamere, the Queen of Knightdorn, is desperate. She has lost all her allies over the course of a seventeen-year war, and now the enemy is at her doorstep. Her bloodthirsty cousin, Walter Thorn, is ready to attack Iovbridge, the capital of Knightdorn, and take over the throne. Sophie knows she has no hope of warding off the impending siege. Everything appears to be over until a mysterious young man named Elliot makes his appearance and requests an audience with the queen.

Sophie and her councillors are taken aback at his arrival but listen to what he has to say. Elliot has a brilliant plan, which is the last hope the city has of being saved from the siege. He aims to draw Walter away from Iovbridge and face him in the stronghold of Wirskworth. He will also attempt to rekindle relations and revive the old alliance between the Queen of Knightdorn and Syrella Endor, the Governor of Wirskworth. Although Sophie's councillors are initially dubious of Elliot, a series of events make Sophie put her trust in the young man. Thus, Elliot leaves Iovbridge and rides south with four companions—Eleanor Dilerion, Selwyn Brau, Morys Bardolf and John, the Long Arm—and dupes Walter into going there.

Elliot's journey proves difficult both for himself and his companions. During their journey, it is revealed that Elliot is the son of King Thomas Egercoll, Sophie's predecessor on the throne and her uncle.

The five companions arrive in Wirskworth, and Syrella is outraged when she finds out that Elliot has drawn Walter to her city. Nevertheless, she decides to help him, going up against Walter beyond her city's walls.

When Walter's army arrives, it fails to enter Wirskworth, so Walter decides to attack the neighbouring City of Heavens. As soon as Elliot finds out, he rides there to save Master Thorold, the last surviving Grand Master in the world. In the City of Heavens, Elliot finds out about the existence of his sister, whose life is unfortunately, lost, however.

At that point, Elliot's anger becomes irrepressible, and he decides to challenge Walter to a duel. Elliot loses the fight and is about to lose his life. Just then, Syrella unexpectedly attacks Walter and his army, forcing him into a retreat. Walter loses the battle, but Elliot loses Morys, one of the companions he had sworn to protect.

After the battle, the truth about Elliot is revealed. He is the last boy trained by Althalos Baudry, the greatest Grand Master of all time. Master Thorold explains to Elliot that Walter will never forgive them for his defeat on Wirskworth's soil and will soon seek revenge. The Master advises Elliot to seek new alliances and try to free the Elder Races who are cursed to remain forever in the Mountains of the Forgotten World.

Furthermore, Thorold reveals Thindor to him, the last pegasus of the world who had been presumed dead for centuries.

Elliot is ready to start his trip to the Mountains of the Forgotten World while his friends have their own missions to achieve. Elliot advises Syrella Endor to invite Queen Sophie to her city, to face Walter behind the strongest walls in the world.

The Blue Light

Velhisya climbed out of a wooden tub and walked to her bedroom window. The moonlight glowed on her body. For a moment, her gaze fell on her pearly white form.

She looked to the sky again, and her thoughts went to a young man. She had expected Elliot to seek her out after their last meeting in the forest, but three days had passed without her seeing him even once. While her heart longed to see him, news had reached her just a while ago that Elliot had left Wirskworth that morning. Anger welled up inside her again, a mélange of sorrow and indignation. He had left without so much as a farewell, and she didn't understand why. Velhisya couldn't comprehend the emotion that had arisen the last time she had caught sight of him. An invisible fire, more powerful than anything she had ever felt before, had been ignited in her soul.

Velhisya thought back to the last time she saw Elliot, in the small forest next to Moonstone when she had felt as though all the love in the world was growing within her. Her father's image and even a blurry memory of her mother had whirled in her mind that day as if all the people she had loved wanted to embrace her. The memory lightened the anger in her heart. The sight of Elliot had stirred everything up in her, igniting a desire to hold him in her arms, kiss him, but she hadn't summoned up the courage to do so. She felt as if she had given her soul to him. Still, something she couldn't explain was missing within her. It was as if she had given Elliot all the pieces of her heart, except for one, which she couldn't give him yet.

Velhisya glanced around, looking into the void for a few moments before an idea popped into her head. *I could try... but would it even work?* she thought, hands clenched at her sides.

She moved across the room, donning a robe from a wooden table. Her eyes then fell upon an ornate sword resting on the cold floor. It was the only item she had from her mother.

The sword reminded her of her mother's fate, bringing to mind all that her father had told her just before his death. She knew that elwyn had the First Light within them and could make such blades glow with their power. *It is worth a try*. Her fingers grazed the steel etched with elaborate symbols and stopped on its cold hilt. She had never been taught the First Tongue and so the symbols were strange and foreign to her. She grasped the hilt with both hands. Time went by without anything changing.

Indignation surged through her as every injustice unfolded in her mind—her mother's fate, the death of her father, the hate-filled stares she had endured for as long as she could remember. A tidal wave of rage was ready to sweep everything away in its wake, and then a faint, blue light fanned out from the blade. Velhisya tried to fix all her thoughts on the silent rage that burned within her, but after a few moments, the light went out, refusing to reappear.

She held the sword a while longer, hoping its light would reignite until the disappointment became too much for her. She shut her eyes, fatigued. Letting the weapon drop to the floor, she returned to the window. The light of the moon caressed her body again as she realised that the feeling of sorrow was now all that nestled within her.

The Night of Memories

Elliot stared at the starry night sky, lost in thought as he sat in the shadow of the Mountains of the Forgotten World. He was in an open field and the ground under him was hard. Pain radiated throughout his body, and his legs itched. He exhaled wearily and rubbed his left foot. The pain from the bite of Walter's tiger hadn't gone away completely. He had wanted to leave Wirskworth right after his meeting with Thorold in Ersemor to reach the mountains as fast as he could. However, his injury had not allowed him to leave as soon as he wanted to. Thorold had advised him to wait, and so he had left the city three days later.

Exhaustion had clung to him ever since he had set off, and the hardship that awaited him would be a lot greater. This journey would not be easy, just like all the journeys he had taken in his short life. His horse, his sole company, had parted from Elliot when he decided to let it go since it would no longer be of any use to him in the mountains. Sitting in the wilderness, horseless and without his companions, Elliot felt the weight of how alone he was.

The slopes of the mountain range were dry, made up of hard rocks and boulders, and there were no pathways leading to the peaks. Master Thorold—the man who had raised his sister secretly in the City of Heavens—had told him that the Elder Races lived in the highest part of the jagged range, which was located on the tip of the central peak. He had to find these creatures. Thorold had insisted that they needed the Elder Races to have a hope of defeating Walter.

Hunger pangs rumbled through his stomach. He reached into his woollen bag and took out an apple. Elliot bit into the red skin and the sweet juices wet his lips. The wind was strong that night, and Elliot glanced at the long sword and the blue cloak with the pegasus that lay next to it. His mind wandered to the plate armour that Selwyn had given him before they set off on their journey to Wirskworth. Now, Elliot had decided to travel without armour. Selwyn, Eleanor, and John took over his thoughts. His former companions had told him they would leave Wirksworth without delay, as soon as he had gone...

He turned his gaze to the stars. Soon, his cousin Sophie would abandon the throne of Iovbridge. Elliot knew that the decrees of Thomas Egercoll ordained that the royal title ceased only upon death. Although he understood why Thomas had set the law that way, no decree would protect the title of a king who had abandoned Iovbridge, and that would complicate things more as soon as Sophie reached Wirskworth. The thought of his cousin brought him some serenity for a moment until he remembered the attempt to murder her some weeks ago. Gervin's blade, the traitor of the Royal Guard, had come too close to the queen. He was lucky that the guard hadn't been wearing any armour that night. Elliot had thrown his sword at him—he had hurled it at him like a javelin. If Gervin had been wearing armour, the sword wouldn't have been able to pierce it.

Panic clenched his chest, and Elliot tried not to worry about Sophie. Althalos crept into his mind and a new surge of emotions overtook him. *Why did you leave me in the dark?* he thought for the umpteenth time.

It had only been a few days since he had found out the truth about Selyn, his twin sister, but the fury he felt toward his old Master had begun to subside. Elliot had tried hard to excuse Althalos' actions and to his surprise, he had succeeded. If he had known about Selyn's existence, his only concern would have been to find her, disregarding his training. The bitter truth was that he would have preferred Althalos to have told him everything, even if it had put the future of Knightdorn in jeopardy. Nevertheless, there were times when his rage about all the things his

Master had hidden from him flared up, and when that happened, it was difficult to tame it. Elliot had hit tree trunks with his sword trying to release this anger.

Once he started thinking about Sophie and Althalos, thoughts of everything else began bombarding him—the centaurs, Aleron, Sophie, his companions on their way to Elmor, his sister, even a dark image of the only memory he had of his mother came to him. Countless memories paraded by his mind's eye until Thindor's form emerged. The snow-white pegasus with its golden eyes and large silver-flecked wings looked at him from afar with a regal air.

Will I ever manage to become his rider?

Elliot didn't believe he would, and the last few days were ample proof that he was not worthy of doing so. His imprudent choices had led Morys to his death, and he would never forgive himself for that.

Elliot finished the apple and threw the core to his right. He took one more glance at the tallest point of the long mountain range and something grabbed his attention. Some stars were so bright that they seemed like small moons.

Two starry-blue eyes came to mind. He had wanted to see Velhisya before he left, but he hadn't found the courage. Elliot couldn't remember feeling that way before about anyone. He knew he had to direct all his attention to his mission and if he had faced her again, he feared he would have decided to stay in Wirskworth.

With his mind filled to the brim, he was sure that he wouldn't manage to sleep, but one last memory appeared—that of Velhisya looking at him as they danced around a majestic hall. He closed his eyes and his body relaxed as he was enveloped in a veil of dreams.

Separate Paths

A strange heaviness clung to Selwyn as he rode behind his companions, their brown horses plodding a few yards ahead. Dusk settled over the landscape as they continued along the Road of Elves. They had decided to avoid the road that went through Stonegate. Walter would soon return to White City, which would make their journey to the north difficult if they travelled along the east road. Selwyn knew that Thorn and his remaining cavalry were still on the Road of Elves. However, they were more than ten days ahead, and were not in danger of coming across Walter's men. Moreover, Sophie would not delay in reaching Elmor. Almost eight days had gone by since the queen had sent a letter via Elliot's hawk to Syrella, informing her that she was travelling southward. Eleanor had told them that she didn't want to come across Sophie on the eastern path. She knew that the queen would not have let her leave for Aquarine. Selwyn's destination was Goldtown, and the western road was a lot faster to reach there.

Eleanor's black hair bounced on her shoulders as she fixed her gaze on the Road of Elves. She was dressed in brown leather, and a crossbow hung on her back. She was the only one who wore a cloak. Its material was blue like the waters of the sea, and the breeze made it flutter behind her.

The young woman was often silent since the death of Morys. It had only been a few days since they had last seen him, but to her it felt like an eternity. Selwyn had expected them to bury Morys, but he had been cremated two days after his death. His family had wanted this rite to take place sooner but the battle at Wirskworth had brought turmoil to the city, resulting in delays. Morys' mother had explained that their family preferred to purify their bodies in flames after death.

Ahead of her, John "Long Arm" was drinking wine from his flask while riding his mare, dressed in a pine-coloured, leather waistcoat with a small sword hanging from his waist. Selwyn flicked the reins, and his horse was soon next to Eleanor's. He knew that he would soon part with her and Long Arm. Nevertheless, that wasn't what scared him.

Selwyn straightened in his saddle while a few warbling sounds reached his ears. The song of the birds seemed like joyous news, but it was not enough to save him from his dark thoughts about his brothers and Morys.

So, what happens after death? he thought. It was one that often echoed in his head as of late.

His brothers hadn't feared death—at least that's what they had told him when they were still alive. But Selwyn *was* afraid of dying, and he had never believed in the life of the spirit after death that the priests promised. If death was eternal absence, this meant that he would never again see his brothers. On the other hand, if the spirit travelled to another world after death, he wondered how time would pass in that place. An incorporeal existence without end seemed like a curse, even if it meant that he would be with his brothers again.

Selwyn gazed at the surrounding trees along the road, trying to forget all that tortured him. *Where could Elliot be?*

The lad had left Wirskworth two days earlier than them, but Eleanor, and even John, had asked for a bit more time before departing the city. He would have preferred it if they had travelled with him, but Elliot wanted to set off earlier despite his wounded foot. Selwyn hadn't wanted to pressure John and Eleanor into hurrying after all that had happened in the last few days. He had considered journeying with Elliot without the others, but he sensed that the son of Thomas Egercoll didn't want company on this trip. Also, John and Eleanor seemed to need him more than the lad did—at least to the extent that he could keep them company since they would soon part ways.

"I haven't travelled so much in many years," John blurted, wiping away the wine that dribbled from his lips.

"Perhaps now that you're travelling again, you could stop drinking so much," Selwyn said.

Long Arm pushed his thick black hair back. "Some habits don't change, Brau," replied the man, laughing. "I'll kill anyone wicked enough to take my wine and women away from me!"

"When you say 'your women', you mean girls in the brothels you frequent day and night?" Eleanor asked.

"Naturally! Such women know how to offer unique pleasure, and I know that they will never abandon me," retorted John.

Eleanor looked at him in disgust. "They'll abandon you when you have no gold left."

"Would that cursed moment never come!" Long Arm exclaimed, stifling a burp.

Selwyn looked at the plains and the few trees ahead of them and then at the Mountains of the Forgotten World on his left. *Is Elliot there already?*

"How high up do you think Elliot is by now?" Eleanor asked, looking towards the mountains.

"He won't have gotten very high up yet. The mountains are quite rugged," Long Arm said.

Selwyn had forgotten that John had been to the Mountains of the Forgotten World. "How long do you think he'll need to reach the place where the Elder Races live?"

"If nothing has delayed him, I believe three or four more days—unless he stumbles and comes a cropper." Selwyn threw John an angry look, and he seemed to take heed. "It is not easy

to scale those mountains," Long Arm added.

"Elliot has been trained by Althalos. I'm sure there is nothing you can do that he can't," Eleanor said.

"True," replied John and took a few more sips of wine. "Even so, I think that there's something strange about Elliot's training. I'd say it wasn't the same as the rest of the men under Althalos received. It seems like Elliot never learned many important things."

"Why do you say that?" asked Eleanor.

Selwyn sat up in his saddle. "The wine has numbed your mind. I do respect your knowledge about the kingdom and its traditions, but I don't believe you have ever served as a soldier, so who are you to talk about Elliot's training?"

John burped and drank a little more wine from his flask. "I don't need to be a soldier to realise that Elliot's training was different."

"Why do you say that?" Eleanor asked again, louder.

Selwyn could see John's frown. "I have heard many times that Althalos created the most accomplished warriors in the history of the kingdom because he taught them everything—not just the art of war. I'm sure that Walter, and others before him, travelled to the Mountains of the Forgotten World during their training, and also went to every city in the kingdom."

Selwyn grunted. "Are you forgetting that Walter was looking for Althalos in order to kill him? If Thorn had found out about Elliot's existence, he would have gone to the ends of the world to find him and murder him too."

"Walter stopped searching for Althalos years ago, believing him dead. No one knew about Elliot's existence to be able to recognise him. Perhaps Althalos was afraid he would be recognised if they travelled together," John said. "Even so, if Althalos wanted to avoid the cities, I don't understand why he didn't show Elliot places like the Mountains of the Forgotten World. I've heard that all his apprentices had journeyed there to see the Elder Races up close. The boy didn't even know the story of the Seven Swords, and I doubt he even knew about the existence of wyverns. There may be many fools in the kingdom who believe that the Elder Races have vanished, but I believe most people know about wyverns..."

"Hardly anyone has seen a wyvern in the sky for hundreds of years, Long Arm," said Selwyn. "There are some stories about their existence from the northerners who have travelled to the Mountains of Darkness, but no one else has seen them in Knightdorn. Don't forget that there are now only a few who have been to the North beyond the North. I'm sure that many believe that wyverns are simply a myth... Even my own father is doubtful of their existen—"

"Your father may be dubious about whether they still exist, but only a few have never heard of them," John interrupted him with an annoyed look.

"Elliot never said that he didn't know about their existence," said Eleanor.

John's face was red from the wine. "Perhaps he knew... It still seems unbelievable to me that an apprentice of Althalos would be unaware of so many truths about the kingdom and its history. That's why I believe his training was different. Maybe Althalos didn't complete his instruction. Also, Elliot may be a worthy lad, but sometimes he behaves like a spoiled kid."

"Elliot is our friend. It's shameful to be saying such things about him," Eleanor said scathingly.

"Really?" retorted Long Arm, leaning forward in his saddle. "Do you believe Walter Thorn, or any other man that Althalos ever trained, would demand that the centaurs follow him into battle after all that's happened, with only the accompaniment of four companions? Nobody would be that foolish. When you want an alliance, you either ask politely, or you make your demands with a whole army by your side. It was a miracle that the centaurs didn't attack us that day in Ersemor."

Eleanor was about to speak, but John continued. "Few would challenge a man like Walter to a duel, alone and helpless, to get revenge. Perhaps some fools would try, but they would surely not be Althalos' apprentices. Really, do you believe that when Walter finished his training, he didn't know about the curse of the Egercoll, the Elder Races, and the

Seven Swords?"

"Do you believe Elliot lied about Althalos?" Selwyn asked.

"No. A lie like that could only bring hardship, as long as Walter is alive. Besides, Elliot's skills would be impossible to get with any other Master. Althalos must have had some reason for not teaching Elliot all that he knew—except for the art of fighting and the value of devotion. He ingrained the latter in Elliot more than he should have," said Long Arm.

Selwyn got lost in thought for a few moments until he saw Eleanor turn her head toward the Mountains of the Forgotten World again, as if she hoped she'd discern Elliot's shape from afar. She seemed disturbed by John's words.

They continued riding for a while, and Selwyn thought about what Long Arm had said. He couldn't judge Elliot's training, but he hoped whatever Althalos had taught him would be enough to defeat Walter Thorn.

"I think the time has come for you to leave us," John said, breaking the silence that had fallen over them.

Selwyn met his gaze. He knew it to be true, too. The time had come for him to continue his journey westward to Goldtown, though he was sorrowful that his companions could not follow him. John and Eleanor had to traverse the whole Road of Elves to reach Aquarine and Tahryn. Each of them had to follow Elliot's orders and seek new alliances while Eleanor would try to take the leadership of the former region of her dead family.

Selwyn stopped his horse and his two companions followed suit. "I don't know when we'll meet again," he said.

"I never expected you'd miss me, Brau," Long Arm teased, smiling.

Selwyn offered a grin. John may have been an uncouth drunkard, but he would miss him.

"I'm sure you'll be successful," said Eleanor, throwing him an encouraging look. "Old man Hale will be convinced by your words."

John did not seem that optimistic. "Take care of yourself," he said in a serious tone even though he seemed drunk.

"All three of us will succeed," said Selwyn, trying to boost their morale—especially his own. "I hope I'll see you soon."

He turned his horse west towards the open plains. A few moments later, he glanced back, wanting to see his two friends one more time. John and Eleanor had not begun riding. They were watching him leave, their mares still on the road. Selwyn's eyes grew wet and then, his greatest fear took root in his heart.

Perhaps one of us will manage to do Elliot's bidding, but it is unlikely that Morys will be the last loss in this company.

The Mountains of the Forgotten World

The strong wind whipped against Elliot's face. It was the fifth day he had been struggling with the terrain of the Mountains of the Forgotten World and now he felt worn out. He looked around and breathed out wearily. The mountain range was made up of seven peaks, and he had started his journey from the lowest one. They were all approximately the same height, except for two in the middle. The central peak was taller than the rest while the one on the left was the shortest.

Elliot regarded the path he had to follow. Three days earlier, he had left the shortest mountain midway. That was where the last footpath led to the tallest peak—the place in which the Elder Races lived. His trip had become more difficult from that point on since the tallest mountain was even more rugged and his injured leg hurt more with each step. As if that weren't enough, the food he had with him would soon run out. Luckily, the last two days had been rainy, so he had managed to fill his flask from some of the running streams on the slopes.

He carried on trekking, and the thorns from a cactus pierced his flesh. He swore loudly. The landscape of the mountain range was dry, despite the rain from the previous days. A little grass sprouted hesitantly where it could. The last summer had been one of the hottest he ever remembered, and perhaps that was to blame for the dry terrain on the mountain. Moreover, the wind was gusting so violently, he feared it would drag him off.

How can they live in this godforsaken place? he thought. The joints in Elliot's legs hurt, but the top of the mountain seemed to be drawing closer.

Time went by torturously slowly, and Elliot decided to stop for a while, staring at the point he was trying to reach. He leaned on the hilt of his sword, a fine blade they had supplied him with in Wirskworth. The wind grew even stronger, forcing him to keep moving.

The sun began to sink, giving way to the moon and the chill of night. Elliot grew disorientated and stopped short, trying to understand where he was. Once he found the path again, he continued walking until something drew his attention. A few miles away, the rocks on the range seemed to have caves among them. Elliot pushed through his exhaustion and headed to the nearest cave entrance. He crept carefully into its interior and stared at the enormous cavern in surprise.

The wind no longer lashed against him, but something seemed strange inside the cave. He gripped the hilt of his sword and drew the blade in one swift movement, turning around. A sword stopped his with a loud clang and then a blue light blinded him. The grip of his sword burned, and his weapon slipped from his hand. Spots danced across his vision as he blinked, and he could make out the face of a man through the light now flooding the cave. His eyes were starry blue, and the light shining around the cave came from the sword he held in his hands.

Fated Love

Reynald put a piece of bread in his mouth while thoughts circled around his mind like storm clouds. Soon, the moment would come when he would meet his old lord, and that filled him with unease. He sat down on the straw and looked around him. He was in the village of Isisdor, a few miles away from Iovbridge. The villagers had agreed to grant him the use of a small stable when he had told them he had run away from the royal capital, fearing the impending siege.

Am I being foolish? he thought, contemplating the decisions he'd made over the last few days.

Elliot had asked him to spy on his old lord, whom he hated. Reynald had never divulged all he had felt for Alice Asselin. He'd intended to take this truth with him to the grave until all was overturned. Alice's son had found himself at Reynald's mercy and he had decided to spare Elliot's life. Many a time he couldn't explain his actions. Elliot may have been Alice's son, but he didn't cease being the son of Thomas Egercoll. Reynald hated the Egercolls.

The thought of Thomas angered him. The second king was to blame for Reynald's house losing its castle and its army. "Liberator of the slaves and tyrant of the lords," the people of his birthplace used to shout out in favour of Thomas. He remembered the moment when his brother had told him that they had to leave Emeroll, their ancestors' castle.

"We can't pay the taxes imposed by Egercoll! If we remain without soldiers, it'll only be a matter of time before we are attacked by some greedy Mercenaries under Lord Hale," Ricard had said.

So, he and his brother had relocated to Kelanger. Reynald remembered Ricard saying that the Asselins were the poison of Oldlands and that he should have had the rulership over the region. Thomas had deprived Ricard of the one thing he was entitled to. The First King intended to appoint Ricard Governor of Oldlands, and just before they got Aymer Asselin out of the way, the Egercolls had raised their war banners and killed Walter's grandfather. Reynald remembered that after Thomas' royal decrees, his brother had once again hoped that one day he would manage to take Oldlands. If the new king had married their cousin, that would have given Ricard prestige, and after the death of old Aymer, the council may have given him the rule of the region, disregarding the House of Asselin. However, when Thomas chose Alice, Ricard lost all hope of becoming Governor of Oldlands.

Reynald recalled his brother's anger at having failed to achieve all that he desired, but nobody ever found out about Reynald's own anger and all that he had wanted. The moment he had first seen Alice Asselin was burned into his mind. He knew that his entire house would have gone against a marriage to an Asselin, and Alice had never shown any interest in him. Nevertheless, Reynald was never able to stop thinking about her. Memories flashed past as he thought of Alice—the boys in the courtyard teasing him because he couldn't hold his sword right and a handful of young lords hitting him, taking advantage of his slight build as a child.

"Leave him alone!" a voice said.

The young lords had taken fright at the face of the furious daughter of the Governor of Oldlands. They had bowed and run far away from the courtyard.

"Are you alright?" Alice had asked him.

"Yes." Reynald had felt ashamed by the way he had lain bloodied on the ground. He hadn't wanted an Asselin to see him in that state.

"I'm sure that one day they won't dare go to battle against you," she had said, her big brown eyes gleaming.

"Do you know who I am?"

"Reynald Karford?"

"I would have expected you to hate me..."

Alice had extended her hand. *"You haven't done anything for me to hate you, Reynald. And I don't care about the foolish hostility between our houses."*

Reynald had taken her hand, pulling himself up. Then the girl had smiled and walked away.

No matter how much time went by, he never forgot that scene. Alice used to smile at him for years until word of his and Ricard's vicious natures reached her ears. Then, she simply gestured briskly whenever she saw him. Reynald was certain that she hated him. He had moved over to Walter's ranks while she became the wife of Thomas Egercoll.

"Alice is not like Thomas—I beg you, my lord, don't kill her."

Walter had become angry. *"Why do you care for that traitress? She is the enemy of your House, an enemy of Oldlands, and an enemy of Knightdorn!"*

"She isn't like the other Asselins... Her father forced her to marry Thomas. We may be able to get her on our side. If we murder her, that will bring great discord to Oldlands," Reynald had said.

"If your brother can't enforce his rule in his region, then he doesn't deserve his title!" Walter had shouted. *"Are you hiding something, Reynald?"*

"No, my lord. I just thought that we could turn her into a valuable ally."

"Traitors never become valuable allies, idiot."

A sound brought Reynald back from his reverie—the whinnying of the black horse next to him. He exhaled, Walter's image still lingering in his mind. His anger towards him had never abated after all these years. He remembered Walter saying that after Thomas' murder he didn't need the weight of Queen Alice's death on his shoulders too. But Walter had tricked him.

When news of Alice's death reached Reynald's ears, he had decided to ask Walter for permission to capture the South Passage on his behalf. To his surprise, Walter had accepted the offer. In this way, he had succeeded in living far away from his old lord for years until the moment when everything changed.

He looked out at the dark sky from a corner of the stable. Elliot may have been Thomas' son, but Reynald felt that he owed him something—retribution for the wrongful death of his mother. Perhaps he was simply fooling himself, and all he wanted was to avenge the love of his life. Reynald was fortunate that Walter had never caught wind of what he felt. Love was an unfamiliar word to him. Nevertheless, Reynald had to be careful. He hadn't met his lord in years, and Walter had just suffered his first defeat. He would soon vent his anger about what had happened in Elmor and the loss of Stonegate. Reynald knew that if he was to appear in front of him now, Walter would most likely kill him.

Reynald could not meet his old lord earlier than was necessary. He had to wait until he sat on the throne. When Walter conquered Iovbridge, he would calm down for a little while. That would be the best time to meet him. Reynald continued delving into his own thoughts, until his eyes slowly started to close, and his body was heavy with fatigue. His dreams were weird and dark, filled with pain and death, until a girl with almond-shaped eyes and wavy hair smiled at him from afar in a clouded courtyard.

The Elder Races

Elliot had been walking for a long time, while the man who had taken him hostage followed, the tip of the sword pressing into his back. He had tried to talk to his captor, telling him that he had been searching for the Elder Races, but the man didn't appear to understand his words. Elliot knew that the man was an elwyn, his starry blue eyes and silvery-blue hair betraying his race. He wondered whether he understood his words or whether he simply pretended not to. He had never thought of asking John or Thorold if the Elder Races spoke Human Tongue. He had assumed they did, considering his meeting with Aleron. Even so, Aleron was but an elwyn.

The man had taken Elliot's blade and forced him to leave the cave. Elliot wondered about the light that had shone from his captor's sword, since it had now returned to a dull steel glint. He had never seen anything like it.

They continued walking in silence, executing a circular route through the mountain's jagged terrain. The sun had set, and the night wind made him shiver. To Elliot's surprise, the man was leading him to a peak to the right instead of to the tallest point of the mountain range. A faint light broke through the darkness, and Elliot saw fires burning along the length of a rugged slope. A familiar anger surged within him. The Elder Races didn't live at the top of the mountain range, and he was sure Thorold had known this. He had been foolish not to ask for John's advice, but he had contented himself with a Master's words. The Masters never spoke the truth. Thorold hadn't told him everything he needed to find these creatures.

After a few moments, countless figures appeared in front of him. He and his captor had reached the lit mountainside, and he felt more confused. Hundreds of creatures with silver-blue hair and starry-blue eyes came towards him, but this wasn't what astounded him. There were other figures who were no taller than three and a half feet. These figures had pretty faces, like the elwyn, but their ears were more pointed, and their hair darker, similar to a lot of humans. Moreover, their eyes seemed to have a reddish tinge. Elliot had never imagined that the elves would be so short.

The elves' clothes were woollen and thick while the elwyn were dressed in lighter fabrics, such as linen. Suddenly, his captor grabbed Elliot by the shoulder, and he stopped obediently. Elliot looked around him, his skin prickling in surprise.

"Aleron!" he exclaimed. He never thought that he would meet this man again.

The familiar, aged figure looked at him with fiery eyes. "I told you we'd cross paths again."

Aleron wore a crimson linen cloak. Elliot could have sworn it was the same one he had worn at their first meeting. He wondered how such an old creature had managed to leave the forest of the centaurs and climb these mountains.

Aleron's eyes narrowed as he looked at him. "Did you not expect to find me here?" he asked as if reading his thoughts.

"I was just thinking that these mountains are difficult to climb."

A smile formed on the elwyn's lips. "Experience is more powerful than youth. I hope you'll comprehend this truth one day." Elliot remained silent as more figures approached him. "What are you doing here?"

"I think you know," Elliot said as Aleron looked him over. "I know now that you knew Althalos... I also know that you knew who I really was before I told you at our first meeting."

"I know a lot that you are ignorant of, young man," Aleron answered.

"However, I wonder what the true reasons are for your presence here."

"I'm here to do what my father failed to do. I'm here to free the Elder Races from the curse of my ancestors!" Elliot replied, raising his voice.

The aged elwyn walked towards him with slow steps. "Do you know how to achieve what you have just uttered?"

Elliot's confidence waned. "I am not sure..."

"So, you came here to achieve something that nobody has ever managed without knowing anything about the curse you wish to break," Aleron told him.

He circled Elliot a few times before he spoke again. "I wonder about the motivations for this desire." The tone of his voice seemed to change. "Are you here at Althalos' request or because you, yourself, want to free the Elder Races?"

Elliot sized up the elwyn, not knowing how to respond. "Althalos barely told me anything about the Elder Races, and he never spoke to me about the curse that haunted them. All I knew was that they had disappeared. The reason I'm here is because I want to free you. I also want to ask for your help in the war of my allies against Walter Thorn. A few days ago, Walter was defeated for the first time on Elmor's soil. I'm certain that he will soon attack again with all his army in Wirskworth, and we can't face him without help."

A murmur rippled through the crowd around him upon hearing these words.

"Do you want to break the curse because you believe the Elder Races must be free or are you here just because you need help in facing your enemy?" Aleron asked.

Thorold's words swirled in his mind. "*Nonetheless, remember that the war against Walter is a war of humans, not of the Elder Races. The Elder Races must be freed, regardless of whether we need allies to defeat our enemy and survive.*"

"The Elder Races must—" He stopped mid-sentence.

The idea that he had travelled to the Mountains of the Forgotten

World to free the Elder Races and that they could refuse to fight by his side annoyed him. If something like that were to happen, this trip would have been a waste of time. He could have stayed in Elmor and journeyed to this place at some other time. Elliot tried to tame the frustration threatening to overflow into his words.

"The Elder Races must be freed, regardless of my enemies. But I believe that Walter Thorn is not just my enemy, but the enemy of every race on this continent," Elliot continued.

"Interesting..." Aleron remarked, stopping in front of him. "My experience with humans has shown that what they say before the word *but* is never what they truly believe. Why is Walter Thorn the enemy of the Elder Races? I don't recall him ever attacking us. Unless you believe he is our enemy because he killed Thomas Egercoll."

Elliot was enraged upon hearing these words. "He killed Thomas Egercoll who tried to free you, and he wants to take the throne of Iovbridge, sentencing the people of Knightdorn to fear and tyranny."

"Thomas tried to free us for the same reason as you. This is also the reason why he failed... As for Iovbridge, nobody in these mountains cares about which human will capture it. Unless you and your allies are prepared to hand it over to us—if you succeed in breaking the curse. I don't know if you are aware that Iovbridge was once the kingdom of the elwyn," said Aleron.

Elliot's anger grew. "If I'm not mistaken, the elwyn left Iovbridge, wanting to move to these mountains and to forge the Seven Swords." He didn't know if this was true, but it was what he'd been told. "I don't think that humans owe Iovbridge to the elwyn. I also believe you should be speaking about Thomas Egercoll with greater respect."

Aleron looked at him, anger reflected in his eyes. "It isn't disrespectful to say that someone failed. Nevertheless, I wonder why you think I should owe Thomas Egercoll respect."

"Because he tried to free your people."

"Only because he needed them."

"Even so, I think your people *owed* him help, Aleron. If I remember correctly, the elwyn, along with the giants and the elves, betrayed my ancestors, and as a result they were slaughtered. This was the reason why Manhon cursed the Elder Races. Your people promised to help my ancestors, by giving them the Seven Swords, but they betrayed them. Since my father wished to break the curse, putting aside the betrayal of the Elder Races, I think they owed him something in return!" Elliot said angrily.

He didn't know whether all he had said was true, but his words seemed to infuriate those present. Elliot noticed two large shapes out of corner of his eye. Two giants—one male and one female—advancing towards him, fists clenched. They towered over him at over twelve feet tall. He had never before seen larger creatures in his life. Still, the two giants were less scary than Aleron's intense gaze burning into him.

"Do you believe that the Elder Races did not pay off their debt towards your ancestors, human?" Aleron shrieked, face reddening in anger. "How many did your ancestors betray during their lifetime? How many innocents have died in the battles of the Egercolls? It's true that Aremor shouldn't have betrayed your ancestors. He believed they didn't deserve to have the power they were given, but this was not his choice. Nevertheless, he needn't have betrayed them. Anyone who knows humans knows that they always destroy themselves. If Aremor had had the wisdom to wait and hadn't been dazzled by the idea of getting his hands on the blood of the pegasi as fast as he could, the Egercolls would have been wiped out of their own accord. Then, he would have been free to study the pegasi and their blood, without their permission.

"I'm a fool to be surprised by your rudeness. I should have known by now that no human is capable of appreciating the hardship that the Elder Races have suffered. If humans were able to understand, thousands would have come here over the years to put an end to the harm their race has caused. The centaurs have asked for forgiveness innumerable times for having helped Manhon unleash this curse. And you, a human, believe that you deserve our help, without even asking for forgiveness. Do you believe that an alliance is a fair exchange for the liberation of the Elder Races from the cruellest torment in the history of the world?"

Elliot was about to speak, but Aleron cut him off. "Humans are responsible for the greatest sins that have ever taken place in this world, and they have never paid for them. But, according to you, the Elder Races deserved this fate for a betrayal. Have you any idea what the curse that haunts us is, descendant of the Egercolls?"

Elliot felt the same way he had felt in Moonland when he had found himself facing the leader of the centaurs. His hot-headed self and the memory of his father had led him astray. He looked around at the creatures surrounding him. Their faces may have been handsome and well-formed, but almost all seemed wearied. Even the two giants, though huge, appeared worn out, as if they had endured innumerable afflictions. Suddenly, his gaze fell upon four figures he hadn't noticed earlier, their build even shorter than that of the elves. These were child-elwyn and child-elves. His thoughts went to Velhisya, and in his mind's eye, he envisioned her as a child. Now, he felt profound sadness.

"I'm sorry about everything that the Elder Races have been through," he said, bowing slightly. "I apologise if my words insulted you and your people. However, it is true that the human race has suffered greatly too because of my enemy. I don't want to fight for castles, land or riches, but only for the freedom of my race from a tyrant. It's impossible for me to help my people without defeating Walter Thorn and for this I need your help." He looked around and wondered about the number of elwyn, giants, and elves in that place. "Nevertheless, as much as I need you all, you have to be freed from the sufferings of the curse whether you help me or not."

Aleron frowned. "You say you want to help humans and you believe that this will be achieved by defeating Walter Thorn, but you forget your enemy got his power from your own kind. Without help, he would have neither the largest army in Knightdorn, nor the power he has."

"Humans made a mistake, as they have done many times in our history. Now, most soldiers are with this man only out of fear. The only ones who are truly devoted to him are a few rich lords who gained power thanks to him. Ordinary people are suffering throughout the kingdom," Elliot said sadly. "I believe you respected Althalos. He wanted me to protect Knightdorn from Walter and for me to achieve this, I need the help of the Elder Races."

"I know you need our help. Even so, I'm not sure whether you deserve it, and I believe Althalos would have agreed with me," the elderly man responded.

"I have told you the truth. I want to free the Elder Races, even if they don't help me in my battle against Walter Thorn."

Elliot looked at Aleron. At this point, he meant those words, even if it meant the end of his people. The defeated look of the creatures around him filled his gut with grief.

"I'm not sure about that, Elliot." The elwyn broke the momentary silence. It was the first time that he had called him by his name. "I believe you *think* you want to free the Elder Races, and moreover you feel an impulsive sorrow for all they've been through. But that is not enough. If you want to achieve your aim, you have to feel the pain that the elwyn, giants, and elves endured. You have to feel the suffering all those surrounding you have experienced over the past three centuries. Only then, will you possibly achieve what you say you wish to."

Elliot thought that Aleron had finished, but he spoke again. "But remember: if one day you feel all that we have felt, the pain will be so great that it may kill you."

Elliot felt bewildered upon hearing Aleron's words. "Can you help me achieve all this?"

"Perhaps." Aleron stared into space momentarily. "I can talk to you, in the hope that all I say will help you. Nevertheless, no one knows whether all that you hear will truly help you," he concluded enigmatically.

Elliot had mulled over this question for a while. "You can begin by explaining the light that came from that man's sword." Elliot turned to his captor who was standing some distance away all this time.

To his surprise, Aleron started laughing. "*Man?*" he asked, looking at him dubiously. "I haven't heard a human call an elwyn a *man* in a long time."

Elliot felt confused and opened his mouth to speak, but Aleron cut him short. "Humans used to call the male and female elwyn and elves men and women centuries ago. But they didn't do the same with giants and centaurs. They had other words for those beings, like 'centaur' and 'centauride' or 'giant' and 'giantess'. They never created words in their tongue to distinguish between male and female elwyn and elves. They used the same words they had for themselves. Do you know why?"

"Because..."

"In the beginning, I thought it was because the elwyn and the elves have a similar appearance to that of humans, so the latter never felt the need to create different words for them. But a few years later, after the curse, the elwyn and the elves were no longer referred to as 'men' and 'women' by humans. From that point onwards, for your kind, we were but some fallen male and female beings. Then, I discovered the reason why humans used to call us men and women was not just because of our appearance."

Elliot waited for him to continue.

"Humans considered us their equals. Giants and centaurs were never their equal in their eyes simply because they were different in appearance. Humans consider anything different to themselves dangerous as well as inferior. In their minds, the elwyn and the elves ceased being their equals when they were considered cursed, steeped in the sin of betrayal. Then, the fact that we looked the same was no longer enough for humans to consider us their equals," Aleron explained.

Elliot couldn't understand whether he had made a mistake in calling his captor "man".

"I don't know whether you called an elwyn 'man' because you consider us equal to your kind or simply because you're new to the world. The future will tell. I hope that one day, the whole of the human race will follow the ideas espoused in the First Tongue," Aleron told him.

Elliot guessed that this was the name of the language of the Elder Races. "What are the male and female humans called in the First Tongue?" he asked.

"Any being that speaks and thinks is called *anir* or *vyli* in our tongue. *Anir* is a man, and *vyli* a woman. So, centaurs, giants, elwyn, elves, and humans are called men and women using the same words in our tongue."

Elliot had been but a short time in the Mountains of the Forgotten World, and he could already perceive how respectful the Elder Races were towards anything different to themselves. Suddenly, much of what John had said came to mind.

"As for the light you saw coming from the sword of your captor, I think it best we walk together a while before I explain," Aleron said.

Elliot noticed the crowd around him beginning to disperse, and even the elwyn who had captured him began to walk away. Elliot looked back at Aleron. The elderly elwyn's gaze had not strayed away from him, and his irises seemed livelier than ever.

Zhilor and Azelor

The chill around Elliot seemed to get stronger as the night stretched on. The darkness was gloomy with only a handful of stars to light their passage. For a moment, the moon drew Elliot's attention—it was full and its colour seemed golden. He and Aleron had moved away from the side of the mountain where the Elder Races resided.

"Have you ever heard about the Light of Life and the God of Light?" Aleron asked, breaking the silence.

Velhisya's image popped up in his mind. *"My mother's name means light in the ancient elwyn language. The power of my race came from the magic of light."*

"I've seen the Temple of the God of Light in the City of Heavens. I've also heard about the magic of the light of the elwyn," said Elliot.

Aleron frowned. The Light of Life is the most powerful force in our world and according to legend, the world was created by Azelor," he replied.

Elliot had never heard that name before. The elwyn watched him closely.

"For humans, Azelor is the God of Life. Many know him as the God of Light, too. The truth is that centuries ago, humans used different names for all their gods. As time went by, these names were forgotten, and the gods were given names which were representative of their powers in Human Tongue."

"Is the First Tongue the language of all the Elder Races?"

"Yes," Aleron replied.

"I thought that each race had its own language," Elliot admitted, remembering Velhisya talking about the ancient tongue of the elwyn.

"There are only three tongues in this world. The First Tongue, Human Tongue, and Mermaid Tongue. The Elder Races always shared the same language," responded the elwyn.

"Do the Elder Races have different names for all gods?"

"No. The Elder Races always believed in the existence of only two gods—Azelor and Zhilor. As I said, for your race Azelor is the God of Life, but most humans are unfamiliar with Zhilor."

Elliot didn't speak, and Aleron scratched his chin. "According to legend, Azelor is the first god of the world while Zhilor is his younger brother. Azelor was all-powerful, and one day he decided to create this world. The Light of Life is his power. When Azelor created the world, he decided to give a small part of his power to some beings."

Elliot listened like a young child waiting to hear the rest of an exciting story.

"The elwyn were the first beings to whom Azelor gave some of his wisdom and so he decided to blow the Light of Life into them. Many know the Light of Life as the First Light or the Light of the First God.

"The elwyn lived peacefully for years until Azelor created the elves. One more being that was not only imbued with a part of his wisdom, but also with a part of his power. Then, Zhilor asked Azelor if he could help him, so that the world his brother had built could be perfected, but Azelor refused. Azelor always thought Zhilor to be sinister and spiteful and so he didn't want his brother to pass on his dark powers to any being in his world. Zhilor got angry with his brother and decided to create some beings in secret. According to scriptures, the first race that he made was that of the giants." Aleron paused.

"Azelor was furious when he realised what had happened and then a war began—one that still rages to this day. Nevertheless, the war between the sibling-gods is not exactly a dual between the two of them. According to legend, the god that will be triumphant will be the one whose powers will prevail in our world. Azelor's powers are those of love and life while Zhilor's force stems from death, hatred, and spite. Some scriptures speak of Zhilor as the God of Death and Darkness."

Elliot watched Aleron, frowning.

"As the centuries passed by, Azelor made other beings, like the centaurs and the mermaids, but although he was able to give them a little of his wisdom, he failed to instil the Light of Life in these beings. Zhilor never succeeded in making another vicious being with intellect and speech, like he did with the giants. Nevertheless, under his brother's nose, he gave life to the tigers of the north and the wyverns. These beings may not speak, but they carry a part of his dark power."

Elliot imagined what this power might be. The pain of Orhyn Shadow came to his mind. "Which of the two gods made the humans?"

A faint smile was reflected in the aged face of the elwyn. "Nobody has the answer to this question. The most widespread myth is that the humans were the last beings with intellect and speech that Azelor wanted to create, but when he was blowing life into the first one, Zhilor tried to instil some of his traits, too. Neither of the two gods was able to give the first human his powers, but both imbued certain pieces of themselves into him."

Anger rose up in Elliot again. "So, this is the attitude of the elwyn towards humans? That they took some of Zhilor's viciousness?" he snapped.

"The truth is that this is what I once believed, too, but I made a mistake," Aleron said.

The elwyn's words made him pause. "What do you mean?"

"Now, I believe that they got all of his viciousness."

Elliot stopped walking and looked at the elwyn angrily. "So, is it only humans who are vicious? What have you to say about the war of the giants and the elves?"

"Truly, that war left thousands of corpses in its wake. But no war can compare to that of humans. Murders of innocent people and children, rapes... None of that ever happened in a war of the Elder Races. It isn't just war, Elliot. Humans have behaved hideously throughout their entire history, even towards their own kind. Humans kidnap other humans and betray them. No other being with intellect has ever dared to carry out such heinous acts."

"Did nobody from the Elder Races kill, betray, or rape someone of their own kind?" Elliot asked.

Aleron frowned. "Some killed and betrayed, but it was exceptionally rare. However, rape is something that has never occurred between the Elder Races."

For a moment Elliot felt sullied, as if his flesh was drenched with all the sins of the world. He turned to the distant sky and saw a bird flying carefree. He wished he too could fly.

"The truth is that I don't really believe what I said before." Aleron's voice was but a whisper. "After living for so many centuries, I now think that whoever it was that created us gave us the will to choose the path we want to follow."

Elliot glanced back at Aleron, his brows furrowed. "What do you me—"

"It may be in the nature of some beings to be more vicious than others, but each creature of this world can choose whether it wants to follow the instincts it is born with," Aleron told him. "In short, even if a human is made to be vicious, he or she has the power to choose a different path. Moreover, the elwyn and the elves, who are made to be pure, can choose to ignore the purity of their kind."

Elliot was enthralled by the wisdom of these words. "Was the light that came from that man's sword the Light of Life?"

Aleron gestured that they should continue walking. "Yes," he replied, gazing at the stars.

"In other words, the elwyn and the elves can create this light?"

"Not exactly," Aleron said, without taking his gaze off the sky. "The Light of Life lives within us, but we can't extract it from our body without help. Centuries ago, we discovered that certain objects could absorb it."

"The sword!" he exclaimed. "The sword absorbed the man's Light and that's how his blade lit up!" Aleron nodded. "When my blade collided with that sword, I felt my hands burn while holding the hilt..." Elliot looked at his palms.

"The Light of Life is a mighty power. Any being not infused with it feels as if it is burning when it comes into contact with it. Some more, some less," Aleron responded.

"And if an elf duels with an elwyn?"

"The Light of Life cannot harm any creature which is endowed with it."

"I assume that the giants feel the burning that I felt," Elliot said pensively.

"Yes... However, they can bear the burning more than humans can—the giants' torso is very hardy. The Light doesn't truly harm most creatures. The burning sensation they experience when an object infused with it touches them, is only in their soul. Their physical body remains unscathed," Aleron said.

Elliot recalled that although he had felt a burning sensation, his skin hadn't blistered. "Are there beings for whom the Light can be more harmful?"

Aleron's lips formed a thin line. "Yes. The creatures that have Zhilor's power will truly burn if they are touched by an object infused with the First Light. They also feel as if they're burning even if they find themselves within the Light's radius."

"The Light's radius?"

"Humans feel a burning sensation if their skin or an object touching their skin comes into contact with another thing infused with the First Light. The beings that have Zhilor's power within them feel that they are burning even if the Light falls upon them without having touched another object whatsoever. Think of it as a poisonous ray of the sun.

However, their physical body is not injured in this case," Aleron explained.

Elliot mulled over Aleron's words. "I bet Zhilor's force is Orhyn Shadow. Which means that the tigers of the north and wyverns must be the creatures most vulnerable to the Light of Life."

"Exactly. Orhyn Shadow is a dark force, so powerful that the beings that can attack with it cannot but be the weakest when faced with the First Light," Aleron replied.

"This venom is the worst there is..." Elliot agreed and glanced at his injured leg. He was lucky that Thorold had healed him from the venom.

Aleron suddenly stopped. "Has Orhyn Shadow been found in your body?" Elliot nodded.

"I'm sorry." The starry-blue eyes of the elwyn seemed saddened.

"Have you also felt the pain that this venom causes?"

"No, my race is immune to all poisons and venoms. Elwyn are immune to poisons and to the elements of nature," Aleron said, and Elliot's eyes widened.

"Elements of nature?"

Aleron laughed. "An elwyn can neither be burned by fire, nor drown. Moreover, we cannot feel the frosty ice or the burning heat on our skin. The Light inside us is so powerful that it protects our bodies from all the elements of nature. Elwyn are also immune to poisons and diseases which kill other creatures. We don't need food, water or air to survive. We can eat and drink, which is fun for us to do, but we don't need it. Moreover, though we can die from our injuries, non-fatal wounds on our bodies heal more quickly than those of humans."

"So, elwyn can only die from injuries?" Elliot asked.

"Not only... An elwyn can die from old age or if they lose the love of their life," the man added.

This confused Elliot more than anything else that night. He looked at Aleron and shifted his weight from one foot onto the other. "If they lose the love of their life?"

Aleron's face had taken on a melancholy look. "Elwyn usually fall in love only once in their whole life. Love is the greatest power of our race. When two elwyn unite through the union of their bodies, they can never fall in love again. Their bond is eternal, and the Light of Life within them becomes one to their death."

"So, if two elwyn unite their bodies, do they stay together forever?"

"Yes," Aleron said with fiery eyes. "Bodily union is not only carnal but spiritual too. When two elwyn mate, they unite their souls, and they are bonded forever. If they haven't bonded, there is a chance they may lose their love for their partner, but this is truly rare and only ever happens when the elwyn they have fallen in love with dies before they are bonded."

"And what happens if two elwyn unite their souls and either of the two dies?"

"I've already told you, Elliot."

Sweat beaded on his forehead. "Does their partner die too?"

Aleron nodded. Elliot's thoughts went to Velhisya suddenly, and his heart throbbed.

"Can an elwyn only fall in love with another elwyn?" He already knew the answer to his question, but he felt he wanted it confirmed.

Aleron's forehead creased. "Theoretically, no. Rarely will an elwyn fall in love with another being."

"Are giants and elves the same as elwyn?"

Aleron shook his head. "Elves also have the Light of Life within them, but it isn't as powerful as that of the elwyn. This is why they have neither immunity to the elements and poisons of nature, nor to Orhyn Shadow. They need food and water to survive. However, they do have immunity to diseases that are fatal for humans."

"And if their mate dies?"

"They stay alive. However, adultery is unheard of amongst their race. They also don't kill or betray their own kind."

"I would have expected the elves to be immune to Orhyn Shadow."

Aleron began walking again and Elliot followed him.

"As I said, the Light of Life within them is not that powerful. However, both the elwyn and the elves can treat a wound steeped in the venom as long as they transfer the Light within them to an object and touch the wound with it."

"And the giants?" Elliot didn't recall ever having asked so many questions in his whole life.

"The giants have an enmity for all other creatures apart from themselves, and are the only race that is devoted to Zhilor. Adultery, trickery, and murder are rare in their race, but not unheard of. I believe that their very nature dictates that they are hostile to everyone, especially to elves. Nevertheless, as I said, each creature has the power to disregard its nature."

"Why are those two giants here?" Elliot asked.

"Centuries ago, giants decided to trust us. Now they are cursed to remain here regretting their decision..."

"I presume that they need food and water, and that they are vulnerable to the elements of nature, poison, and the Orhyn Shadow," Elliot said.

"Right, except giants are immune to Orhyn Shadow."

Elliot started with surprise. "But you said that only the Light can give immunity to the power that was given to our world by Zhilor. I thought that the giants didn't have the First Light within them!"

"They don't have immunity because of the Light. Their immunity stems from the fact that they are born with Orhyn Shadow in their blood." An inexplicable fear washed over Elliot. "Giants, like the tigers of the north and wyverns, are immune to Orhyn Shadow because it flows in their veins."

"Then I would have expected giants to be vulnerable to Light, like wyverns and the—"

"No," Aleron cut in. "That happens only to creatures that can attack with the venom. Giants have Orhyn Shadow in their blood, but they can't attack with it. The tigers of the north have the venom in their teeth, and the wyverns have it in the spikes that cover their body. Legend has it that Zhilor gave a number of his own traits to giants, but he failed to give them the ability to attack with his power. Nonetheless, those beings that can attack with it are the giants' natural allies."

They continued walking in silence for some time, Aleron's words filling Elliot's mind until he felt his head was ready to burst. Elliot observed the mountain range that spread before them. A few stars appeared to touch their tips. *Where is he taking me?*

After a few moments, Elliot stopped. "What is the truth about Manhon's curse?" he asked.

Aleron looked at him strangely, and for a moment, Elliot could have sworn that he had seen Velhisya come to life in his gaze.

The Brave Soul

The gold snakes on the left and right of the Governor of Elmor's seat seemed to come alive under the light of the torches. Velhisya didn't know why she had decided to go to the great hall in Moonstone. Darkness had fallen a while ago, but she wasn't able to sleep. She walked around, contemplating the events of the last few days. Walter would never forgive them for his defeat in Elmor and would soon attack again with every man he had. It would be nigh impossible to beat such a large army.

As if the size of the enemy forces weren't enough, they also faced the most capable warrior and commander that the world had ever known. Velhisya knew that all this was the reason she felt such tension. It seemed like a premonition—a premonition of death. The fact that she would die soon filled her mind with questions of what she should do with the last few days of her life.

At first, she had thought about her aunt's suggestion—leaving for the Mountains of the Forgotten World. However, she didn't feel there was anything that connected her with the elwyn. If her mother were there, things would have been different. However, Velhisya knew that she had died years ago, a fact that she had never told anyone. Her father had told her that her mother could not live in a world without him. Then, a little before his death, he had confessed all that he knew about the elwyn.

Velhisya often wondered whether she was more like the elwyn or humans. It was obvious that her appearance came from her mother's side, but she felt that her deeper nature was human. This was confirmed by the fact that she hadn't observed any gift of the elwyn within herself that her father had told her about. Nevertheless, she wondered about the invisible power she had felt the last time she had seen Elliot. This frightened her. She feared that her destiny was intertwined with his, just like her mother's with that of her father.

Velhisya glanced at the ornate ceiling of the hall. Wirskworth was the only home she had ever known. People had looked at her with eyes filled with scorn ever since she could remember. The superstition surrounding the Elder Races may have haunted her skin, but each person with the name of Endor had treated her as if she was family. Syrella, Linaria, Merhya—all of them had embraced her from the very beginning.

This is my home. I'll fight for it, and if need be, I'll give my life, I will! she thought.

For the first time, the idea of death gave her some momentary joy. She was sure that when she left this world, she would meet her parents again, her uncle Sigor, her cousin Henry, and many other relatives.

She tried to put dying out of her mind. She was still alive, and she had to help the family that remained as much as she could.

"What are you doing here?"

Velhisya turned in surprise. Linaria had come into the hall without her realising it.

"I can't sleep," Velhisya told her.

A smile was painted on Linaria's lips. She wore a blue, linen cloak. "Neither can I."

"Are you afraid of death?" Velhisya suddenly blurted out. She had never asked her before.

Linaria seemed calm. "No... The only thing I'm afraid of is that I may not be able to take enough Ghosts with me when I die."

They remained silent until Velhisya started laughing and Linaria joined in. She observed her cousin. Linaria and Merhya were always brave and warlike, as if the God of War himself had sent them both to Syrella's womb.

"What is keeping you awake?" asked Linaria.

Velhisya glanced at her. She loved Linaria like a sister. "I want to help... You are the only family I ever had. This is my home!" Her voice had strengthened. "Syrella won't let me figh—"

"Velhisya..." The woman cut her short. "Ability in battle is not everything. You aren't a warrior—at least not on the battlefield."

"I know I'm weak... I was never skilled with the sword."

"You aren't weak. You're one of the bravest women I have ever met."

Velhisya couldn't believe her ears. "Me?"

"Yes... you!" Linaria moved closer. "You grew up in a place filled with superstition and stupid legends about the elwyn and yet you never hid who you were. You could have left everything behind, you could have demanded every person in Elmor to forget your origins... You could have just been an Endor!" Her eyes were shining as she faced Velhisya.

"You never did that," Linaria continued. "You always supported your father's choices, even if he was forced to take you away from your mother. I don't know why Arthur came here without your mother. I don't know why he never wanted to take you to the Mountains of the Forgotten World while he was alive. But you accepted everything with courage and decency. Even now, you want to fight, though you know that would mean your death. Your courage is greater than anyone else's in our House!"

Hot tears poured from Velhisya's eyes.

"I often wonder whether I or Merhya are suited to ruling this place."

"What do you mean?" Velhisya asked.

Linaria touched her arm softly. "My sister and I were born for the battlefield. Neither of us would be capable of governing Elmor."

"It is your duty! One of you will have to do it!" Velhisya's voice echoed through the great hall.

"Not necessarily... Nobody knows who the council would choose if my mother were to die."

"Elmor belongs to the Endors! Nobody will—"

"We're not the only ones with that name," Linaria butted in.

Surprise coursed through Velhisya.

"I always believed that none of us was capable of leading Elmor. My mother and my sister only have the honour of battle on their mind, just like me. Henry and Sigor were stubborn, while your father wanted to live free, far from any responsibility. You are the only logical one, and at the same time you're braver than you think. If you truly understood all that I have said, perhaps one day you'll help this place more than you can ever imagine."

Velhisya hugged her tightly, and Linaria reciprocated.

"I don't think I'll manage to help Elmor much... Soon we'll all die," Velhisya said after a while.

"But we'll die together." Linaria squeezed her hand.

Velhisya smiled. "I think this time we need the biggest Dance of Blood that has ever taken place!"

"I hope your escort will have returned by then," Linaria teased.

Velhisya felt herself going red. She knew that everyone had seen her dancing with Elliot, and that was the last thing she wished to discuss. "It was just a dance," she said defensively, lowering her gaze.

"I've never seen you dance with anyone, except for Sadon Burns and Johan."

"He asked me to dance, and it wouldn't have been polite to refuse." She blurted a lie with ease.

"I don't know much about love and passion, but I'd swear he wasn't the only one who wanted that dance."

Velhisya lifted her eyes and looked at her cousin boldly. Linaria was smiling.

"Elliot is a brave lad, but he is a man too."

Velhisya was troubled by her words. "What do you mean?"

"You may be unaware of this, my dear cousin, but men are afraid of us. Soon, Elliot will pluck up the courage to ask for more than just a dance," she said, laughing.

Velhisya smiled too. She adored Linaria. With just two phrases she had succeeded in relieving her from torture.

"Go to your room, cousin. And when you can't sleep, remember that I, my sister, and my mother will always be by your side."

With one last smile, Linaria walked away with her long black hair dancing along her back. Velhisya stood alone for a few moments until she decided to follow Linaria's advice. She walked down the dark passages of the castle, contemplating her cousin's words. She hadn't felt such love and affection in a long time. Moments later, she opened the door to her room, while Linaria's words were still on her mind.

"I don't know why he never wanted to take you to the Mountains of the Forgotten World while he was alive." Linaria's words drifted through her mind over and over.

The truth was that Velhisya had blamed her father for this. She had asked him innumerable times to travel to the place where her mother lived, but he had never agreed. Velhisya grew up believing that her mother had left him, and that was why he never wanted to see her again. However, when her father was on his deathbed, he had told her everything and the truth had broken her heart into thousands of pieces. That memory popped into her mind.

"Why didn't you ever take me to the Mountains of the Forgotten World?" she had asked.

Arthur looked tired. His face was sweaty and his eyes full of pain. *"Ellin asked me to swear that I would never take you to see her in that place... She didn't want you to see her imprisoned and weak. She wanted you to imagine her as she imagined you... Proud and brave."*

Tears poured down Velhisya's cheeks one more time that night.

"I'll make you proud," she said softly to herself, and then a blurred image of her mother appeared in front of her eyes.

The Invisible Curse

Aleron watched Elliot. "The truth about Manhon's curse?" he repeated. "What do you mean *what's the truth?*"

"Is it true that the Elder Races can't leave these mountains?" Elliot wanted to hear the truth from an elwyn.

"The fact that the Elder Races can't leave this place is the least of their problems compared to the rest of the consequences of the curse." The elwyn's starry-blue eyes radiated a white light as they observed him. "From the moment that the Elder Races were imbued with the curse, they haven't aged, and they also can't die in any natural way."

Aleron's words had caused an indiscernible anxiety within Elliot. "What do you mean?"

"Elwyn may not need food and water to survive, but that doesn't apply to giants and elves... Nevertheless, they can't die of hunger, of thirst or even from the cold, as long as there is the curse. Moreover, the Elder Races don't age with the passage of time—they are compelled to be here eternally, no matter how much they are tormented."

Elliot's legs deadened and the true weight of the curse rested on him. "Is there no way of dying with this curse?"

"Only from an injury, which means that someone has to kill you, or you have to put an end to your own life."

Elliot couldn't imagine anything worse than this. He pictured himself being hungry and thirsty eternally, having no other option but to take his own life to put an end to his misery. "Is there any food and water in the mountains?" he asked.

"There are ways to collect water, but food is rare. The centaurs take care to bring food as often as they can—it's not easy for them to travel with carts from Ersemor, so they bring supplies only every few months. Elves are able to endure the torment of hunger, but the giants suffer the most. All have died except for two. Adur and Aiora are the only ones left.

Elliot felt sorrow.

"The truth is that after the Battle of Wirskworth there were no more than three hundred giants left. Most of them survived the first centuries of the curse—but, as time went on, they became certain that life would continue eternally. So, more and more began to jump from the tops of the mountains, till only two were left."

Elliot's eyes grew wet. "How did Manhon manage to unleash such a powerful curse?"

"I was there," Aleron mumbled, staring into the void. "Manhon killed Aremor, my brother, as soon as he gave him the Sword of Light. Then he unleashed the curse with the help of the centaurs. Manhon would not have been able to tame such powerful magic without them."

"The centaurs didn't know that they would be able to use this magic. Their legends have it that there was a terrible curse they could unleash only once during their existence. However, they needed a mighty object to succeed—this object was the Sword of Light. Nonetheless, the centaurs had not realised what the repercussions of the curse would be. When they realised, centuries were not enough time for them to forgive themselves, even if humans forgot. For most of your kind, the Elder Races are now just a myth..."

Elliot was mystified. *Aremor was Aleron's brother.* "At least the elwyn don't feel the torment of hunger and pain," he murmured.

"That's true. But, the elwyn lost the most precious thing in their life. The power of love," Aleron said. "Since the curse, the elwyn remain alive even if their other half dies, unable to join their love in death. This is the worst torment they can be subjected to."

Elliot remained silent under the weight of the grief settling on him.

One more question nagged at him. "How did you manage to break the curse and go to Ersemor?" His voice was but a whisper.

"Nobody knows... I was also imprisoned in these mountains for two centuries until one day I was able to leave. Since then, I have started to grow old again. Nobody ever knew why I was free from the curse, and I'm the only one who has managed to escape it. Sometimes, I travel to Ersemor to speak to the centaurs, but most of the time, I remain here—my people need me."

Elliot exhaled, fatigued. He didn't know whether Aleron was telling the truth, but it didn't matter. "I want to free your people. I'm sorry about everything the Elder Races have been through," he said, and he meant it. "They don't deserve this kind of punishment."

The elwyn smiled. "Thomas Egercoll said the same thing. However, it isn't enough... You have to feel the pain the Elder Races felt all these years. As I told you before, if you manage to feel this pain, it may kill you."

Elliot sighed deeply. "I need Thindor... Thorold told me that only the Rider of Fate can break this curse. If I had the pegasus, I might be able to break it," he whispered remembering the Master's words.

"Only two humans know about the existence of this creature." The man spoke sternly. "I would advise you to forget Thindor and never speak about him to anyone, unless truly necessary. He is the last thing you need to achieve your purpose."

Elliot was bewildered—the fact that Aleron was aware of how many humans knew about Thindor meant that he had heard about his sister's death. Selyn had known about Thindor. Althalos had even confided the truth to Aleron but not to Elliot himself. "Did you know about Selyn?" he asked.

Aleron closed his eyes and exhaled mournfully. "I'm sorry about her death."

Elliot was irate—he didn't want to talk about it any longer. "What am I going to do in this place until I discover whether I can break the curse?" he asked.

"You'll be trained," Aleron told him with the shadow of a smile on his lips.

It was Elliot's turn to smile. "That man may have disarmed me, but I didn't know about the Light of Life. With all due respect, I'm sure that now that I know, I can beat any man of your race."

Aleron's eyes were fiery. "Your arrogance is out of control! I believe we can do something about that. I know that Althalos never taught you how to fight against a creature of the Elder Races. Your old Master told me that he taught this kind of combat to all his other apprentices, except for you. I think that this training will be to your benefit."

Elliot's smile was wiped off his face, and he felt a familiar anger. "Why didn't he teach me?"

"I have no idea." Aleron looked away, as if he was hiding something. "Perhaps you need to discover for yourself some of the motives of your former Master. Now, it's time to turn back. Your training will begin soon."

The elwyn began to walk away hurriedly, leaving Elliot in the depths of his raging thoughts.

The Oak Tree and the Snake

The midday light made the interior of Syrella Endor's room in the Tower of Poisons shine. Innumerable worries circled inside her mind. The events of the last few days filled her with fear. *Walter will not forgive all that happened on Elmor's soil. He'll return and kill us all,* she thought.

A loud sound brought her out of her reverie.

"Who is it?" she called.

"Egon, Your Majesty," a voice answered from the other side of the door.

"Come in."

The man, one of the Sharp Swords, came in and the rays of the sun reflected against his steel armour. Syrella could make out his chain-mail under his plate armour while his heavy yellow-black cloak almost touched the floor. Egon held his helmet in his right hand.

"I bring you news, Your Majesty. Thousands of people are approaching the city carrying the banner of Isisdor," said Egon.

Syrella straightened. "Open the gates and inform the council and my guard to gather in the great hall. Lead Sophie Delamere there as soon as she enters the city."

The man nodded and left the room in a hurry. Syrella looked at the spot where Egon had been. *How will my first meeting with Sophie go?*

Collecting herself, she turned and walked decisively out of her room.

Sophie glanced at Peter as he rode silently next to her horse. The Lord of the Knights seemed tireless in his armour. He and the other three men in the Royal Guard had surrounded her throughout their journey. Sophie breathed out wearily and rubbed her forehead. She couldn't remember the last time she had ridden for so many hours. She had told Peter to ride with Laurana who was just behind. But her former general had ruled out any such thing.

"*My wife is safe. I have seen to that. My oaths compel me to protect the queen.*"

Sophie had remained pensive after hearing his words. *So, am I still queen?*

She had neither throne nor crown, only some decrees that protected her title for as long as she was alive. Nevertheless, it was the people who chose which leader they would follow, and Sophie knew that their choice was always based on loyalty, or on fear. Nobody was afraid of her, and only those from Iovbridge who had chosen to leave their land and travel by her side were still devoted to her. Nevertheless, the continuous defeats over the last few years, along with her choice to leave Iovbridge, would erode the trust of even the most devoted of her supporters over time. Syrella's leadership traits could gain the loyalty of the people of Iovbridge, and then she would be transformed into a simple lady. Sophie had thought through this days ago, but she had decided to follow Elliot's plan—or rather Althalos'.

Sophie looked ahead and felt a sense of wonder at the huge gate of Wirskworth. Her horse neared the gate slowly, followed by thousands of people, the majority of whom were on foot. *Soon I'll meet Eleanor again.* The joyous thought lifted her spirits a bit.

She also wanted to see Elliot. She would have preferred that he would have told her who he really was at their first meeting, but the gratitude and affection she felt for him overshadowed all else.

A prolonged metallic clang vibrated in the air as the gate of the city that once belonged to the elves rattled open. The banners of the House of Endor flapped in every corner of the city's walls. She remembered that every time she had visited the capital of Elmor, she had always admired the moonstone used for buildings throughout the city. In contrast, the golden snake heads on top of the enormous gate of Wirskworth had always provoked a sense of fear in her.

How many bodies were burnt by the burning oil that poured out of the mouths of these reptiles?

She had heard stories of the first King of Elmor even habitually pouring burning-hot sand from these snakes' heads since oil cost more. Sophie didn't want to imagine the feeling of burning sand on a body clad in steel armour.

"Stay close to me," Peter said.

Sophie saw dozens of guards at the entrance to Wirskworth. She rode slowly into the city while the men with the yellow-black cloaks made room for her and her people to come in. As soon as she entered, a horse stood in front of her.

"Good evening, Egon," Peter called out to the man of the Sharp Swords.

Egon took off his helmet with a smile. "It's been a long time since our last meeting, Lord Peter. The governor is expecting Lady Sophie and her councillors in the great hall of Moonstone. The rest of the people of Iovbridge will be led to a place in the city that we have prepared for them."

"Very well," replied Sophie, noting that Egon had addressed her as "lady" and not as queen.

Sophie signaled to Peter and began riding uphill followed by her guards. Moreover, the Lord of the Knights made haste to inform the men in the council to continue on to Moonstone. Sophie discerned an untold number of people crowding in the narrow streets of the city, watching her arrival. She continued riding, watching Moonstone getting larger and larger before her. Time went by painfully slowly, and the people of Elmor were swarming the narrow alleys up to their governor's castle.

Peter returned to her side on his brown destrier. They crossed the city until they reached the east tower of the castle of Endor. Sophie dismounted and handed the reins to a stable hand. The Royal Guard and councillors did the same.

A little further off, Egon dismounted his horse, too. "Follow me," he said.

Sophie and her entourage followed Egon to the entrance of the castle. Five guards were standing out front and moved aside immediately as they approached. They navigated the well-lit corridors leading to the great hall. The door was open, and Sophie admired the architecture of Moonstone once more.

Egon entered the great hall. Sophie threw a furtive glance at the ornate ceiling, the marble floor and the animal furs hanging here and there on the walls. Nothing had changed since her last visit. Her eyes fell on the tall stone seat encircled by two gold snakes. The Scarred Queen was looking at her from afar with the rest of the men of the Sharp Swords standing around her. A little further off, the governor's councillors were seated at a majestic table along with her daughters and one more figure—a figure with silver-blue hair and shiny starry-blue eyes. Sophie always felt joy mingled with sorrow upon seeing Velhisya, remembering the stories she had heard about the woman's mother. But despite the sadness, seeing living proof that the Elder Races still existed in the world filled her with inexplicable joy.

Sophie stopped a few yards from Syrella and Egon approached his ruler's side. Sophie looked around, but didn't see Eleanor, Selwyn or Elliot anywhere. Anxiety flared inside her.

"I never expected to see you in this castle again." Syrella's voice was loud and strong as it rang across the great hall.

"The truth is that I didn't expect to find myself here again either," Sophie replied.

The Scarred Queen smiled. "I'm glad you and your people arrived safely in my city. However, I must confess that I feel bitter about certain decisions you have made while sitting on the throne."

Sophie saw Peter taking a step forward. "We're grateful for your hospitality, Syrella," the Lord of the Knights said, "but don't forget that Sophie is still Queen of Knightdorn," he said raising his voice.

"Your words are daring, Lord Brau. Sophie left her city and her crown. I'd say this changes things somewhat..."

"You know the laws of Knightd—" Peter began to say, but the governor interrupted him.

"Do you believe that a decree gives you power?" she asked with sarcasm in her voice. "I imagine you consider yourself quite clever to think such a thing."

"You're right. But I saw the letter you sent to Iovbridge a few days ago with my own eyes. If I'm not mistaken, I think you sent an invitation to the *Queen of Knightdorn*. Or did you perhaps never intend to recognize the laws of the kingdom and wished to mislead us?" Peter asked.

"How dare you!" a voice shouted from the table where Syrella's councillors sat. Sadon Burns stood up and strode towards Peter. "The Governor of Elmor agreed to accommodate Sophie Delamere and her people even though the Queen let the men of Wirskworth get slaughtered at the Forked River! Moreover, a few days ago, you sent Walter to our doorstep to save yourselves."

"I'm glad to see you again, Sadon. I'm sorry I sent Walter to your city, but this way we achieved a great victory against him. I'd also say that my decision not to send the Royal Army to the Forked River proved correct. The death of your son is proof of the danger posed by an unnecessary battle with Walter in an open field," Sophie said.

"How dare you!" Sadon screamed, spit flying from his mouth. "If you had sent your army to help us, perhaps my son would not have died. You lost the throne and the cities of your allies, and even now your men carry the banners of the pegasus. The only thing you have left is devotion because of the name of the Egercolls... But now, you're just a Delamere, lady of Felador, nothing more."

Sophie watched in horror as Peter drew his sword and at the same time, the men of the Sharp Swords touched the hilts in their belts.

"One more word, Burns," the Lord of the Knights said, face red with rage.

"You think I'm afraid of you, Brau?" the ineffectual lord shot.

"Enough!" shouted the governor.

"Syrella." Sophie's voice remained steady as she moved towards the governor. "You know that your decision to fight Walter at the Forked River was wrong. I have also made many mistakes while sitting on the throne. Nonetheless, my having said no to that insanity, was not one of them."

"Everyone in this room has suffered enough from Walter Thorn. Both of us know that we have no hope of defeating him without our being united. I don't care if your people call me 'queen' or 'Your Majesty'. I don't care whether my men carry a banner with an oak tree, a snake, or a pegasus. The only thing I want is for an end to the death that has plagued our people all these years. Are you with me or not?" She stopped in front of the Scarred Queen and looked into her black eyes.

Syrella got up swiftly and all sound died down in the hall. "Sophie Delamere is the Queen of Knightdorn. Let everyone in this hall remember this, but also let all those beyond it know it too."

Sophie extended her hand, and Syrella squeezed it hard. Hundreds of pairs of eyes gazed at the two women with a look of unparalleled awe.

The Alliance

Sophie let go of Syrella's hand, and Peter returned his blade to its sheath. The tension in the air shifted, the knot in Sophie's stomach loosening.

"What happened when Walter reached Wirskworth?" Sophie asked Syrella.

A man took a step forward, and she recognised him immediately. Jahon never left Syrella's guard.

"He tried to get into the city, but we forced him to retreat," the commander of the Sharp Swords said.

Syrella began to recount all that had happened over the last few days. Sophie listened carefully, and pain rooted in her soul when she heard what had happened to the Hewdars. She couldn't imagine having people tortured in wooden horses outside her gates. The events bewildered and worried Sophie, bringing many questions to the forefront of her mind.

"Is Master Thorold alive?" she asked.

Syrella nodded and gave her a sharp look that meant she should not interrupt her again. Sophie remained silent until Syrella finished her narrative. She sat in immense sorrow over the extent of the deaths that had befallen the City of Heavens, especially over the loss of Morys. The governor hadn't said a word about Elliot, Eleanor, and Selwyn. Even so, Sophie was sure that if something had happened to them, she would have mentioned it. She pondered a while over everything she had heard. The fact that Walter had attempted to contaminate Elmor's main source of water was a rather brilliant strategy. Sophie remained lost in her own thoughts until a question came to mind.

"When your men saw Thorn's soldiers leaving Wirskworth, you spoke to Elliot. Did he hasten to the City of Heavens to save Thorold?" she asked.

"Yes," the governor responded.

"Why did Elliot presume that Walter would go there? Thorn had ridden to Elmor without carts to draw food from the capital of Elirehar, and they had no idea that Thorold was alive."

Syrella remained silent, and Sophie was perplexed. It was as if the governor didn't want to speak about this.

"Where are Elliot, Eleanor, and Selwyn?"

Syrella didn't answer once more.

"Are they alive?" Peter's voice spoke aloud the worry Sophie carried.

"Yes," Syrella told them. "I would like to speak to the queen alone."

Sadon turned to the governor. "You can turn away Delamere's entourage, but you shouldn't bear secrets from your council, Your Maje—"

"Enough," Syrella said, giving him a look sharp enough to cut steel. "I've told you before that some things do not concern the council."

The lord began to distance himself, enraged, while the rest of those present followed suit. Sophie gestured to Peter, and he followed the crowd, anxiety mirrored in his eyes. Heavy silence hung over the empty hall when everyone except the two women had left.

"So?" asked Sophie.

"My City Guard caught sight of someone coming into the city through a secret passage, but they failed to catch him because it happened when they were changing watches." Irritation coloured the governor's voice. "The odd thing is that no man of Walter's could have a key to this passage. Even if somebody in this city had sent the key to Walter, it would have been well-nigh impossible for one of his men to pass by the guard unnoticed, unless he did so at the changing of the watch. This is a worrying coincidence."

"Perhaps somebody sent Thorn a key along with a letter with information about the times that the guards change watches."

"It wouldn't have been enough. The watch changes take place at unspecified times of the day and are decided only by me. This is so no one in the city knows when the guards change watch."

"I'm sure that neither you nor I believe in coincidence. So, the only thing left to assume is that someone in Wirskworth, who knew about the guards' watches, left the city and returned after a while," Sophie said.

"It appears to be the only reasonable answer," admitted Syrella.

"I have always been suspicious that one of your close advisers is a man of Walter's. I may have thought it foolish for you to have set up your men at the Forked River, but it is remarkable that Thorn learned of the plan."

The governor looked at her in a way that showed that she agreed. "For the time-being, Walter is quite a few miles away, but sooner or later he will attack Wirskworth again. We have to be careful until the spy is caught."

"I doubt it is only one," Sophie said.

Syrella pursed her lips into a fine line and then she spoke of William of the Sharp Swords and his attempt to free Reynald Karford.

"Elliot caught William freeing Karford?" she asked, her eyes wide. Syrella nodded. "And Elliot killed William?"

The governor frowned. "Not exactly... Elliot didn't have a sword, so he found himself at William's mercy. But the guard gave his sword to Karford to kill the boy—"

"And?" Sophie felt impatient, waiting for her to continue.

"Reynald killed William instead of Elliot."

"What? Reynald spared Elliot's life?"

"Yes. Elliot went to see Karford in his cell after the incident, but he didn't tell me what they discussed."

Sophie was troubled. "Is Karford still in the dungeons?"

"No. Elliot let him leave the town, Nobody knows why, but your cousin must have entrusted him with a mission. I asked Elliot many times about it, but he refused to divulge either the mission, or why he had entrusted him."

Sophie was very confused. She remained silent a while, then decided to mull it over again later. There were more important questions that needed answering. "Where is Elliot?"

Syrella avoided eye contact to evade this question. "He's gone. Selwyn, Eleanor, and Long Arm left the city a few days after him," she finally said.

Sophie felt a pinch of fear. "Where did they go?"

The governor took a deep breath and began to speak—Sophie felt as if an invisible hand tightened her chest with every word.

"Selwyn went to ask for an alliance with the Mercenaries and Eleanor went to Felador!" Sophie's voice pitched higher in disbelief. "The Mercenaries will never take the side of those with the smaller army, and Felador has only a few dozen men. The only soldiers in its capital will be the boys who survived Walter's attack seventeen years ago."

Syrella was composed. "Elliot believes that Felador has remained without a governor for a long time. He told me that each region in the kingdom that isn't under Walter's rule must be protected and must acquire a leader. He didn't send Eleanor there to bring us soldiers but to give them hope. He told me that in order for a place to be reborn, a prudent leader is essential, otherwise it will remain forever in the shadows."

Sophie feared for Eleanor's safety, and she also knew that Peter would panic as soon as he found out where Selwyn was going. Nevertheless, if Eleanor reached Felador, she would be safe, which was not a given for anyone in Wirskworth. The capital of Felador was the last place in the world that preoccupied Walter—this thought brought her momentary peace.

"Why should they accept Eleanor as their ruler in Felador? Why should they listen to a scoundrel like Long Arm in the Ice Islands?" she asked. "Moreover, the idea of the Mercenaries fighting with us is insane even if we promise them all the gold in the world. The Mercenaries take gold only from future victors, not from future losers."

Syrella remained silent, but nodded.

"Elliot's plan to lure Walter to Ersemor was Althalos' plan. Now, Elliot is acting on his own and he may not be ready," Sophie told her.

The governor closed her eyes for a moment. "I thought the same, but Thorold seems to agree with his decisions. You can speak to him."

"I still can't believe that Thorold is alive and has been in hiding all these years. Perhaps Elliot should have sent someone to rule the City of Heavens instead of Felador," Sophie said, irritated as she thought of Walter's attack in the birthplace of Thomas Egercoll.

"No one remained in the City of Heavens. They're all dead," Syrella said and Sophie understood what she meant. It would take time for that place to regain people who wanted to live there, even more so, a ruler.

"You haven't told me where Elliot has gone," Sophie said.

"Into the Mountains of the Forgotten World."

Sophie's jaw dropped. "Does he believe that the Elder Races will fight with us?" If Elliot could make the creatures fight by their side, it would be an immense help. Legends said that the Elder Races possessed unique powers.

"There's more to his mission. If the myths about the Elder Races are true, this means that he is either unaware of them, or that he doubts their veracity. Unless he thinks he can break the curse..."

Sophie got lost in her thoughts. She was aware that Syrella knew a lot about the Elder Races. She had once confided in Sophie that although she didn't believe the legends, she wondered why her brother hadn't brought Velhisya's mother to Elmor. The fact that Arthur had returned alone to Wirskworth with a baby in his arms meant that either the tales about the curse were true, or that some other unfortunate incident had occurred.

"Who else knows where Elliot and his companions are?" Sophie asked.

"Thorold and me. Elliot asked me to swear that I wouldn't divulge the truth to anyone except you. He even told me to ask you not to disclose this information to Peter. Elliot was sure that you wouldn't be able to avoid speaking to him about Selwyn, so he advised me to only inform the Lord of the Knights about his son's mission. As for Karford, word has it that he has left the city, but nobody knows why."

Sophie stood, gaze unfocused as she stared at the governor's seat, until Syrella's voice was heard again. "Elliot asked me not to reveal where Selwyn and Long Arm are until we have news of them. If they manage to forge new alliances, they will send an emissary and then their missions can be revealed. He also told me that if he managed to retake the road with new allies, he would send news with his hawk. But Elliot doesn't want anyone pinning their hopes on new alliances without their first being a given. It would be best that these secrets not reach Walter's spy in the city earlier than necessary. As for Eleanor, your cousin believes that few need to know where she is."

Sophie sighed. "Okay," she said.

"I heard that Lord Ballard travelled to Elmor with you" Syrella told her.

Sophie recounted all that had happened in Iovbridge the last few days, speaking about Walter's spies, Giren Barlow and the victory in Ramerstorm.

Syrella seemed pensive. "Althalos' plan was ingenious and the victory at Ramerstorm was hard won. I'm glad that Giren Barlow finally escaped from Walter."

"Me too," Sophie exclaimed.

Both women remained silent for a while until the Scarred Queen cleared her throat. "I heard you revived the institution of the knights. Perhaps now I too could name the men of the Sharp Swords *knights.*"

Sophie didn't answer, preoccupied by only one thought that had taken over her mind. *Will Elliot be our saviour or our destruction?*

The Black Vale

Selwyn rode while the sun was still in the sky, but soon it would yield its place over to the moon and the stars. He felt tired as he thought of John and Eleanor. Five days had passed since they had parted. *Are they alright?*

Selwyn glanced at the road he was crossing. Goldtown, the capital of Vylor, was a place that the Paths of the Elder Races did not reach. He'd had to ride in the plains between the Mountains of the Forgotten World and the Lonely Mountain. He was very close to Goldtown, and on the right he could make out the Mercenary River. Selwyn often wondered what kind of reception he'd have when he reached his destination. He had never found himself in the city of the Mercenaries before, but he remembered his father talking about the greed and compulsions of these people, which led them to destruction throughout their history.

Selwyn had heard that many years back, Vylor had been an affluent region. Its northern part bordered the fringe of the Iron Mountain and the foot of this mountain was rich in metals and gold. So, the first King of the Mercenaries had constructed mines, exporting the treasures of this majestic mountain. The greatest part of the Iron Mountain belonged to Oldlands, and its ruler knew nothing about the mines of Vylor that had been dug along its borders. As soon as he became aware, he was close to starting a war. However, the King of the Mercenaries claimed that the mines he had constructed were on his own land. Oldlands accepted his assertions since the Iron Mountain could cover the needs of both former kingdoms.

While the King of Oldlands had left the mines of the Mercenaries untouched, it wasn't enough for them in the end. Some years later, the men of Vylor had extracted almost all the metals and gold in their mines, and the last was wasted. Then, the first King of the Mercenaries decided to acquire riches by supplying various conquerors and tyrants with swords at a price, which his successors continued to do for the rest of their history. Furthermore, the rulers of Vylor were in the habit of looting villages and castles, stealing their harvests and gold.

Damned Hales. The House of Hale ruled over Vylor from the time when the first humans set foot in Knightdorn. Nevertheless, its members did not seem to learn from the mistakes of the past. Each new ruler from the House of Hale was always more greedy than the last.

The sun set slowly, and Selwyn could now see the wall of Goldtown. The capital of Vylor was large, but the wall that surrounded it didn't look strong, and there was no moat around it. Selwyn discerned its small, wooden gate as he rode closer.

This city could easily be conquered. The entrance to the capital of Vylor was fortified with steel in some parts, but still looked old.

Selwyn leaned into his stirrups and pulled on the reins of his mare, breaking speed. He looked up and spotted a dozen guards positioned in the passage behind the walls' ramparts. He had drawn their attention and one of them headed hurriedly down to the interior of the city.

He stopped his mare a short distance from the entrance to Goldtown and waited. A little later, the gate began to open with a creaking sound and five riders headed toward him. Selwyn remained still as they neared him. The guards of Goldtown were not wearing any armour, but large swords hung from their belts. A few moments later, the five men stopped in front of him, and he noticed their woollen jerkins.

"We don't accept peasants in our city. Turn back to your land!" one of the guards said in a commanding tone. His hair was sparse and his look sleazy.

"I'm not a villager. I'm an envoy of the Queen of Knightdorn," Selwyn told them.

The guards started laughing.

"I don't know whether you know where you are, but this is the last place the Queen of Knightdorn would send an envoy. *If* she's still queen... I think Walter Thorn was ready to attack Iovbridge some time ago."

Selwyn knew that news of the recent days' events wouldn't have travelled to Goldtown yet. "Walter Thorn left Isisdor, and attacked Wirskworth where he was defeated."

The guards started laughing even louder.

"I am here on the Queen of Knightdorn and the Governor of Elmor's orders. I carry a letter from Syrella Endor, for the Ruler of Vylor!" Selywn said in a loud voice. Then he raised a letter with the wax seal that looked like a snake. "I would advise you to accompany me immediately to Liher Hale."

Their laughter stopped abruptly, and the man with the sparse hair stared at the letter. "Very well," he said.

He turned his horse while the other four men surrounded Selwyn's mare. They rode towards the city and passed through the ancient door.

Selwyn's gaze wandered over the city's interior. The ground in Goldtown was made up of sand and a few cobble-stoned alleys that spread along its length. Their horses moved at a slow and steady pace while men and women walked by unhurriedly. Most were dressed in threadbare clothing. Sunlight darkened and drunken shouting filled the air. The city teemed with life, which Selwyn hadn't dared to imagine. The people of Iovbridge had all been retreating to their homes before sunset for many years. Isisdor had been at war for decades while Vylor was a forgotten place without problems of war to trouble its inhabitants.

They continued riding towards the northern part of the city, and people went in and out of the small taverns lining the narrow streets, their faces flushed from drinking. A little further off, a cackling sound caught his attention. He saw a man fondling the buttocks of a young simpering woman. Selwyn knew that the city of the Mercenaries had a reputation as the place with the most bastard kids in the kingdom since the institution of marriage did not exist in Vylor. Many in the kingdom called the army of the Mercenaries "the Army of Bastards."

A castle with rounded turrets came into view. The Goldtown Castle was small in Selwyn's eyes. The guard with the sleazy-looking face stopped his mare, and Selwyn did the same. The rest of the guards dismounted and pulled their steeds to a small stable on the right. They tied up their horses and moved towards the deserted entrance of the castle.

One of the guards opened the wooden door of the building and Selwyn entered it, surrounded by the others. They passed dark rooms and damp corridors until they found themselves in a bigger room. A few lit torches nailed to the walls flickered and Selwyn noted some rusty armour hanging on the walls of the hall. He had heard about this room from his father. It was the vestibule to the great hall of Goldtown Castle, decorated with the armour of all the Hales who had led Vylor in the past.

In the far corner of the room was a door that for the most part was gold-plated. Then, a feeling of fear mixed with impatience overcame him. One of the guards opened the door and Selwyn found himself face to face with about ten women swaying naked along the length of the great hall of the castle. The light of the fire imparted a reddish-hue to their bodies while a little further off a few men beat a handful of wooden tambourines. There was quite a crowd in the hall, and the entry of the guards and Selwyn drew a few stares. Selwyn stared at the women who moved sensually, dancing an unknown dance. He looked more closely at their faces. None of them looked a day over sixteen summers.

The great hall of the Goldtown Castle was quite simple, without wall paintings and ornate domes. A large wooden table stood in its centre, behind the young dancers. Selwyn counted a dozen figures eating and drinking gleefully. To their right, the men with the tambourines kept rhythm for the women dancing, while behind the majestic table stood two armoured guards.

The guards led Selwyn to the table, and a man sitting at the head raised his hand to them. The sound of the tambourines immediately fell silent, and the young women stopped swaying.

"What's going on? Who is this?" the man at the head of the table asked in a gruff voice. His amber-coloured hair was curly and thick. A long beard covered most of his face while his eyes were small and wild.

"This man just arrived in the city, my lord. He asked to speak with you. He is an envoy of the Queen of Knightdorn," one of the men accompanying Selwyn replied hurriedly.

All eyes were upon him. Liher Hale—the man with the curly hair—got up off his seat with a look of incredulity reflected in his steely features. His clothes were made with gold thread with a coat of arms sewn to his chest. Selwyn knew the symbol. It was a rusty coin, the emblem of Vylor.

"An envoy of the Queen of Knightdorn?" Liher repeated.

Selwyn sized him up. The man was about the same age as his father. "I am Selwyn Brau, son of Peter Brau."

"I know who your father is, but I wonder what you're doing in my city and what the *queen* wants of me." Anger burned across the man's face.

Selwyn took note of his sarcastic tone as he pronounced the word queen. "The Queen of Knightdorn and the Governor of Elmor have sent me here with the purpose of asking for an alliance with the Ruler of Vylor." Liher stood still. "Sophie Delamere and Syrella Endor are prepared to offer a sum of gold in exchange if, of course, the Ruler of Vylor were to accept to ally with them."

Elliot had advised him to journey to Goldtown with a small amount of gold to tempt Liher Hale. Nevertheless, Syrella had told him that it was foolish to offer anything to the Governor of Vylor without having him agree to help first. Otherwise, Liher would steal the gold and throw him out of the city.

A faint smile had formed on the governor's lips. "Do you know who I am, boy?" he asked.

"The Governor of Vylor."

"I am Liher Hale, descendant of the House of Hale. You can't trick me."

"That was not my intention," Selwyn replied.

"Really?" Liher said. "I know well that Elmor abandoned its old alliance with Isisdor a long time ago. I also know that Walter Thorn is outside Iovbridge with sixty-five thousand men, ready to take the Palace of the Dawn. I would say you need to choose your next words carefully." His tone betrayed a veiled threat.

"The queen rekindled her old alliance with Elmor. Walter heard about this and rushed to attack Syrella Endor with a few thousand riders before she united forces with the Royal Army. Walter's army received an unexpected attack from the men of Wirskworth and was defeated, resulting in his retreat. By now, he must be in Ballar again." Selwyn hesitated for a moment. "Also, The Guardians of the South fought on the side of Syrella and the queen."

"Reynald Karford fought on the side of Elmor?"

"Reynald Karford is no longer the Guardian Commander. He was defeated in a duel and lost his title."

"Reynald Karford, defea—" Liher stopped short and walked in a circle around Selwyn. "By whom?"

Selwyn took a deep breath. "By Elliot Egercoll, son of Thomas Egercoll and Alice Asselin, who was being trained in secret by Althalos Baudry all these years."

"HOW DARE YOU UTTER SUCH LIES BEFORE ME!" Liher shouted.

"I have a letter from the Governor of Elmor that confirms my words."

"From Syrella Endor? I thought you were an emissary of the queen..."

Selwyn looked him in the eye. "The queen sent me to Elmor days ago, so that I could inform Syrella Endor about her decisions and help in the battle against Walter. When Walter was forced to retreat, the governor sent me here with the permission of the queen so that I could pursue an alliance with the Ruler of the Black Vale."

"You said there is a son of Thomas Egercoll whom Althalos trained?" Liher asked.

Selwyn nodded. He felt awkward revealing this information, but Elliot had told him that after all that had happened, the news would travel round the whole kingdom sooner or later.

"Give me the letter," the man said.

Selwyn took the parchment from his belt and extended his hand. Liher approached him, took the letter, and broke the wax seal. His eyes seemed blurry under the torchlight as he read the parchment.

"Unbelievable!" he shrieked.

"It's true," Selwyn told him.

"I think we need to consider Elmor's proposal," someone said from the wooden table nearby. A man, younger than Liher, stood. His voice was not heavy, but he too had curly and thick hair.

"Sit down, Lothar. You may belong to the House of Hale but as I've told you thousands of times, *I* am the ruler of this land!" Liher shouted.

Lothar sat down in his seat, his expression cross. Selwyn remembered that name—his father had once told him that the younger brother of Liher and Lain was the most prudent.

"Thomas Egercoll and Alice Asselin couldn't have children," the governor said after a while.

"That's what everyone thought, but Alice gave birth to a son before her death."

"She had a son in secret, and he grew up with Althalos Baudry," Liher said to himself. "And years later, the son of Egercoll appears in the kingdom, beats Reynald Karford, and forces Walter Thorn to a defeat with the help of the army of Wirskworth... These are just some of what this letter from Syrella Endor says."

Liher studied Selwyn's face. Selwyn didn't look away and nodded.

"And you accompanied Elliot Egercoll to Elmor?" Liher went on.

"Yes."

"Is he such a capable warrior?"

"He's the greatest I have ever seen." Selwyn felt confident. He realised that the man opposite him was putting the tidal wave of information he'd just heard in order. Liher would want to take the side of the most powerful if he chose to return to war for the throne of Knightdorn and now the scales had turned.

"I know that Iovbridge doesn't have gold," the governor said again.

"The war has depleted the queen's gold, but Syrella Endor is prepared to reward Vylor and everybody knows that Elmor's gold is the most valuable in the kingdom. Sophie Delamere will also restore the right of the Governor of Vylor to vote for the King of Knightdorn," Selwyn said.

Liher muttered something nonsensical. "Yes, that's what Syrella's letter states," he remarked and started walking around Selwyn again. "If I fight against Walter, will I have to march my army to Isisdor or to Elmor?"

Selwyn hadn't expected this question. *Liher may be a savage, but he knows about war.*

Selwyn bet that the man opposite him knew that Iovbridge would fall more easily than Wirskworth in a siege. A new alliance between Isisdor and Elmor could bring the Royal Army to the east-south. With Stonegate in the hands of the queen, that would be easy. This presupposed that the queen would leave the throne to Walter without a battle. Nevertheless, Syrella and Sophie's armies behind the walls of Wirskworth would be more difficult to defeat. Walter's reign would be undermined as long as the two women remained alive. Liher seemed to know all of this, and it wouldn't surprise him if Sophie chose to take her armies and head to Elmor, abandoning the throne.

"To Elmor," Selwyn told Liher. Syrella and Elliot had advised him to tell the truth. Besides, the news would get around sooner or later.

"Will Sophie Delamere leave Iovbridge?"

Selwyn nodded.

"So, soon she won't be queen! You say that Sophie Delamere will restore the Governor of Vylor's right to vote to choose the king though she won't be sitting on the throne any longer. I don't know where Walter is, but I'm sure he'll take Iovbridge before he marches to Elmor to kill his enemies. Thorn will restore the male line of succession the moment he puts on the crown..." Liher looked enraged.

"You're right... But Sophie may beat Walter, and then she will fulfil all of her promises."

"So, the tradeoffs being offered for me to ally with the *queen* will only be given if Walter is defeated?"

"No. Elmor's gold will be given immediately. Then, if Walter is defeated and the queen remains on the throne, she will keep her word for the rest," Selwyn told him.

The man smiled and he shook his head with a shudder. "Okay, I'll fight on the side of Sophie Delamere and of Syrella Endor," he replied.

The governor approached and extended his hand. Selwyn shook it, feeling a mix of relief and joy.

"I know your father," Liher said, looking at Selwyn as he squeezed his fingers. "He's the most trusted man of the *queen*, but he always disregards reason."

Liher smiled, and Selwyn felt that something wasn't going well. Time stood still for a moment and then a thump cracked against the back of his head, wrapping his thoughts in a dark vortex.

The Path of Fate

Eleanor stole a look at John as he rode a few yards away from her. Now they were close to the Road of Steel, and the view of the Lonely Mountain had been accompanying them for almost a day. The stars were like pearls in the night sky and her cloak kept the chill of night away.

Morys' face appeared in Eleanor's mind. He seldom left her thoughts. She had prepared for a lot when she left Iovbridge, but love was not one of the things she could have predicted. She remembered her father telling her that love and lust always came when you least expected them.

After all, he was right. Life plays strange tricks on us.

She recalled the traces of fear she had felt before leaving the place where she grew up. She knew that if the Guardians caught her and her companions in the Land of Fire, their future would be bleak. Rape, torture, death were some of the things she thought would happen to her if she fell into the hands of Reynald Karford. Nevertheless, she never dared to imagine that she could have fallen in love on that journey.

She and Morys had lived in Iovbridge for years without ever having spoken to each other until they journeyed to Elmor. The "unprepossessing Morys" was what she had thought about him in the beginning. And yet, the day he offered to fight Reynald Karford for her sake, everything changed. Sometimes Eleanor wondered whether she would have loved Morys forever if he had stayed alive. She knew that the years took their toll on people's emotions, and they would go their separate ways, but now she would never have an answer to this question. One thing that was certain was that she missed Morys more than she could bear and each time she thought of him, she felt an invisible hand squeezing her stomach.

Eleanor had felt the same despair when her brother had died from an illness no one in the kingdom had seen before. Sophie had tried to bring in every healer on the continent, but nobody had been able to figure out what caused Bert to have trouble breathing. Until one day he left this world forever and a piece of her soul left with him. Morys, too, had taken a piece, and she wondered how much longer her soul would hold out in this world with it being so torn apart.

"I insist that you follow me until the Three Heads," John said in a steady voice, breaking her thoughts.

Eleanor was puzzled. Long Arm was seldom serious. "I told you before, if I ride between Oldlands and Ballar up to the Vale of Flowers, I'll reach Aquarine sooner," she said.

"And I told you that this road may be faster, but it's very dangerous. Walter's scouts will keep watch around Ballar, and his allies are located near Yellow River. If you come across them, you're dead."

"If I ride up to the Three Heads, it'll take almost two days longer."

"Yes, but you'll stay alive!" Long Arm shouted. "The later you reach the crossroad between the Path of Shar and that of the Wise, the more likely you are to avoid a meeting with Walter's men."

"I want to reach Aquarine as soon as possible."

"Why? Elliot isn't expecting allies from Felador. He only sent you there because he believes that place needs a new ruler. Two days won't make a difference!"

"I don't like travelling. I detest riding," Eleanor responded. She was lying. She just wanted to be alone.

"And you prefer to die rather than ride two more days?" John burst out.

"The road you want to cross is more dangerous than the one I want to follow. The Three Heads are surrounded by the cities that have allied with Walter," she argued.

"Walter's allies are marching towards Iovbridge."

"Do you think they won't have left anyone guarding their regions?"

"They're not expecting an attack in the north!" John said. "No one has any reason to send scouts to the land of the northern regions. Moreover, there are several inns where we can rest up along the Road of Steel. In contrast, the journey through the countryside is very dangerous."

"I think you want to cross the Road of Steel for the inns and *especially* the brothels along the route. You couldn't care less whether you get to your destination faster, all you care about is having a good time. Elliot may not need help from Felador, but he does from the Ice Islands," Eleanor said with a measure of annoyance.

"If I die trying to get to the northern isles, Elliot won't gain any new allies. It's more important that I reach my destination safe and sound. What's more, I think the reason you want to ride this route is that you seek danger," Long Arm said.

Eleanor turned to face him for the first time that night. "What do you mean?"

John frowned. "You want to be alone to pursue a dangerous journey because you miss Morys. You want to risk your life because one mistake could send you to him."

Eleanor opened her mouth in surprise. Long Arm knew how to read people more than she realised. "You're mistaken," she said after a while.

"Your eyes say more than your tongue, Eleanor. I know you miss him. I know that a voice in your head tells you to take a chance and if you fail, you will simply return to his arms. But that voice is making a mistake. If they catch you, they won't just take your life. You'll suffer. I'm sure that Elliot would prefer that you listen to me. If you recall, even he trusted me as his guide. I know you're not short of reason. My company may not be the most pleasant, but I'm sure that even for you, it's preferable to such recklessness."

"Your company doesn't bother me. You are one of the few men I trust.

I just want to reach my birthplace as soon as I can."

Eleanor looked up at the sky. Long Arm's words had caught her unawares. She had been feeling the need to do something reckless for a long time—to risk her life for a new adventure. It would remind her of the journey with Morys. It would be as if they were together again. Moreover, she had wanted to be alone for days. She was consumed with sorrow each time she bid farewell to one of her companions, but a part of her sought loneliness. Eleanor bet that only John understood how she felt.

"Remember that the dead are not waiting for anyone to come into their arms. They only live through our memories. As long as these remain in the world, they too are alive. Only when they are forgotten by those alive, do they really die," Long Arm said.

Tears pricked Eleanor's eyes and she lowered her gaze. John was brimming with wisdom, a trait that seemed to be contradicted by his vices. "And if the living want to find themselves in the embrace of the dead?" she murmured.

"Fate must decide that, not you. Don't forget that there are people in this world that need you. For as long as you fight for them and Morys stays in your thoughts, he too will be with you. At some point you'll meet him again. The path of fate will send you to him when the time comes."

Eleanor realised that he wasn't drunk at that moment. Silence spread between them and their horses' hoofbeats were the only sounds carrying on the light breeze of the night.

"Thank you for everything, John. The time has nevertheless come for me to make some decisions on my own. You're free to follow my path if you wish," Eleanor said.

John pulled his horse to a stop and looked at her with fiery eyes. "I consider what you want to do reckless. But you may be right... Perhaps you need to make this decision on your own. You remind me a little of myself when I was young, but that's not a compliment, since it's a miracle that I managed to make it to my age."

Eleanor slowed her horse, too. They were at the point where their paths would part. She glanced at him, trying to smile.

"Bye, John. I hope we'll meet again one day." Sorrow ignited in every cell of her body as she said goodbye. She didn't want to break down crying—she kicked her horse and took off as fast as she could before any tears could fall.

Invisible punches hit her chest as she moved away. She had never gotten close to another person before except for Sophie and Bert, and yet, Elliot, Selwyn and John had almost become like family to her. The tears flowed freely, while joy sparked within her. She may have been alone now, but it was the first time that she decided for herself.

The Imprisoned Soul

The morning breeze blew over the mountain slopes. Two days had passed since Elliot had spoken with Aleron, and a day had gone by without any instructions. He had expected someone to come and find him the previous morning to "train" him, but the only person he had interacted with was the elf woman who had brought him a rabbit to eat.

What am I doing in this place? he thought.

Elliot watched the Elder Races for hours, and all he could conclude was that they spent their time in a very boring manner. The elwyn would go for walks on the mountain slope, gazing at the sky and collecting wild greens and mushrooms. The elves did the same and read from a few well-worn books alongside the elwyn. The two giants seemed the weariest and most depressed beings in the settlement. They spent most of the day sharpening their enormous swords, and they ate of the small amount of food there was more frequently than any other being there.

What a boring life... Elliot looked at the sky and the distant hills past the slopes.

A faint screech brought him out of his reverie. He turned and spotted an eagle soaring wondrously through the air. A memory came to mind—Hurwig's squawk above his head just before Walter's men caught him on the outskirts of Elirehar. His spine prickled as he recalled the terror he had felt as soon as he saw his companions were captured by the enemy's men. He sighed, remembering the pain from the bump to his head from where Walter's soldiers had hit him with a stone. He had woken hours later in Wirskworth after his horse had carried him there, unconscious.

I should have been more careful.

"I think you have lazed around enough," a voice said, bringing Elliot out of his thoughts. Aleron stood nearby, fiery eyes boring into him. "I see you like the view."

Elliot nodded. "I was wondering which region of Knightdorn the Mountains of the Forgotten World belongs to."

Aleron smiled. "To Isisdor, the largest region in the continent. Ersemor and the Rock Mountains are also a part of it."

"The Rock Mountains?"

"The mountains next to Stonegate," the elwyn explained.

Elliot was unaware of this information. "Is it true that the elwyn built the Palace of the Dawn?"

"Yes. The Palace of the Dawn and the Temple of Azelor are some of the most beautiful buildings my race ever made."

Elliot was perplexed. "The Temple of Azelor?"

Aleron nodded. "The temple of Iovbridge was built by the elwyn in honour of Azelor until George Thorn converted it to the Temple of the Unknown God. People can still honour Azelor in the City of Heavens. The Egercolls always honoured the God of Light."

"Naturally! The Egercolls were the only ones to bond with the pegasi—one of the first beings that Azelor created," Elliot said, thinking of the wall paintings he had seen in the temple of the City of Heavens.

"I don't think that's true."

Elliot frowned and was going to argue, but something else caught his attention. An elf stood behind Aleron. He hadn't noticed him before, hidden as he was by the silhouette of the elwyn.

"The elwyn lived for thousands of years before the existence of humans and none ever came across a pegasus in the Age of Light," Aleron told him, not seeming to notice the elf behind him. "I know that in the temple of the City of Heavens the elwyn and one pegasus are depicted receiving life together from Azelor. However, the Elder Races believe that this creature is one of the newest in our world. Precisely when and by whom it was created is difficult to ascertain."

His words got Elliot thinking, but as much as he tried, he couldn't find any answers. He took a closer look at the elf behind Aleron. He had long chestnut-coloured hair. His face was fierce and beautiful at the same time. A small sword hung from his belt. Elliot gathered that this man was a warrior.

"That is enough of this talk, I think. The time has come to see what Althalos taught you," Aleron said.

Finally! His injured leg hadn't hurt for the last two days, and he was ready to practise fighting. Elliot took hold of his sword, which the elwyn had returned to him, and stood up.

"Alaric is a great swordsman—one of the best of the Elder Races," Aleron said and gestured to the elf.

The elf pulled out the sword that was hanging from his belt. Quite a few elwyn and elves were gathered around, staring at them. Elliot lifted his sword and watched the small-bodied creature opposite him.

Alaric approached, and Elliot looked at his opponent's legs. The grass he stood on seemed to stand still but moved as soon as the elf took a step forward. Alaric moved suddenly, but Elliot avoided his blow and darted to attack. His opponent was very quick. With a twist, he moved to the right, leaving Elliot's sword to cut empty air. Elliot readied himself for another swing, but the elf aimed at his feet, and Elliot almost lost his balance to repel Alaric's attack. The elf continued to move at great speed, delivering repeated blows to his lower limbs. Elliot could foresee his moves, but the elf's speed made it difficult for him to counter the blows.

Alaric made a swift move and the sword barely missed Elliot's knee. *Damn!*

He didn't want the leg that had just healed from Annys' teeth to get wounded again. Alaric continued the attack, forcing him into a defensive posture. The elf's sword tore through the air before he took a giant leap, twisting his torso. Elliot was caught off guard and he almost lost his footing. He lifted his sword to deflect the attack, but the elf struck the blade with such force that Elliot stumbled backwards. He was about to lift his sword again, but his opponent had already approached him. Then something strange happened—Alaric's sword emitted a red light.

Elliot took his sword in both hands and made a swift slash downwards. As soon as the blades clashed, Elliot screamed as the sword slipped from his hands. He grimaced in pain. He tried to withstand the feeling of the burning hilt, but in vain. He looked at his hands for blisters, but remembered the burning sensation wouldn't leave any wounds.

Aleron's laugh rippled through the air. "I should think that, knowing the effect of the Light of Life by now, you would have been more careful," he said playfully.

Elliot was about to object. *How can I fight against a blade I can't repel? It's unfair.* The exercise reminded him of the early years of his training when he constantly complained to Althalos about the hardships he was subjected to.

He had decided not to protest, but still had questions. "Why was the light that enveloped the sword red? I thought that the Light of Life was blue."

Aleron scoffed. "The Light of the elwyn is blue, but that of the elves is red."

Elliot took a deep breath, lifted his sword and looked at his opponent. The light on the blade of the sword was the same shade as the colour of his irises. Aleron may have been laughing, but Alaric had the stance of a warrior with a look that said he would rather die than be defeated. He was waiting for Elliot to attack.

Elliot ran towards him, but the elf was prepared. Alaric's small body shifted to the left while the lit sword went for Elliot's feet again. He lifted his right foot and avoided the blow, knowing he couldn't repel the elf with his sword as long as his opponent's blade shone. The elf prepared to attack his legs again, but just before he extended his hand, Alaric turned and went for his neck. Elliot pulled back as fast as he could, avoiding the sword. His opponent hastily attacked again, but this time an enraged Elliot bent towards the elf and pushed him with all his might with his left hand. Alaric hadn't expected this move. He took several steps back, trying to keep himself upright.

Elliot didn't run towards the elf, although he could have taken advantage of his clumsy step. He threw Alaric a look full of hatred. The elf's last blow had aimed to kill. Elliot knew that during practice swordsmen never attacked such body parts unless they held wooden swords. Alaric stood a few feet away. In theory, things were simple—he couldn't use his sword to repel a blow as long as Alaric's sword shone. So, he had to avoid any attacks. At the same time, if he attacked, he had to be sure that his blow would find its target instead of hitting the lit sword to prevent the hilt of his blade from burning him.

The elf rushed at him, and Elliot threw his sword at his opponent's face. Alaric opened his eyes wide and dodged the sword in a clumsy move. Elliot tackled him and threw him to the ground. The sword slipped from the elf's hand, losing its red light. Alaric tried to escape Elliot's grip and threw a punch at his ribs. The pain radiated up Elliot's side, but he headbutted the elf on the nose.

"ENOUGH!"

Aleron's shout rang in his ears, but he didn't care. He was about to throw another punch at Alaric when something pulled him away with superhuman strength. Elliot fell onto his back. Pain spread along his backbone and then he saw the huge figure that had pulled him off Alaric. A male giant looked at him with rage. His black hair was long and dirty, and his eyes had narrowed in his face. His body was covered with a huge coat made of wolfskin. The giant lifted his hands, ready to attack again. Elliot wasn't scared. He had learned not to be afraid of death.

"Enough, I said!" Aleron's lithe form stood in front of Elliot's fallen body.

Hundreds of eyes had watched the scene unfold, and Elliot felt as if they were looking at him in anger. His attack on Alaric had infuriated them.

Elliot got to his feet and his anger continued to simmer. "So, the elwyn and the elves use the Light of Life to kill," he said with a huff.

Aleron turned towards him. "You must decide which path you wish to follow, my lad."

"What do you mean?"

"You must choose whether you want to follow the path of hatred or not."

"He tried to kill me!" Elliot snapped.

"No! He knows you have been trained by Althalos. One of the first things he taught you was how to face a sudden hit to the throat," Aleron said.

This was true, but he didn't care. "I have never received a swing from a sword that I can't repel," Elliot protested.

"If I remember correctly, the swift blows that aim to cut your throat are always best avoided with manoeuvres, and not with your blade. At least, that's what I think Althalos taught you."

Elliot looked at the elwyn angrily, irritated that he knew so many things about his training. "It doesn't matter. When you face something for the first time, it's customary to improvise."

"Really?" Aleron said, raising his eyebrow. "Do you believe that Althalos would agree with that?"

Elliot knew the answer but nevertheless didn't care. "The elf should also have known how to defend himself if somebody throws a sword at him."

"Naturally, but in a practice duel, the fighters do not throw objects."

"And they *don't* aim for their opponent's throat."

"Do you mean to say that over all the years you were being trained, no opponent aimed for your throat during practice?"

"Certainly not with a steel sword!"

"That's a lie."

Elliot was bewildered. At the beginning of his training when he was a child, he used to counter blows aimed at his neck with his blade. Althalos would tell him to avoid them, wanting to prepare him for such time as he didn't have a sword, but Elliot never managed to follow his instructions. Then, Althalos had commanded he avoid the blows of a peasant holding a steel sword while he was unarmed. He had been terrified and had asked Althalos to at least use a wooden sword, but his Master had refused. When the peasant attacked him, it was the first time he'd succeeded in avoiding blows aimed not only at his throat but other parts of his body.

"It should have been made clear that such blows were allowed before the duel began," Elliot said.

"Do you know why Althalos made you avoid the blows of that peasant with the steel sword when you were young?"

How does he know all this? Elliot didn't know but felt strange. "Why?" he asked.

"Because fear is a useful emotion. It keeps you on the alert and prepares you so that you can face any imminent danger. Alaric knew that blow would frighten you and force you to concentrate. It would make you realise that there was a risk and that this wasn't a typical training. Only then would you find a way to deal with the danger and retaliate. If you had failed to avoid the blow, he would not have injured your neck."

Elliot threw a look at the elf who looked at him with a fury that didn't seem to confirm Aleron's words. "Then the same applies to my attack, too."

"In a practice duel, objects should not be hurled. At least, not by those who have trained under Althalos. Nevertheless, I didn't try to stop you because of that," the elwyn responded.

Elliot remembered Althalos telling him countless times not to hurl his sword when practising. He'd asked him why he was so unbending about that rule. His Master had told him that while a good throw of the sword was a useful skill, the aim of the training was for him to learn how to fight holding the blade in his hand. Althalos had argued that throwing a sword was rather dangerous since if it didn't hit its target, the swordsman who'd thrown his weapon would be left unarmed.

"Why did you try to stop me then?" he asked.

"Because you attacked with a vengeance."

Elliot couldn't believe his ears. "Nonsense! I attacked in self-defence because my opponent tried to kill me."

"You attacked with hatred. Hatred is not welcome here. The hatred of Manhon Egercoll is responsible for all the suffering of all those who surround you," Aleron told him as the group of elves and elwyn watched Elliot. "What do you believe the Elder Races would do to you for all that they have suffered, if they let their hatred blind them?"

A soft breeze blew on the mountain slope, and Elliot's anger died down. He threw one last glance at Aleron. Elliot approached Alaric and extended his hand. The elf stared at him with his steely eyes, but, to his surprise, returned his handshake.

"Walk with me." Aleron's voice was hard.

Elliot turned and fell in step alongside the elwyn while those present seemed to return to their everyday tasks.

"Hatred will never help you, Elliot," Aleron told him. "Hatred makes you feel invincible, and it also makes you see things in a short-sighted manner."

Elliot wished to disagree, but he knew that his hatred had made him make several rash decisions over the last few days. "And is fear ever useful?" he asked.

"It depends. A lack of fear certainly makes you more powerful. However, there are certain times when fear is a useful emotion, as I said earlier. It helps you react to danger."

"Althalos always told me not to be afraid of either pain or death."

"Life is complicated... If you're overly afraid of pain and death, it will be impossible to continue fighting. A cowardly warrior is a bad warrior. If, however, you forget about your fear altogether, then you can waste your life. Fear is useful as long as it doesn't make you a coward."

Elliot thought about this. "Hatred and rage also make you overcome your cowardliness," he said.

"No." Aleron stopped and looked him in the eyes. "To vent your fury may at times calm your soul, but hatred will never help you. Hatred is a slow, oppressive rage that tortures the soul. It makes one seek revenge, poisons one's thoughts, and always leads one to make the wrong decisions."

Elliot stood still, taking in Aleron's words.

"When Walter revolted against Thomas, he was about seventeen years old, and yet, his soul was filled with such hatred rarely seen in anyone so young. Nevertheless, he was cunning and knew how to hide his hatred from Althalos. I wonder about your feelings... Do you want to free your hatred by killing Walter or do you want to help the people of Knightdorn?" asked Aleron.

"I want..."

The old man had taken on a strange look, one that Elliot had never seen on his face before. "You need to think about this question carefully. I can tell you with certainty that Walter won't be the last tyrant of this world. If what your heart desires is to fight for the people, one day you'll be so powerful that your name will go down in the annals of the history of your race for perpetuity. But if you decide to fight for revenge and hatred, there will come a day when you'll be worse than those you're trying to overturn," Aleron told him.

"I don't want to be like Walter," Elliot said after a few moments.

They remained silent for a while until the elwyn started moving again, and Elliot followed. The mountain ground was rough and dry, but the view and the song of the birds imparted a strange beauty to the area. Elliot wondered about their destination. The mountain slope was on an incline, and he noticed a couple of mauve flowers. Their blossoms seemed to contain a liquid. He bent and picked one, and brought it to his nose. Its scent was magical, and he felt the need to drink the juice of this flower.

"Don't." Aleron caught him by his wrist. "It is the Flower of Desire. Its smell is addictive, but its juice brings intense stomach pain."

Elliot had never heard of anything like it—he threw the flower to the ground, and they continued walking. A soft splashing noise reached his ears. Elliot looked around to find the source of the sound. Aleron climbed towards the right, and Elliot saw a thin stream rapidly flowing down the mountain slope.

"This is the source of the river that lies at the edge of the mountain—the Cursed River," Aleron said.

Elliot felt strange hearing the name. "Cursed River?"

"This river didn't have a name for centuries. It got its name from your race, after the curse of Manhon. If nothing else, humans have a sense of humour," the man said with an icy tone.

"Why did you bring me here?"

Aleron looked to the right, frowning, and Elliot followed his glance. A stone building stood near the stream. Elliot got closer, taking slow steps before he realised what it was—a stone tomb. He touched the icy stone and noted a few symbols inscribed in an unknown tongue.

"This is the tomb of Aremor," Aleron said.

Elliot was surprised. "Why did you bury him here?"

"He always liked the sound of the stream. Even so, we didn't bury him." Aleron took on a strange look. "As soon as Manhon killed Aremor, he took his body and brought it here. The elwyn and the elves wanted to attack him and keep the corpse. However, Manhon had come to the mountain with his whole army, the centaurs, and a pegasus. The truth is that we didn't know what he intended to do. Had we known, we may have decided to fight..." Aleron paused.

"As soon as Manhon brought Aremor here, the centaurs helped him build this tomb. A few years later, my race engraved these words on its stone."

Elliot eyed the inscription. "What do they mean?"

"'May you one day be freed'."

Elliot didn't understand. "Be freed?"

"When Aremor's corpse was placed here, the magic of the centaurs along with the Sword of Light sealed the grave. Then, the curse drenched every being of the Elder Races. Manhon didn't trust any of us."

"How can the curse be broken?" Right then, it was the only thing that mattered to Elliot.

"Aremor's soul must be freed and travel to the realms of the dead."

"The soul be freed?" Elliot repeated, bewildered.

"According to legend, the soul of every being hovers above their body for seven days after their death. Then it travels to the realms of the dead. The magic of the centaurs kept Aremor's soul imprisoned in our world, inside this tomb. As long as Aremor's soul remains imprisoned, the Elder Races will also be imprisoned in the Mountains of the Forgotten World."

Elliot struggled to get the information in order. "And how can his soul be freed?"

"The sword that imprisoned it must free it, breaking the tomb."

"The Sword of Light?" Worry overcame Elliot when Aleron nodded. Thorold had already told him that he needed this sword, but he had no idea where it was. "I don't have the Sword of Light!"

"Because you are not yet worthy of holding it."

Irritation ran through Elliot. "I would say that the elwyn and the elves are the ones who don't deserve the Light of Life. They don't deserve such potent magic in order to attack with it," he said, thinking of Alaric's attack.

"The elwyn and the elves use the Light for protection, not to attack."

Elliot was dubious, but did, however, remember one more question that had been troubling him over the last few days. "Are there many objects that can absorb the Light of Life?"

"No. Only the Aznarin have this power," Aleron explained.

Elliot had never heard this word before. "What is the Aznarin?"

"The only metal that can absorb the Light of Life. The swords of the elwyn and of the elves are made from it."

"Aznar's Gate," Elliot said to himself.

"Exactly! Aznar discovered this metal and its powers. He was one of the first wise elwyn. When Iovbridge was built, the elwyn decided to give his name to the gate of the city and later humans kept this name."

"Are the wise of your race the equivalent of human royalty?"

Aleron took a step forward. "The elwyn always chose the wisest amongst themselves as their leader. Being a sage does not mean having a title like those that the rulers of humans have."

"Does the chosen sage of the elwyn take decisions on behalf of your people?"

"Yes. However, their decisions are for the good of our kind and not for personal gain. Of course, the elwyn are free to ignore them if they wish," Aleron said.

Elliot threw a look at Aremor's tomb and exhaled wearily. "My trip here was purposeless. I don't have the sword. I can't break the curse." He'd hoped Aleron would know where his father's sword was, but it appeared he was mistaken.

"Even if you had the sword, it would be useless. You need one more thing. Nobody can use the Sword of Light to break the curse without Thindor having given him the power to do so first."

Aleron moved behind the tomb while Elliot wallowed in dismay. Now he was sure that his mission was impossible. He had neither the sword nor Thindor. *It's pointless... All of this was for nothing.*

"I'd say that getting the sword is the least of your problems. The most important is for Thindor to make you master of the sword. Only then will its blade be able to break the tomb," Aleron went on.

"But without the Sword of Light, how will..." Elliot trailed off.

Aleron pulled out an enormous sword from behind Aremor's tomb. Elliot stared at the emerald hilt and the ornate blade as the sunlight made the sword glitter like a star in the night sky.

The Game of Power

Syrella touched a flower, its petals soft and comforting. Its sweet aroma filled her nose. The small forest next to Moonstone was one of her favourite places. In all the years of her hegemony over Elmor, she would always go there whenever she wanted to get her thoughts in order. The colourful flowers, the scents, and the happy singsong of the birds were like medicine for her—medicine for the mind.

Syrella gazed at the view that Wirskworth offered. All morning she had been struggling to tame her thoughts. She felt that the decisions she'd made were right, but something tormented her. Most of her councillors had insisted that she not accept Sophie Delamere as queen since she had abandoned the throne. They repeated over and over that all Sophie's plans depended on Elmor and that the queen had abandoned them in the battle of Forked River. Syrella hadn't recovered from either the death of her brother or her nephew in that battle, and neither had she got over her husband's death. She may not have desired Sermor Burns, but his death had shaken her. Despite all that, she'd ignored her councillors, and that decision haunted her.

What should I do now? she thought. *Will I come to regret this decision?*

She glanced at the plains before her until another worry took hold of her thoughts—her secret affair with Jahon. The fact that she was the Governor of Elmor, but had had to hide for most of her life seemed odd to her. Syrella had often thought of marrying Jahon and of making their relationship public in Elmor. But she was the Governor and was afraid of what the people would think. Tongues wagged about the esteem she always held for her general and if she formally announced their relationship, many would perhaps suspect that they had slept together secretly even before the death of her husband. She had decided that she would never allow this secret to become public knowledge, not for her own sake, but for the sake of her daughters.

Syrella put these thoughts aside and focused on Sophie Delamere. Nobody doubted that the queen had abandoned her in the battle of the Forked River and was simultaneously powerless. Iovbridge would soon fall into Walter's hands, and there was no more gold and silver in Sophie's hands. The only possessions that the queen had were the remaining men in the Royal Army and a few of Ballar's soldiers. Syrella knew that it wouldn't be difficult to persuade those men to change sides and choose her as their leader.

She stepped deeper into the forest. Undoubtedly Sophie seemed powerless, not only in the eyes of Syrella's lords and councillors, but to all of Elmor. The queen had about twelve thousand men under her command, though she had no food to sustain them. What's more, Selwyn had travelled to Vylor with the intent of offering Elmor's gold to Liher Hale. No one in Elmor understood why Sophie remained queen in their land since she depended on Elmor's wealth, and she had given up her crown.

Althalos knew you would do the right thing, a voice whispered in her head. *Althalos was the one who urged Peter to support Sophie in the succession of Thomas.*

Syrella wondered whether such a weak leader was what the kingdom needed against a conqueror like Walter. *Did Althalos know what he was doing?*

Such thoughts troubled her often. Syrella believed that the Master expected her to accept Sophie on her land as queen, agreeing to carry out the plans he had confided to Elliot. Although she respected Althalos' prowess in war, she questioned his views on matters of leadership. Syrella believed that Knightdorn needed a more powerful ruler while Althalos appeared to think that might could be defeated by innocence.

Sadon had been the most vocal in opposing her decision to proclaim Sophie queen on their soil. Jahon kept telling her she had done the right thing. It was a fact that Jahon detested giving anything without receiving something in return, such as food for the men of Isisdor and gold for Liher Hale. But her general admired Althalos more than anyone else and since he had asked for Sophie to be on the throne, Jahon believed that they should submit to his wish.

"*Do you want the throne of Knightdorn? Even if we beat Walter, you have never wanted to rule Knightdorn, only Elmor. Why try taking advantage of the situation if you don't want the crown?*" Jahon had asked her.

Syrella agreed with him, and the House of Egercoll had fought on the side of the Endors countless times throughout history without ever asking for anything in return. Sophie may have been a Delamere, but the blood of the Egercolls flowed in her veins, and the Endors owed much to the House of Pegasus. For a moment, she had clarity about her decisions. She had to make the queen seem powerful in the discussions that would take place about the imminent war. Walter would not delay returning to Wirskworth, and Syrella knew that her councillors and lords would question both her and Sophie's decisions until Thorn arrived in the city. Fear always brought dissension, and she too had to appear more powerful than ever.

She took one more look at the beautiful view, and her gaze fell upon Elves-Mountain. That mountain range belonged to Elmor, but it was of little importance. The mountain in whose heart Wirskworth was built was one of the richest in the world while Elves-Mountain had nothing valuable. Syrella had often thanked her lucky stars that her city always had a bountiful amount of gold, steel, and silver, turning her into the richest ruler of the south.

Where could Walter be? Where is he hiding? she thought.

Logic said that he ought to have reached Ramerstorm by now. However, he may not have attacked Iovbridge yet. If news of Sophie abandoning the throne hadn't reached his ears, it was a given that he would wait for his allies before heading for the royal capital.

Syrella felt joy for the first time. Their recent victory against Walter was the most important battle that she had won in all her years of ruling. Quite a few had maintained that they should have gone after him as soon as he retreated, however, she had said they were foolish. They didn't have enough horses, and if her small cavalry chased after the six thousand remaining riders of Thorn, they would have met with a tragic death.

"I knew I would find you here," came a voice.

Syrella turned and saw Velhisya standing in front of her. Each time she saw her, her younger brother came to life in her memory.

"It would appear that all the Endors come here when they want to be alone," Syrella said, trying to smile.

"I wanted to ask you if you have thought about what I told you," Velhisya said.

Syrella's joy turned to irritation. She didn't want to have this conversation. "You're not a warrior, Velhisya." She loved her as much as her daughters, but that didn't stop her from being very different to them. "You never learned to fight... Why do you want to fight now?" Syrella asked.

"I told you. I want to fight for you! I want to fight for my land and for my sisters!" The starry-blue eyes of the woman didn't falter.

"I don't understand why it's so important this time..."

Velhisya's jaw clenched. "It's the last battle! It's my duty to figh—"

"No," Syrella interjected. "This war is not yours, my dear niece." She walked slowly towards her.

"Did you say the same to your daughters?"

"I wish that I could without them threatening to kill me." Syrella smiled, taking Velhisya's hand. "Leave the city... Find your mother!"

The woman pulled her hand away and tears glistened in her eyes. "My mother is dead."

Surprise tore through Syrella. She had tried countless times in the past to speak to Velhisya about her mother, but she had never managed to get a word out of her. "How do you know?" she asked.

"I know."

"If that's what Arthur told you, perhaps he made a mistake... Did he see your mother dying?"

A strange smile appeared on Velhisya's face as her tears threatened to spill down her face. "My mother could not live in a world where my father did not exist."

"What does that mean—"

"It makes no difference," Velhisya interrupted. "My mother is dead. I know that I will never have the respect and devotion that those who bear the name of Endor have, but I don't care anymore. This city is my home, and you and your daughters are the only family I have. Nobody will stop me from fighting for whatever remains for me in this world!"

Syrella embraced her in a way she never had before, trying to show her the thousands of unsaid emotions she felt. Velhisya returned her embrace, and her aura brought a sense of magic to Syrella's mind.

Syrella gently broke away and looked Velhisya in the eyes. "I have always considered you my daughter, and anyone who treats you as if you're not a woman of my House won't live to see this world again. However, you're not a warrior—nor am I any longer. You can help in the war, even if you're not on the battlefield. Help me retain the devotion of the council and the noblemen until Walter reaches Elmor... Help me find a way to beat our enemy," she said.

Velhisya wiped away her tears, and Syrella felt an invisible force while observing her niece. It was as if her irises had filled with silver-blue flames.

"You have my word," Velhisya said sharply. She turned and began to leave the forest, but stopped. "Where is Elliot?"

Syrella was surprised. Velhisya was the most beautiful woman she had ever seen but had never shown an interest in anyone, man or woman. Syrella had seen her dancing with Elliot the night of the Dance of Blood, but she hadn't thought it important. However, now she saw a strange anger in Velhisya's eyes. She recognised this anger—the kind that accompanied love.

"I know that you know," Velhisya said.

"I can't tell you. It has to remain secret," Syrella responded.

"I swear nobody will find out anything from me. I swear on the memory of my parents."

Velhisya had never sworn on the memory of her parents, and she avoided even mentioning them. Syrella knew that she had said those words to show how important it was for her to know. "If your mother were alive, Elliot would be near her now."

Syrella could have sworn that her niece's irises lit up. She expected her to ask why Elliot was in the Mountains of the Forgotten World.

"Thank you." Velhisya said nothing else, leaving the forest and disappearing from sight.

Syrella remained deep in thought for a long time before thoughts of Jahon overtook her mind. She was prepared to give up everything so that her daughters and niece could follow their hearts and not live a life of lies and fear like her.

The Sword of Light

A ray of sunlight fell on Aleron's face, making his eyes appear golden-blue, and the legendary sword seemed to radiate light in his hands. Elliot looked at the ornate weapon, speechless. Thousands of questions milled around in his head, but only one came to his lips.

"May I hold it?" he almost whispered.

Aleron extended his hand and Elliot gripped the sword, bringing it before him. The pommel of the hilt had a blue-green ruby the size of a fig, and its cross-guard had three small diamonds at each end, two yellow ones and a blue one. In the centre of the cross-guard, there was a matching ruby the colour of the sea. The size of the sword was such that the hilt balanced its long blade. Elliot had presumed that its weight would have forced anyone holding it to use both hands, but it was lighter than he expected. He looked at the hilt more closely. It was padded with blue leather that was soft to the touch, and there were no stains from sweat or blood. The tip of the blade was fine so that it could cut easily, while in the steel he could discern a few indistinct grooves.

"This sword is very light for its size," Elliot said.

"Of course. The Sword of Light, like each blade of the Seven Swords, is made from Aznarin. Aznarin is lighter, stronger, and sharper than any other metal in the world. However, it can only be found in these mountains," Aleron told him.

"Was this the reason the Elder Races travelled here when they agreed to make the Seven Swords?"

Aleron nodded. "The elwyn and the elves had been making blades from Aznarin for centuries. However, at some point they had made so many weapons from it that they no longer needed to forge any more. So, there was no longer any Aznarin in Iovbridge to make the swords that Aremor had promised the Egercolls, since the elwyn and the elves hadn't made any new weapons for thousands of years. However, Aznarin is not the only reason the Seven Swords had to be made in these mountains."

"What was the other?"

The elwyn smiled. "In the mines, Aznar discovered a highly flammable stone in the depths of these mountains—the Stone of Fire. It's a stone that can sustain extraordinarily hot flames. Only this stone can create heat capable of forging a weapon from Aznarin, and it cannot be found anywhere else in the world."

"Do humans know about this stone?"

Aleron shook his head.

Interesting. "So, humans could make weapons from Aznarin if they were aware of these secrets," Elliot said.

Aleron frowned. "Yes. However, humans discovered neither Aznarin nor the Stone of Fire. Althalos and Thorold were the only ones I chose to share these truths with."

"I'm sure Althalos confided these secrets to most of his apprentices," Elliot mumbled with some disappointment.

"No—the only apprentice of Althalos who ever found out about this is you."

Elliot looked at him. "Why?"

"I've decided to trust you even though I'm not yet sure about you."

"Althalos didn't trust me!" Elliot said, lowering the sword. "Even if he hid this information from all of his apprentices, I'm sure he confided the truth about the Elder Races to them. He may have even brought them here during their years of training." The words wounded his soul.

"Althalos never brought anyone to our slope. His apprentices would come with him to the mountains and observe us from afar—"

"They knew everything!" Elliot cut him short and threw down the sword.

"Althalos loved you. Whatever he did, he had his reasons."

"He didn't love me... If he had loved me, he would have trusted me. If he'd loved me, he would have told..."

"One day, the answers will find you," Aleron said in a calm voice.

Elliot breathed out wearily. "Did the people of the Elder Races want to follow Aremor when he decided to come here?" he asked.

"In the beginning, only the elwyn and the elves travelled with him."

"And the giants?"

"The giants had heard about the pact with the Egercolls and wanted to see the weapons we would make for them with their own eyes. Their animosity for the elves had not died down, but the death that the Battle of Wirskworth left in its wake made them think that this was a chance to ask for a truce since the war had proven a painful solution."

"And the elves accepted them?"

"Yes... Then, we decided for the first time to pass on our knowledge of forging a weapon with Aznarin to the giants."

Elliot was taken aback. "The giants didn't know how—"

"No. They never discovered how to utilise this metal and make weapons with it, just like humans. The truth is that neither the elwyn nor the elves wanted to teach them. Their hide is already quite resistant to the Light of Life. If they held enormous swords made of Aznarin while riding wyverns, they would be even more dangerous. Nevertheless, we decided to trust them."

For a moment, the winged monsters came to life in Elliot's imagination. He bent down and picked the sword back up, seeing no damage on it.

"I expect you're wondering how this sword came to be in my hands," Aleron said.

"My father gave it to Althalos, and he in turn gave it to you. Althalos would never leave the only hope of freeing the Elder Races to fall into Walter's hands." Elliot could have sworn that, for the first time, Aleron had looked at him approvingly. "But I have one more question. How many men, women and children made up the Elder Races when they arrived here?"

The elwyn's face darkened. "Why do you want to know?" His voice was heavy with sorrow.

"Just..." Elliot faltered. "I was thinking that if the entire Elder Races once travelled to this place... I would have expected there to be more of you," he confessed—it was a fact that he'd hoped for more beings capable of fighting.

"When the curse haunted our races, there were more of us. However, the elwyn, the giants, and the elves had already been significantly reduced even before the curse." A sigh escaped Aleron's lips. "The Elder Races stop having children in times of war."

"The Battle of Wirskworth..." Elliot said to himself, and the man nodded.

"The hostilities between the giants and the elves before that battle were evidence that war would soon be upon us. The births among the Elder Races almost stopped during those years. Then, the death toll in the Battle of Wirskworth was so immense that decades would be needed for all these casualties to be replaced. Even so, the war was not the only reason why the elwyn and the elves stopped having children..." Aleron said. "The elwyn and the elves avoid conceiving children when they feel that the future is bleak."

The warbling of the birds seemed like a dirge. Aleron's words sounded strange in Elliot's ears. "I don't under—"

"A few years before the Black Death Age, the Elder Races numbered over a hundred thousand souls. At some point, something changed. The Light of Life seemed to fade within us... It was as if it was warning us that something terrible was about to happen. So, the elwyn and the elves stopped having children long before the Battle of Wirskworth. After the battle, once humans had reached Knightdorn and the pegasi filled the skies, the Elder Races no longer numbered more than twenty thousand souls," Aleron continued.

"Even one hundred thousand is not a great number."

"The Elder Races never used to have lots of children. We're not like humans," the elderly elwyn said. "Most humans spawn kids, even if they don't love them. For the Elder Races, and even for the giants, the birth of a child is sacred. They don't procreate if they don't feel they want to give their all to their offspring. Moreover, no one of the Elder Races would ever inflict harm on a child."

Elliot understood what he was hinting at about the calibre of humans with his last point. Aleron's words made him feel dirty. "Didn't the giants kill any children from the race of elves when they attacked Wirskworth?"

"No! The innocent were taken to a safe place before the battle, but this isn't the most important thing. If the giants had taken the city and found children, elderly, and women within it, they would neither have killed nor raped. No one of the Elder Races would have committed such atrocities..." Aleron pointed out with a note of irritation.

"I'm sure that in some war of the Elder Races, heinous acts must have taken place. War blinds the mind."

"The Battle of Wirskworth was the only war that ever occurred between the beings of the Elder Races," Aleron replied.

Elliot couldn't believe his ears, his grip tightening around the hilt of the sword. "Had the elves and giants never ever fought before that battle?"

Aleron frowned. "The elves had tried to defend themselves against some of the giants' raids in small villages, but they had never fought a big battle."

"The giants have attacked many a time in the past!" Elliot remembered John's words. "They killed humans and centaurs, along with the elves. You're telling me that in all those attacks they never hurt the weak and innocent?"

The eyes of the elwyn sparked. "Giants never killed children or feeble, elderly people, nor did they rape women during their raids. They followed their nature, which commanded they attack anything different than themselves, but they never behaved as savagely as humans."

"And did elwyn never fight in a war?" Elliot asked.

"They never fought in the whole of their history, and they forged weapons only for their protection. Giants invaded villages where elwyn and elves lived, looting and stealing their harvest. My race chose not to attack them, knowing full well that war was not the answer. Nevertheless, the elves decided to fight against them when they'd had enough of Magor."

Elliot remembered that name. Long Arm had told him about Magor the Terrible. "I've heard that the giants used to kill humans for pleasure when they united under Magor."

Aleron breathed out wearily. "That isn't completely true. Unfortunately, as soon as most of the tribes of the giants decided to unite under the leadership of Magor, it was as if he had convinced them that the murder of beings from any other race was their life's purpose. Nevertheless, giants didn't kill humans for pleasure. It was simply that the latter started arriving in Knightdorn for the first time during Magor's rule, and he had convinced the giants that humans could attack them in order to take over their land."

"What hope was there for humans against giants mounted on wyverns?"

"Giants think differently, Elliot. Many times, they feel that anything different to them must be eliminated, irrespective of whether it's dangerous or not. I also think humans had some hope of defeating giants when the seven Egercolls rode the pegasi—the giants didn't know about these winged creatures back then. When the pegasi appeared in the skies of Knightdorn for the first time, the giants had been butchered, so they had no interest in attacking humans.

"Now, the Elder Races number about ten thousand souls. Half of our people ended their lives in the early years of the curse, and there are only four children in these mountains. Two from the race of elves and two from the race of the elwyn. These were the only children that existed before the curse too, and they have remained children for three hundred years... As if this wasn't enough, the curse has hindered all beings of the Elder Races from procreating for centuries. Even if we could reproduce, no one would want to give birth to a baby that would remain an infant eternally."

Elliot felt horrified. He wished he could break Manhon's curse that very moment. Nevertheless, something else puzzled him. Velhisya's mother was able to give birth, and her daughter had not remained a baby. He put this thought aside. There were other things he had to find out more about.

"I always wondered why the Elder Races travelled in their entirety to this place to forge the Seven Swords," he said.

Aleron looked even more sorrowful. "The first elwyn and elves lived here for centuries before moving to Isisdor and Elmor. Most ancient myths claim that we were created in these mountains. Before the Battle of Wirskworth, we felt the Light of Life slowly fading within us. After the battle, it was as if our souls had been enveloped in darkness. We felt the need to come here... To live in the land of our birth for a while. We believed that the creation of the Seven Swords was the fateful impetus for our return to this place and that perhaps here our Light would be reborn. We would never have come had we known the fate awaiting us." His eyes were full of pain.

"Did no one stay behind?" Elliot asked.

"No, not that I know of," Aleron replied.

"Had any of the elwyn or elves not come to this place, would they too have been under the curse?"

Aleron closed his eyes for a moment. "No one can be sure, but I believe not. The curse should only haunt those who were here."

"Were the giants also created here?"

The elwyn shook his head. "According to our old scriptures, their existence began in the Mountains of Darkness. Nevertheless, when they decided to travel to the Mountains of the Forgotten World, there were no more than a thousand. Most had perished in the battle against the elves. So, all those that had survived decided to come here." Aleron paused and extended his hand. "I say we should return now."

Elliot understood and returned the sword even though he felt it rightfully belonged to him.

"If one day you deserve to hold this sword, I promise you will have it," the man said.

He wanted to protest, but he didn't. They started walking and hadn't got far from Aremor's grave when Elliot stopped.

"I don't know how to break the curse. I don't know how to make Thindor give me the power... I'll fail, just like my fa—"

"Never think of either success or of failure," Aleron interrupted without stopping. "The only thing that matters is being willing to try—wanting to try so much, that you would sacrifice everything. Would you sacrifice everything to break the curse?"

Elliot was torn. He may have felt deep sorrow for all that had happened to the beings in this place, but there were many who depended on him. There was the queen, his companions, the people of Knightdorn. He feared that if he sacrificed everything for the Elder Races, he would leave the people who depended on him in darkness. Velhisya looked at him sadly in his mind when she thought of her mother.

"Yes," he said. "I promise you I will do all I can, Aleron."

Aleron slowed, glancing back at him. "Don't promise me anything, only yourself."

Elliot looked at him and nodded curtly. "I need to know one more thing. I've been wondering for days about the powers of the pegasi... Thorold told me that a pegasus is truly immortal. It may die the moment its rider passes away, but then it is reborn out of the light of the God of Life, ready to bond with a new master. I've also heard stories about the power of the seven Egercolls who rode on these winged horses... However, I'm not sure what the true powers of the pegasi are and how these made the Egercolls so powerful."

Aleron frowned. "Thorold was right about what he told you. As for the powers of the pegasi, nobody knows what they truly are. It's practically impossible for anyone to study them, and as I said before, this creature must be relatively new to our world."

"You surely know more than anyone else." Elliot pressed.

Aleron weighed him up carefully. "I have never been a rider of a pegasus, but the seven Egercolls said that their senses increased infinitely when they bonded with these creatures. They could see things before they happened, and they no longer felt fatigue or pain so easily. Moreover, the hide of the pegasus is impenetrable, which gives its rider a huge advantage. Imagine being on the back of an immortal flying creature while being able to see everything before it happens. Rumour has it that ten thousand archers weren't able to hit even one of the seven Egercolls in the Wars of the First Kings. Nevertheless, the pegasi are not warmongering beings."

Elliot's spirits lifted as the news eased some of the heavy sorrow hanging over him.

"Everything points to them having been made from a massive build-up of the Light of Life's power, which means they were somehow made from love itself. Some legends say that the pegasi can even communicate with beings in the realms of the dead. Nobody knows why they chose the Egercolls as their riders," Aleron continued.

"Could anyone without the blood of the Egercolls running through their veins bond with a pegasus?" Elliot asked.

Aleron seemed torn. "No one can say for sure... But I'd bet they couldn't."

"Can Aznarin pierce the hide of a pegasus?"

"No," Aleron replied sharply. "As I told you, their hide is impenetrable."

A few of Long Arm's words came to Elliot's mind. "Legend has it that the Seven Swords killed six of the seven pegasi. I thought that Aznarin gave them this power."

"The Seven Swords are not unique because they were made of Aznarin. The swords of the elwyn and the elves cannot kill a pegasus. Six of the Seven Swords were forged in the mines of this mountain, drenched with the blood of an equal number of pegasi. This blood gave them special powers," the man explained.

Elliot shivered. "What?" It was the only word he could force himself to say.

"The six Egercoll riders let Aremor draw the blood of their pegasi so that he would make these powerful weapons—swords they wanted more than anything else."

"But you said the hide of the pegasi is impenetrable!" Elliot said.

"Their hide ceases to be impenetrable if they themselves allow you to pierce it... The pegasi obeyed the will of their masters, and they allowed Aremor to draw their blood," Aleron replied.

Elliot remained silent a while. "The six riders? And the seventh?"

"The seventh was Manhon," the man said wearily, appearing older. "Aremor believed that the tears of a pegasus are more powerful than its blood. A myth said that the tears of a pegasus contained the most powerful magic in the world. So, when Aremor had made the six of the Seven Swords, he decided not to use Thindor's blood and to ask Manhon for some of his tears. It had become an obsession of his to try to make a weapon forged with the tears of a pegasus... Manhon accepted his wish, and Thindor obeyed his master, dropping a few tears into a container—the tears that drenched the Sword of Light."

Elliot was confused. "Are the tears of a pegasus so powerful?"

"There are legends which argue that they can even reverse death. The myth goes that a sacrifice could perhaps unlock this magic."

"A sacrifice?"

"A sacrifice is the ultimate act of love."

"I still don't underst—"

"No one completely understands all of this. Moreover, no one can be sure which legends are real and which aren't. The only thing that's indisputable is that the tears of the pegasi are imbued with mighty powers. Aremor succeeded in proving this without of course expecting that his soul would forever be imprisoned in a stone tomb..."

"Does the seventh sword, the Sword of Light, have different powers from the rest?" Elliot asked, remembering John saying that Manhon's sword was the most powerful of the Seven Swords.

Aleron nodded, and Elliot expected to hear what these powers were, but the elwyn continued walking again. He followed him and the thick silence weighed on them.

"The blades of the swords that were drenched in the blood of the pegasi are so sharp that they are capable of killing any being in the world," Aleron said after a while as they headed downhill. "These swords are capable of cutting into the torso of giants, and they can even penetrate the body of a mermaid in the water. I've seen these swords pierce armour and wound the hide of a wyvern with ease. Their strongest power is that they can kill a pegasus."

"And the seventh sword?" Elliot asked.

"It has the exact same powers as the rest. However, if someone succeeds in becoming the master of the sword, he gains more benefits that none of the other Seven Swords can grant him."

Aleron had repeated this phrase and Elliot didn't understand what it meant. "Master of the sword?"

The man looked at him. "The murderous abilities of the Seven Swords are the same no matter the hand that holds them. The Sword of Light has a few more powers which can only be used by its master."

Elliot wanted to know more. "What powers?"

Aleron frowned. "The master of the Sword of Light cannot be injured by it. If someone attempts to attack him with it, its blade becomes intangible. Moreover, this sword can absorb the Light that lives within Thindor since it was he who gave his tear. Thus, the rider of Thindor can make the blade light up with the Light of Life."

"How can one become the master of the sword?" Elliot asked.

"Only if Thindor chooses him, as long as he leaves a tear on the sword the moment it is in the hand of a being. The master of the Sword of Light is the only one who can break the curse that haunts us, and no one has succeeded in becoming the master of this sword after the death of Manhon."

Elliot's enthusiasm evaporated. He felt he would never manage to break the curse. "How will I make Thindor shed a tear on—"

"Forget about Thindor. Forget about everything I told you. If you are destined to succeed, everything will fall into place when the time comes."

Elliot breathed out heavily. "It's just that..." He choked the moment he began to speak. "It's just that, only with a creature like Thindor would I have any real hope of overthrowing Walter."

"Really? When you began your journey, you never imagined that there was a live pegasus. Why did you decide to fight if you believed that you had no chance?"

"I thought..."

"Humans are very talented in calling greed, need. Be careful, Elliot. Don't let your dark self lead you astray," Aleron told him. "Always try to succeed with what you've been given. If you are fated to become Thindor's rider, nobody will be able to stand in the way of destiny."

They continued walking as Elliot tried to put his thoughts in order. "Do the Seven Swords protect the hands of a swordsman from the burn of the Light of Life?"

"Yes. They're the only objects that have that power. The blood of the six pegasi and Thindor's tear are responsible for that."

"Perhaps I could hold the Sword of Light while I practice with the elf."

"Interesting," Aleron remarked. "I thought you were an unbeatable swordsman."

Elliot felt enraged and the man smiled.

"I believe that it would be useful for you to learn how to dodge blows of a sword without parrying and to learn to—"

"To attack only when you're sure that your opponent will not be able to retaliate," Elliot said completing the sentence wearily. "Could an elwyn or an elf light up the blade of one of the Seven Swords?"

"No," Aleron replied abruptly. "The seven pegasi gave a part of themselves to the Aznarin of these swords. No creature can get their Light to pass through them. Think of it like the metal that made the blades is protected from the magic of every other being. The only sword that can be enveloped in the Light of Life is the one I'm holding in my hand. However, it can only absorb it by Thindor's soul."

Elliot thought that Aleron had finished, but he spoke again.

"Even if the Seven Swords hadn't been forged with the blood and tear of the pegasi, the elwyn and elves would have to touch their blades directly in order to get their Light to run through them. Our swords have a thin layer of Aznarin which starts at the pommel of the hilt and reaches up to the blade. This layer of metal allows the Light to travel from the hand of an elwyn to the whole sword. When we made the Seven Swords, no one expected that a human would be able to pass the Light of Life to their blade since it doesn't inhabit their souls. So, we never put Aznarin in the hilts of the Seven Swords. However, the Sword of Light can absorb the Light of Thindor without him even touching it."

"Can Thindor be hurt by the sword?" Elliot asked, looking at the weapon in Aleron's hands.

The elwyn frowned. "Yes. It's strange that the sword cannot hurt his rider, but it can kill him."

They were walking up the path that had led them to the tomb of Aremor when Elliot decided to ask one last question. "Why did you take the sword from the grave?"

"Why not?"

"One might say that its place was there for quite some time..."

"There are some things I'd like to try out," Aleron responded nonchalantly.

Elliot was sure he was hiding something, but he decided not to push things. "When I left the village I grew up in, I believed that my destiny was to fight for the freedom of Knightdorn. Althalos had always told me that I was the only hope the queen had, which was an unbearable burden for a child. Now, I also feel the weight of the freedom of the Elder Races on my shoulders... I don't know how I'll manage. I have no idea where Thindor might be..." he said, uttering all the things that kept him awake at night.

Aleron caught him by the shoulder, his fiery gaze piercing through him. Elliot could have sworn that for the first time he saw pity in his eyes.

"I know..." Aleron muttered. "But if to succeed is the deepest desire of your heart, you will find a way."

Elliot felt a few drops of courage within himself. "I can understand why the Elder Races chose you as their leader. You are truly wise."

The elwyn scoffed. "The elves were so devastated after the Battle of Wirskworth that they decided to devote themselves to the leader of the elwyn. However, the giants never chose to embrace the views of any sage of my race," he said sorrowfully.

By now they had reached the mountain slope where they had started, and Elliot saw Alaric sitting cross-legged, gazing at the cloudy sky. The elf noticed them and without saying a word, drew the sword from his belt.

How much do I want to fulfil the deepest desires of my heart? Elliot thought. The memory of Morys came back to him. He walked slowly until he stood in front of Alaric. He took one last look at Aleron and raised his sword, more decided than ever.

The Fallen Queen

Sophie felt crushed. A whole day had passed since they had arrived in Wirskworth, but her body still hurt from riding. She glanced around her room in the Tower of Poisons. It was decorated with kilims and rugs. To her right, there was a wooden table with bread and fruit on it, but she wasn't hungry. She was tormented by her demons—the same demons that had warned her not to leave Iovbridge.

"May I come in, Your Majesty?" Peter's voice pulled her out of her reverie.

"Yes," she said, and the door opened and closed loudly. The man was dressed in a fine cherry-coloured silk jerkin and looked weary and sleepless. "I'd say you didn't have a peaceful sleep."

The bright light of day reflected on the walls of the room while Peter was grim. "I can't believe everything you told me," he said.

Sophie had expected that. She knew that Peter would panic as soon as he found out where Selwyn had travelled to. As if this weren't enough, he had accused her of not trusting him when she had refused to reveal where Elliot, Eleanor, and Long Arm were.

"None of this was my decision," Sophie said once more. "I set foot in Wirskworth at the same time as you. I couldn't stand in the way of Selwyn leaving the city."

"How could Syrella let him go to the Black Vale?" the man said in a low voice.

"Selwyn is not a child nor is Syrella his mother... We now know that Elliot was carrying out Althalos' orders. Perhaps he told him to send someone to Liher Hale's doorstep."

"I'm not sure that Elliot is still following Althalos' advice. Nevertheless, Syrella could have ordered thousands of men to carry a letter to Goldtown. Why my son?"

"You know the answer. Selwyn went to ask for an alliance on behalf of the queen. No man from this city could have travelled to the Black Vale to ask for an alliance on my behalf. I don't think Elliot would have trusted anyone other than Selwyn."

"Why didn't he send Eleanor or Long Arm?" Peter asked.

Sophie was enraged. "Would you ever send a woman to a place like Goldtown?" she shot. Peter seemed to regret his words as he looked away, jaw clenched. "Still, if a man like Long Arm went to Liher Hale to ask for an alliance on my behalf, he'd most likely lose his head."

"Why didn't Elliot go himself?"

Sophie started to lose her patience. "We've discussed this before. He's trying to build another alliance."

"With whom?" Peter raised his voice. "Who else is left in the kingdom?"

"I thought you were devoted to Althalos. I told you, Elliot asked Syrella not to reveal where he and his companions are."

"This was Elliot's request, not Althalos'!"

"How can you be so sure?"

The man breathed out angrily.

"I told you to speak to Thorold. Syrella reassured me that he agrees with Elliot's decisions."

Peter shook his hands as if he was trying to shake off an annoying fly. "Thorold..." he said to himself. "A coward... He remained hidden all the years we risked our lives, and he didn't train even one boy."

"I believe he'd seen enough boys he had trained falling dead at the hands of Walter."

"Then we should stop the war and surrender without a fight—"

"Enough!" Sophie interrupted him angrily. "I understand that your fear for Selwyn has blinded you, but we too have problems to deal with. All that we have found out is very important."

"What do you mean?" Peter asked.

"When Walter unexpectedly left for the City of Heavens, Elliot assumed that he would go there. He believed that he wanted to kill Thorold." Sophie had told Peter all that had happened during Thorn's stay in Elmor.

"Naturally," the Lord of the Knights said under his breath. "Everyone knows that Walter killed every Grand Master. If anyone had revealed that Thorold was alive, Thorn would have certainly rushed to kill him..."

"Why did Elliot want to save Thorold?"

The man seemed troubled. It was the first time since he'd heard the news about Selwyn that he assumed his military look. "Do you believe that Thorold communicated with Althalos?"

"I'm certain of it. I don't know whether Elliot knew about this, but I'm sure that something made him rush to save Thorold—something we don't yet know about. I think the two Masters secretly communicated with each other, and Elliot either knew about this or realised when he accidentally found himself in the City of Heavens. Thus, he wanted to save a friend of Althalos. However, Thorold will never admit this," Sophie felt irritated momentarily.

Peter frowned. "I don't know what Elliot knew nor what the two Masters were hiding. However, none of that is important in the forthcoming battle."

Sophie sighed heavily. "I don't think we'll manage to find out anything more about Thorold and Althalos." This bothered her, and something inside her told her that the hidden secrets surrounding the two Masters were important. "However, we must be careful and appear to be strong while we're here."

"Are you afraid of the spy who entered Wirskworth?" Peter asked.

Sophie nodded. "We've been suspecting for some time that some man of Walter's is close to Syrella. I'd bet that the same man is responsible for whoever came into the city."

"You're right. Whoever it may be, he will try to create friction between you and Syrella," the Lord of the Knights said thoughtfully.

"Exactly!" Sophie said and nodded. *At last, Peter understands what is happening.* "I'm a queen who left the throne and her crown while she walked south like a smuggler without gold or a capable army. I don't have the capacity to feed my own soldiers... The alliance with Vylor will depend on the gold of Elmor. Without Syrella, we stand no chance against our enemy. As if that weren't enough, we're in a place we left without help when Walter attacked. How long do you think it will take before the people, the lords, and the councillors of Elmor convince Syrella to cast me aside?"

It was the first time Sophie had given voice to everything that scared her. Peter remained silent, immersed in thought.

"Syrella can take the Royal Army and the men of Ballar under her command whenever she wishes. All she needs is someone whom she trusts to convince her to do it," Sophie added.

"If something like that happens, I'm sure she will also claim the throne of Knightdorn should we win," Peter said.

Sophie laughed. "She can have it. I don't want to sit on that damned throne again. However, my opinion must not be given less weight in the discussions about the forthcoming battle. In this place, foolish decisions have been made before, and I don't want what happened at the Forked River to happen again. I have to remain queen for some time still."

She saw Peter looking at her with a strange expression. She bet that the man opposite her hadn't expected her to be so indifferent to the throne.

"I agree," said Peter. "However, I don't know what we can do to prevent Syrella from changing her mind."

"Perhaps now that we are here, you may be able to find out more... I want you to go round to every tavern and brothel and find out about all the gossip being spread in Wirskworth. We may hear about something useful—something we can use if Syrella changes her stance."

Sophie knew that Peter would find that a genius idea. He had told her innumerable times in the past that in those places, one could hear whatever was being whispered about in a city. Most of that gossip may have been nonsense, but there were always particular rumours that eventually proved to be true.

"I'll inform you as soon as I have any news," Peter said curtly, which showed that he had found himself again.

Momentary silence spread between them.

"Perhaps we shouldn't have left Iovbridge," Sophie said.

The man shook his head. "We had no hope there."

"We even left our fleet..."

Peter waved his hand to dismiss the statement. "Our seventy ships would not have helped us. If Thorn had decided to attack from the sea with the Shiplords of Tahos, we wouldn't have stood a chance against a thousand ships. Moreover, our fleet would have been useless in a siege on land."

Sophie frowned. "Try to find out whatever you can about Reynald Karford, too."

Peter's face darkened. "That is really strange," he said.

Sophie knew what he meant. She couldn't find any reason why Elliot had let a murderer like Reynald leave on an unknown mission.

"I'll see what I can find out."

With that, Peter headed towards the door. Just before he left the room, he turned once more towards her.

"Please, let me know at once if you get news of Selwyn," he asked with an imploring tone.

"I promise you'll be the first to know whatever reaches my ears," she told him.

The man nodded curtly and left the room. Sophie remained lost in thought for a while. She really missed Eleanor. She was the only person that brought her peace when she felt the demons tormenting her mind.

She gazed at the chimneys and the houses of the city through her window. She would have given everything to have been able to travel to Felador and live with Eleanor in the land of their birth. She knew that she could do so, if she left her men to Syrella and forgot the war forever. However, Walter would never rest unless he killed her. She sighed heavily, wearied. That wasn't the only reason that she wouldn't go away, leaving everything behind. Something inside Sophie told her that she still had some role to play in the battle for the Kingdom of Knightdorn. Perhaps the fact that a man like Althalos wanted her on the throne made her feel responsible for the kingdom and its people—a responsibility she couldn't part with until the end.

Are you sure you didn't make a mistake? she thought, looking at the aged Master's image in her mind. She wished she could talk to him, to ask him all the questions that plagued her. However, it was no longer important. She knew that whatever fate had in store for her, she would soon find out.

The Heretic's Fork

A soft gnawing sound reached Selwyn's ears. His eyelids were heavy, and he had lost all sense of time. It felt like a long time had gone by since the last memory he could recall—Liher Hale's sardonic smile.

His head was killing him. He tried to open his eyelids and dizziness washed over him. He vomited, managing to open his eyes to find himself in darkness. Selwyn wiped his mouth and looked around. There was little light as his eyes grew accustomed to the dark, finally noticing a barred steel gate. He was in a cell. He heard the gnawing sound again and turned his gaze to the right. A rat was munching on a small piece of wood a few feet away from him.

Selwyn tried to get up. His legs shook, but he managed to stand. He stumbled towards the gate and held onto the icy metal to support himself. He looked down the passage in front of his cell—he bet he was in the dungeons of Goldtown Castle. A few torches nailed to the stone walls glowed softly. There were no windows, so he had no idea whether it was day or night.

How long have I been here?

He turned towards the interior of his cell. He wondered how many were in these dungeons, as he spotted a chair with broad arms in the corner. Selwyn approached it, and he was overcome with horror. The arms and the legs had straps, and it was nailed to the floor. He knew what that meant. There were many kinds of torture that could be carried out in such a chair.

He tried to remember the last moments before he was enveloped by darkness. He had spoken to Liher about the queen's offer. Then, as he was shaking the hand of Vylor's Governor, everything had gone dark with a crack of pain. The throbbing ache in the back of his head betrayed the fact that someone had hit him with something heavy. His stomach rumbled. It was a strange sensation, like he was nauseated and hungry at the same time.

Selwyn moved away from the chair and sat on the stone ground. He knew it would be difficult to get out of the cell alive. He was beset by a familiar fear of death while the way the end would come frightened him even more. He always imagined that he would lose his life in a battle like his brothers. A sudden death with a sword, an arrow or a spear, was much better than a slow death through torture.

Time passed and his terror grew. There was no way he could escape. He tried to keep his panic in check as he took deep breaths. Surely there was something he could do.

What would Elliot do?

Angry voices in the distance snapped him from his thoughts.

"Think about what you're about to do!" a male voice boomed.

"I will do whatever I please! Who told you I was coming to the castle dungeons?"

All talk ceased a for few moments until the first voice spoke again. "No one."

Now the quarrelling men were outside Selwyn's cell, and their shadows stretched across the stone floor. He saw Liher Hale with Lothar while two guards stood behind them with expressionless faces.

"Go, before I order the guards to drag you kicking and screaming to your chamber," Liher said.

"If they dared to touch me, they would not live to see the next morning," Lothar replied angrily.

"I will not tolerate your insolence any longer. You may be my brother, but that won't save you forever," Liher told him.

Lothar's face flushed under the dim light of the torches. Liher turned his gaze towards the inside of the cell and a smile appeared on his lips.

"At last! I'd started to believe that my healers were idiots and that you would never wake up... Do you know that you have been unconscious for two whole days?" he asked Selwyn.

Selwyn looked at him, the terror within him growing ever greater. "Water," he murmured weakly.

"Of course," Liher said, still smiling. He motioned to the two guards and one of them inserted a long, narrow key into the door of the cell. It rattled open and the four men advanced towards Selwyn.

The guard grabbed a flask. He held out his hand, glancing at Selwyn apathetically. "Drink."

Selwyn took the flask and emptied it at once. The water was lukewarm, but he didn't care as he downed every last drop. The liquid hit his empty stomach like a rock.

"I want you to tell me the truth," Liher said.

"The truth?" Selwyn repeated, licking droplets from his lips.

"Why did Sophie Delamere and Syrella Endor send you to my land?"

"I told you the truth."

Liher sneered. "Sophie and Syrella would never ask for my help. They would never trust me. They know that if Thorn offered more, I would betray them at any time. Were you sent to spy on me?"

"No."

"Did they want you to kill me?"

"How would that help in the war against Walter?"

The man looked at Selwyn, and his eyes narrowed. "They know that my brother is foolish... Perhaps they want me out of the way in the hope that Lothar will take over the rulership of Vylor and fight for them."

Selwyn was bewildered.

"You've lost your mind," Lothar said. Liher looked at his brother with eyes that sparked with wrath. "Would they send a man on his own to get you out of the way? Even if he succeeded, how could they hope for an alliance if they treacherously assassinated the Ruler of Vylor?"

"You know nothing!" Liher shouted. "The rulers of this kingdom are cunning schemers. Having failed to make me subservient to them, they would try with my brother next. If they failed, they would get you out of the way, too."

"So that's the real reason you want to torture him... You see enemies everywhere, brother. Why didn't you tell me about your fears?" Lothar asked.

"I'll say whatever I want to whomever I want! I don't care what you think," Liher spat.

"I didn't lie! Sophie and Syrella sent me here because they wanted a new alliance with Vylor!" cried Selwyn.

"LIES!" Liher's voice echoed through the dungeons.

"Think, brother." Lothar caught the governor by the shoulder, ignoring his angry demeanor. "Walter has sixty thousand men. There is no one left in Knightdorn to fight for Delamere. They know that the Ruler of Vylor only fights for gold, so they sent the son of a queen's officer to offer gold for an alliance... Killing you would not bring a new alliance, but a new enemy who could take Thorn's side."

"Really? Do you remember how Walter killed Lain and then I fought by his side? Do you remember how he promised me gold and lands for me to do so and I followed him?" Liher had taken on an air that made him look insane.

"Did you follow Walter out of greed or fear?" Lothar asked. "I always thought you did it out of fear. If you did it out of greed, then you aren't my brother..."

Liher made a sudden move and grabbed Lothar by the neck. "I knew Walter was using me, brother. I knew he would never give the returns he'd promised, but if I'd refused to follow him, he would have killed me. It was fear..." Liher said, his cheeks a fiery red.

"I know what you'll say, Liher. Delamere doesn't scare anyone. However, perhaps she thought she could get my younger brother, whom everyone in the kingdom knows is weak, on her side. I know you hate

Walter for what he did to Lain, but you forget that neither Delamere nor the Endors will ever become your allies."

Lothar tried to push his brother away, but he pushed him back more forcefully. "Maybe Delamere wants to get me out of the way, maybe not... Even if you're right and she only wants an alliance, do you believe that if she wins the war, she'll pay off her debt? Have you forgotten who barred Vylor from choosing a king? No one has shown any interest in us for decades. We have neither allies, nor friends, Lothar... Who paid for Lain's death? Who paid when Thomas took away our rights in the kingdom?'

Liher pulled back his hand, freeing Lothar.

"Do you really think that if Walter takes the throne, he'll allow you to rule over Vylor? Have you forgotten that you abandoned him in the middle of the war?" Lothar asked.

"Walter doesn't care about Vylor," Liher told him.

"Because the only thing he desires is the throne! If he gets it, he may attack us," Lothar insisted.

"And Delamere will help us protect our land?"

"If we fight on her side, we may be able to defeat Walter," Lothar said.

Liher took on an expression of disdain. "You're a fool for believing that. No one can beat Walter."

"Perhaps Thomas Egercoll's son can! He has already done it once before in Elmor—he's a man who has been trained by Althalos."

Selwyn looked at Lothar, feeling a strong headache that blurred his thoughts. *Had the news reached Vylor, or had they just taken his word for it?*

Liher laughed. "You're an idiot, Lothar. Will a random lad overthrow Walter?" Lothar was about to speak, but Liher broke in before him. "I will never fight for anyone again, and any man who fought against us who falls into my hands will pay. This scoundrel will pay for Delamere not having restored our rights in Knightdorn all these years. He will pay for what Thomas Egercoll did to our House. Now, everyone will learn that betrayal of Vylor is paid for in blood, not with alliances."

"Think carefully, Liher. Your decisions will determine the future of Vylor," Lothar insisted.

Liher was expressionless. "I'll send emissaries to Elmor to ask for gold for his release. If they refuse, he'll die in these dungeons. Even if they give the gold, Selwyn Brau will pay for Delamere's and the Egercoll's betrayal, even if he doesn't pay with his life."

Horrified, Selwyn saw him signal the guards. The two men approached him immediately. He tried to push them away in vain. They pushed him towards the chair, and started to tie his arms and legs with the straps. He began screaming, unable to control his fear.

The guard punched him in the face, and Selwyn's voice died. Something was shoved into his mouth—a dirty cloth. Selwyn's arms and legs were tied up. His eyes darted to Liher who was looking at him impassively. Then he saw a strap with a strange object in the middle in the governor's hands.

Selwyn started panting, knowing what awaited him. His father had told him about the Heretic's Fork. This object was a metal rod with two pointed ends that looked like forks. The rod was attached to a strap that was tied around the neck. The result was that if the victim succumbed to sleep, the pointed ends would be driven into their jaw or sternum. His father had told him that many men went mad from the insomnia brought on by this torture.

He thrashed in the chair. They had tied him so tightly that he could barely move. Lothar watched him, frowning.

One of the two guards took the instrument of torture from Liher's hands and began to tie it round Selwyn's neck.

"Stop moving if you want to live until we find out whether the *queen* will pay for your hide," Liher said.

The strap tightened around Selwyn's neck and the pointed ends poked his jaw and chest.

"I'm sorry they sent you like a lamb to the slaughter." Liher's look contradicted his words. "But someone must pay for the treachery of the Egercolls."

Liher turned and left the cell. Lothar threw one last look at Selwyn and followed his brother. The two guards left the cell, locking the steel door behind them.

Selwyn felt that his heart would stop. He tried to move and immediately felt the pointed ends pricking his skin. He was sure the metal rod of the instrument was filthy, and if it pierced deep into his flesh, it would cause sepsis. Tears fell, and for a moment, he wished he had lost his life in the battle against Walter. That death would have been far better than this that awaited him. Tears continued falling, as he closed his eyes. If he could put an end to his life, he would, instead of enduring this torture. He tried to visualize his two brothers. Their figures emerged before him, seeming to smile at him from afar.

Give me strength... Give me strength and soon we'll be together again...

The Green Gate

John wiped away the wine dribbling from his lips and put his goblet on the wooden table. He looked around at the inn. One man was eating bread and porridge, lost in thought, and a little further off two young men were giggling while drinking beer. John loved these places—it had been many years since he had travelled to the kingdom, and he felt young again.

I've always liked the Green Gate. This inn was one of his favourites in the Three Heads.

A golden ponytail caught his attention. A young girl was eating fish and olives next to an ugly-faced man. John looked at her more closely. He bet she was a whore. His gaze drifted to her bosom until a thought swirled in his mind. Her hair reminded him of Selyn. He felt momentary sorrow. Althalos had behaved cruelly towards Elliot. He had tried to talk to the lad about his twin sister, but he was unwilling to say a word.

"*I don't want anyone to find out about Selyn,*" Elliot had told him, Eleanor, and Selwyn one day before leaving Wirskworth for the Mountains of the Forgotten World.

John knew that it didn't matter who else found out about the secret. But it was as if Elliot believed that if everyone forgot about his sister, it would be as if she had never existed.

He took another sip of wine. He often wondered if Selwyn and Eleanor were safe. Caring for someone other than himself was so new to him and felt strange. He had tried to convince Eleanor to ride along the same road as him, but he hadn't succeeded. The woman's soul was wrapped in sorrow and that was dangerous.

John was sceptical of Elliot's decision to send Eleanor to Felador. He bet that the remaining people of Aquarine wouldn't easily accept her as their ruler. Moreover, John didn't know if Eleanor was capable of ruling a region. She had never seemed to possess leadership qualities in his eyes.

His thoughts turned to Selwyn. Who knew what reception he had got in Goldtown. Liher Hale was vain, but at the same time vicious and cunning. John wondered if it was wise for Selwyn to travel to such a place.

He glanced at the cheese and meat on his table. He wasn't very hungry. It was as if he could live on wine alone. He carried on drinking, thinking of Selwyn and Eleanor, until Elliot came back to his mind. Worry clouded his thoughts whenever he thought of the son of Thomas Egercoll. Undoubtedly, many things seemed strange about that boy. Elliot was extremely skilled and courageous, but at the same time immature and hot-headed. The latter two were quite rare for apprentices of Althalos and that scared John.

The door of the inn opened and closed loudly, and four men entered. John watched them carefully. Long swords hung from their belts, and one of them wore a jerkin with a tiger sewn in the centre.

Gaeldeath soldiers.

The men strode proudly towards the back of the inn, looking over the faces of the inn's patrons.

"Every man in here should be in our king's ranks!" the soldier with the tiger on his chest said.

John noticed his angry look and his coarse features.

"You!" the soldier spoke again, looking at one of the two young men who had been chuckling earlier. "Why aren't you fighting for King Walter?"

They're looking for deserters, John thought, panic rising within him.

The young man crumpled with fear. He lowered the mug in his hand and spoke hesitantly. "I am a peasant from Oldlands, my lord. I have never held a sword in my hands. The king ordered that men like me not fight since they can only cause trouble in battle."

The soldier looked disgusted. "Is everyone here a villager?" he asked.

"Seems so, Emil," one of the newcomers said. "Look at their bony builds."

"This one isn't so bony," Emil replied.

John saw the soldier's gaze turning towards him. "I'm very old," said John, raising his goblet.

Emil carried on looking at him, and John realised what had caught his attention. His clothes—a gift from Syrella Endor—looked a lot more expensive than those of the villagers who boozed at the Green Gate.

"Are you a lord?" Emil asked.

John knew that all of Walter's lord-allies would have travelled with his army even if they didn't intend to fight.

"Me?" John pretended to look behind him. "I have been many things, but I have never been a lord."

Emil touched the hilt of his sword. "Villagers don't wear silk jerkins."

"Who told you I'm a villager?" John asked nonchalantly. The soldier seemed to be waiting for him to continue. "I'm just a merchant who knows how to sell his merchandise to good hands."

"Are you a man of the north?"

"No. I'm from Oldlands."

"Oldlands' merchants usually sell their wares to trash like the Mercenaries..." Emil said with a hint of insolence in his voice.

"Not me... I've always preferred to do business with northerners," John told him.

"What do you trade?"

"Spices and perfumes." John raised his goblet again. "Today was a good day. I managed to sell all my wares."

Emil approached, his hand staying near his sword. "Then, perhaps you could treat us to a couple of drinks too..."

"Of course!" John knew what he was trying to achieve. The lords who deserted quickly spewed forth as soon as they were overcome with fear.

"You remind me of someone," Emil told him.

"I don't think I've ever sold you anything, my lord."

"No... You remind me of a bounty hunter... His name was John *the Long Arm*."

Panic gripped his chest. He hadn't expected anything like this. *Damn*. It had been a long time since he had spent time in the north. He didn't expect anybody would remember him. He too had tried to forget everything that happened the last time he was in the Three Heads.

"I'd heard that John lived in Iovbridge in recent years."

John did his best not to look rattled. "I've never met him. I haven't been to Iovbridge for a long time."

"Really? You really remind me of old John. In the north, we don't accept those who have betrayed us and then hidden in Delamere's ranks."

John stood up abruptly, jostling the table in front of him. "Don't ever call me a supporter of the usurper!" he shouted. Emil stopped short, taken aback. "My governor almost lost everything because of Thomas Egercoll! I have always been a man loyal to Ricard Karford! I won't accept any insults concerning my loyalty!"

One of the other men who had entered earlier caught Emil by the shoulder. "I don't think that this man is John the Long Arm," he said.

Emil frowned. "What's your name?" he asked, watching John carefully.

"Morys."

"Your next drink will be on me, Morys," Emil said with a nod and went back to his companions. The four soldiers headed for an empty table.

John breathed out, relieved but threw furtive glances at Walter's men. Now, Eleanor's words to him just a few days before didn't seem so irrational after all. He had to be more careful. It was logical that Walter should have left a few men in the northern regions.

John had paid for a small room, wanting to spend the night in Green Gate. However, he didn't want to leave his table yet. If he did, it could raise suspicions. He had felt unexpected grief saying Morys' name. He may not have taken to him during the early years of their acquaintance, but things had changed lately.

We'll meet again soon, old friend, he thought. *Probably sooner than later...*

Finishing his wine, John got up from his chair and headed to his room. He climbed the creaking stairs, followed a small corridor, and found the door the innkeeper had pointed out to him earlier. He pushed the rusty key into the lock and turned it wearily. The door opened with a dragging noise. A few candles lit up the room, and a narrow bed stood at its far end. He closed the door and lay down on the bed with his clothes on. He may have liked the northern inns, but sometimes he missed Iovbridge. He was getting too old for all these trips and hardships.

He turned on his back and looked at the ceiling. For some time now he had been trying to fathom what it was that wasn't right about Elliot. John may not have been a warrior or a Master, but he had heard much about Althalos. Even if only half of it was true, the conclusion he came to was the same. Something was strange about Elliot's training, but he couldn't tell exactly what. He ruled out the possibility that Elliot was lying about who his Master was. That would have been foolish.

How could Althalos not have confided so many things to an apprentice of his? He couldn't find an answer to this question. *Perhaps the old man had started losing it.*

It wasn't an irrational thought, but it didn't convince him. The Grand Master had taught Elliot the art of war. Nobody could deny that. If Althalos had lost his mind, John would have expected Elliot to have insufficient training in battle, too.

Althalos didn't want to tell him everything... He wanted to keep some secrets. That was the most logical answer of all and the simplest. *If that's true, why had he chosen to train Elliot? Perhaps Althalos never wanted Elliot as his apprentice. He may not have trusted him, but he felt guilty about everything that Walter had done to Thomas Egercoll.* That thought may have been the most logical, but this didn't seem like Althalos at all.

John tried to put Elliot out of his mind. He wouldn't find any answers, no matter how much he wracked his brain. Then he thought about his journey's end. His voyage would be long and difficult. The Cold Sea separated the Ice Islands from Knightdorn, and the autumnal storms were worse than the winter ones. He had to get to the nearest point in Knightdorn from the northern islands before he looked for a ship. If he attempted to travel a long distance by sea, it was more than likely that the ship transporting him would be wrecked at that time of the year. Stormy Bay near Tahos was the best place from which to set sail for the Ice Islands but also to find a ship to carry him. There were several small merchants and smugglers who anchored there.

John sighed. As much as he admired the politics of the Ice Islands, he would have preferred to have been in a brothel in Iovbridge. Nonetheless, he had decided to help Elliot. If anything, he didn't want to be in Iovbridge when Walter entered its gates.

He considered everything he had promised to do. Syrella had given him a letter in which she called on Begon to ally with Sophie, and revealed the existence of a descendant of Thomas Egercoll. John suspected the queen wouldn't find allies in the place he was going to, even though he wished he was wrong.

John felt the effects of the wine spreading through his body. He closed his eyes and began to sink into a warm darkness. His dreams were pleasant and colourful, full of lush green forests and beautiful mermaids swimming in deep blue seas.

Death and Hope

Selwyn's head felt ready to burst. He brought his hand near his face and rubbed his temples lightly. He was very thirsty, his throat burned. Selwyn had lost all sense of time. He could have sworn that the Heretic's Fork had been tied to his neck for days before the guards removed it. It was the worst kind of torture he'd ever experienced. He wondered how long he could hold out. He felt like he didn't have much longer.

Two men had come into his cell a while before and had removed the Heretic's Fork from his neck. Then, they had left without a word. Selwyn knew—Liher didn't want him to die, at least not yet. He needed to wait until his envoy reached Wirskworth and asked for a ransom. Until then, Liher had to keep Selwyn alive.

He had napped a few times, trying to keep his neck still with the Heretic's Fork tied around it. No matter how much he tried, the steel prong had pierced his flesh, waking him up. He was afraid he'd go mad from the torture. Moreover, hunger gnawed at him, and thirst numbed his body. He was lucky that his head didn't hurt anymore.

How long will I last?

He may not have known how many days he had been jailed, but he was sure that this torture would continue. The trip from Goldtown to Wirskworth took approximately nine days, which meant that weeks would pass before word from Sophie reached the Black Vale. He bet he hadn't been in this cell for long, even if the Heretic's Fork made each moment seem like an eternity.

Elliot would find a way to escape, Selwyn thought. *But I don't know how...*

Selwyn felt the need to stretch his body. His legs wobbled as he rose, and his back cracked as he straightened. He moved slowly like a baby taking its first steps. Selwyn touched the icy steel of the cell door. Torch fire lit the dungeons, and not a single sound could be heard.

His thoughts wandered to Elliot's sister. *It would have been a thousand times better if I'd gone like that.*

He knew he didn't have the courage to end his life, even if he found a way to do it. He also knew his parents would collapse as soon as they heard the news. He remembered telling Elliot that he wasn't afraid for his life. He was only afraid of the pain he would cause his parents if he died, and he wanted to protect them. But Selwyn *was* afraid of death, and he hadn't found the courage to confess to Elliot, John, and Eleanor.

Father will move mountains to save me as soon as finds out what has happened, he thought.

Selwyn had no idea how much gold Liher would demand for his release, and Sophie no longer had any gold. His father couldn't do anything. It all depended on Syrella and even if the Governor of Elmor wanted to help, she would meet with great resistance from her council since Walter's army loomed in the distance.

Selwyn heard voices whispering in his mind. Half assured him that his father would find a way to save him while the other half told him he wouldn't make it. The feeling of hope and the fear of death alternated continually in his soul. Once, his elder brother had told him that hope keeps a person alive. Selwyn tried to hope. Even when he was tormented by thoughts of death, he thought of his brothers. The idea that if he died, he'd see them again gave him some faint hope even if he didn't want to spend an eternity in the realms of the dead.

He let go of the bars of the door and walked around the perimeter of the cell. With each step, he felt his legs gradually recover and his heart beat stronger.

Soon the guards will come again. He knew that they were allowing him to rest a little until they subjected him to torture again. He had thought of attacking them and trying to escape, but he didn't know the way to leave the dungeons, and he was very weak.

Selwyn sat on the icy floor again and glanced at the chair a few yards away. *Humans are the worst beings in the world... We keep searching for the most imaginative and painful ways to torture each other.* He bet the elwyn, the elves, even the giants, would never think of causing so much pain.

"My race is the oldest of this world, human. A world that your kind almost destroyed... The human race is our world's biggest sin," Aleron had said.

Aleron was right. And yet, the Elder Races had almost been destroyed, leaving the world at the mercy of humans. Selwyn had never cared about the Elder Races before leaving Iovbridge, but now he believed that the legends about the curse of Manhon Egercoll were true.

Will Elliot make it? Many times he wondered why the lad had decided to go to the Mountains of the Forgotten World. *How will Elliot manage to break the curse?* He didn't know, and the odds were that he would never find out. The sunset of his life would come in this tiny cell.

A loud sound caught his attention. He turned his gaze and saw the rat that had been running round his cell. The tiny creature moved towards him with slow steps, and Selwyn extended his hand. The rat approached hesitantly, smelling his fingers. It climbed into his palm and looked at him with its beady eyes.

"Hello. You'll probably be my last friend in this world," Selwyn muttered. The creature remained still in his hand. "Are you afraid of death?"

The rodent studied him a while and then jumped off his palm, disappearing into the shadows.

I'm losing my mind. He never expected to be talking to a rat. He glanced at the door of the cell and wished he could open it with his mind—that he could get out of the dungeon and kill all of them using his mind only. He had never been a sadist, but now he wanted to cause pain. It was as if the Heretic's Fork had changed a part of him.

Selwyn closed his eyes and began to pray. Not to the gods he knew but to something unknown—to an invisible force. He prayed that this torture would end, either with death or with his release. His father's expression just before he left Iovbridge came to mind. Peter had been afraid—more afraid than he dared say.

I love you father, Selwyn thought and wished his father could hear him, wherever he might be.

The Little Thief

Elliot woke suddenly in the night. He looked around with bated breath, but he didn't detect the slightest movement. He shut his eyes wearily, trying to forget his nightmare. He'd seen someone drawing near him, holding a knife.

It was only a dream.

The night breeze made him shiver. He was sleeping in a small cave which the Elder Races had granted him the day he arrived in the Mountains of the Forgotten World. Elliot had seen the elwyn, the giants, and the elves sleeping in the open air on the mountain on woollen blankets. He wondered how they withstood the autumn cold. He recalled Aleron saying that the elwyn were unaffected by the cold—nevertheless, the same did not apply to giants and elves.

Elliot had also seen a cave near the slope where the Elder Races lived. The four children that lived in the settlement slept there—the beings that had remained as children for entire centuries. There were other caves along the length of the mountain, but their terrain was rocky and inhospitable. Thus, nobody could sleep in those. An elwyn had told him that the mountain had more caves hundreds of years before, along with mines and forges; however, an earthquake had destroyed everything. The caves that remained were very small and rocky. The Elder Races had tried to carve new caves, but every time they did, rocks detached from the mountain.

The stars shone brilliantly in the sky. He was able to see them from the entrance of the cave, a few yards away from him. Elliot was tired and his body hurt from training, but his thoughts wouldn't let him sleep. He had been in these mountains for five days now and as time went by, he felt himself losing faith more and more. He doubted whether he would ever succeed in freeing the Elder Races.

Elliot spent his time duelling with Alaric, and whenever they stopped, he gazed at the view from the slopes of the mountain. That morning's training had gone on for hours until he could no longer feel his hands from the numbness. He had improved quite a bit at dodging the elf's blows, and he now only attacked when he was sure that his opponent wouldn't be able to fend him off. Alaric now had to fight harder to disarm Elliot since the elf had already been defeated twice.

None of that made Elliot particularly happy. Even if he were to become the greatest swordsman in the world, it wouldn't be enough to liberate the Elder Races or to defeat Walter. Elliot believed he was wasting his time, and Aleron hadn't spoken to him since their last meeting. Elliot hadn't seen the Sword of Light again either. He had been irritated when Aleron had taken the weapon with no intention of handing it over to him.

It belongs to me! he thought. The sword had come down through the generations to his father.

Elliot tossed and turned under his blanket. Althalos should have given him the sword instead of Aleron. However, his former Master's act didn't surprise him. If anything, it had proven that he didn't trust him.

He trusted you to save the queen. This thought was some consolation, but not enough. Althalos had disappointed him even though Elliot had loved him as a father.

Elliot often stewed in his own thoughts. Sometimes he felt untold grief for the plight of the Elder Races while at other times he cursed everything—Althalos, the Sword of Light, the place he found himself in. Aleron telling him he was too consumed by hatred angered him more.

Suddenly, he remembered Reynald Karford. He had to write to him soon. Elliot wondered where he was, and he also wanted to find out whether Walter had reached Iovbridge.

He heard footsteps outside the cave, and wondered who was out walking at such a late hour. He bet it wasn't anything exciting, but he was so bored that he decided to take a look. He got up nimbly and moved towards the exit of the cave. Elliot listened and cast a furtive glance around. The noise had subsided for a moment before he heard more footsteps. He walked out of the cave and proceeded to the right. A figure appeared through the darkness—a figure walking on tiptoe. Elliot might not have been in a castle, but the scene reminded him of Moonstone when he had heard the man of the Sharp Swords rush to free Reynald Karford.

He advanced silently and saw the figure a little more clearly under the moonlight. He'd thought it was an elf, but it was an elwyn who was only slightly taller than the elves.

What's he doing in the middle of the night?

The elwyn was moving away from the hillside where the rest of his tribe slept, taking a path Elliot hadn't explored. He followed him like a shadow, trying not to get any closer than was needed.

The elwyn trod on, glancing around. Elliot continued to spy on him, ducking behind large boulders whenever the elwyn stopped abruptly to look around. Elliot realised that the figure he was spying on was a man.

He may suspect he's being followed.

The elwyn eventually reached the edge of a cliff. Elliot had lost all sense of time, but he was sure he had gone quite some distance from his cave. The elwyn extended his right foot into the void, as if he was getting ready to jump. Elliot tried to see better, but darkness obscured the elwyn. He took a few silent steps and shuddered in fear at the sheer cliff. He couldn't even see the bottom of it. It looked like an abyss.

What's he doing?

Elliot remained frozen in place, watching the elwyn nearing the edge of the cliff again. For a moment he thought of running and grabbing him, but he was afraid he would scare him and in that moment of panic, he would accidentally fall. On the other hand, it would have been impossible to go near him without being spotted.

Suddenly, the elwyn appeared ready to jump, and Elliot felt his breath stop. At the last moment, the man seemed to change his mind. Elliot continued watching the elwyn until he heard a sound—the elwyn's muffled sobs in the cold night air.

The man wept inconsolably and then Elliot understood. He wanted to die, to put an end to the torture of the curse. However, he was afraid of jumping into the void.

Elliot felt pain and that he was responsible as if he himself had unleashed the curse. *Why me?* He remembered feeling the weight of responsibility that he carried throughout the years of his short life. He hadn't known even one carefree moment—the throne, the queen, Walter, and now the Elder Races. Everything depended on him. *Why should they think I'm the chosen one?*

He had been orphaned from the moment he was born, and he had even been deprived of his sister. And all this, for what? To save a kingdom from a tyrant and to break a curse he hadn't unleashed? Almost three centuries had gone by since the death of Manhon Egercoll. Why had no other ancestor of his broken the curse? Why should it be him? He felt anger, but at the same time guilt weighed on him more than he could bear. There were so many things he had to accomplish, and he feared it was only a matter of time before he failed something.

The man's sobs grew louder, and tears began to pour from Elliot's eyes. Before the elwyn was the worst dilemma in the world—death or a torturous life. He wanted to run back to the hillside, to find the hiding place of the Sword of Light, and lift it up in the air, yelling. He wanted to see Thindor landing in front of him and making him the master of the sword. He wanted to break open Aremor's tomb and free himself of this guilt forever.

He got up and took a step towards the elwyn. He had decided to approach him. Then, a thought kept him rooted to the spot. *When someone seeks death, even if you stop him, he'll find a way to try again.* Sweat poured down his forehead as the guilt crushed his soul.

"Now, you know," came a whisper.

Elliot stumbled back in surprise. He turned, and saw Aleron's starry-blue eyes through the darkness.

"Now you know what this curse means," Aleron told him.

Elliot was bewildered. The elwyn on the edge of the cliff didn't seem to have heard Aleron. "What are you doing here?" he asked in a whisper.

Aleron cast a look at the elwyn standing just a few yards away from them. "His beloved, Eshina, jumped years ago... Since then, Erin has come here every night, trying to find the courage to follow her. The elwyn never put an end to their lives until the curse of Manhon. They always believed that we should honour the sacred gift of life that was given to us by Azelor. Eshina couldn't stand the suffering any longer. She tried for years until one night she lost all hope and jumped into the void, leaving Erin behind."

Elliot's mouth grew dry, hot tears streaming down his cheeks.

"There were others who jumped too. Many couldn't brave the last one hundred years. Erin is the only elwyn who hasn't found the courage to do it, since his mate fell off the cliff. The rest of my race who lost their soulmates followed them to their death shortly after. The giants and the elves began to jump too when they saw that many elwyn had lost all hope." Aleron's voice betrayed his grief. "One day he'll do it... Death is a little thief—a thief of souls. When he fails to take a soul, he always finds a way."

Elliot couldn't answer as the sound of Erin's sobs rang in his ears. He looked at Aleron. His tears appeared violet as they rolled down like dewdrops from his starry-blue irises.

Unlawful Love

Sophie felt carefree as she walked along Brass Road. The merchants' stalls and the smells wafting through the air cheered her up. However, this wasn't the only reason she felt her burdens had lightened that day. She'd expected the council of Elmor to oppose her every word after all that had happened since her arrival and that Syrella herself would have been met with resistance from her councillors about the battle tactics they would use against Walter. But the last few days had gone by without the slightest disagreement. Syrella had announced to the Elmor council that she would base her defence on the mighty walls of Wirskworth and nobody had opposed her.

Sophie continued looking at the merchants' wares. It was fortuitous that the councillors hadn't protested. She was afraid they might demand a different strategy, something that would reveal bravery and foolishness at the same time. The councillors had agreed that even with sixty thousand men, Walter would have difficulty breaching the gate of Wirskworth. So, they had decided it'd be best to rely on their walls without taking risks.

Walter knows that the walls of the city are strong. That frightened Sophie. She suspected that her cousin would try to draw them out of Wirskworth and was afraid he might succeed.

Stop being pessimistic, she told herself. For the time being, everything was going better than she could have hoped. Syrella had supported her, declaring that she was the Queen of Knightdorn, while nobody had tried to suggest anything foolish about the siege that was fast approaching.

"I don't believe it!" a voice shouted. Sophie turned and met with Peter's frightened look. "You're walking alone in the city!"

"I wanted to think," Sophie responded sharply.

Peter's face was flushed. "Your Majesty, we're not in Iovbridge!"

A shrill laugh came out of her mouth. "Do you mean to say that in Iovbridge I was safe?"

Peter seemed about to protest, but he didn't. "I want us to talk," he said, scratching his chin.

"I'm all ears."

"Not here."

Sophie breathed out. "Alright."

Peter caught her hand and pulled her to the right. Brass Road was crowded with people that day. They walked a while, passing through narrow alleys while innumerable voices filled the air. Merchants shouted, trying to sell their wares. People formed queues in front of their stalls to see the various goods better.

The Lord of the Knights turned into an alley, and Sophie followed him. Their boots echoed in Sophie's ears as they walked on the cobbled streets. Peter stopped suddenly, and she did too.

"What's wrong?" Sophie asked.

"I did what you told me to. I spent the last three nights in the taverns and brothels of the city."

"I hope you enjoyed it," Sophie remarked and noted his angry expression. "That was a joke made in bad taste. Did you find out anything noteworthy?"

"Maybe," Peter replied. The man seemed troubled, and she knew that wasn't a good sign. "I heard a lot... I heard a rumour that Velhisya stole the ancient beauty of the elwyn by using magic potions. Moreover, many say that Walter is undefeated because when he was a child, his mother fed him with the entrails of wyverns. Furthermore, nobody knows the slightest about Reynald Karford."

Sophie felt irritated. "And you felt the need to share this *interesting* information with me?"

Peter shifted. "There's more," he said, frowning.

Her patience started to run out. She had told him a thousand times that he should get to the point faster.

"Many in the city think that Jahon has always been Syrella's secret lover," Peter said.

"What?" Sophie's eyes widened. "Do you believe this nonsense?"

"In the beginning, I reacted the same way as you... But then I began to think about this rumour more carefully."

"Have you lost your mind?" Sophie hissed, looking around to see if anyone was listening nearby.

"Listen to me." Peter took on a serious expression he usually reserved for his men. "I remember Syrella from way back, many years before you were born. She made eyes at Jahon when she was a young woman. He may have been a worthy soldier, but I can't say that he was the most skilful in the court of Wirskworth. However, as soon as Syrella took over the governance of Elmor, she named him Lord of the Knights of the region."

Sophie was unconvinced.

"Have I told you that Syrella's father decided to give her Elmor just before his death?"

"Yes."

"After, Edward forced her to marry Sermor Burns."

"I know all that, Peter," Sophie said, exasperated.

"Think. Edward wanted to unite his house with that of the richest lord in Elmor, but Sermor was never a man you would have expected to see by Syrella's side."

"You're telling me that all these years Jahon was the secret lover of the Scarred Queen under the nose of all of Elmor?" Sophie asked.

"It wouldn't be impossible..." Peter said.

"I think you must give up wine. It clouds your judgement!"

"Syrella never managed to fall pregnant for years after her marriage..."

"And?"

"And suddenly she gave birth to twins! Have you ever taken a closer look at Merhya and Linaria?"

"YOU'RE TELLING ME THAT HER DAUGHTERS ARE—"

"Don't shout!" Peter hissed, eyes darting around. A few people looked their way but didn't pay them any mind.

Sophie's face felt hot. "You're telling me that her daughters are Jahon's bastards?" she whispered.

"I'm sorry to say so, but the truth was in front of our very eyes..."

"But—"

"I think that you'd also expect Syrella would want a different man by her side," Peter cut in. "A lord that only loved riches and banquets doesn't seem the ideal match for her... She may have tried, and when she realised that she couldn't, she gave in to her true love." He seemed to be speaking more to himself. "She may have fallen pregnant by Jahon the moment she realised she would never succeed in loving Sermor."

"And she slept with Jahon under everyone's nose? Even that of her husband?"

"It's not impossible."

Sophie breathed out wearily. "Even if it's true, how is that useful to us?" she asked.

"This secret could bring down Elmor!" Peter told her. "Syrella would be accused of adultery, and her daughters would become bastards overnight, just as Sadon would become her greatest enemy. If it's true, the Scarred Queen would do anything you asked so that you wouldn't reveal everything. She wouldn't dare to strip you of your rank as Queen of Knightdorn no matter who tried to make her change her mind."

"Even if they are bastards, Linaria and Merhya have Endor blood in their veins," Sophie said.

"Naturally, but you must admit that a lot of things would change if such a truth was revealed. Adultery isn't tolerated in Elmor, and the names of Linaria and Merhya would be soiled. Nobody would believe that they were Sermor Burn's daughters any longer."

Sophie cast a look at Peter. The man was right. However, she was troubled. "I can't use something I have no proof of. Even if I used it, Syrella would deny that it was true, and she could order my execution to keep my mouth shut. If it's a lie, she'd punish me for sullying her reputation."

"First, we need to make sure that it's true... If we succeed, we'll think about how we can use this secret, if need be."

"How will you find out if it's true?"

"I'll get someone to follow her."

"Someone that you want dead?" Sophie asked and watched the surprised look appear on the man's face. "If your spy is caught, his head will adorn the spikes of the city."

"I'll think of something..." said the Lord of the Knights.

"If all you heard is true, that means that nobody has caught them all these years even though..."

"And if someone has caught them?"

"What do you think? That they were afraid to talk or that they were killed?"

"I've given this a lot of thought. Walter may be an excellent commander, but I think it impossible that he expected Syrella to hide her army at the Forked River. Her plan was so foolish and risky that it was unlikely anyone could have predicted that she would do that. Now, I'm sure that there's a traitor by Syrella's side, and that everything that happened during Walter's stay in Elmor leads to one conclusion," Peter said.

"So what?"

"Think. Why would someone want to betray an Endor? The Endors have always been worshipped in Elmor, and Syrella is one of the most beloved rulers to ever pass through these lands."

"Do you believe that someone saw her with Jahon and then decided to betray her?"

"It wouldn't be unreasonable..."

"Perhaps William of the Sharp Swords sent information to Walter about the battle at Forked River," Sophie said.

"I thought of that. However, William became a member of the Sharp Swords after that battle. Before that, he was just a soldier, and the plan wouldn't have reached his ears early enough for him to divulge it to Walter."

He was right. Sophie remembered this, too.

"I bet William was one of those who lost a loved one at the Forked River and decided to betray Syrella for her failures. Whoever betrayed her before that battle must have had a motive, and her secret affair with Jahon is the only one that I can think of."

"Perhaps someone simply admired Walter," Sophie countered.

Peter crossed his arms. "Perhaps, but it seems strange to me. How many have supported Walter in this land all these years?" he shot.

Sophie cast a look down the narrow alley where they stood. *Did Peter discover a great secret or is this likely to bring us more trouble?* "Don't tell anyone about this. For the time being, Syrella is on my side. Let's hope she doesn't change her mind. In the meantime, try to find out as much as you can."

Peter nodded sharply.

Sophie watched him and only one thought dominated her mind. *Peter was right about one thing. If this secret is true, it could bring down the whole of Elmor.*

Alone in the Dark

Eleanor stared at the stars while she sat on a woollen blanket spread out on the wet soil, feeling a strange longing. Morys had told her that the stars were the Eyes of the Dead, and she felt that if she looked at them for long enough, she might make out his face in the night sky. But as much as she hoped to see him again, she had to accept that Morys was gone forever.

She glanced at her horse tied to a log. The morning rain had left the ground damp while the humidity clung to her skin. Eleanor had crossed countless plains and small forests over the last few days, trying to reach Aquarine. She tried to avoid the Paths of Shar and the Wise and to her surprise, she had succeeded. Long Arm had warned her not to approach places where Walter's men might be. So, she had ridden carefully through the Vale of Flowers. The sound of footsteps had reached her ears some days before. She'd seen countless soldiers marching towards Ramerstorm; however, she'd managed not to be seen. Then, she'd ridden as fast as she could towards Yellow River. John had told her that there was a small bridge that went across it to the opposite bank of the river, east of the Path of the Wise. She had followed his directions, so now she was nearer than ever to her birthplace.

Eleanor felt lonely in the dark, but a part of her told her that loneliness was what she truly needed. Perhaps she *had* to be alone to process Morys' loss. Perhaps if she thought about it over and over, she would be able to get over his passing.

She sighed. *Maybe I'm cursed. Anyone who's loved me and wanted to protect me has passed away.*

It was a fact that her short life was full of death. She had lost her father, her mother, her brother, and a few days ago, the man she loved. All of them had fought to save her. Her parents had ordered her brother to get her out of Felador and take her to safety in Iovbridge before Thorn's attack. Moreover, they themselves had decided to fight on Thomas Egercoll's side. Bert had told her that they wanted to fight so that their children would be free from a tyrant like Walter.

She kept sitting in the dark, observing the stars. *What strange feelings passion and love are*, she thought. She had never been in love before. She remembered a few smug boys eyeing her, but none had managed to draw her attention. She'd believed she would die alone, and yet, she'd fallen in love at a time in her life when she least expected it.

She shivered, remembering the blow of the short man of the Trinity as it struck Morys. The sound was like a breaking branch. Short Death was notorious for blows that crippled his opponents. Eleanor had seen his sword being unsheathed. She knew that moment, while she had been stripped of her tunic in front of Walter's men, that Morys' spine had been shattered. She had tried to run in front of Morys to shield him, and to go and find her family in the realms of the dead. But she hadn't succeeded.

Why did you do that? She thought, unable to find an answer.

Elliot would have challenged Walter to a duel sooner or later and he would have agreed. It was only a matter of time before Elmor's army attacked. If Morys hadn't rushed to save her, he would have been alive now. His bravery had cost them a life together. Eleanor now believed that if he'd remained alive, they would never have parted. She was certain that their destinies had been united that night they had spent together in the plundered City of Heavens—united in the midst of pain and death.

Eleanor tried to forget Morys for a moment and focus on travelling to Felador. She had wanted to go to her birthplace for years, but now that she was making her dream come true, the only thing she felt was fear. Something inside her was scared of seeing the place where her parents had lived and died—she was afraid that the memory of them would haunt her. But she wasn't a coward. She'd decided that she would do what Elliot had asked of her, and until now, she'd coped better than she'd hoped.

Eleanor tried to make herself comfortable on the woollen blanket. Earlier, she'd seen a small village north of Yellow River. She'd thought that there she could have rested up in a more comfortable place, but she'd decided that the safest was to stay alone. She knew she wouldn't be able to sleep as another worrying thought took root within her.

Will I succeed in taking the rulership of Felador?

She didn't know, and she wondered if she was fit to rule. Elliot's trust filled her with gratitude, but she wasn't sure whether she could do what he had asked of her. Eleanor knew that a ruler should always put their people above all else, and she intended to do that if Felador became hers. However, having seen how Sophie ruled, she knew that it was a burden that only a few people could bear. Eleanor also had doubts as to whether the people of Felador would accept her as governor. The only reason for them to choose her as a ruler was that her father was a lord of Aquarine and that Elliot and Sophie wanted her for that role. Eleanor knew that neither of those reasons would be enough in Felador. She had decided to try. Her brother had once told her that people with the gift of ruling should sacrifice themselves to help others even if they didn't want to. If Elliot had seen the virtues of a ruler in her, it was worth trying even if the burden would be heavy.

An unfamiliar voice snapped her out of her thoughts. Eleanor picked up the bow resting at her side and grabbed an arrow from the quiver. She got up stealthily and listened to the darkness.

"Move." This time, there was no doubt she heard a voice. A few groans were heard in the night. "Bring this scumbag, too."

Eleanor grew fearful at the harsh tone of the voice. She took a few steps until she saw a shadow under the light of the stars. Figures appeared among the trees. Two armoured men in red cloaks pushed two stooping captives in front of them. Neither of them wore helmets. Sweat bathed her brow. Walter's men. She took a closer look at the silhouettes in front of the soldiers—a girl and a boy. The boy suddenly tried to grab the girl's hand, and one of the soldiers delivered a blow to his neck. The lad fell in a heap.

"I thought you understood by now that your girlfriend is ours now," the man who had thrown the punch said with a chuckle. His companion laughed.

The boy got up, staggering, while the girl tried to help him. "Don't touch him!" the soldier behind the girl shouted.

"Please! I beg you..." The girl's voice shook with terror.

"I like women who beg." The soldier laughed and touched the hilt of his sword. "However, I know... I know that you want to be our whore. It'll be better than what you have done with this scumbag."

Eleanor was horrified. The two captives couldn't escape the fate that awaited them. *What are these soldiers doing here? I saw Walter's men marching towards Ballar. Perhaps Thorn had left some men to patrol the roads to the north.*

"I think it's pretty quiet here," said the soldier who had beaten the boy.

"You're right, Egil."

Egil delivered one more punch to the boy, throwing him to the ground while his companion caught the girl by her shoulders. Nausea roiled in Eleanor's stomach. The two men fondled the girl's breasts while trying to tear her dress. The boy tried to get up, crying, but Egil kicked him in the face.

"Be quiet if you don't want to miss the spectacle." Eleanor saw Egil's sardonic smile in the dark.

"You shouldn't have left your village in the middle of the night..." the second soldier said, looking at the girl as he grabbed her between the legs. "But you'll see. You'll enjoy this more than you think."

The girl started screaming and the soldier covered her mouth.

"Hold her tight," Egil told his companion and unbuckled his belt and lowered his trousers.

Egil was about to reach his hand across her thighs when an arrow pierced his skull. Eleanor aimed carefully at the second man.

"WHO'S THERE?" The remaining soldier pulled out his sword and held the girl in front of him as a shield.

Eleanor tried to aim for his face, but she couldn't see clearly. The girl blocked his head.

"YOU'RE DEAD! THERE ARE MORE OF MY COMRADES NEARBY AND AS SOON AS WE CATCH YOU, WE'LL PUT YOUR HEAD ON A SPIKE!"

Eleanor moved amongst the trees, watching the soldier.

The man brought the sword to the girl's throat. "IF YOU DON'T SHOW YOURSELF, I'LL KILL HER."

Eleanor could see the side of his face clearly now. She lifted her bow and pulled the string back. She wanted to shoot but was afraid. It would be easy to miss. A loud scream broke the silence. The boy got up and crashed into the soldier. The man and the girl tumbled to the ground, and the boy grabbed the soldier's hand that held the sword. The girl broke free and ran a few yards away. The soldier punched the boy and raised his sword. An arrow lodged in his open mouth, stopping him in his tracks. Eleanor came out of her hiding place and ran towards them.

"Leave! Run to your village and if you see more soldiers, run towards Aquarine," Eleanor told them.

The lad got up from the ground with blood covering his entire face. "Who are you?" he asked.

"That's not important! Leave."

The girl approached the boy, grabbed his hand and they sprinted into the trees.

Eleanor looked at the corpses of the soldiers. She felt such strong hatred that she wanted to shoot more arrows into their dead bodies. She turned and ran back to her campsite. She collected her things hurriedly and freed her horse. In one swift movement, she climbed onto the saddle and rode away from the carnage as fast as she could.

The Empty Throne

Walter sat on the throne of Iovbridge with its two golden pegasus wings protruding from its sides, lost in his thoughts. The Royal Hall didn't seem majestic to his eyes. He remembered the first time he'd seen it when he was still a young boy and had been in awe. Now he didn't feel the same admiration as he sat in the chamber.

He made himself more comfortable in his seat, thinking about the events of the last few days. He'd wanted to sit on this seat for decades but now that he'd accomplished it all he felt was hatred and rage. They'd left him an empty throne—a throne that had fallen in his hands at a time when he'd been defeated. He'd taken the bait riding to Elmor, and his rage had led to his first mistake. He'd ignored his men's fatigue as soon as he realised Althalos had been alive all these years. He felt irritated thinking about his old Master. He recalled fat and slimy Sadon Burns telling him that the boy who beat Reynald Karford had been trained by Roger Belet.

Roger Belet, he thought angrily. Althalos had tried to trick him.

Once he'd journeyed with his former Grand Master to a small village in Mynlands. There, in Althalos' birthplace, a peasant had told him that when the Master was young, he'd wanted to go to Mermainthor to train for battle. The aged peasant had laughed as he recounted the story.

"Althalos feared that no Master would train him unless he came from a noble lineage. So, he intended to go to the capital of Mynlands as Lord Roger of the House of Belet. He thought no one would bother to find out whether his House was real."

Althalos didn't know that the villager had told him this. So, as soon as Walter heard Sadon's words, he knew the truth. He knew that his old Master had escaped him and had trained the son of Thomas under his very nose. For a moment, the image of Alice Asselin's dead body flashed through his mind. The healer had told him that she had drunk poison, and her body bore no signs of having given birth recently.

That healer was foolish or a liar.

Walter took one more look at the Royal Hall. He should have returned to Ballar as soon as he realised what Elliot's plan was. However, his rage upon hearing that Althalos had trained him right when he found out Thorold was alive too had overshadowed all sense of reason.

He got up off the throne and went down the steps. His eyes wandered to the nine councillors' seats a little below where the king sat. He didn't need a council. The Trinity of Death was enough. He walked down the empty hall, and his rage grew fiercer with each step. They had lured him east-south and had decided to hand over the throne. As if this wasn't enough, Delamere had killed the men he'd left in Ramerstorm. It was undoubtedly the greatest defeat he'd suffered.

The soldiers that had attacked in Ramerstorm had even taken his slaves. He hadn't found any of them alive or dead. He'd thought that some of the slaves had conspired with Delamere, opening an underground passage to Ramerstorm for her soldiers to enter. His men had found the secret gate of one of the tunnels open, and it was obvious that no one had besieged White City.

Perhaps there was a traitor—someone who wasn't a slave.

It was possible, but he didn't think so. Still, he'd heard that Sophie had killed all the hostages taken during her attack. That could be heard in every corner of Iovbridge. Undoubtedly that lack of compassion was something he hadn't expected from his cousin.

For a moment, he thought of when the Guardian of Stonegate had arrived in Ramerstorm. He'd wondered why Sophie had sent him the Sword of Destiny. Now, he knew... It was all a ruse so that his cousin could retreat, but not in a cowardly way. She wanted to retreat, forcing him to accept his first defeat. She wanted to wound his pride.

He felt the need to touch the hilt of his sword. Walter knew that the news of the death of half his horsemen, coupled with the slaughter of his men at Ramerstorm, would bring discord amongst his allies. However, this wasn't as important as the existence of a descendant of Thomas who Althalos had trained.

He tightened his grip on the hilt of the Blade of Power. He wanted to kill. He'd been thirsting to take revenge, to hang Sophie in the centre of the city next to the headless body of Elliot Egercoll, but he had been tricked once more. He'd waited for his allies for days before attacking the palace and when he was ready to wreak havoc and death on Iovbridge that morning, the gates had opened, without a battle.

Walter heard footsteps approaching and felt his anger spike. He glanced at the door of the hall and a huge man entered. Anrai.

"I ordered that no one disturb me," Walter said, wanting to draw his sword and kill Anrai.

"I have a letter for you, Your Majesty. A letter from Sadon Burns," the giant man told him.

This he hadn't expected. "Who brought this letter?"

"A villager. Old Sadon always finds a way to send an emissary under Syrella's nose."

"Have you read what it says?"

"No. I thought it best only you read it. The men are holding the messenger. If the wax seal is fake, and the letter is from some supporter of Delamere, they'll put his head on a spike."

Walter approached Anrai, taking the letter. He broke the wax seal, and read carefully. When he'd finished, he felt even more enraged. "The boy is searching for allies in the kingdom."

Anrai laughed. "He's foolish." Walter gave the giant man a hard stare until Anrai's face became serious. "I mean, there's no one left in the kingdom who would fight for him. At least, no one who has a capable army…" Anrai added, swallowing.

"Sadon says that the boy and his companions left Wirskworth a few days ago. His spies overheard that they're trying to forge alliances, but they were unable to find out where they're heading. Syrella Endor didn't tell anyone where they went or why they left. She's begun to suspect that some man close to her is spying on my behalf." Unease sprung up inside of him, a disquiet he hadn't thought of up to now.

"The only ones with a capable army are the Mercenaries, the Ice Islands, and the Western Empire. None of them will fight for Delamere."

Walter didn't speak. For the first time he felt a trace of fear. *Was that your plan, Althalos?* "There is still someone else…" His voice came out almost in a whisper.

Anrai frowned. "Who?"

"The Elder Races…"

Anrai seemed bewildered. "But how… No one can free the—"

"I need the wyverns," Walter interrupted. He'd wanted to become their master for years, but now this wish was more important to him than ever before.

"I know that you want the wyverns on your side, Your Majesty. I wish I could help you."

He looked at Anrai who was one of the few beings in the world who perhaps had something that Walter desired. Something that you couldn't get without being born with it.

"Where is Leonhard?"

"I don't know, Your Majesty. I'll find out and let you know as fast as I can."

"Tell my commanders that we'll be leaving Iovbridge soon. I want every man to be ready to travel."

"Everyone expects that we'll be marching to Wirskworth."

"No. Not everyone…"

"What do you mean?"

"The riders of Gaeldeath, along with those of Ylinor, will travel with me. I will speak to Gereon myself."

"Where?" Anrai asked.

"To the Mountains of Darkness."

The giant appeared not to believe him. "It's dangerous to approach the wyverns, Your Maje—"

"It's not just the wyverns I want from that place! When I set out to kill Delamere, I didn't expect the last battle would be in Elmor. Wirskworth is a strong city. I want to saturate every arrow and every blade of my men with Orhyn Shadow."

Walter was pensive. A couple of hundred branches from the Night Trees would be enough. Leonhard had told him that boiling these branches could produce large quantities of Orhyn Shadow.

"Your Majesty... If we ride to the North beyond the North, we won't be back in time for the battle in Wirskworth," Anrai said hesitantly.

"You're mistaken. The rest of the men will march west since it's unwise to attack Stonegate. We must not lose a single man before the final battle. My soldiers will travel by the Road of Elves and if necessary, camp along it until we return. I won't exhaust my horses. However, they can't wait for us here. That would delay our trip to Elmor too much. We'll meet them near Wirskworth."

Anrai seemed ready to say something.

"I don't want any objections."

The gigantic man shut his mouth and nodded curtly.

"In addition, I need to train you, the rest of the Trinity, and a few trustworthy Ghosts in a new kind of battle."

"A new kind of battle?"

"The Elder Races have some special powers. My men need to be ready to face them. Do as I've told you."

Anrai bowed sharply and left the Royal Hall.

Walter remained lost in his own thoughts. *The time has come for me to meet the wyverns.* Something told him that he would achieve what he'd longed for for years in the Mountains of Darkness.

The North beyond the North belonged to Gaeldeath, and that place was destined to give him all he needed to be rid of his enemies once and for all. Sometimes, the name sounded funny to his ears. He remembered the first time his father had told him that all the places north of the capital of Gaeldeath belonged to the North beyond the North. People feared that land—the old home of the giants. However, he had seen it as a boy without feeling a single trace of fear.

Walter touched the hilt of his sword again. The fools in the kingdom thought that he did everything he did because he was vain. They were wrong. The crown was rightfully his. His grandfather had united the kingdoms of men for the first time in history and then he had been attacked treacherously by the usurpers and the weak. He wouldn't forget this. He had seen with his very own eyes a letter from the First King to his father.

"Cowardly are those men who do not fight for that which was stolen from them." Walter would never forget what his grandfather had said. His father may have been a coward for not claiming what was his, but he wasn't. He had been born with a gift, an invincible power, and he would use it to put an end to his enemies' lives. He would use it to show everyone that the Thorns of the north would remain sovereign rulers forever.

The Secret of the Mermaids

Walter walked hastily inside the Palace of the Dawn. A few moments after Anrai had left the Royal Hall, a man had told him the whereabouts of Leonhard, and he had rushed to find him. The healer might have answers and Walter needed them. He cast furtive glances around as he walked. He liked Tyverdawn, the capital of Gaeldeath, more than Iovbridge. Rockspire, the Thorns' ancestral castle, seemed far more beautiful than the Palace of the Dawn.

Every time he saw Rockspire, he felt an incomparable power envelop him. The huge castle with the pointed top was the symbol of his House's power. In contrast, the old palace of the elwyn may have been a more ornate building, but it lacked grandeur. Walter headed to the Tower of Courage, eventually finding the chamber he was looking for. He pushed hard on the door and stepped inside. The morning light didn't reach the room, and a handful of torches propped against the walls were required to illuminate the space. An aged figure stood in front of a strange creature.

Walter approached the man and looked at the chained mermaid. The scales on her waist glistened, and her breasts were pure white. Her tail was submerged in a wooden tub with water while her arms and torso were chained to a metal cross nailed into the ground. Walter's gaze went to the mermaid's face. She was watching him with hatred in her eyes. He derived pleasure from this spectacle every time he saw it.

"I think I've found the answer," Leonhard Payne said, breaking the silence, his eyes bright. Walter often thought that Leonhard had unprecedented energy for his age.

"I wish we were only looking for one answer." Walter hoped the healer had good news, otherwise this time his old head wouldn't be spared.

"We're searching for truths that no one has even dared dream of. In order to discover great things, patience is required."

"And what great things have you discovered this time?"

"Mermaid blood makes you invulnerable to anything they are invulnerable to in their natural environment," Leonhard said.

"In their natural environment?" Walter asked.

"Mermaids are only invulnerable in water."

"My natural environment is land... So, I guess I am invulnerable in my natural environment while I will lose my strength if I find myself in water?" Walter asked.

Leonhard smiled. "That's what I also thought! However, my hypothesis wasn't correct. I experimented on dozens of land animals and their bodies remained impenetrable even in water after receiving mermaid blood. In short, mermaids might be invulnerable only in water, but their blood makes you invulnerable wherever you are."

"Let's prove it," Walter approached the tub.

The violet eyes of the mermaid watched him carefully. He put one hand into the water and extended the other towards Leonhard. The aged man looked at the extended limb and then tried to pierce it with a sharp metal object. Walter saw him go red from the effort, but he didn't feel the slightest pain. A little later, he pulled his arm away.

"So, am I vulnerable only to fire?"

"No, there is one more thing that can harm you..." Leonhard walked towards the back of the room. There were thousands of drawers and wooden counters around the dark chamber. Shortly after, the man returned, holding a large object. Walter recognized the Sword of Destiny.

"Extend your hand."

Walter obeyed, feeling strange. Leonhard placed the blade on his forearm and then he felt pain. Walter's skin was sliced in two and blood gushed from the wound.

"According to my experiments, you are vulnerable to the Seven Swords and fire, just like our dear guest."

Leonhard made a sudden move and slashed below the mermaid's chest. She screamed as blood ran down her body. The creature looked at Walter and Leonhard with such hatred that it seemed its eyes would pop out of their sockets. It began speaking in an unknown tongue—Walter knew it was cursing them.

"I only discovered yesterday that the Seven Swords can cut the invulnerable body of a mermaid," said the healer.

"Let it be," Walter said, gazing at the wound on his arm.

Walter thought about their countless experiments. It had taken them a long time to discover how they could draw a mermaid's blood. Legend told that the blood of this creature turned into a colourless liquid as soon as its body came out of the water, which they had verified for themselves. The only way to draw a mermaid's blood was to pierce her skin while she was in her natural environment— water. However, this was impossible, as her body then became impenetrable. They had tried everything without any success until Leonhard found an old myth which said that mermaids' impenetrable bodies were only vulnerable to fire. It was an interesting theory, which was difficult to prove—they couldn't burn a mermaid while she was in water.

Nevertheless, the devious healer discovered that a mermaid's entire body didn't need to be submerged in water to become impenetrable. A few drops on one part of her body was enough. Then, he had devised the structure that stood before them. The way the mermaid was tied, they could burn part of her body while her tail was in the water. The skin that got burnt from the fire became vulnerable, so a sharp object could pierce it and give them the precious blood. The blood that gave Walter youth and strength—the blood that made him immortal.

"I don't care to know what can kill me as much as what can make me even more powerful!" Walter said after a few moments.

"I'm now sure that wyverns only bond with giants because Orhyn Shadow flows in the veins of the latter..." said Leonhard, throwing the Sword of Destiny to the floor.

"This we had surmised from the beginning. I need more than that."

"I can't allow you to meet the wyverns before I'm able to put the venom in your veins!" said the aged man.

"You told me you were close." Walter's face was inches from Leonhard's.

"And when did I ever go back on my word?" Leonhard moved to the back of the room again. When he came back, the healer was holding a cage in his left hand.

"What's that?" Walter had difficulty discerning the contents of the cage in the faint light.

"A rabbit."

"A rabbit?"

"A rabbit with the venom of your beloved tiger in its body."

Walter was bewildered. A while ago, Leonhard had asked him to stick a needle with a strange vial at the back of it into Annys mouth. It was a miracle that the tiger had not devoured him.

"How?" was the only word that came out of his mouth.

"This rabbit drank plenty of our beloved guest's blood," Leonhard pronounced, looking at the mermaid. "Then I put Orhyn Shadow in its blood."

"And?"

"And nothing!" The man's voice betrayed a paranoid glee. "It didn't even make a sound until a month had passed."

"A month?"

The man nodded. "The rabbit began to gasp with pain about thirty days later. Then, I gave it a little more of the mermaid's blood."

"And did it help?"

"Yes. As soon as another thirty days passed, the same thing happened, and then I gave it the antidote."

"So, is Orhyn Shadow no longer found in its blood?" asked Walter.

The man nodded. "This means that in order to withstand the venom in your body, you must drink mermaid's blood about every thirty days. Otherwise, you will have to take the antidote. Of course, by taking the antidote, the venom will cease to be in you, and we don't want that... You need Orhyn Shadow inside you all the time to hope to bond with the wyverns."

Walter remained silent for a few moments. "In short, I'll have to drink mermaid blood for the rest of my life."

"This is essential even if you don't want to tame the wyverns. Without this, you will lose your immortality. However, if my experiments are correct, I think you no longer need to drink the blood daily and still remain immortal."

Suddenly, the mermaid started screeching in an unknown tongue. Walter gave her a blow, and she fell silent.

"If you speak again, I'll pull you out of the water and leave you in the chamber until you die," Walter said in a calm yet menacing tone. Something told him that the creature understood his language.

The mermaid lowered her gaze—he had just threatened her with the worst torture for her. A mermaid died a martyr's death if her body didn't touch water for a few days. Leonhard had told him it was like a human who couldn't find air for his lungs.

"How long before Orhyn Shadow ceases to exist in my blood if I don't take the antidote?" Walter asked.

"Never! Unlike mermaid blood, this venom doesn't spoil, nor can it be expelled. Without the antidote it will be inside of you forever," Leonhard said ecstatically.

Interesting. Things had proven simpler than he'd expected.

"What is the antidote?" Walter couldn't remember the answer.

"Drowning Poison. It can be found only in the flower of Myr".

Walter smiled. A poison was the antidote to a venom. Nevertheless, the fact that he was defenceless against the Seven Swords irritated him. He didn't care about fire; he believed he could easily avoid it. Walter glanced at the Sword of Destiny lying on the floor. He felt vulnerable looking at it, and suddenly the Blade of Power on his belt felt heavier.

Don't be a fool, a whisper in his head told him. No man would be able to hurt him with a blade, whether it was one of the Seven Swords or not.

Suddenly, a memory from the past came to him. The last apprentice Althalos had trained had managed to cut his palm in one swift move. He remembered Elliot staring in surprise at his intact arm.

If Elliot had been holding one of the legendary swords, that battle would have been dangerous. It was sheer luck. Neither Elliot, nor anyone else can beat you. The voice of arrogance in his subconscious was louder than the others.

"I have a huge army, the ships of the Mynlands and Tahryn, the steel of Oldlands, and soon I will have the help of the wyverns..." Walter said to himself.

"Moreover, you're immortal as long as the mermaid blood flows in your veins," Leonhard added.

"Even if the boy gets the Elder Races to side with him, he can't stop me..." Walter said.

The old man frowned. "Do you think he'll be able to accomplish something like that?"

"I received a letter from Sadon Burns." Walter scratched his chin. "The letter said that Elliot and his companions have left Wirskworth. Sadon's spies heard that they're looking for allies, but they didn't find out where they planned to go. I've been wondering who's left that could help them... Who would dare fight against me? Until I remembered that Althalos always spoke of the Elder Races. He admired the elwyn and the elves, and he had spoken to me of legends that say that only an Egercoll can break the curse."

"No Egercoll has managed to free the Elder Races for centuries. Do you believe that the boy will travel to the Mountains of the Forgotten World and manage to break the curse?"

"I don't know how many Egercolls have attempted to free them. As for whether the boy will manage to do so, that's a good question. When I was young, I wondered whether the legend of the curse was true… Althalos reassured me that it was, but when I asked him how the curse could be broken, he replied that he didn't know. I doubted the truth of his words until Anrai assured me about the legends, but he also didn't know how the curse could be broken. Of course, I've never taken an interest in freeing the Elder Races, but I have been curious."

"I know nothing more about this," Leonhard said.

Walter frowned and contemplated his plan. "I'll order my men to start out for Wirskworth while I ride to the Mountains of Darkness. There, I'll try to find the wyverns and take branches from the Night Trees. I need a lot of venom to saturate every blade and arrow with Orhyn Shadow. Afterwards, I'll catch up with the rest of my armies before they attack Elmor. Some of my men need to be taught how to deal with elwyn and elves. No one will be able to stop me from killing Delamere and Thomas' son this time! Ultimately, I need the wyverns."

"If you are to fight the elwyn and the elves, the few Seven Swords you have will come in handy," Leonhard mumbled.

"True. However, there aren't many swords like mine. The men must be trained with the weapons they have."

"Giants are even more dangerous," Leonhard added.

"Giants would never side with an Egercoll. If they throw themselves into battle, they'll only do so for me because I'm the enemy of the Egercolls. However, if what I know about the elwyn and the elves is true, those creatures will never fight on my side."

Leonhard cast him a look. "Even with the Elder Races, it'll be impossible for them to beat you, Your Majesty."

Walter remained preoccupied. "I need the wyverns. Let's see if your experiments willwork," he said.

Leonhard seemed to understand what he meant. He walked towards the back of the room and retrieved the needle with the glass vial attached to it—the needle that had been sunk into Annys' jaw. Walter looked at the black liquid in the vial.

"Why can't I drink it?" he asked.

"Most venoms don't work if you drink them. They must go into the veins," Leonhard replied. "I should put it in this wound before it heals." He pointed to the still-bleeding wound that the Sword of Destiny had made.

Walter extended his arm. "Will this give me all the wyverns?"

The man looked him in the eye. "I don't know."

"Let it be so."

Leonhard stuck the needle into the wound and black liquid flowed into Walter's veins. He expected to feel pain, but he felt nothing except for an insuperable power rising within him. He was foolish to have had doubts. Leonhard was right. His enemies couldn't stop him.

Power and Wisdom

Elliot raised his sword and looked at Alaric. The elf was still, waiting for his attack. *I won't make it easy for him,* he thought.

Practising with Alaric had taught him not to ever attack first. The secret was to wait for his opponent to make the first move and search for the right moment to strike. It was one of the few ways to avoid clashing with the elf's sword.

Alaric took a step forward, lifting his blade, and Elliot watched carefully. The elf's short stature and speed made it more difficult for him than the fact that his sword could fill with the Light of Life. With a sudden move, the elf ran towards him and aimed for his legs. Elliot avoided the blow and stepped backwards. Alaric circled him, attempting to cut his shoulder. Elliot dodged and brought his blade down, aiming for the elf's left arm. Alaric took the hit and fell to the ground with a scream. The elf had a tear in his woollen clothing, and thick blood flowed from his shoulder.

Elliot dropped his weapon and tried to pick his opponent up. "Are you alright?" he asked, and Alaric shot him an angry look. "I didn't mean to hit you!"

"Why not?"

Alaric had never spoken to him before—Elliot thought he didn't speak Human Tongue. "You aren't my enemy! We're just practising."

The elf stood up suddenly. "If I'm not your enemy, why did a man of your house curse me and my whole race to stay in this place forever?"

"I'm not Manhon Egercoll!" he shouted angrily. He was tired of being blamed for the actions of an ancestor of his hundreds of years ago. It was as if every creature of the Elder Races saw Manhon in his face.

"Do you think you're any different?"

"Yes!"

"Would you sacrifice us to defeat Walter Thorn?"

Elliot hadn't expected this question. "No, I wouldn't ask you to sacrifice yourselves," he said.

Alaric looked at him, face expressionless. "Remember this, Egercoll."

Their eyes crossed, and an image of an elwyn trying to find the courage to jump off a steep cliff flashed through Elliot's mind. "I'll remember," he promised.

"One could say you've changed since you first came to this place."

Elliot turned, and saw Aleron. The man was smiling.

"There was a lot I was unaware of when I came to the Mountains of the Forgotten World."

"I'm sure of that," Aleron replied.

Elliot remembered the rage he'd felt when he arrived at this place. However, after seeing that elwyn trying to jump into the void, that rage had died down. "Now, I know..." he said.

Elliot's gaze turned to Alaric. The elf's brow was furrowed as he tried to make out if what Elliot was saying was true.

"However, there is something I want to know," Elliot added. "How did you manage to break the curse?"

The elwyn frowned. "I've already told you. I don't know!"

"I don't think there's much you don't know, Aleron."

Alaric turned to the old man. The elf seemed to be wondering about this too.

"There are countless things I don't know," Aleron said.

"You want me to believe that one day, after two centuries, you were just able to leave this place without any explanation. What made you try to leave the mountains?"

Aleron breathed out wearily. "I felt that something had changed. I don't know how to explain it… I felt that I was free."

Elliot frowned. "I don't understand."

"For as long as the curse haunted me, I felt captive, as if an invisible force prevented me from leaving."

"I know what that's like," Alaric said. "For three hundred years now, I've felt that my flesh is imprisoned. I feel like I'm being held captive. I'm sure that if I were free again, I would know."

The familiar painful guilt stirred up in Elliot's gut. "Something changed." Elliot's eyes went to Aleron again. "Something changed and you were able to leave. If I find out what, maybe I can succeed in breaking the curse."

The elwyn took on a sad expression. "I'm sorry, Elliot… I think you're looking for the answer in the wrong place. I don't know how I got free, but I do know that no matter what happened, it won't help you break the curse. I believe there is only one way, and I have already shared it with you…"

"I don't know how to become the master, either of Thindor or of the Sword of—"

"No," Aleron cut in. "I didn't mean that… Remember what I told you when you got here."

Elliot didn't understand. He tried to think back over everything Aleron had told him since he arrived in the mountains until a memory came to mind. "I have to feel the pain of the Elder Races," he muttered.

Aleron's eyes lit up. "Exactly."

"I feel the pain… I've been feeling it for days."

"No." Aleron now looked serious. "You feel remorse… You feel responsibility now that you know about our woes. But you haven't felt the slightest pain yet."

Elliot was exhausted. He wanted Aleron to stop the riddles and just tell him what he wanted to know. Suddenly, two large figures came into view. The giants were watching their conversation from a hillside. They looked angry. Elliot wondered if they wanted to kill him and Aleron had convinced them not to.

"Perhaps the curse broke because you're the oldest out of all of us," Alaric said.

Aleron cast him a doubtful look. "I don't think age can affect such strong magic."

Elliot started to believe that the elwyn was telling the truth. *He doesn't know how he was freed. If he did, he would have confided in Alaric.*

"Perhaps your wisdom is so powerful that it broke the magic of the centaurs," Elliot said hesitantly.

Aleron smiled again. "Wisdom isn't enough to break such a strong curse. However, I thank you for respecting my knowledge." Silence spread between them for a few moments. "If only Manhon had also respected my wisdom... I tried to convince him not to do what he wanted to and to put his anger aside."

"He lost his siblings. The pain blinded him," Elliot responded.

"Not the pain—hatred and revenge," Aleron corrected him.

Elliot wanted to disagree. "His enemies killed his siblings and their pegasi! He lost six brothers to the Seven Swords—the weapons your race had promised his house!"

"You're right. However, my race never killed anyone. We have never attacked Manhon's siblings—Thomyn, Arne, Albous, Edric, Annora, Eira... None of them died at the hands of the Elder Races!"

"You shouldn't have given the swords to the enemies of the Egercolls!" Elliot insisted.

Aleron sighed deeply. "Aremor made a mistake. Nevertheless, he was just one elwyn, and Manhon decided to punish three whole tribes for his mistake. Hatred and revenge have always blinded humans."

"Perhaps he didn't know exactly what the cur—"

"The curse did exactly what he'd hoped it would do!" Aleron's angry voice snapped through the air. "I still remember his words: 'All of you will be punished. You all deserve to be cursed!' The centaurs may not have realised the real repercussions of the curse, but Manhon wanted us to be punished forever."

Elliot grew sorrowful. "Not all humans are like Manhon."

Aleron frowned. "That's what I also thought. However, over the last three hundred years I've begun to lose my faith in them..."

"I know that the history of my race is steeped in blood, but there are good humans, Aleron."

The elwyn looked at him with endearment. "I'm glad you have faith in humans. But if you had seen all that I have seen, you might have lost your faith in them, no matter how hard you tried not to..."

"You're mistaken. Not all humans are bad or evil."

Aleron breathed out wearily. "Humans respect nothing but power, and that's their biggest problem. They also don't care about anything beyond themselves."

Elliot was about to protest, but Aleron spoke before he could.

"Why are human wars so brutal? Why do the powerful exploit the powerless, even when there is no war? Why didn't half the people in the kingdom want Sophie on the throne simply because she was a woman?"

Elliot had no answers.

"No man or woman ever dared to disparage Annora and Eira Egercoll while they had two pegasi at their side. When the army of the First King of Oldlands killed their pegasi, he ordered they be raped before they were murdered. Without the pegasi—without power—they were mere objects in his eyes," Aleron continued.

Elliot had never heard of this before. Manhon Egercoll may have made the wrong decisions, but Elliot understood the pain his family's plight had provoked in him.

"Humans will never respect anything but power. No being of their race ever valued either wisdom or knowledge. That's why when Manhon came to these lands and took the Sword of Light, he felt he had to take revenge—felt he had to impose his newfound power on the weak. I thought he would regret what he did, like the centaurs, but even until his death, he used to say that he had made the right decision..."

Elliot wanted to respond, but he couldn't find the words. Out of the corner of his eye, he saw a male elwyn approaching silently with a wooden plate in his hands. The newcomer held out the plate to him. Elliot looked at its contents—a freshly roasted hare and some fruit.

He took the plate and bowed slightly. "Thank you."

The elwyn nodded and left.

Elliot cast a look at Aleron and Alaric and he started walking towards the giants. The two enormous creatures seemed to be aware of his presence. Elliot looked at the face of the male giant. It was wide with a thick beard and menacing black eyes. In contrast, his mate had softer features, even if her size was over ten feet tall. He bet they were thinking of killing him, but the two giants looked at him as if they were waiting to see what he wanted.

Elliot held up the plate before the male giant. "Take it," he said, not knowing if he understood his language. "You need it more than I do."

The giant extended his enormous hand and took the wooden plate with a strange expression. He looked at the food first and then at Elliot. A moment later, he turned to the giantess and offered her the food. She glanced at him with an affectionate look. Elliot had never imagined he would see such sentiment in two such huge creatures. The giantess nodded curtly to Elliot as if to thank him. He responded with a nod and turned back towards Aleron.

"My practice isn't over yet for today," Elliot said, grabbing the sword he had thrown to the ground earlier.

"You're right," Aleron said, watching him with an impressed expression. "But I think you now need a new challenge."

Elliot was bewildered. Alaric turned to the left, and he noticed one more elf. An elf-woman walked towards them and gave Alaric a smile. She had long hair and fierce red eyes.

"I think it's time you faced two elves at the same time!" Aleron said. "However, I advise you to be careful. Alysia is capable of killing anyone who upsets her mate."

Elliot was taken aback. He had no idea Alaric had a mate. He let out a sigh and raised his sword as Aleron walked away. The red eyes of the two elves glared at him. For a moment, he saw Althalos in his mind. He might have felt anger towards his old Master, but something told him that Althalos could see him from wherever he was. He was sure that his Master wanted him to succeed.

I'll make you proud. Elliot brought the sword up in front of his face, ready for battle.

The Free Captive

The sharp ends of the Heretic's Fork had been driven into Selwyn's chest and jaw, his eyes flying open at the fiery pain. He'd fallen asleep once again, having tried in vain to keep his head still.

You must hold on, he told himself. Something within him hoped he would leave the Black Vale alive and that all he needed was to hold on a little longer. He heard footsteps approaching him. This sound was his only relief—relief from pain for a few hours.

The footsteps got louder until a figure stood in front of the door of the cell. Selwyn looked at the guard, but he couldn't make out his face properly through his blurred vision. The newcomer opened the door with a clang and approached him with long strides. Selwyn flinched as Lothar Hale stood before him.

The man removed the Heretic's Fork from Selwyn's neck and untied the straps of the chair. Selwyn tried to stagger to his feet, but his legs couldn't support his weight, and he fell to the ground. He brought his palm to the pain along his sternum and glanced at it under the dim light. His fingers were red. The Heretic's Fork had gashed the skin on his chest. He hoped it wouldn't get infected.

"What do you want from me?" he asked, mouth parched.

Lothar held his hand out, and Selwyn saw a small flask. He grabbed it and emptied its contents in one gulp. He wiped the water from his lips, staring up at Lothar.

"Why did you come to Vylor?" Lothar asked.

Selwyn mustered up what little strength he still had to stand before answering. "I've already told you. Whatever I told your brother is true."

The man began to pace the cell, holding his chin. "My brothers were always hot-headed, arrogant and greedy. Lain died because of his arrogance when he decided to risk the leadership of Vylor in a duel against Walter..." he said.

Selwyn took a closer look at Lothar as anger spread across the man's face.

"As soon as Walter executed Lain, Liher took over the rulership of the region, agreeing to fight on Thorn's side! I couldn't believe it. He decided to forge an alliance with the man who had sentenced our brother to death!" Anger arose in his voice. "Walter would have killed us if we hadn't allied with him, and I told Liher to let him do so! In Vylor there is deep devotion to my house. No one would have fought for Thorn if he'd murdered all the Hales!"

Selwyn didn't understand why he was telling him this. It was as if Lothar had wanted to vent about this for some time.

"Liher told me I was naïve, and he believed that Lain had behaved foolishly. In his opinion, we had to fight for Walter. It was certain he'd become the new king, and if we were with him from the beginning, we would enjoy his favour. He also told me that Walter would give us more gold than we had ever imagined.

"I told my brother that he was making a mistake! I told him that Walter would never give us all he dreamed of. However, Liher didn't listen to me, and a few years later he realised that I was right. When Thorn eventually acquired a huge army, Liher understood at last that he would never pay him for his help. After allying with Ricard Karford, Walter didn't need us."

Lothar breathed out angrily. "For years Liher blamed Lain for all his decisions. The looting and attacks from our older brother not only enraged George Thorn but Thomas Egercoll too. Liher believed that Vylor should at last come out from under the shadows that Lain had condemned it to. So, he decided to fight for Walter, thinking that this would restore the glory of our land while also bringing him plenty of gold. At the same time, he didn't want to die since Walter wouldn't leave Vylor without its men. Back then, he needed us... However, I knew." Lothar's eyes looked off into empty space. "Walter would never forgive our house for not helping his grandfather. The fact that Lain didn't send an army to the side of the First King in the Pegasus Rebellion will never be erased from his memory. Walter doesn't forget..."

"Why are you telling me all this?" Selwyn didn't know what else to say. The pain in his body prevented him from thinking clearly.

Lothar frowned. "Because I know I'll never trust Walter, but I think I can trust Sophie Delamere."

"Your brother is holding her emissary captive, demanding gold!" Selwyn wanted to raise his voice, but he didn't have the strength. "Liher Hale is subjecting the son of the most important officer of the queen to torture! Do you think that is how a new start between Vylor and Sophie happens?"

"No, but I want to know... Is it true that Sophie wants a new alliance with Vylor, or is it simply a trick?"

"A trick?"

"Perhaps all she wants is to use us for as long as she needs us."

Selwyn laughed, and pain shot through every muscle in his body and his jaw ached. "You say Sophie isn't like Walter. You say you trust her. Yet you want to know if she sent me to your land to lie to you and your brother? You trust no one, Lothar, just like your brother."

Selwyn placed his hands on the icy floor and tried to get up with a jerk. A few moments later, he managed to stand up straight. "Because of Lain Hale, many in the kingdom don't trust the men of your house. However, Sophie chose to trust Liher, sending the son of Peter Brau to ask for an alliance. She trusted your brother. She trusted your house. If you want a new beginning, you have to start trusting, too."

Lothar remained silent. "I'll talk to my brother," he said.

"He won't listen to you."

"Perhaps not. But I can try."

Selwyn laughed again. "Even if Liher changes his mind, do you think the queen will forgive him for torturing me?"

"She'll have to try. Sophie Delamere is no longer seated on the throne of Knightdorn. The news has travelled throughout the kingdom... If she wants to remain *queen* for some, she'll have to be prepared to forgive. Our history doesn't allow new alliances to be built easily," Lothar said. "I can't free you."

"I understand," Selwyn responded.

"I'll try to get my brother to see the truth. Perhaps, if I try hard enough, he'll understand and realise the mistake he's about to make."

Selwyn was puzzled. "I didn't expect you to want a new alliance with Sophie so much. Most in the kingdom think the only mistake is to be against Walter."

Lothar smiled. "When Walter sits on the throne for any length, he'll get bored. Taking a throne is far more interesting than keeping it and ruling a kingdom. He'll look for new enemies and those who didn't fight by his side will be slaughtered. We have no hope against Walter alone."

Selwyn studied the man. *If anything, Lothar is quite a bit smarter than his brother.* "If you want something to change, you don't have much time."

Lothar frowned. "It won't be easy to convince my brother, but I have time. Sophie cannot attack Goldtown now. Walter will reach Elmor soon to destroy his enemies once and for all. He won't forgive his defeat at Wirskworth."

The news had truly travelled throughout the kingdom. "I didn't mean that," Selwyn explained.

Lothar stopped short. "What did you—"

"You're right. The queen will not waste men to attack Vylor at this moment in time. However, if you delay changing your brother's mind, only two things can happen. Either Walter will win the battle, and one day he'll kill every person in Vylor, or Sophie will win the battle and do exactly the same thing. I won't endure this torture for long, and if I die, Sophie will never ally with a Hale. Even if I live, I think the queen won't forgive my torture if you don't help her in Elmor."

Lothar watched him for a few moments. He moved towards him, and, to Selwyn's surprise, held out his hand. Selwyn squeezed it, trying to figure out whether it was a trap.

"I trust you, Selwyn Brau. I'll do all I can for the good of both of us," Lothar said.

Selwyn nodded. "You must be quick, Lothar... I don't know how much longer I'll last."

The man looked thoughtful. "I'll replace the guards with some men who are loyal to me. I'll try to make sure this damned thing doesn't go round your throat again," he said, looking at the Heretic's Fork in his hand.

"Thank you," Selwyn murmured.

Lothar turned and walked towards the door of the cell. For a moment, he stopped short and turned to Selwyn again. "Do you think Elliot is capable of beating Walter?"

"Yes." The answer had rolled off Selwyn's tongue without hesitation.

"Why?"

"Who else has succeeded in forcing Walter to retreat in all these years? Who else has succeeded in devising a plan to kill six thousand riders from Gaeldeath?"

Lothar stared at him. "I hope you're right."

With these words, he left the cell, locked it, and disappeared from sight. Selwyn could hear his boots echoing on the ground until the sound faded away. He felt strong hope welling up within him. He thought of his brothers, his father, his mother, Morys, Eleanor, even Long Arm, until his mind travelled to Elliot—the only person who was capable of overthrowing Walter.

I'll get out of here! Together we'll manage! He thought. Suddenly, Selwyn felt free inside his small cell—free of all the fear, death, and pain that had been haunting his mind.

If you fear death, you'll miss the opportunity of living a real life, his older brother's words resounded in his head. He'd told Selwyn this when he had confided in him how much he feared death.

Selwyn straightened and walked towards the entrance of the cell. He gripped the icy bars and looked at the torches that lit the hallway. His body may have been held captive, but his mind had at last been liberated from his demons. He felt an unprecedented strength, one he never imagined he would find. Now, he knew that no matter what they did to his body, nothing would be able to imprison his mind again, and that meant he would be free forever.

The Old Friend

Reynald waited beside his destrier. Suddenly, the horse neighed, and he pulled the reins, bringing it closer to him. He stroked it gently on the head and the beast closed its eyes at his touch. Reynald was uneasy. He'd pondered several times whether his coming to Iovbridge might mean the end for him. Walter's guards had let him enter the city and had ordered that he wait until they heard whether his old lord would agree to meet with him. Three guards stood before him, awaiting orders.

He hadn't been in Iovbridge for many years. He remembered the capital of Knightdorn having an aura of grandeur. However, it didn't feel the same anymore. It was as if the veil of war had swallowed up all the hope of this once glorious city. He felt his anxiety flaring up. At times he wondered why he had agreed to spy on the most dangerous man in the world—the man who wouldn't hesitate to feed him to his tiger.

I'm a fool, he thought again. He remembered the fear from the very first day he had set foot in Isisdor. However, his fear that morning was greater than ever. He'd seen Walter's armies arrive in Iovbridge, and he'd known that the time had come to meet his former lord.

"The King will see him now in the Royal Hall," a voice said. Reynald saw an overwrought guard with short hair and a wide face to his left. "I'll accompany him," the newcomer spoke again.

The three men watching Reynald all this time nodded curtly, and he began to walk, pulling his horse along.

"Leave your horse here. A stable boy will take it," said the guard.

One of the three men held out his hand, and Reynald swiftly handed over the reins. Then, he began to follow the newcomer. His eyes fell upon the cloak of the guard as it gently fanned out behind him. A tiger was sewn in its centre. The wind had picked up, and it would soon be dark.

Reynald observed the people of Iovbridge as they passed. Their faces looked grim as they gathered in their homes. He felt pleased he had spent the last seventeen years in Stonegate. The Guardians of the South hadn't been plagued by worries in decades. Instead, the men of the north marched from battle to battle while Sophie's allies had spent the last few years in misery and death.

They moved through several deserted alleys until Reynald saw the gardens surrounding the Palace of the Dawn. The scent of flowers eased his anxiety as they approached the entrance of the ornate building. Two armed guards stood in front of it. The man accompanying Reynald motioned to them, and the guards stepped aside. Reynald had forgotten how high the ceiling of the palace was, and his eyes wandered over it as he stepped inside. Reynald felt strange as they walked through deserted and dark corridors.

Is this the end of me? He would soon find out.

After a while, Reynald found himself in front of the entrance to the Royal Hall. The door was open, and he passed inside the room with his escort. His eyes suddenly fell upon the throne and then he saw him. Seventeen years had gone by, yet Walter looked as if he hadn't aged at all since their last meeting.

Walter had a smile on his lips, two golden wings springing up behind him from the throne. Reynald knew that smile. It was the smile of death. Four figures were seated below the king's throne. Reynald would have preferred to see Walter without the Trinity of Death and Berta Loers. For a moment, he almost laughed. Berta, Walter's lifelong lover, had for years hoped that her lord would one day honour her with a place amongst the Trinity of Death, but Walter would never bestow such an honour upon a woman. Reynald's gaze shifted to a giant man—the man who had replaced him in the Trinity.

He continued to approach his former lord, while his eyes wandered to the ceiling of the hall. The gods of Knightdorn were depicted along its length in such detail that they seemed to be contemplating the decisions of the king of men.

Walter rose from his seat quickly. "I didn't expect to see you again, my old friend!" he said.

"It's been years since we last met, Your Majesty." Reynald bowed deeply. "I'm glad to see you again, especially in the seat I've always wanted to see you in."

Walter's smile got even wider. "The truth is that I would've preferred you to have been by my side all the years I fought to get this throne."

"I was, Your Majesty," Reynald replied. "I established your rulership in the South Passage for a full seventeen years."

"You know that I didn't want you there. You were the one who wanted that mission."

"Few would have wanted that mission, Your Majesty." Reynald met Walter's gaze. "You wouldn't have been able to hold Stonegate without a man of yours remaining there. I stayed in the castle, ruling it in your name. It wasn't easy to make the Guardians turn their back on the Oath of the South. I think no man of yours would have wanted this duty."

"That's true..." Walter said.

He began to descend the stairs slowly, and it was then that Reynald noticed some men standing to the right of the Trinity. His attention had been so focused on Walter that he hadn't been aware of them until then. His eyes widened as he noticed Ricard Karford. His brother looked back at him with a strange expression.

"However, the Guardians shouldn't have defied the Oath of the South. If they had come to the aid of Elirehar and Elmor a few years ago when I attacked the southern regions, I would have killed them all." Walter came up to Reynald. His eyes were cold.

"That's true. But that way, Stonegate would have remained deserted, and this would have allowed Delamere and Endor to establish their dominance in the south. My rule over the castle prevented their alliance."

The blond man sized him up. "You're not mistaken about that." Reynald bowed again. "But not long ago, you failed to hold the castle, and this led to my first defeat in seventeen years."

Reynald braced himself for the blow. He had seen Walter draw his sword with superhuman strength and separate heads from human bodies countless times.

"I'm sorry about that, Your Majesty... I shouldn't have accepted the challenge to that duel."

"You shouldn't have. However, I too, made mistakes. I was mistaken in leaving Ramerstorm, and I should have returned there as soon as I found scorched earth in Elmor," Walter said brusquely.

"Sometimes mistakes make us wiser."

"Yes. If you stay alive. I wonder, how did you get here?"

"That's a long story..."

"I'm all ears," Walter replied. "My informants tell me that you killed William of the Sharp Swords while you were held prisoner in the cells of Syrella Endor. You killed him instead of killing Elliot Egercoll who found himself at your mercy."

"That's true." Reynald had expected the news would have reached the ears of the new king.

"Why?" He saw Walter grasp the hilt of the Blade of Power and felt a trace of fear.

"I wanted to gain his trust, Your Majesty."

Walter's hand remained on the hilt as he raised an eyebrow. "Really?"

"I was curious. I thought that if I saved his life, he would tell me the truth. I wanted to know who trained such a skilled swordsman. I wanted to find out whether he was the son of Alice Asselin and Thomas Egercoll."

"Do you know now who trained him?" Walter asked.

"I heard the guards of Elmor talking about that..." Reynald replied.

"So, he didn't tell you himself. He didn't trust you."

"Not immediately, but later he confided in me the truth."

"Does he trust you now?"

"I think so."

"Didn't he wonder why you saved him?" Reynald nodded. "What did you tell him?" said Walter.

"That when I decided to fight for you, I hadn't realised who you really were. As soon as I saw the slaughtering of Thomas and how brutally you treated his allies, I detested you and decided to leave, having requested that I conquer Stonegate and remain there. I also told him that I'd never wanted to fight against you because I knew that that would have meant the end of me."

"And he believed you?"

"Yes."

"Did he let you leave Wirskworth?" Walter asked.

"He was the one who set me free," Reynald told him.

"Did you tell him you would return back to me?"

The question took Reynald aback. Walter waited expectantly for him to continue, his hand still resting on the hilt of his sword.

"He sent me to spy on you," Reynald said and felt the tension in the room thicken.

Walter's blue eyes were fixed on him with a strange expression. "And you accepted?" he asked.

"If I hadn't accepted, I don't think I would be here right now."

"Your cunning remains to this day, my old friend. That was a very clever way of escaping. However, if you had let William free you, it would have been easier. As for Elliot, sooner or later you would have found out everything about him. Such news rarely remains a secret."

"William was a fool. There was no way he would have succeeded in getting me out of Wirskworth. The City Guard was on the alert the moment they heard you may have been riding to Elmor. There were guards everywhere, and William had failed to even get me out of the dungeons of Moonstone without being spotted by anyone!" Reynald felt an ounce of courage. "If I hadn't won the boy's confidence, I would've been dead. Had I died, I wouldn't have been of any use to you. Now I can offer you my sword while the boy thinks I'm his spy. We can take advantage of this."

The blond man seemed troubled, as if he was trying to come to a decision. "How?" he asked.

Reynald was stunned. "By giving him false information!" he replied.

"I didn't mean that. How did he intend for you to communicate with each other?" Walter clarified, head tilted to the side. "He's miles away..."

"He has a hawk that obeys him only."

Walter let go of the hilt of his sword with a jolt. "A hawk?"

"Only the centaurs can have given such a gift," a voice said.

Reynald turned and saw an aged figure. Leonhard Payne. He hadn't seen him in years.

"The centaurs are helping the boy," Walter said.

"That wouldn't be strange. They allied with Thomas in the past," Leonhard spoke.

"True," Walter said and grinned at Reynald again. "However, now we have the right man to help us! Lord Karford has killed many centaurs in the past." Reynald smiled back. "Where's Elliot now?"

"In the Mountains of the Forgotten World."

The blond man seemed puzzled. After a while, he turned his gaze towards Leonhard.

"You said you wanted to offer me your sword..." Walter said.

"Of course," Reynald replied with another bow.

"But you no longer have a sword." Walter turned and made a motion that was barely visible.

Leonhard walked towards them, and it was then that Reynald saw something shiny in his hands. He immediately recognised the ornate hilt of the Sword of Destiny.

The aged man walked to Walter's side and held out the sword to him. He took it, his eyes never leaving Reynald. "This sword was the reason I rode to Elmor. If you lose it again, I'll make sure it's the one that takes your life," Walter said and held the weapon out to him.

Reynald bowed once more. "I won't disappoint you again, Your Majesty," he replied and reached for the sword.

"We'll discuss every word you send to Elliot together."

"Of course."

Walter smiled. "Every one of my allies is in Iovbridge except old Launus Eymor... I'm sure you'll have plenty to say after seventeen years."

Walter headed for the door of the hall. The hinges groaned as the door opened and the king left. Reynald turned his gaze to those still present. Everyone looked at him with suspicion as if they hadn't believed a word he'd said.

"It's my pleasure meeting you all again after so many years, my friends!" he said loudly, keeping a grin on his face.

With that, he left the hall with his head held high, gripping the Sword of Destiny as tightly as he could.

The Lost Brother

Soft candlelight enveloped the chamber, and Reynald gazed at the landscape beyond the window. There were no stars in the sky that night over Iovbridge. A thump on the door made him turn his gaze. He got up, opened the chamber door and found Gereon Thorn standing before him.

"To what do I owe this pleasant surprise, Lord Thorn?" Reynald asked.

Gereon gave him a hard stare. "One would expect that you'd have a lot to say, after so many years," he replied. He was old, with white hair and a wrinkled face.

"Doubtless. Most of it only concerns your nephew," Reynald said.

Gereon reddened with rage. Walter's uncle did not arouse the fear that his nephew induced in people, nor did he command the slightest regard in the kingdom.

"I think Walter is wrong to trust you. This will be one more mistake after all those he has made recently," Gereon said.

"And why don't you share your thoughts with him?"

Gereon adopted on an angry expression. "No need. I'll be watching you. If you try to subvert Walter's reign, I'll kill you. If you were loyal to our king, you wouldn't have stayed in a castle in the south for seventeen years."

Reynald smiled. "At least I stayed in a castle that belongs to Knightdorn, and I managed to conquer it in Walter's name. If I remember correctly, your own castle doesn't even belong to the kingdom, or do you intend to bring Ylinor under the new king's jurisdiction?"

"Ylinor will belong to Knightdorn for as long as Walter sits on the throne."

"I never expected you to make such a decision," Reynald said in a cheerful tone.

"Ylinor of the House of Thorn is the most prestigious castle on the continent. It must belong to a kingdom with a man of my house sitting on the throne."

"Then why did you refuse to make it a part of the kingdom when your father wore the crown?"

Gereon's jaw clenched. "At that time the institution of one king had just begun. I waited to see if the First King would be able to—"

"You're pathetic."

Gereon thrust his face into Reynald's. "How dare you!"

"If you don't step back, you'll regret it," Reynald said without flinching. The man's face was contorted with rage. Nevertheless, he took a small step backwards. "I know why you didn't relinquish Ylinor to the kingdom when George sat on the throne. I know that you never wished to be subservient to anyone. You weren't afraid of your father, but you're afraid of Walter since you're afraid of telling him your thoughts about me."

"I never included Ylinor in the kingdom until I believed in one king!"

"Naturally. I think that if Thomas Egercoll or George Thorn had attacked your castle, you'd have changed your mind."

The man laughed. "If Thomas Egercoll had dared march to the North beyond the North, he would have met with an even more horrendous death than that which awaited him."

Reynald returned the smile. "You're brave only when you're up against those you know cannot harm you, Gereon."

"At least I had the courage to fight for Walter while you hid in Stonegate for—"

"You're a liar." Reynald cut him short. "You refused to fight for Walter when he took Gaeldeath from his father! When he came to your castle with the men from Tyverdawn, you chose a duel instead of a battle because you knew that your army had no hope of winning. You hoped Walter would be defeated in the duel. When your champion fell, you saw who Walter really was, and your fear didn't allow you to refuse him anything ever again. Where was your bravery when you betrayed your own father in the Pegasus Rebellion?"

Gereon reached out and grabbed Reynald by his jerkin. "I won't tolerate any insults from you, Karford."

"Don't you touch me." Reynald's voice rose.

Gereon released him. "My father made mistakes, but I'll make sure Walter doesn't do the same. I'll watch your every move."

"As you wish."

"You must feel proud that for seventeen years you stayed in a castle, then you lost to a young lad," Gereon said gleefully.

"At least I fought that young lad myself. You were afraid to duel against Walter for Ylinor, putting someone else in your place—"

"I came to warn you. Walter may have welcomed you back, but I don't trust you. If you're hiding something, I'll find it, Karford. Remember my words." Gereon said and left the room.

Reynald sat on his bed and glanced at the ceiling of the chamber despondently, trying to calm down. He hated Gereon Thorn. He took a few steps and sat back down on his bed, trying to calm down. *Coward.* He could have sworn that Gereon was the most spineless man to ever pass through the House of Thorn. Walter had once told him that his father hated Gereon—Reynald had never before met more mismatched siblings than Robert and Gereon Thorn.

Reynald remembered that Walter's father. Robert Thorn, the firstborn son of George, had had the courage to defy the First King, deserting him in the Pegasus Rebellion. Moreover, he had decided to fight against Walter even though he knew that he was the most skilled swordsman in the kingdom. Reynald admired Robert's courage in going against his father and son, as well as the traditions of his house. The fact that he had decided to marry Thomas' sister—an Egercoll—was living proof of that.

Reynald glanced at the chamber door. His anger at Gereon hadn't subsided. Walter's uncle had boasted that he was a descendant of the most illustrious house in Knightdorn, the house that was meant to dominate the entire continent. However, as soon as George took the throne as First King, Gereon claimed that he didn't want the castle of Ylinor to obey anyone but himself. Even so, Reynald knew that George had a soft spot for Gereon and would indulge his whim. Thomas, too, had allowed him to keep Ylinor separate from the realm. Reynald was certain that if King Egercoll had asked Gereon to bring his castle under his jurisdiction by threatening him with war, he would have agreed without a fight.

Coward. He backed out of helping even his own father—the father who loved him. Reynald knew how brutal George Thorn was. The fact that he had let Gereon keep his castle independent of the kingdom meant that he adored him.

Walter had confided in Reynald that he wanted to kill his uncle over his decision not to help the First King in the Pegasus Rebellion. They were both aware that the reason Gereon had made this decision was because he knew George would lose. However, Walter had a lot of blood on his hands after killing his own father. As if that wasn't enough, he needed trustworthy men in the regions under his rule, and Ylinor needed a Thorn as a ruler.

Another knock on the door forced Reynald out of his reverie. He felt his anger rising. This time he wouldn't hesitate to hit Gereon. He opened the door with an abrupt movement, and it was then that he saw a figure he hadn't expected to face.

"Good evening, brother. I would have thought you'd have a lot to tell me after so many years," said Ricard Karford. He was tall with thick hair and big black eyes.

"If you'd wanted to talk to me, you could have always visited me in Stonegate," Reynald replied.

"And you could have come to Kelanger. I thought you would have wanted to return to the land of our house." Reynald didn't speak and Ricard entered the room. "I wonder why Walter allowed you to stay in Iovbridge. You didn't fight on his side all these years, and you even lost Stonegate!"

"Why don't you ask him yourself, brother?" Reynald asked, closing the door. "We both know that I can offer him more than you in battle."

Ricard frowned and suddenly burst out laughing. "You, one man, can give him more than the army of Oldlands?"

"You're older than me, and yet you haven't learnt anything, Ricard..." Reynald laughed in turn. "I'm the man who took Stonegate alone. The man who commanded the armies of the Mercenaries by slaughtering the centaurs. The man who belonged to the Trinity of Death."

"I thin—"

"Walter gave you Oldlands and me a position in the Trinity for the very same reason our father gave you his castle and me the Sword of Destiny," Reynald interjected. "You may be the one who can govern, but I'm the one who can fight."

"Since your contribution to the battle will be so significant, I want to see if you'll accomplish more than my men when we attack Wirskworth."

"I'm sure that Walter will give me the command of your men in this battle."

Ricard almost choked. "You've always thought you're great, Reynald, but you're not."

"I agree... I'm simply a Karford who never lost a battle."

"Except to a boy... The son of Thomas Egercoll."

"That boy was trained by Althalos."

"I would not have expected such a skilled warrior as yourself to be looking for excuses." Reynald remained silent. "You are forty-five years old now... The truth is that you've grown old, Reynald, even if you won't admit it. Perhaps you're not the man you used to be."

"You may leave now, Ricard."

"Listen to me! I don't know what happened to you... None of us ever understood why you decided to stay in Stonegate all these years. But Walter doesn't easily forgive. I don't know why he accepted you back, but you must be careful."

"Thank you, brother. However, I can look after myself."

"No, you can't. This was always your greatest flaw. I came here to warn you... Much as you don't believe it, I've always loved you." Reynald frowned, throwing him a look.

"Why did you stay in a castle in the south for seventeen years?"

"Sometimes gifts become curses, brother. I was tired of killing," Reynald told him.

"And now you've decided you want to kill again?"

"Yes... This boy will pay," Reynald said.

"Walter only respects the men who fight for him, and he doesn't want those who only fight for themselves at his side."

Reynald's laugh sounded like a howl. "Then, he would have killed you years ago, Ricard. Have you forgotten that if Thomas had married our cousin, we would have fought alongside him all these years? Have you forgotten how you so wanted him to choose Jeanne instead of Alice? You may have come to hate Thomas when he deprived you of your soldiers, but you knew that if he married Jeanne, you might have been able to take over the rulership of Oldlands from the Asselins one day! You lost all hope as soon as he chose Alice, and when you got the opportunity, you allied with Walter to get what you'd always wanted... The only reason you found yourself on his side was because he gave you Oldlands, and I'm sure he knows that."

"And you, brother? Have you always wanted to fight for Walter?"

For a moment, Reynald got lost in his own thoughts. "Yes," he said after a while.

"But not any longer... Now, you just want to redeem your honour because it was sullied by the son of Thomas Egercoll."

"I've nothing more to tell you, Ricard."

"You were always stubborn, and you have never thought of anything else except yourself. You have never thought about the future of our house."

"Really? I think it was the highest honour for our house when I got into the Trinity of Death."

Ricard scoffed. "I expected you to say that... However, you've forgotten that members of the Trinity cannot have children."

"I've never wanted children, Ricard."

"And what will become of our house?" his brother blurted out angrily.

"What do you mean?" Reynald asked.

"You're foolish!" Ricard had gone red. "You know I can't have children, so you're the only one who might be able to continue the family name."

"I'm a sworn fighter. I don't want children, and no child would want me for a father."

"I don't care. You fought for Walter and yourself all these years... As soon as we destroy the last of the King's enemies, you'll do something for our house, too. You no longer belong to the Trinity."

They remained silent for a few moments.

"Be careful... As I told you, Walter doesn't forgive easily. You have to prove your dedication," Ricard told him before he left the room, closing the door behind him.

Reynald sat back on the bed as his thoughts raced. He loved his brother. However, he was a man who wouldn't allow anyone to take away what he longed for more than anything else—Oldlands. If he dared tell him the truth about Elliot—dared tell him how he felt about Alice—he was sure that Ricard would either betray him or kill him. His older brother knew that Walter was capable of killing every man of the House of Karford to get revenge if he found out about these secrets.

Reynald stood. He'd always expected that he and his brother would die young. Their father, as well as their uncle, had died of the same disease before they turned fifty years of age. He, his brother, and their cousin were the only Karfords alive.

Me, a father? he asked himself, thinking of his brother's words. He'd never wanted sons or daughters, like Ricard and Jeanne. However, his remaining relatives hadn't managed to have children, no matter how hard they'd tried all these years.

Ricard's words swirled in his mind. It was a fact that Walter was unforgiving, and he punished the powerful men he believed could betray him. He had to be careful. He remembered William Osgar, the last Lord of the Knights before the order of knighthood had been banned. William and the four royal knights had been Walter's men for some time before the Battle of Aquarine, giving Thomas a lot of wrong advice. So, King Egercoll had decided to ride to Aquarine without his allies.

William and his knights got the fate they deserved. They betrayed the king they had sworn allegiance to.

Reynald remembered Thomas yelling at William, asking him to help him escape when he had lost the battle. William had laughed and hit him while holding him in place until Walter cut off his head. Sometime later, Walter had William and the royal knights murdered in their sleep. He had said that since they had betrayed Thomas, they might betray him too. However, Reynald knew that his lord wasn't telling the whole truth. William was the only living man who had been trained by Althalos, aside from Walter, feared that he might have been capable of overthrowing him.

The last men Althalos trained had no honour. The thought terrified him. *Is Elliot any different?* He didn't know. The boy hadn't told him that Althalos had trained him until Reynald asked in his last letter. He might have heard the truth from the guards in the dungeons of Wirskworth, but something made him want to hear it from Elliot as well.

Reynald wondered why Elliot had decided to go to the Mountains of the Forgotten World. Elliot had written that he wanted to free the Elder Races and convince them to fight by his side. Reynald had heard about the curse that haunted those creatures, and so he questioned how the boy would accomplish such a thing. He wasn't sure if Althalos had advised his last apprentice to journey to that place. Reynald had also asked Elliot if he wanted him to reveal his whereabouts to the new king, and the boy had advised him to do so. He had to give Walter valuable information about Thomas' son. After all, the king couldn't harm Elliot where he was. Moreover, the boy was certain that Walter had a spy in Wirskworth—Elliot had asked him to find out who he was.

Reynald didn't have the slightest idea about the identity of the spy. However, the information in Elliot's letter had prepared him for his first meeting with Walter. Reynald had expected the new king to know about what had happened with the man of the Sharp Swords in the dungeons of Moonstone. If Reynald lied, and the truth reached the king's ears, it would cost him his head.

Reynald scratched his chin. He remembered one of Walter's letters where he had confided that one man of the Sharp Swords had become his spy just after the battle at the Forked River. However, Walter hadn't mentioned any other informant in Wirskworth who had collaborated with him before that battle. Reynald was sure that the king had other spies near Syrella. That would explain how Walter had guessed her plan for the battle of the Forked River so perfectly. Nevertheless, Reynald had never heard who they were. He had to try and find out.

He pushed aside all these thoughts and tried to calm himself down. Things had gone better than he'd expected since his head was still attached to his body. He'd considered whether he should have fought against Walter all the years he'd spent in Stonegate, but he knew that if he'd attempted to do so, that would have been the end of him. There was no hope of his winning. Now, however, there was a glimmer of hope that he could take revenge—a hope that he could pay homage to the memory of ill-fated Alice Asselin.

The Kingdom of the Wise

Eleanor took in the wall of Aquarine looming before her. It was lower than that of Iovbridge and the ten-feet-tall city gates were wooden with metal layers. The night sky was empty while the torches on the round towers of the city gave off the only light in the atmosphere. She felt a spark within her as she set eyes on her parents' home for the first time.

Eleanor pulled on the reins of her mare and approached the gates. She searched for guards in the passage behind the parapets of the wall. There was no one to be seen. Eleanor drew ever closer to the entrance of Aquarine and spotted movement in the turret to the left of the gates. A figure began running behind the battlements. She slowed her horse, trying to figure out what was going on. More figures moved quickly on the wall.

Eleanor noticed a few arrows pointing at her. *They may not allow me into the city.* Nothing happened for a moment before the gates opened. Two horses galloped towards her, the green cloaks of their riders billowing behind them.

"I told you, it's a woman!" came a voice.

The horses approached Eleanor, and the armoured riders frowned at her.

"Who are you? What are you doing in Aquarine?"

"I'm Eleanor Dilerion, daughter of Lord Jackin Dilerion and sister of Bert Dilerion," she said. The men seemed taken aback. Eleanor bet they had no idea who she was. Both of them were very young. "I have a letter from Syrella Endor, Governor of Elmor. Who rules in Aquarine?" Eleanor raised the letter in her right hand.

"High priest Andrian," one of the men said.

"May I speak to him?"

The horsemen looked at each other, not knowing what to do. The first man who had spoken approached and inspected the seal on the letter closely.

"Alright, follow us," he said while the other nodded tersely.

Eleanor rode behind them into the interior of the city. Aquarine was cobbled, and a few trees were dotted throughout the city. A dozen chimneys were smoking, and there was absolute silence. She followed the two soldiers through the deserted alleys, riding slowly until a huge building stood before her. Its architecture was the most impressive she had ever seen. Eleanor was sure it was the Temple of the God of Wisdom, the place where all Knightdorn's healers had been trained. Sophie had told her many times that she had always dreamed of being trained in that place and becoming one of Knightdorn's most famous healers.

She carried on riding and saw yet another impressive building—the Castle of Knowledge, which was the ancestral home of the House of Delamere. She took in the gardens near the castle filled with flowers and small ponds, while on the opposite side was the largest fountain she had ever seen. She remembered her brother talking about this fountain. Bert believed it was the biggest in the world. Eleanor couldn't help but admire Aquarine. The little light there was didn't allow her to see every detail of Felador's capital, yet she thought it was beautiful.

The two men stopped their horses and dismounted in front of a small stable. Eleanor got off her horse and tied it next to theirs. She followed them in silence towards the entrance of the castle. The wooden gates of the building were unguarded, and the two men pushed against them forcefully, revealing a dark corridor behind them. Eleanor felt uneasy. She didn't know what awaited her when she met the high priest. It seemed strange to her that he resided in the ancestral castle of the Delameres instead of in the temple of the city.

The soldiers turned into a corridor with more light than the rest. A low door stood to their left, and they stopped in front of it. One of them knocked softly. The door opened immediately, revealing a short man with white hair and a good-natured appearance standing behind it.

"What's the matter?" the man asked.

"We have a visitor with a letter from Syrella Endor, high priest," one of the soldiers said. The man seemed astonished and looked at Eleanor behind the two guards. "We were thinking about sending someone to inform you, Lord Andrian. However, after the news of what happened in Isisdor and Elmor, we thought it'd be best to bring the messenger to you immediately. This is Eleanor Dilerion."

"Eleanor?" Andrian looked at her as if he had seen a ghost. "I don't believe it!"

The high priest motioned to the guards and stepped aside. Eleanor entered the room. It wasn't very large, and a few candles illuminated the white walls. A wooden table, a chair and a small bed were the only furniture inside. The door of the room shut with a soft sound.

"I never expected to see you again, Eleanor," he told her

"I'm sorry, Andrian... But I don't remember you," Eleanor replied.

"Naturally!" the aged man said. "What news does Sophie send me?"

Eleanor wasn't expecting this question. "How did you...?"

"Aquarine may have been destroyed after Walter's battle against Thomas, but it's still rich in harvests. Most merchants of the north steal them and trade them in the northern regions. However, a few are honest and pay the price they should. Moreover, they inform us of the news in the kingdom." The man smiled.

"As you might have guessed, we know that Walter has taken Iovbridge, and that Sophie has left the throne and journeyed to Wirskworth. We also know that Walter lost men in Elmor, and some in Ramerstorm. I assume, therefore, that Sophie sent you here. However, I wonder why Syrella wrote a letter."

"Sophie hadn't reached Wirskworth yet when I set off on my journey to Aquarine," Eleanor responded. Immediately after, she held out the letter to the high priest.

He looked at her thoughtfully. He took the parchment, broke the wax seal, and began to read. His eyes widened. When he finished, he looked back at her and asked, "Is it true?"

Eleanor nodded. "It is."

"The son of Thomas and Alice... Trained by Althalos," Andrian muttered, trying to digest all the information he'd been given. "I heard that Walter had suffered a defeat in Wirskworth, but the existence of Elliot hadn't reached my ears."

"The news will soon travel throughout the kingdom. The truth is that neither Sophie nor Syrella were the ones who sent me here," Eleanor said.

The man seemed even more bewildered. "Elliot?"

"Yes." She'd decided to tell the truth. She imagined that the word of the queen would be stronger than any other in Aquarine. However, lies weren't the best start in the city she hoped to rule.

"'*Queen Sophie believes that Felador needs a new governor*'," the man said, reading from the letter.

"The Governor of Elmor wrote this. I'm not sure whether the queen finds these words wise, but Elliot thinks they are. Syrella and Thorold agreed with him."

The old man seemed stunned. "Thorold? The Grand Master?"

Eleanor explained to him that the Master of Elirehar had been alive all these years.

"Did Elliot's plan force Walter to a defeat?" Eleanor nodded again. "Then, perhaps there is still hope..." the man said. "Although I don't doubt Elliot's motives, I'm certain that the people of Aquarine are free to choose the governor they want." Andrian looked her straight in the eyes.

"I don't want Aquarine to fight for—"

"Aquarine cannot fight for anyone," the high priest cut her short.

"There is no army on these soils. Furthermore, the few lords of Felador have chosen me to govern this region because of my wisdom."

"I didn't know that Felador had a council."

"The truth is that it doesn't..." Andrian said. "The sons and daughters of the lords who survived Walter's massacres conceded many of their crops to the people of Felador all these years. Thus, they gained the respect of the common people, giving them the right to choose me to lead them into the future. They chose me in the hope that one day this land would recover from the deaths of a hundred thousand of its people at the hands of Walter's armies. Sorry to say, Eleanor, but Isisdor forgot about Felador for decades. I'm afraid that its people won't accept you as their new governor even if Elliot Egercoll and Sophie Delamere sent you to their land. I knew your father; he was an honest man. One of the most honourable lords in Felador. However, not even that will be enough for you to win the region. Syrella might have written in that letter that you would become a leader with compassion, but you have never been a ruler, and the people of Felador won't trust you. I bet they wouldn't even accept Sophie herself to rule them after what has been happening all these years."

"And you? Would you want me for Ruler of Felador?"

"I don't know," Andrian said. "However, that's not important. There's only one important question, and you're the only one who can answer it. Do *you* think you're able to rule Felador?"

Doubts gnawed away at her like bloodthirsty rodents, and she turned her gaze away, not knowing how to reply. *Was Elliot right to have assigned me this mission?*

Stormy Bay

John shivered through his clothes against the icy wind blowing through Stormy Bay. He felt relieved that he'd managed to make it to Tahryn without any other unexpected surprises. However, the autumnal stormy seas hadn't subsided, so it seemed impossible that he'd find a ship that would take him to the Ice Islands. There were no inns for him to rest in in the port city, and if he slept outside, he would freeze from the cold. John had spoken to a couple of fishermen from the northern isles, asking them if they could transport him to their land. They had told him that the winds had strengthened, and they didn't think their ships would be able to sail again for a few days.

Damn. I've only been here a few hours, and I already want to leave.

John had thought that the Harbour of Tahos would be much more welcoming than the small port of Stormy Bay. However, he didn't know how easy it would be to enter Tahos—a city under Walter's rule. As if that wasn't enough, he knew not many ships from the Ice Islands would have docked in Tahos. He'd heard that Eric Stone had restricted trade with the men of the northern islands since he'd taken over the rulership of Tahryn. John was more likely to find somebody to transport him to his destination from here.

He began to look for someplace where he could sleep. He was certain that the wind would strengthen as the night grew, and the sun had all but disappeared from the sky. He walked hurriedly through the port, looking at the ships moored in the bay. Perhaps if he paid, some captain would allow him to sleep in his hold.

A neigh reached his ears, and he caught sight of a horse tethered a few yards away. He had sold his mare a little while ago since he didn't want it in the Ice Islands. The gold he got for her was more useful to him. The wind whipped his face, and raised voices sounded on his right.

About ten soldiers with a ship sewn into their cloaks were walking around the harbour. *Why does Tahos have soldiers in Stormy Bay?* His instincts told him to leave, but something made him walk towards them.

"Are you the captain?" shouted one of the tall soldiers with a thick beard, his voice authoritative.

"Yes," said an ugly-looking man standing in front of a small wooden ship. He was bald with small eyes, a big head and rotten teeth.

"What are you carrying?"

"Fish and spices."

"Are you from the Ice Islands?"

"Yes. From the Grand Island."

"Show us your wares."

John watched the man's ship as it swayed with the dancing waves. The captain seemed annoyed by the orders of the soldiers, and John wondered why they wanted to inspect his ship.

"Why has Tahryn sent an army here?" asked the captain. "They haven't searched my ship before."

"Governor's orders!" one of the soldiers told him.

"I'm sure you know why," the man pressed.

"Step aside!" shouted one of the soldiers as he boarded the ship. "Do you have a crew?"

"Of course. Five men. They've walked to Tahos to buy supplies for the return journey. They'll be back by dawn."

The soldier searched the ship from end to end, and John continued watching. Soon after, the soldier from Tahryn got off the ship. "I didn't find anything."

"What did you expect to find?" asked the captain.

"Weapons or soldiers in your hold!" said the man in an angry tone.

The captain seemed puzzled. "Weapons or soldiers?"

"King Walter will soon start the last battle against Sophie Delamere, and the Ice Islands wanted to fight on the side of the usurper at one time!"

"That happened fifteen years ago!"

"Once a traitor, always a traitor," the soldier said and spat on the ground.

The captain glared at him with rage contorting his face. "Did you think my ship would carry enough men to overthrow Walter?"

"There may be many of you carrying soldiers on your ships! We're checking every vessel in the bay," said another soldier.

"I don't think the Ice Islands have enough men to stop your king from getting what he wants!"

One of the soldiers cast a threatening look in his direction. "If we check your ship again, don't object if you value your life." He left, along with the rest of his companions.

"Damn you! We should have fought for Delamere and sent you to the bottom of the Cold Sea!" the captain muttered once the soldiers were out of earshot.

So, did the soldiers mean Walter's battle for the throne of Iovbridge, or were they talking about a battle in Elmor? John thought. He didn't know if Walter had taken the throne, but thought that such news would travel quickly throughout the kingdom. The wind picked up, and John felt like it was going to blow him away. He stepped into view. "The truth is that perhaps you should have fought for Delamere," he said.

"Who're you?" The captain looked at him perplexed.

"An emissary of Sophie Delamere, and I want to get to the Ice Islands as quickly as possible." The men of the Islands hated lies and he had to be careful. If he was caught lying, he would lose his head.

"Do you bring news from Sophie for Begon?" John nodded, and the man laughed. "Really, does Sophie Delamere expect that the few men of the Ice Islands will save her? Even if it were possible, I'd say it's too late for that."

"Are you really a captain?" John asked.

"Yes," said the man.

"Take me to the Grand Island."

"What do you want from Begon?"

"What is your name?"

"Raff."

"Sophie's words are to be heard only by Begon, Raff."

The man looked at him suspiciously. "What is your name?"

"John."

"You remind me of someone."

"I'm John the Long Arm."

Raff's eyes widened. "I never expected Long Arm would want to travel on my ship!"

John was aware that a number of people knew him in the kingdom, but he hadn't expected a man of the Ice Islands to have heard of him.

"You caught a pirate as a favour to my father years ago. That scoundrel used to tear our nets," the captain said.

John laughed. Finally, luck was on his side. He didn't recall anything of what the man was telling him, but he had taken on many such jobs in the past. "Will you help me?" he asked.

"We'll set sail in the morning," Raff told him.

"A few fishermen told me that the sea-storms are quite dangerous. Perhaps we should wai—"

"You've changed, John," Raff said, smiling. "My father would tell me that John the Long Arm always thirsted for wine and adventure. What a pity that now you're just a grouchy messenger... I've travelled in worse storms than these. If you want to set sail with me, we'll set off at dawn tomorrow." The captain made a move as if he was welcoming John aboard his ship.

"Dammit," John swore under his breath. He was destined never to live a quiet life.

Aleron's Secrets

Elliot was on the lookout, holding a bow that Alaric had lent him, but he hadn't managed to find any prey. He'd decided to hunt that day since food was not plentiful in the Mountains of the Forgotten World. He felt guilty each time he deprived the elves and giants of a meal. Aleron had told him that the centaurs would bring supplies in the coming days, but Elliot bet that their food would run out before then. Autumn was approaching, and the cold brought more hunger.

He continued walking for hours and disappointment enveloped him. His hunt had proved fruitless. The sun began to set in the afternoon sky, and it was then that he decided to take the road back. He was very hungry, and the thought of returning empty-handed angered him.

The sound of rustling caught his attention. He looked to the left and was stunned. A deer stood a few yards away. He raised his bow and grabbed an arrow from the quiver hanging over his shoulder. He pulled the bowstring as slowly as he could, and then the animal's eyes turned in his direction. The arrow shot out at great speed and struck the deer in the head. The unfortunate animal fell to the ground with a thud, and Elliot approached.

"I'm sorry," he whispered above the lifeless body. He never liked killing animals.

The deer was small, so he lifted it onto his shoulders and made his way back. After a while, his back hurt. He hadn't considered how difficult it would be to carry an animal on uphill slopes. Sweat bathed his forehead as he struggled to continue.

The scant rays of the sun were still shining as he approached the hillside where the settlement was. He tried to pick up pace when he suddenly heard a loud roar. He turned and lost his balance, the deer slipping off his shoulders. A huge monster was flying a few yards from him, startling him. Its body was pitch black and its wings, trunk, and tail were full of thorns.

Elliot saw the monster land on the ground in front of a tall figure. He looked a little closer and then he understood—it was the male giant. It was the first time he'd seen a wyvern, and he couldn't even imagine how someone would be able to fight the beast. He got up slowly, put the deer on his shoulders, and walked towards the slope in order to get away from the wyvern. It wasn't long before he reached Alaric and Alysia next to the outskirts of the settlement.

"I saw you fall," Alaric said, grinning. "Have you never seen a wyvern before?"

"No," Elliot replied. He considered that from the moment he'd offered the food to the giants, the elf had been more friendly towards him.

"From what I can see, your hunt bore fruit," Alaric spoke again and looked at the deer.

Elliot nodded and threw the animal to the ground.

"I can help you cut it up and roast it," Alaric said.

Elliot hadn't expected him to help. "That would be great," he said.

A loud sound made him look in the direction of the wyvern once again. The enormous creature had taken off and a few moments later flew far away.

"Can't he take him away from the mountains?" Elliot asked and looked at the giant.

"No... Adur tried to years ago, but as soon as he climbed onto Belhyor, he couldn't fly. However, Belhyor has remained faithful to Adur all these years that he has been trapped in these mountains," Alaric said.

"How many years does a wyvern live?"

"About four hundred. Belhyor was very young when he became

Adur's wyvern, but he's old now. Occasionally, he comes here to meet his old master."

"Could he find a new master?"

"Not as long as Adur is alive. However, wyverns can only be bonded with giants and now only Adur and Aiora remain."

Elliot saw a grief-stricken look on Alaric's face, and felt pangs of guilt once more —guilt for actions that were not his own. "Are there many wyverns in the Mountains of Darkness?" he asked, recalling John mentioning that the creatures lived in the north.

The elf shook his head. "Belhyor is one of the few remaining wyverns. Most were killed in the Battle of Wirskworth, and those that survived died of old age as the years went by. After the curse, the wyverns stopped reproducing, and no one knows why."

Elliot heard footsteps approaching and turned to see Adur a few yards away from him, looking at the deer on the ground.

"We'll roast this deer with Alaric. You and Aiora can eat with us," Elliot said. *He could kill me with one move*, he thought, unsure if Adur understood him.

Adur looked at him as if he was contemplating the offer. Then the giant turned his enormous body and began to move away, in silence. He saw him heading towards the edge of the slope where Aiora was.

"I wonder how Manhon managed to curse the Elder Races. If you had attacked him along with the giants and the wyverns, he wouldn't have had any hope," Elliot said, looking at the two elves.

Alysia laughed. "Manhon travelled here with all his soldiers, the centaurs and one pegasus. They had four times the warriors as us. As for the wyverns, they fear the pegasi, and no one knows why."

"Do wyverns fear the pegasi?" Elliot had never heard that before.

"I think so, yes... When Manhon came to the mountains, not many giants remained, and only a few dozen of them had a wyvern under their command," Alaric said. "I remember the wyverns flying far away as soon as Manhon appeared before them astride Thindor. Perhaps the decimation of their kind in the Battle of Wirskworth had weakened them. In the days before then, they may have attacked him."

Elliot didn't know what to add and silence enveloped their company for a few moments.

"Let's roast this poor animal," Alaric said suddenly, and Elliot nodded, mouth pursed.

Elliot's stomach was full and warm. The deer had proven very tasty. A little further away, Alaric and Alysia were licking their fingers.

"The supplies are dwindling day by day. The more animals we find, the better things will be," Alaric said.

"Tomorrow, I'll come hunting with you," Alysia said and looked at Elliot.

He smiled and nodded sharply, realizing there was no one around. The people of the Elder Races had gone to sleep; it was late.

"Alysia is the best with the bow," Alaric said.

"She's good with the sword too," Elliot added, the memory of the morning popping into his head. He had duelled with both elves for hours, and many times Alysia was so agile that she gave him a harder time than Alaric.

Alysia finished her food and then leaned over towards her mate and hugged him. Elliot saw Velhisya in his mind's eye. He wished that one day he could hug her just like Alaric did Alysia. Elliot couldn't get Velhisya out of his mind. No matter how many elwyn women he had seen in these mountains, she was the only one he longed for.

He sensed something approaching and turned. Hurwig landed next to him with a small parchment wrapped round his right foot. *About time.* He stroked the hawk's feathers and pulled the parchment free.

"Pretty hawk," Alaric said.

"A gift from the centaurs," Elliot replied with a smile.

"The centaurs are generous... News from your friends?" the elf asked.

Elliot nodded. He hadn't told anyone that he was exchanging letters with Reynald Karford. He unrolled the parchment and read its contents. Walter had taken the bait and accepted Reynald in his ranks, and soon they would be riding to the Mountain of Darkness. Walter would go there with the riders from Gaeldeath and Ylinor only, while the rest of his armies would march to Elmor. The new king wanted Orhyn Shadow to drench every weapon of his men before the battle in Wirskworth.

Clever plan.

Elliot read the parchment one more time, mouth pursed. Walter had asked Reynald to show him every letter he would exchange with him. This was a problem, but Reynald had proposed a solution. Elliot would send a large parchment, which would have a smaller one hidden within it. The large one would be presented to Walter while the other—the one with the real message—would remain a secret. Reynald would do the same. It was reasonable to assume that Elliot wouldn't need to show the letter to anyone, but it would be best to be prepared. The trick was simple and clever, however, he wanted to think in peace.

"I'm exhausted," he said to the two elves and stood up. "We'll hunt with the first light of the sun," he added to Alysia.

The elves bid him goodnight, and he hurried to his cave, lost in his own thoughts. Elliot was pleased with the information Reynald had sent him. His idea had worked better than he had dared to hope. He had revealed several truths to Reynald in the letters they exchanged. The man had asked him if Althalos had trained him, and Elliot had confirmed it. He thought about whether he wanted to tell Reynald about his sister. He felt that a man who had loved his mother should perhaps know this secret. However, something prevented Elliot from telling him. Reynald may have loved Alice Asselin, but he hated his father.

Elliot looked at the letter again. He had to reply as soon as possible. Walter's journey to the north gave him time, but Elliot had to find a way to achieve everything he wanted to accomplish in the Mountains of the Forgotten World. Otherwise, no matter how much time he had, it wouldn't be enough.

A light shone into his eyes, and he looked to the left. There was a small cave there, one he hadn't seen before. Curiosity got the better of him, and he walked slowly inside. A figure sat in the centre of the cave, holding an object that emitted a bright light.

Elliot approached and took in the figure carefully, his jaw dropping. It was Aleron. The elwyn's eyes were closed as if he was sleeping. Elliot tried to discern what he was holding. It looked like an orb. He felt the urge to touch the object, but a voice inside him warned him not to.

The light will burn me.

He was about to leave, but a longing awoke within him. Aleron seemed not to be aware of his presence. Elliot was torn as he bent down and lowered his hand towards the orb. He gently touched it, and a painful burning sensation made him jerk his hand back. For a moment, he felt that everything had gone dark.

It's only in my head, he said to himself. Something commanded him to endure the pain. He had to keep touching the orb for longer to find out what the darkness that enveloped him was.

He mustered all his strength. He'd learned from childhood to endure pain. Elliot touched the surface of the orb again and didn't pull away. The pain shot through his very core until his body was lifted into a cloud. Terror flooded his soul as he tried to move his limbs. It felt as if he were travelling through the sky, destined to fall and crumble until his feet touched the ground again.

He touched his body to make sure he was all in one piece, relieved that nothing was amiss. He looked around and found thousands of figures standing before him. Elwyn, giants, and elves were gathered in a familiar place—the Mountains of the Forgotten World. Elliot moved forward and saw more figures. Centaurs and humans were standing still while a man raised a large sword.

He rushed towards the man and was about to push a figure out of the way, but his hands went through it. Elliot stopped, unable to believe what he'd seen. He didn't understand what was happening. He tried to run towards the man with the large sword again, but a few moments later found himself in front of Aleron. Another elwyn stood next to him. Aleron looked younger, but something else caught his attention. Thindor was there.

How is this possible?

"Listen to me, Manhon! I'm sorry about your siblings, but killing will not bring them back," Aleron said to the man with the sword.

Elliot couldn't believe his ears. Aleron was begging. He had found himself immersed in a memory—the moment Manhon Egercoll had taken the Sword of Light from Aremor.

"I don't care. A sword isn't enough to repay for the lives of my siblings!" With one move, Manhon stabbed the elwyn next to Aleron in the chest.

"No! Aremor!" Aleron screamed.

Elliot wanted to help, but he didn't know how. Then, he was enveloped again in clouds that swept him into a formless maelstrom. His body spun endlessly until his feet touched the ground again. He looked around and saw a tomb and some men placing a lifeless body in it. He recognized it as Aremor's tomb. Elliot saw Manhon again a few yards away and ran towards him. He had to stop him.

"Don't do it," Elliot said and moved in front of him. The man didn't appear to hear him. Beside Manhon stood a centaur he'd never seen before. A few men closed the tomb, and Manhon raised the sword just as the centaur started to say a few words. Behind him, hundreds of centaurs spoke in the same unknown language.

"Don't do it, Manhon! We're not to blame for what Aremor did to you—you got your revenge! I swear that we will not make such weapons, nor will we ever get involved in the wars of humans again!" Aleron shouted.

"No one should have to go through what my house went through again! The Elder Races have always wanted the end of the pegasi, and they must be punished ."

"For how long?"

"Forever!"

"We can't fight you! There are more of you, and you have a pegasus. I beg of you, don't do it!" Aleron cried.

Manhon looked away and raised the sword higher just as the centaurs' voices grew louder.

"NO, NO, NO!" Elliot tried to touch Manhon, and then the ground disappeared from under his feet again.

He fell through the vortex until he landed on solid ground once more. He found himself in the Mountains of the Forgotten World again. A fallen body lay before him. A human woman had fainted, and her white dress was torn with red between her legs. Blood. He bent over the woman as he heard a voice behind him—a voice filled with pain.

"WHAT HAVE YOU DONE?!" Elliot saw Aleron, the elwyn's face transformed by anger. "WHAT HAVE YOU DONE?"

Elliot realised where he was looking. A giant was standing a short distance away from the fallen woman.

"She got what she deserved for all that humans have done to us!" the giant told him.

"YOU DESERVE TO DIE FOR THIS, ADOR!"

A hand grabbed Elliot by the shoulder. Everything went dark, and he fell to the ground. He opened his eyes and saw the figure of the real Aleron before him. The elwyn's eyes were wide, his mouth agape.

"What did you do? What did you see?" Aleron asked.

"I've been listening to you talk about my kind for days. You say no race is worse than that of the humans!" Elliot seethed with rage.

"What did you see?"

"WHO WAS THE WOMAN THE GIANT RAPED? WHERE IS SHE NOW?"

The man closed his eyes, sighing and shaking his head. Silence spread between them before Aleron said, "Ador and Emy are now dead."

The Giant Man

Anrai followed the winding hallways of the Palace of the Dawn. He had to find Reynald as soon as possible. A moment ago, he had knocked on his door, but no one had answered. So, he had entered the room and searched it, but Reynald wasn't there. Anrai wanted to speak to Reynald as soon as possible. Walter had assigned him a mission, and he didn't want any kind of delay that could annoy his king. A day earlier, Walter had told him that the Elder Races might fight against them, and Reynald had confirmed that Elliot was in the Mountains of the Forgotten World. He couldn't digest this information.

How will Elliot manage to free the Elder Races? he thought.

Anrai knew that they were doomed to stay in the Mountains of the Forgotten World forever, and that they had never fought for humans in all their history. As if that wasn't enough, Elliot was a descendant of Manhon Egercoll—the man who had imprisoned the elwyn, the giants, and the elves in torment for hundreds of years.

Anrai had no answers, so he continued to search for Reynald. The Elder Races wouldn't leave his thoughts until his parents came to his mind—the parents he'd never met. His father was imprisoned in the Mountains of the Forgotten World and Anrai, despite only being seventeen years old, had never decided to travel there to meet him.

Moreover, he often felt sad about his mother. She had died in childbirth as his infant body had been much larger than she could bear. He'd found out years ago that his father had raped her, and it had been a miracle that she survived. Sometime later, his mother had discovered that she was pregnant. Thus, Anrai came into the world by taking the life of his own mother.

Anrai couldn't get his parents off his mind. He remembered the moment he found out about their story—the moment he'd hated the Egercolls with all his soul. He may have taken his mother's life, but the Egercolls were responsible for everything. If Manhon hadn't cursed the Elder Races, his father wouldn't then have looked to avenge himself on humans and he would never have raped his mother—thus Anrai wouldn't have been born. In his opinion, that would have been the best for everyone.

His thoughts remained fixed on the Egercolls, the humans he hated more than anything else. From the age of ten, he'd sworn to take revenge for the fate of his father. He'd sworn that he would take the life of every man with Egercoll blood in his veins—except Walter. Anrai remembered everything Walter had told him about Thomas Egercoll's moment of death. He had felt unrivalled joy upon hearing that story; however, his joy hadn't lasted long. His anger at the fate of his parents hadn't faded, even after the death of Thomas. He hoped that if Sophie and Elliot died, he would at last find the peace he was looking for. He found it unbelievable that the son of Thomas Egercoll had forced them to their first defeat.

Soon he'll pay. He was sure of that. *Did Elliot see my father in the mountains?*

He often wondered whether his father was alive, but he didn't want to see him. A pervasive anger simmered within him for what he had done to his mother, even if he was unable to admit this to himself. His father had raped his mother to get revenge on humans. Anrai would rather he had taken revenge on Thomas Egercoll, crushing his skull with his very own hands.

Anrai knew that Egercoll blood ran through Walter's veins too, but he respected him for his courage in defying his own parents and fighting Thomas. He'd decided to follow him from the age of thirteen, and Walter had welcomed him with joy. A sudden thought made him smile. Walter hadn't been able to find anyone to take Reynald's place in the Trinity of Death for years. So, he had gladly accepted Anrai when he had asked for the honour. Anrai could have sworn that Walter wanted to include him in the Trinity earlier, however, he had been too young.

Anrai continued to search for Reynald throughout the palace, but couldn't find him anywhere. His irritation bubbled into anger, and he decided to go the Royal Hall. It was the only place he hadn't searched yet.

He carried on along the corridors taking long strides until he reached the Royal Hall. He stepped inside, and found Reynald staring at the throne from afar. The man was alone.

"I've been looking for you," Anrai said irritably.

Reynald faced him. "I didn't know you wanted to talk to me, Anrai."

"You know my name?"

"I may have left the Trinity seventeen years ago, but rumour of a giant man who replaced me reached my ears."

"Why did you leave? I would never leave Walter to live in Stonegate," Anrai snapped.

Reynald smiled. "You're very young. Things change over the years."

"Walter told me to inform you we'll be leaving as soon as night falls. Most of the men will march to Elmor, but we will ride—"

"I know the plan," Reynald cut him short. "My brother confided it to me this morning."

"I didn't know."

"Walter will destroy Wirskworth with Orhyn Shadow," Reynald said in a cheerful tone.

"And the wyverns," Anrai added.

Reynald's brow furrowed. "The wyverns?"

"Walter wants to go the North beyond the North to try and tame them. Didn't you know?"

"No," Reynald admitted. "Do you have anything else to tell me?"

Anrai shook his head.

Reynald threw one more look at the throne. "Sometimes I think that all of this is going on only because of one damned seat."

With that, he took one last look and brushed past Anrai, leaving the giant man lost in his own thoughts.

Truths and Lies

Elliot looked at Aleron. He struggled to catch his breath, anger like a furnace in his chest. "That giant killed that woman!" he shouted.

"No, he didn't kill her," the elwyn told him.

"I don't believe you."

"She survived, and she became pregnant," Aleron mumbled.

For a moment, Velhisya's voice came to Elliot. "*Giants slept with humans throughout the ages. But the elves and the elwyn never loved anyone outside of their race. My mother was the only one of her kind to fall in love with a human.*"

"Did she die during childbirth?" Elliot asked. Aleron nodded. "And the baby?"

"It survived."

"Where is it now?"

"I think you've seen Ador and Emy's son."

Elliot was so bewildered that he stumbled in surprise. He saw Anrai, the giant man of the Trinity of Death in his mind's eye. "How did that baby end up with Walter? Who was his mother?"

Aleron breathed out and rubbed his forehead. "Emy was one of Thomas Egercoll's maids."

Elliot didn't believe what he was hearing. "And how did she end up here?"

"She belonged to Thomas' entourage when he journeyed to the Mountains of the Forgotten World in an effort to free us. Emy wanted to take a walk one night, and Ador attacked her."

"And how did her son find himself by Walter's side?"

"Emy was from Tahos. As soon as she discovered she was pregnant, she returned there to be close to her family."

"And did Anrai grow up in Tahos?"

"Yes. I never met the boy. I heard he had become a member of Walter's elite soldiers a few years ago," Aleron replied.

Naturally. Tahos was one of the regions that had submitted to Walter—Thorn would never have left such a distinctive man out of the Trinity. "He's shorter," Elliot said.

"Shorter?"

"Shorter than the two giants who are here."

"That's to be expected. He's half giant and half human. Moreover, I'm sure that his life will be shorter than that of a pure-blood giant," Aleron said.

"How long does a pure-blood giant live?"

"As long as an elf—about two hundred years. However, giants take on an adult appearance around sixteen years after their birth. The elwyn and elves need a little longer to mature."

"As long as an elf." That phrase got Elliot thinking. "Do elwyn live longer?"

Aleron nodded. "An elwyn usually lives twice the number of years that giants and elves do."

"What happened to Ador?" Elliot asked after a while.

"He jumped into the void."

"Because of his guilt over what he did to Emy?"

"I don't' think so... His beloved had jumped a short time before the incident. At some point, he decided to follow her," the man said sadly.

Despite his anger, Elliot felt sorrowful. "So, it's not just humans who are evil, Aleron."

"Elliot..."

"You told me that rape is one of the most heinous sins of our world, which has only been committed by my race. You told me that it has never happened amongst the Elder Races."

"I meant that no giant has ever raped another giant."

"IS THE RAPE OF HUMANS BY GIANTS INSIGNIFICANT?!"

"I never said that. If only I could stop it, Elliot."

"I'm sure it wasn't the first time. In Wirskworth I heard that the elves and the elwyn never slept with humans throughout the ages but that the giants did. Now, all I believe is that giants simply raped humans..."

Aleron looked down. "The giants did much while they were united under Magor."

"This woman was raped after Magor's death. I know the elves murdered that giant before the Battle of Wirskworth... before the curse," Elliot said, remembering some of Long Arm's words.

"You have to understand... The giants suffered the worst torture in the world when they were imprisoned here. Their entire race began to leap into the void..."

"And did this woman have to pay the price?" Elliot asked angrily.

"No... If only I could change the past." Aleron seemed unable to get over these memories.

"You lied to me... You told me that only humans have committed the most heinous crimes... No, Aleron. Humans have also suffered at the hands of the Elder Races and their actions."

The elwyn didn't speak.

Elliot breathed out wearily. "I no longer care to blame any race for what happened in the past... All I want is a better future."

Aleron looked at him as if he momentarily admired his words. "If that's your goal, I swear I'll try to help you."

Elliot's eyes stayed fixed on him for a few moments. "How did this happen? I was in your memories!" he said.

Aleron wore a puzzled expression. "You're the only human who's ever achieved such a thing."

"What's that object?" He pointed to the orb in the elwyn's hand.

"It's Aznarin. When I am engrossed in my memories and my Light is funnelled into this orb, I can relive them. For this purpose, a spherical object is more convenient than the metal of a sword."

"And how did I come to be in your memories?"

"The elwyn and elves can touch Aznarin wrapped with the Light of another creature and see the memories they have recalled in their mind. However, I believed that this would be impossible for a human... The pain that the Light would cause would be unimaginable."

"I can withstand the pain," Elliot said, his jaw set.

Aleron gave him a contemplating look. "No doubt..."

"Who was that centaur? The one who was next to Manhon."

"That was Areos—the leader of the centaur tribe at the time. Several years have passed since his death. Areos died full of guilt about what he did that day."

"How did he manage to get away?" Elliot asked.

"To get away?"

"Anrai! I would have thought that the curse would have kept his mother here, at least while he was in her womb," Elliot said.

Aleron laughed. "His mother was a human. The curse cannot imprison anyone of your kind—Anrai is only half-giant. I believe his human nature would allow him to escape the Mountains of the Forgotten World but also to grow as time went by. Nevertheless, the curse would have no effect on him since he wasn't born here."

"No child should have to be born in such a place..." Elliot said.

"Perhaps... The truth is that only one baby was born in these mountains in the last three hundred years. It was the only day that all of us felt a resurgence of hope," Aleron responded.

Elliot opened his mouth, but two starry blue eyes flashed through his mind, looking at him in a hall the colour of blood—eyes he longed more than anything else to see again.

Venomous News

Unease coiled in Velhisya's stomach that morning. She was trying to go to the great hall of Moonstone as fast as she could. She'd heard that an emissary from Vylor had arrived in Wirskworth and had requested an audience with Syrella. She couldn't believe her ears as soon as she heard the news.

What could Liher Hale want from Syrella?

Velhisya hurried through a dozen corridors until a commotion reached her ears. She quickened her pace and arrived in front of the great hall. She entered and found dozens of people there. She saw Sophie Delamere, Peter Brau and Elmor's council in the centre of the hall. A little further off, Syrella was seated between two gold snakes while her daughters and the Sharp Swords stood beside her. Velhisya walked to the centre of the hall and passed by several people, trying to get closer to her aunt.

Syrella looked at Velhisya, gesturing brusquely, and she hastened to get closer to her cousins. It was then that she saw a man of medium build standing between Syrella and Sophie. He had to be the messenger from Vylor.

"What is your name?" Syrella asked in a loud voice.

"Agor," the man replied.

"What news does Liher Hale send me?" the governor said, throwing him a vicious look.

About time. Looks like I haven't missed anything important, Velhisya thought.

"My ruler has sent me to negotiate the terms for Selwyn Brau's release."

A commotion spread through the room. Velhisya was bewildered, countless questions forming in her head. She knew Selwyn had left the city, but she hadn't the faintest idea how he had ended up in Vylor. The sound of a sword being unsheathed echoed in her ears, and Peter Brau moved towards the messenger.

"Lord Peter!" Syrella shouted.

The man remained still. His face had gone red while a woman nearby broke into tears. That woman must have been Peter Brau's wife.

Syrella spoke once more. "Have you got some sort of letter from Lord Hale?"

Agor smiled. "No."

"How do I know you're telling the truth? How do I know Liher has Selwyn?"

Agor drew a sword from his belt, and the men of the Sharp Swords unsheathed their blades.

"This is Selwyn's sword," Peter said in a heavy voice.

Velhisya felt pain looking at him. His face had gone white, and she could have sworn his hands trembled.

Syrella rose from her seat quickly. "How do I know he's alive?"

"Dead he would be of no value... However, I don't know how much longer he will stay alive," Agor replied.

"What does your lord want?" came Sophie's voice.

Agor smiled again. "Gold!"

Velhisya wanted to kill the messenger. His eyes shone as he uttered the last word. He was a sadistic Mercenary just like his ruler.

"Selwyn Brau offered Vylor gold for an alliance, and Liher chose to keep our emissary prisoner?" Syrella walked toward Agor.

"The Governor of Vylor will not ally with either Syrella Endor or Sophie Delamere, and he wants a lot of gold to free Selwyn Brau. This is the message he ordered me to deliver." Agor threw Selwyn's sword to the ground.

"May all of you in Vylor be damned!" Peter screamed, brandishing his sword.

Velhisya was sure that the Lord of the Knights wouldn't keep himself in check for long.

"Why did you send Selwyn to ask for an alliance with Vylor?"

Velhisya knew who that voice belonged to. Her gaze found Sadon Burns a few yards from the governor.

"I came to the decision that we needed new allies," Syrella replied.

"From Vylor?" Sadon asked. "The council was never told about that, and I doubt they would have agreed."

"I'm free to share only what I want with the council, Lord Burns."

Sadon turned red. "The men on the council have always been on your side. It's disrespectful to keep things a secret from the coun—"

"It's disrespectful to say all these things to the Governor of Elmor, my lord." Linaria took on the look of a beast of prey.

"Silence!" Sophie suddenly screeched, her rage mirrored in her gaze. "Selwyn is being held as a hostage!"

"How much gold does Liher want?" Syrella asked, throwing a look at Sophie.

"All of it," Agor said.

"All of it?" Syrella pressed.

"All the gold in Elmor."

Silence spread around the hall.

"That's outrageous! You ought to die for the words you bring before the governor!" Sadon broke the silence.

"Lord Burns, I'd like you to remain silent," Syrella said.

Velhisya knew that her aunt's voice may have been calm, but if someone disobeyed her at that moment, they would meet with a torturous death.

Sadon looked angry but bowed his head without speaking.

"And if Elmor doesn't give all its gold, will Selwyn Brau die?" asked the governor.

"Yes."

"I've never heard of such blackmail before! Blackmail for an emissary who only asked for a new alliance!" Syrella snapped.

"My lord knows that soon Walter will attack Elmor with sixty thousand men. You have neither the soldiers nor the time to attack Vylor. If you don't accept his request, Selwyn Brau will die sooner or later," the messenger blurted.

Syrella's eyes sparked. "Sooner or later?"

"He may lose a few parts of his body by the time he breathes his last."

A bellow echoed through the hall, and Velhisya saw that Peter was running towards Agor, sword raised. A man of the Sharp Swords jumped in front of him and pushed him back. Peter stepped back, the sword slipping from his hand. The Lord of the Knights straightened and hastened to attack when Jahon tried to restrain him.

"YOU'LL DIE AND SO WILL LIHER! I SWEAR THAT BEFORE I DIE, I'LL SEND EVERY MAN WITH THE NAME OF HALE TO THE GRAVE!" Peter shouted.

"The Braus will go into the grave by Walter's hand much sooner than the men from the House of Hale," Agor said, laughing.

Syrella grabbed Peter's sword off the floor in a flash and plunged it into the messenger's throat. Velhisya felt her heart stop, seeing the look of surprise on Agor's face. The man gasped for air while clutching his blood-soaked neck. The messenger continued to choke on his own blood until he fell to the ground convulsing before falling still.

Everyone had frozen in place, even Peter. Velhisya saw her aunt looking at the red blade she had just used. Syrella Endor knew full well what the decision she had made meant—war.

"What are we going to do?" Sophie's voice broke the silence. She didn't seem to believe what had just happened.

Syrella didn't speak, and Peter was released by the men restraining him. "The murder of the emissary means war," the man said, looking at Agor's lifeless body.

"We cannot possibly send an army to the Black Vale while we expect Walter," Linaria pointed out.

"IF WE DON'T SEND AN ARMY, MY SON WILL DIE!" Peter's head looked like it was about to explode.

"I'll order the Royal Army to march to Vylor. There's no other solution..." Sophie said.

Velhisya looked at Syrella, who remained still with the sword upright in her hand. She wondered what her aunt would do. The situation was very difficult, and there weren't many options. The decision she took could even lead to a civil war within Wirskworth.

"Liher knows that if he touches Selwyn, we'll kill him. The only thing he wants is gold, so killing the lad will serve him nothing." Syrella's voice was hoarse.

"So, you're suggesting we do nothing?" Peter asked.

"We'll deal with Liher when we force Walter to leave Elmor—when the siege is over."

"And what if Liher kills my son by then?"

"He won't. As I said before, it wouldn't do him any good..." Syrella looked certain.

"Liher knows that the chances of our winning the battle are slim. Why should he wait? If we die, Selwyn is useless to him. He knows his only hope of getting gold is before Walter attacks!" Peter spoke to Syrella as if he thought she had lost all reason.

Velhisya sensed that a civil war in Wirskworth was imminent. Her face and palms began sweating. She wanted to help, but didn't know how.

"Liher is a coward. He'll worry that if we win, we'll kill him and every man in Vylor. He won't hurt Selwyn until he knows who won the battle. Should we win, I believe he'll release him immediately, fearing reprisals," Syrella said.

"And what if we lose the battle?!" Peter screamed.

"Then, Selwyn would die even if he was here, Lord Brau."

"How can you be so sure that Liher will wait until he finds out what the outcome of the battle is?" Peter asked angrily.

"I know how men like Liher Hale think."

"Like you knew that Walter would fall into your trap at the Forked River?"

"HOW DARE YOU!" Syrella turned her sword towards Peter. "How dare you speak about the battle in which you and the queen betrayed me!"

"No one betrayed you, Syrella," Sophie said. "That battle was lost. I tried to tell you, but you wouldn't list—"

"My son died at the Forked River fighting in the name of the queen—the queen that didn't send an army to Elmor. You want my men to save the son of Peter Brau when yours were in Iovbridge at the time mine was breathing his last?" Sadon shouted.

Sophie turned to the lord slowly. Her eyes narrowed, and Velhisya felt that conflict could no longer be avoided.

"I'm sorry about your son, Lord Burns, but your men belong to the Governor of Elmor. She will order what the soldiers of the city will do, not you. King Thomas' decrees were not changed while I sat on the throne."

"You no longer sit on the throne."

"One more word, Lord Burns. One more word, and I'll make sure you're dead before sunset," Sophie said menacingly.

Sadon was about to speak when Syrella turned to him. "Leave the hall."

The lord's eyes widened. "What?" he asked.

"LEAVE NOW!"

Velhisya feared that Syrella would also cut Sadon's throat if he didn't obey. The lord gave her an angry look and walked away hastily.

"By staying in the past, we become weak. We cannot hope for a victory against Walter unless we put aside our differences," Syrella said, breaking the silence as soon as Sadon left the hall.

"I agree," Sophie said and walked over to the governor. "Peter lost two sons in the wars over recent years. Selwyn is his only son left."

A sob escaped from Peter's wife, and pain took root in Velhisya's soul. Selwyn's mother couldn't stop her tears.

"I'd send my army to Vylor today even if Walter wasn't marching to Elmor," Syrella said.

"We can't be sure whether Walter will march to Wirskworth," Sophie replied.

Syrella laughed. "You killed his men in Ramerstorm... Moreover, my soldiers killed half of Gaeldeath's riders, and Elliot Egercoll, a man trained by Althalos, is on our side. Do you think Walter will let us live in peace in Elmor?"

"We cannot wait! After the siege, it may be too late!" Sophie glanced at Peter as she spoke.

"We cannot fight two battles. There isn't—"

"There may be another solution." A voice Velhisya didn't recognize interrupted Syrella.

She searched for the man who had spoken and saw a lanky youth with red hair and a pockmarked face. It was Giren Barlow, the son of the ill-fated Aghyr Barlow. Giren took a step forward.

"What solution?" Sophie asked.

"Knowing Walter, I'm sure he'll march his men to Elmor as fast as he can. However, we may not need an army to free Selwyn."

"We cannot give all of Elmor's gold," Syrella told him.

"We can do what we did in Ballar," Giren said.

"How?" Peter looked at the young man with anticipation on his face.

"I was forced to be in Walter's servitude for a long time. I remember clearing tables years ago when he was talking to Liher Hale. Liher had told him that Goldtown had only one secret passage leading out of the city. This passage started somewhere in the dungeons of Goldtown Castle and ended outside the west tower of the city wall. I'm sure Selwyn will be held in the dungeons of the Hales' castle."

"You were the one who opened the underground passage in Ramerstorm. In Goldtown, there's no one to help us," Peter told him.

"We may not need anyone. Goldtown trades with few regions in the kingdom. Most men who bring merchandise to this land are petty traders who spend the night there. I'll arrive at its gates as a merchant, and with some gold, I'll manage to get into the city."

"And how will you get to the dungeons? How will you get past the guards?" Peter seemed unconvinced. "Furthermore, how will you find the entrance to the passage and open it without a key?"

"The Mercenaries love gold. If you pay them, you can accomplish anything... As for the passage, the entrance and exit may not need a key to open them. If they do, I'll find a way to get the key and go to the dungeons. From there I'll be able to free Selwyn."

"There'll be guards in the dungeons! No one will risk their life to take you there no matter how much gold you offer. It will be impossible for you to open the passageway under the guards' noses," Syrella said.

"The Mercenaries would even sell their children for gold. I'll find a way," Giren insisted.

"It's unlikely you'll succeed, and if you get caught, you'll die," said the governor.

Velhisya agreed with Syrella. She saw many holes in this plan.

"It's better than doing nothing. We don't need many men for this plan." The young man seemed determined.

Velhisya felt admiration for Giren Barlow. It was well-known that the man had suffered all his life, and yet his bravery hadn't been extinguished from his heart.

"I can ride to Vylor with ten soldiers. That'll be enough to keep us from being attacked by itinerant mercenaries and petty thieves," Giren said again.

"You might die," Sophie said.

"Your Majesty, you and Lord Brau rescued me after years of slavery. I want to help."

Velhisya looked at both Sophie and Peter. Despite the tension hovering over the great hall, they seemed touched.

"You were the one who helped us, Giren. You don't owe me your life," Peter said.

Velhisya knew by now that Peter Brau was an honourable man. Even now, having heard that he might lose his last son, he wouldn't give up his principles.

"I want to do it! It'll be an honour," Giren said boldly.

Syrella exchanged glances with Sophie, trying to come to a decision.

"I can give you ten men from the Royal Army," Sophie said.

"No," Syrella said. "I'll give you ten of the most able soldiers in Elmor. I can even give you twenty. I'm sure they will be more effective than the lads of the Royal Army. I'll think about who will lead the mission."

"I want to lead!" Velhisya couldn't believe that she'd found the courage to speak. All eyes in the hall turned to her.

"Your place is in Wirskworth." Syrella seemed to get more infuriated upon hearing her words.

"Selwyn risked his life to bring allies to Elmor! He took a risk so that we have some hope of winning! I would like to take a risk for him too!" Velhisya protested.

"NO!" Syrella shouted.

"Soldiers are mindless and foolish. They need someone they won't dare disobey. Otherwise, while Giren is in Goldtown, they might end up in a brothel."

"My men obey my orders!" Syrella snapped in a tone that showed she wouldn't put up with any objections. "But, I'll find a suitable commander for the mission. Your place is in Wirskworth."

"You need the commanders here, but you don't need me. I'm an Endor. No soldier will dare disobey me."

"This plan is doomed to fail! You, Giren and the men who follow you will die!" Syrella flung in anger.

"I'll wait outside Goldtown. If Giren doesn't succeed in freeing Selwyn, I'll return with the soldiers to Elmor!" Velhisya told her,

"NO! It's too dangerous. You will not risk your life!" Syrella said once more.

"I'll do so," Peter said.

"I need you here," Sophie said brusquely.

Velhisya saw the quandary in Peter's eyes. The man was Lord of the Knights and his oath stated that he was first and foremost charged with the protection of the queen and not of his family.

"If Linaria or Merhya were in Selwyn's place, you would want to lead the mission yourself! I know what my duty is, and you won't stop me!" Velhisya looked at her aunt. She had decided that no one would stand in her way this time.

"Linaria and Merhya would die for you! Where was Selwyn when our men were slaughtered at the Forked River? They betrayed us and you'll die for them!" Syrella yelled.

"And you'll die fighting Walter in the name of the queen!" Velhisya retorted.

"Even without the queen, Walter would have killed me at some point. I've decided to fight by her side!"

Velhisya was furious. "So, this alliance is only founded on self-interest and not on devotion!"

"I didn't betray the Crown! It betrayed me!"

"YOU BETRAYED EVERYONE IN ELMOR!" Sophie's voice echoed throughout the hall.

"HOW DARE YOU!" Syrella pointed the sword she held towards the queen.

"We need to talk alone," Sophie said.

Velhisya could have sworn that Sophie's voice revealed more of a command than a plea.

"If you don't listen to me, civil war will break out in Elmor, and we'll die before Walter gets to your land," Sophie insisted.

The scar on Syrella's face was taut, and her lips became a thin line.

Velhisya wondered what decision her aunt would make.

"LEAVE US!" Syrella's voice boomed through the air, and Velhisya saw those present moving towards the exit as fast as they could.

Syrella was furious, and she still clutched Peter's sword, its blade stained with blood. "How did you dare talk to me like that?" she shouted.

Sophie crossed her arms and looked at her as if she was contemplating how to begin. "You've never wanted a new alliance with me... The only reason you accepted me in the city was because you knew that only united would we have even a slim chance against Walter."

"You betrayed El—"

"You said that dwelling on the past makes us weak, but you're the one who hasn't put it behind you," the queen said, cutting her off. "I wanted to fight by your side, but your plan would have wiped out all the men I had left."

"Your plans cost you every ally in the kingdom! How dare you say that a single failure in battle is a treasonous act against Elmor?" Syrella said, seething.

Sophie looked as if she wasn't sure what to say. Syrella's patience was wearing thin. The queen's words had angered her so much that she was ready to throw Sophie out of her city.

"When I said you betrayed Elmor, I didn't mean by your decisions at the Battle of the Forked River," Sophie went on.

Syrella took a step forward and prepared to strike the queen with the sword in her hand. *I've sacrificed everything for this place and Sophie dares to challenge me after she abandoned me?*

"Will you kill me?" Sophie asked.

"No, not if you ask for forgiveness."

To her surprise, Sophie started laughing. There wasn't a trace of fear on her face, and she looked insane.

"Do it!" the queen suddenly shouted. "Kill me! Maybe then I can finally escape from the kingdom I've never wanted. You've been accusing me of treason for years even though I wanted to help you. I sent Peter to reason with you before the Battle of the Forked River... I tried to explain to you that no matter how clever your plan was, Walter would find out, and slaughter your men! My cousin has eyes and ears everywhere".

"I might not have known if there were spies in Wirskworth, but I was afraid that Walter would find out about the plan. His scouts would ride to every corner of Elmor before he attacked, and he always finds conspirators in the cities of his enemies. I was right, and I tried to explain to you that you would lose, but YOU WOULDN'T LISTEN! NOW YOU ACCUSE ME OF TREASON. YOU ACCUSE ME FOR THE ONLY RIGHT DECISION I'VE MADE WHILE SITTING ON THAT DAMNED THRONE!" Sophie took a breath before continuing. Syrella was certain that she had wanted to say all these words for a long time. "I know that you believed you would win, but you made a mistake... Just like you made a mistake in telling the people of Elmor lies all these years."

"LIES? I'VE GIVEN MY WHOLE LIFE TO THIS LAND!" Syrella shouted.

"WHO IS THE FATHER OF LINARIA AND MERHYA?!"

Syrella took a step back, her soul filling with a strange emotion. She'd forgotten that fear could grip her so quickly. She had no idea how Sophie had found out about her secret. "I don't understand," she managed to say.

"It's true..." Sophie said.

"What's true?"

"You didn't expect me to find out about this secret. If it was a lie, you would have already killed me... The fear on your face confirms it."

Syrella felt helpless. She had to find her self-control and kill Sophie. *Perhaps others know, too.* The terrifying thought poked its way into her mind. She had to find out how many knew and kill them all. If this secret got out of the great hall, civil war could break out in Elmor.

She tried to regain control of the situation, but something within her made her resolve crumble. Tears rolled down her cheeks before she could stop them. The years of lying had become an unbearable burden, and she couldn't bear to carry it any longer. She wanted to bare her soul to someone.

"How did you find out?" Syrella's voice came out in a whisper.

"In every tavern in Wirskworth, it is whispered that Jahon has always been your secret lover. I thought it was a silly rumour, but the truth was right in front of my eyes. Your daughters could never be the daughters of Sermor Burns," Sophie told her, and Syrella's mouth grew dry. "I knew you might kill me, but I decided to talk to you."

Syrella's eyes were still tear-filled. She felt she had to kill Sophie, but at the same time she wanted to finally throw the weight off her shoulders. "I've loved him for as long as I can remember." She couldn't believe she'd just uttered the words.

"Why didn't you marry him?"

Syrella wiped her eyes. "My father insisted that I was the only prudent one amongst his children. He wanted me to rule, and he believed that the House of Endor should be united with that of the Burns. He feared that the reign of the First King would bring war, and he wanted Elmor to remain strong."

"So, you married Sermor..."

"I tried for years to forget Jahon. I tried to love my husband, but I never succeeded. And each time I fell pregnant with Sermor, I miscarried. One day, I couldn't stand it any longer and lay with Jahon. It was about a month later I realised, I was pregnant. When I gave birth to twin daughters, I knew they were Jahon's. My husband never figured it out." She looked at Sophie. The woman was no longer looking at her with anger but with sorrow.

"You shouldn't have listened to your father. I fell in love with Bert the moment I saw him, and when every councillor objected to my desire to marry him, I remained with him. I may never have married him, but we stayed together, and I never wed a man I didn't want," Sophie told her.

"Have you ever regretted not pursuing a strong alliance through marriage?" Syrella asked.

Sophie took a step towards her. "No."

Syrella let out a weary breath. The anger had abandoned her. "I made a lot of mistakes, and I was arrogant..." she said. "I thought everyone in Elmor was only loyal to me and my house. I never believed that Walter would find spies in Wirskworth... When Elliot told me what William of the Sharp Swords had done, I was furious. A man in my own guard was a traitor, and shortly afterwards, I realised that there was another rat in Elmor. My arrogance had got the better of me. I was looking for someone to blame for my defeats. Someone responsible for the death of my brother, my nephew... even for that of my husband. Blaming you was the easy way out."

Sophie approached slowly until she stood in front of her. "We both made mistakes. No one teaches you how to rule." She embraced Syrella. "Your secret is safe with me."

This move was so unexpected that Syrella lost her footing and the sword slipped from her hand. She knew that everything that had happened was very dangerous. Sophie could destroy her whenever she wanted with this information. However, she felt the need to trust her. Before she'd realised it, she returned the embrace.

The two women separated and a fear took root in Syrella's mind. "Who else knows?"

"Peter and half the population of Elmor."

"The people of Elmor have always made up stories that few consider real. However, Pet—"

"Peter will never speak about this. You have my word."

Syrella's every instinct told her that she should kill them before it was too late, but a small, albeit powerful part of herself, decided to trust Sophie. That way, she would no longer feel so alone.

"Why didn't you marry Jahon after Sermor's death?"

Syrella laughed. "You've only been in Wirskworth a few days and already, rumours have reached your ears. Just think what would have happened if I'd married Jahon after the death of my husband... I'm doomed to live a lie forever. Elmor depends on my misery."

The queen looked at her strangely. Syrella could have sworn that Sophie had a look of compassion.

Syrella gazed at the dead body of the messenger, his blood congealing on the great hall floor. "Giren's plan is our only hope of saving Selwyn's life. Walter will arrive in Elmor soon and we can't fight two battles. I'll send twenty skilled men to ride with Giren to Vylor. The men of the Royal Army are just unseasoned lads now," Syrella said. She'd decided to help Peter's son as much as she could.

"You're right. Thank you," Sophie replied. "However, it will be difficult for Giren to succeed."

Syrella breathed out wearily. "It will be impossible for him to succeed... That's why I don't want to let Velhisya head the mission! If she dies..." Her voice broke. "She's all I have left of my brothers."

The queen took her hand. "Over the years, I've lost everything... My parents, Felador, Bert, even my very own dreams. All I have left is Eleanor."

Syrella knew this. She had been taken aback when she had first seen Eleanor in Wirskworth with Elliot. The journey from Iovbridge to Elmor was far too dangerous for the queen's protégée.

"Nevertheless, we must let our loved ones decide their own fates. We can't keep them with us forever... We can only love them for as long as we're alive." Sophie managed a smile.

Syrella's tears ran down her cheeks again, and she looked at the queen whose blue eyes were tear-filled too. She and Sophie had more in common than she thought. Sophie wiped away her tears, and headed for the doors of the great hall.

Syrella looked again at the corpse of Vylor's emissary a few yards away.

"We'll be together until the end," she said.

The queen stopped, and glanced back at Syrella. "Until the end," she said.

Syrella bowed deeply. It was the first time in her life that she had done so of her own free will.

The Song of the Endors

Velhisya paced around her chamber. Her rage had not subsided. She might have felt endearment for Syrella's attempt to protect her, but she was no longer a child. She wanted to fight for whatever she had left, and no one would be able to stop her. She worried about what had happened in the great hall that morning. It was one of the few times she had seen her aunt that angry. Velhisya wondered what she'd discussed with Sophie when they stayed behind to talk alone, and whether civil war would break out in Wirskworth. She wished that Syrella, and the queen would cast aside their differences. The lives of thousands of people depended on their decisions.

She looked out of the window of her chamber as the rays of the sun lit up the sky. The waters of the Forked River seemed to shine, the beautiful view easing her anger a bit. She'd liked the river as far back as she could remember. Suddenly, a memory flashed through her mind.

"*Why is it called Forked River?*" she had asked her aunt.

"*Because its waters end up in a fork before reaching the Sea of the Sun.*"

She knew her aunt loved her. Many times, Velhisya felt that Syrella wanted to protect her for her father's sake. She was the only thing he had bequeathed to the world. However, no one could protect anyone. Walter would reach Wirskworth sooner or later and that would be the last battle—the battle between freedom and death. Velhisya wanted to fight for a free Knightdorn. Her mother's fate had taught her that freedom was the most important thing in life, and she had decided that she would give anything to be free. She wouldn't die like a coward, trying to flee.

Suddenly, her thoughts flew to Selwyn. Velhisya had never spoken to Peter Brau's son. However, she'd assumed that Elliot and his friends had left the city to bring help to Elmor. She had realised that the moment Syrella had revealed the whereabouts of Thomas Egercoll's son to her. She was certain Elliot wanted to free the Elder Races and convince them to side with him. Velhisya believed he wouldn't succeed in doing either. She also hadn't imagined that Elliot and his companions would have sought an alliance with Liher Hale, and she wondered whether her aunt truly wanted the alliance since everyone in the kingdom knew how unreliable the Governor of Vylor was. As for Eleanor and John, she had no idea where they were. Nevertheless, there weren't many left who were able to fight with them.

It doesn't matter whether they manage to bring help, wherever they are, Velhisya thought.

Elliot and his companions had risked their lives to reach Wirskworth. They had taken Stonegate, had managed to build a new alliance between Sophie and Elmor, and now they were risking their lives again trying to find other allies. Four companions had achieved so much while she was imprisoned in Wirskworth. She was imprisoned because Syrella didn't trust her to do the slightest of things.

Now, rage overwhelmed her. She sat on her bed until she began to feel she was suffocating in the room. She had to go to the little forest next to Moonstone. It was the only place she could find peace when she felt nothing could calm her. She put on a robe and a pair of boots, casting one last look at the view from the window of her chamber and strode to the door. She opened it and a figure appeared in front of her.

"It appears I came at the right time!" Syrella snapped.

Velhisya was bewildered. "What are you doing here?"

"I want to talk to you." Syrella had her familiar brusque tone about her.

Velhisya moved aside and her aunt entered the chamber. She closed the door behind her and looked at Syrella, in silence. A while ago, a guard had told her that her aunt had ordered that the Dance of Blood be cancelled. She agreed with Syrella's decision to cancel the dance. There were far more serious issues that demanded their attention. Still, seeing her aunt now stoked her anger.

Syrella looked at her strangely. She wore a silver tiara, and her dress was a soft lilac colour. "I've always admired you..." the woman said.

Velhisya wasn't sure she was speaking to her. "Me? Why?" she asked.

"Because you're brave... You know you'll die in a battle, but you're not afraid to fight. Moreover, you're willing to give your life for those who deserve it, and you have never been vain. I dare say you'd make a great leader."

Her words reminded Velhisya of Linaria. "I don't want to hear about my virtues. I want to fight," Velhisya said.

She expected Syrella's familiar angry look, however her aunt just smiled. "Do you remember the song of Edgar the Devoted? He was the high priest of the first King of Elmor."

"Edgar?" Velhisya was annoyed. She wanted to fight, and her aunt was talking to her about the old songs of a priest. "No."

Syrella didn't lose her smile. "Edgar believed in the God of Souls more than anything. He was his most devoted servant. One day, he spread the word that he'd seen our god in his dreams, and he'd given him a message."

Velhisya had no idea why she was telling her all this. Syrella might have pretended that she respected the gods, but she knew that her aunt had never been particularly devoted to them. Most people in the kingdom worshipped the gods, and the priests and Syrella thought it wise to show that she honoured them as well.

"The message of the God of Souls was that one day, people would be enveloped in pain and death. Then, just before their end, an Endor would save them from their suffering. An Endor would show them how to create a better world." Syrella looked out the window to her left.

"Edgar so believed in this dream that just before the end of his life, he lost his mind. He used to tell the King of Elmor that the Endors were the descendants of gods and attacked those who didn't worship our house. Shortly before he died, he wrote a song."

"Why are you telling me all this?" Velhisya asked.

"I'm sure you remember the song."

"I've never heard it before!"

To her surprise, Syrella opened her mouth and began to sing a melancholy tune. Velhisya wondered if her aunt had lost her mind until the chant began to sound familiar.

"As the dark of the night grows
Life in the kingdom will be filled with woes
And when men's end is near
An Endor will deliver them from their fear"

Velhisya listened to the words and tried to remember where she'd heard them.

"Your father would sing it to you when you were a baby. He'd hold you in his arms, look you in the eyes and say it over and over," Syrella told her.

Memories flooded Velhisya's thoughts. It was as if this memory was so deeply embedded in her mind that she saw it through a tunnel. Her eyes watered and the last image she had of her father emerged.

"Arthur loved you more than anything in the world. He thought you were the most special being ever to be born," Syrella said and moved towards her. "I always tried to protect you... I felt I had failed to protect my brothers. I felt it was my life's purpose to make sure nothing bad happened to you. You are all that I have left of them, but I may have made a mistake..."

Velhisya couldn't speak as a river of tears ran down her cheeks. She looked deep into her aunt's black eyes. It was as if the scar on Syrella's face shone with the soft rays of the sun falling on her cheek.

"Perhaps Arthur was right..."

"About what?" Velhisya asked, her voice cracking.

"Perhaps you're the Endor that will save us, and I'm simply an obstacle in your life."

Syrella threw another grin at her and moved towards the door. "I hope you and Giren make it."

Her aunt was about to leave when she turned back again. "Whatever happens, remember that you're unique... Remember that I'll always believe in you till my last breath."

Velhisya heard the door close, and she felt her body being deluged by power—an unadulterated power that fanned out like a tide through her. She saw her father once more in her mind, and then another face came to her—a face she'd never managed to see so clearly. Her mother's starry-blue eyes looked at her with a tearful smile, and an endearing voice spoke in her head.

I love you, Velhisya.

The House of the Owl

The Castle of Knowledge was freezing cold and quiet, despite the sunlight seeping through a few tall windows lining the corridors of the Delameres' ancestral home. Eleanor was looking for the great hall, Andrian had told her he'd gather the lords of Felador to speak with her that morning. She walked stooped over, shoulders bent under the anxiety that had taken root within her. She hadn't been able to sleep since arriving in Felador, and she couldn't get her conversation with the high priest the night before out of her mind.

She looked around and quickened her pace. *Will this meeting go well?* A large door came into view, and Eleanor slowed her pace, feeling afraid. *This must be the great hall.*

She hesitated a few moments before regaining her nerve and strode decisively towards the hall. A statue near the door caught her attention. The bust of a tall man scowled at her. In his right hand he held a long sword, and his stance showed that he was ready for battle. Eleanor thought he must be some knight from the past. She stared at the statue, and a memory came to mind.

"Why aren't there any knights anymore?" she had asked as a child.

Sophie had breathed out dolefully. *"Because they betrayed their oaths."*

Eleanor adored stories about knights when she was young. She'd always imagined the knights being brave and fearless, ready to fight to save Knightdorn. However, while growing up, she had found out that all of that only happened in fairy tales.

Her eyes turned to the entrance of the great hall again, and she realised she'd been standing in front of the statue for quite some time. She headed for the door taking quick strides, pushing open its two panels and stepping inside. A dozen figures stood before her. The great hall was not as impressive as the Royal Hall in Iovbridge. A few green banners with a golden oak tree hung from the walls while another large statue stood beside a table. Eleanor headed towards the centre of the room. High Priest Andrian sat at the head of the table surrounded by several men and two women.

"My dearest Eleanor!" Andrian exclaimed. "I hope you had a good rest."

Eleanor came to the front of the table and bowed to those present. "Thank you for your hospitality, Andrian," she said.

"Sit with us," the high priest said. His tone was good-natured.

Eleanor could have sworn that every eye at the table was fixed upon her. She sat in an empty chair to the right of the priest.

"I was telling the lords of Felador that you arrived in the city yesterday with a letter from Syrella Endor on behalf of the Queen of Knightdorn," Andrian said.

"Sophie Delamere is no longer Queen of Knightdorn," came a voice.

Her gaze fell on the man who'd spoken—a lad near her own age. "I never expected Felador would kneel to Walter Thorn," she said.

"In fact, it doesn't matter who sits on the throne, Lady Dilerion. No one in Iovbridge cares about Felador," continued the man.

Eleanor's sense of unease was driven away as anger set in. "Sophie Delamere never forgot—"

"Really?" the young man replied.

Eleanor faltered. She knew Sophie had ignored Felador for years. "What is your name?" she asked.

The young man looked at her, indifference resting on his face. "Solor Balkwall."

"Sophie Delamere sat on the throne when she was still a child, Lord Balkwall. For years she tried to defeat Walter and bring peace to Knightdorn. However, she made several mistakes trying to do so. On behalf of the crown, I seek the forgiveness of the lords of Felador. Sophie should have helped your land."

"Sophie's father and King Thomas lost most of the soldiers from Felador. This was the reason why the queen never took an interest in our land all these years. There was no army here to help her," Solor said.

"Sophie had to fight against Walter! She had to fight to save Knightdorn from a tyrant!" Eleanor said.

"And what did she achieve in the end?"

Eleanor remained silent. Solor had managed to irritate her. The rest of the lords were the same age as him, and they were looking at him approvingly. Eleanor looked a little closer at those present. None of them were dressed in expensive silk, as was the case with the lords of Iovbridge.

"It isn't easy to defeat a man like Walter." Eleanor broke the momentary silence. "However, now there's hope—a hope that was unheard of for all these years."

"Elliot Egercoll?" a young woman beside Solor asked, and Eleanor nodded. She wore a yellow dress and had brown bushy hair like Sophie. All the nobles at the table were young; they were the sons and daughters of the former lords and ladies, and they were now the only surviving nobles in Felador.

"Was it he or the queen who sent you here?" the woman asked.

Eleanor looked at Andrian. She didn't know how much the high priest had told them.

"Eleanor confided in me that Elliot asked her to travel to Felador. He believes that this place has been without a ruler for several years," Andrian said.

Eleanor frowned. Clearly Andrian didn't want to keep secrets from the nobles. "Sophie would welcome Elliot's decision," she added.

"Why did she forget about us all these years then?" The woman rose from her seat with rage etched across her face.

"Lady Alarie!" Andrian's voice was sharp.

The woman sat down, her cheeks flushed. Then, Eleanor stood up quickly and looked at her in anger. "Sophie Delamere was half your age when she took the throne. One of the most powerful men of all time opposed her—a man whom no one has managed to beat on the battlefield. Of course, she has made mistakes, but the brunt of the burden she has had to bear has been so heavy that most of us would have given up years ago."

"Perhaps she too should have given up and left the throne," Lady Alarie said.

"To whom? Who would have come between Walter and Iovbridge? Who would have dared? Unless you mean that she should have given up the crown to Walter..."

Silence followed her last words.

"You said that no one has succeeded in beating Walter on the battlefield," Lady Alarie said. Eleanor nodded. "However, we heard that he was defeated in Elmor a few weeks ago."

"That's true."

"Who won that battle?"

"I think the news has arrived in Aquarine," Eleanor answered, looking at the lady.

The woman smiled. "We heard that the soldiers of Wirskworth attacked Walter and forced him to a retreat, but nobody spoke to us about the existence of Elliot. Was he the one who truly defeated Walter?"

"The men of Wirskworth won the battle. However, Elliot's plan was what brought a weakened Walter to Elmor. Moreover, his plan earned Sophie the loyalty of Stonegate."

"What?" Andrian's voice was filled with wonder. "Is Stonegate now devoted to Sophie?"

"Yes," Eleanor said curtly.

"How?" asked the priest in amazement.

"Elliot defeated Reynald Karford in single combat and took the castle. After his victory, he gave leadership of Stonegate to a Guardian and asked him to guard the passage for Sophie and her allies. The Guardian agreed, but didn't want to fight for the crown. However, a few days later, the Guardians witnessed Walter's brutal attack on Lord Hewdar's castle, and they decided to march to Wirskworth and fight."

"There are a lot of things that seem strange... Why did Walter decide to go to Elmor just before his attack on Iovbridge?" Andrian asked.

Eleanor took a deep breath. She recounted everything about Elliot's plan, and the events of the last few days. When she'd finished, she felt that her voice had become hoarse. She sat in her chair again, touching her neck.

"Walter will never forgive what happened in Elmor. He may be seated on the throne, but the news will travel to Knightdorn and will overshadow the fact that he took the crown. Thorn will endeavour to kill every shadow of doubt over his power," Andrian said.

Eleanor nodded. "The last battle between Walter and Sophie will take place in Wirskworth. We all believe that Thorn will march there with all his forces."

"That would be a correct assumption. Will the Guardians of Stonegate fight by Sophie's side again?" the priest asked.

She didn't know if Elliot had spoken to the Guardian Commander before the latter had left Wirskworth. However, the leader of Stonegate must have seen Sophie and her people marching to Elmor. So, he must have heard the news and have had the opportunity to decide what he wanted to do.

"I'm not sure... but I believe that they will," Eleanor said.

Andrian looked thoughtful. "What happened to Reynald Karford?"

"Elliot spared his life and let him leave Wirskworth. However, I haven't the slightest idea where he is."

Andrian looked puzzled, but she didn't care. Eleanor had decided to tell the truth. If she was destined to lead Felador, she wouldn't achieve it with lies. She looked at the people around the table; they frowned and whispered among themselves. She wondered what they thought of her.

"I hope that if he captures Walter, he doesn't let him go, too," Solor said, and a few laughs echoed around the table.

"I'm sure Elliot had his reasons for doing what he did," Eleanor said.

"Elliot may be a virtuous lad and a fearless warrior trained by Althalos, but he doesn't have the right to appoint the Governor of Felador," Solor continued.

"Lord Balkwall..."

"Neither Sophie Delamere nor Elliot Egercoll have that right."

"You're right, my lord," Eleanor said.

Solor stared at her. "Moreover, Elliot is just a lad. If what you told us is true, he is responsible for the death of every person in the City of Heavens."

Eleanor was enraged. "Only Walter is responsible for that."

"You said that some traitor in Wirskworth confided in Walter that Thorold was alive! Only Elliot and his companions knew this truth if I've understood correctly." Solor appeared pensive.

Eleanor sighed. "Elliot revealed this to Syrella's council."

"Then he's a fool!" the lord shouted. "Walter killed every Grand Master in the kingdom. If he heard that both Althalos and Thorold were alive, and that a descendant of Thomas was, too, it was certain that his wrath would be unleashed. Elliot shouldn't have spoken."

"Elliot didn't kill those people."

"Our actions have complex consequences, Lady Dilerion." Solor's eyes met hers. "Althalos may have been wise, but Elliot isn't—at least, not yet. I'm sure that he'll make many mistakes and Felador cannot afford any more mistakes. I'm sorry, but I don't trust his judgment for the rulership of this land, nor him himself."

"Elliot managed to beat Walter in one battle! What have you accomplished, Lord Balkwall, other than being a lord who sells his crops?"

All eyes at the table fixed on Eleanor. She could see the rage on the faces of those present.

Solor seemed angry too. "My parents died when Walter's men ransacked Aquarine... They died in the name of King Thomas. I grew up an orphan, and my whole life, I've given my crops to the people of Felador. Moreover, I sold some for gold, like every lord at this table. This gold helped us rebuild our ruined city."

Eleanor knew she'd overstepped the mark. "I'm sorry—"

"I may not be a warrior," Solor interrupted, "but I, and all those seated around you, have done everything in our power to help Felador. Elliot may be great, but he, like you, has done nothing for this land. I think it would have been wiser for Elliot and Sophie to have tried to help Felador all these years. Nevertheless, Elliot decided to send his choice of ruler here. This is the greatest of insults to all of us who have given our all for this place."

"Elliot didn't want to impose me on Felador as governor." She felt anxiety as the people in the room stared at her. In her anger, she had said things she shouldn't.

"Then why are you here?" Lady Alarie asked.

"He believed that the people of Felador would choose me for what I am! He believed that you would choose me as ruler." Eleanor felt the urge to lower her eyes, but she didn't.

"Why did he think we would choose you?"

Eleanor felt anxiety. She didn't know how to reply.

"Why did he think Felador needed a ruler? What does he want of Felador?" Lady Alarie spoke again.

"This place has been without a ruler for many years... Elliot believes it's time it got a new one."

"Nonetheless, this place has a ruler," Solor responded.

"He didn't know."

"Did you accept this mission happily?" Solor said.

Eleanor turned to him. "At the beginning, I wanted to stay in Elmor and fight Walter by the queen's side, but Elliot convinced me to travel here."

Solor looked doubtful as he fixed his gaze on her. "I think Elliot sent you here for another reason," he said. "Everyone knows that Felador has no army. Most of the lads in the city have never held a sword in their hands. After the deaths brought about by Walter's attack seventeen years ago, few here have wanted to learn to fight. We have no Masters nor officers, and I'm sure Elliot knows all this."

Why is he telling me all this? Eleanor thought.

"I think Elliot sent you here to save your life. We know your house and that your brother was always Sophie's lover. Perhaps that's why Elliot wanted to save you. Sophie herself may have asked him to do so. I can't think of any other reason for you to be here other than your safety. I can't believe Elliot really cares about Felador's rulership at this time. Admittedly, he has far more important problems..." the lord continued.

Eleanor felt knives piercing her body. She had had the same thoughts but had refused to admit them to herself. The idea that Elliot had lied to her made her chest feel tight.

"Perhaps he thought that if he told you to save your life, you would refuse, so he told you that Felador needed a new leader. He probably realised that the people of Aquarine wouldn't accept you. But he had to say the right thing so that you would listen to him," Lady Alarie said.

Eleanor was about to say something but choked. It was as if her lips had been sealed.

"Nevertheless, if all this is true, I might say that we at least know one thing about you," Solor said again.

"What's that?" Eleanor managed to get out.

"You're brave... Otherwise, he wouldn't have needed to convince you to leave a city that will be besieged by Walter Thorn."

Eleanor took a deep breath. "Perhaps... But he may truly have believed that I can help Felador." She could have sworn that Andrian was smiling at her.

"So be it," Solor said. "The House of Dilerion has the respect of the nobles of this land. You may stay as long as you wish, but the rulership of Felador will remain with Andrian. His wisdom is greater than all of us at this table and wisdom is the only thing we need for a better future on this soil."

Eleanor's eyes fell upon the banners at the end of the great hall. She hadn't noticed them until then, but she recognised the coats of arms belonging to the nobles of Felador. One had an owl against a white background—the symbol of her house. She didn't know why, but it filled her with courage.

"Very well. I'd like to take a walk around the city now," Eleanor said and got up off the table. She bowed slightly and strode boldly towards the door.

She was on winged feet as she left the great hall without looking back. Everything that had happened in the meeting suddenly crashed into her. Her heart beat incessantly, and her palms had become sweaty. She felt angry with Elliot. If his intention was to save her, he should have told her the truth.

He chose me to accompany him on his journey to Elmor, she thought, sorrow growing within her. *Perhaps Morys' death shook him and so he wanted to save me. Elliot knew that I was the weakest amongst the companions. That was most probably the reason why Selwyn, John, and Elliot had travelled to forge alliances while I was sent to a place where there was no army.*

"*How do you know they will choose me as their governor? Do you think they'll give me Felador because I come from one of its dead noble houses, or because the queen was in love with my brother?*" she had asked Elliot.

"*They won't choose you for your name, but for who you are...*" he had replied.

Eleanor let out a weary breath. She couldn't be sure of Elliot's motives, but she had decided to stay in Aquarine. It was her parents' home, and as long as she was there, she'd do everything in her power to help its people.

The Grand Island

John was trying to hold onto the ropes of the ship, but the wind was very strong, and his stomach was turning. The waves were powerful and sprayed his lips with salty mist. He hadn't been at sea for years. He remembered yearning for such an adventure during his time in Iovbridge, but now he felt that he hadn't really missed going on voyages in stormy waters. He was tired of spending his nights with sailors, singing pirate songs.

How far are we from the damned Islands?

Three days had gone by since they'd set sail from Stormy Bay. Raff had told him that within the day they would reach the Grand Island if the sea wasn't stormy. With the waves, they were bound to be delayed. A dozen sailors ran around while Raff turned the ship's helm, smiling.

Bastard, John thought, looking at the captain.

He let go of the rope and tried to walk towards him. The ship swayed to and fro, and John struggled not to lose his balance. After a few moments, he reached Raff's side.

"It's the first time I see a captain smiling in such a storm."

Raff shot him a look without losing his smile. "The sea is the most beautiful woman, Long Arm, and women always want to put obstacles in our way."

John snorted contemptuously. "You are a fool... I hope you don't end up at the bottom of the sea one day."

"I've always wanted to die in the bosom of a woman!" Raff said.

"I thought we'd reach the Islands today."

"You're more impatient than I expected." John's face took on a look of dismay. "Look to the right," Raff said.

He cast a look and saw something looming in the distance—something that looked like a hill. "What's that?"

"The Grand Island!"

John took a closer look and realised that Raff was right. The Ice Islands consisted of five neighbouring islands, and the Grand Island was the largest of them. That island was home to Begon, the Leader of the Islands.

John was momentarily relieved. *Finally. I thought we'd never reach land.*

"Have you lost your tongue?" Raff asked.

"I hope there are pretty whores on the Grand Island still..." John retorted.

Raff laughed again. "I hope the years don't make me like you, Long Arm. You've forgotten the adventure of the blue bewitcher. You've forgotten the magic of the sea. Brothels and wine are boring companions."

John moved away, staring at the Grand Island while a few memories came to mind. He had spent five whole years on pirate ships, stealing loot and gold from petty merchants and fishermen. He remembered loving the sea those years. John surveyed the landscape; the best spoils for pirates were always to be found in this region.

Suddenly, a big wave slammed into the ship, but John managed to stay upright. It was a true miracle that he had crossed the Cold Sea during the autumn storms. The wind whipped his face and then a crow passed in front of him.

Lucky bastard. He would give anything to be able to fly to his destination at that moment.

Time passed, and the Grand Island grew bigger. However, the waves seemed to get stronger as they got closer, pushing them away from the harbour.

Damned wind. John had promised himself that after so much hardship, he would sleep with at least three women once he set foot on land.

A voice in his head told him, *You must speak to Begon, you must give him Elliot's message.*

Something scared him each time he thought about all the things he had to say to the Leader of the Islands. Perhaps he'd kick John out as soon as he heard his words. John knew that when Begon's gladiator lost to Walter, the Leader of the Islands swore he would never fight against Thorn.

Begon had also sworn to Sophie that he would fight for her before the duel against Walter, and he went back on that oath.

John let out a weary breath. Begon had had no choice. Walter had arrived on his land with thousands of soldiers. He had choosen single combat to spare his men, otherwise they would all have been slaughtered. John remembered Begon's gladiator. Byron the Sturdy was considered a great warrior. However, rumour had it that Walter had killed him with three thrusts of the sword. John wished he could have seen the duel with his own eyes.

The Grand Island was now very close, and John headed towards the bow. Suddenly, the ship jolted so violently that he lost his balance. John hit the ground hard and felt a sharp pain in his left leg.

Damned storms! he thought and got up, swearing and cussing. John saw a sailor a few yards away holding his belly with laughter. "Stop laughing or I'll punch you."

The sailor went back to his work without losing his smile. John stood near the bow and waited patiently until the ship entered Merynhor—the harbour of the Grand Island. He heard the anchor going down into the depths of the sea with a rattle while the sailors threw some ropes to two men who were standing on the harbour. John was worn out, but he was glad to have reached his destination. He glanced at the cloudy, morning sky. The ship docked in the harbour and John prepared to set foot on land again. He longed for solid ground instead of constant swaying.

"At last, the brothels will reward you," Raff said behind him with his familiar, obnoxiously jovial manner.

"Maybe we'll meet at one of them," John shot back.

"I'm a married man, Long Arm! Sometimes I miss the old days, but after escaping pirates all these years, I don't want my wife killing me."

"How can a dirty rascal like you be married?"

"Why not?" exclaimed Raff. "My bride's father owned this ship and gave it to me to wed his daughter."

John couldn't understand how a scoundrel like Raff had managed to find a bride who had a ship in her possession. "The more men get wed, the more whores there'll be for me."

"Until you run out of gold." Raff's words reminded him of Eleanor. "I can ask Begon to speak to you."

John looked at him in bewilderment. "I'll request an audience from his guards myself."

"I don't think he'll agree to speak to an emissary of the queen. However, if I ask him, you may have some hope." Raff's tone grew serious.

"I didn't know you were such a close friend of Begon..."

"My father was a good friend of his, and you helped my father years ago. If you want, I can do you this favour, Long Arm."

If nothing else, my past has its rewards. "Thank you, Raff. However, you've already returned the favour I did your father when you took me on board your ship. I wonder if you want to help me because you have other intentions."

John stood on the gangplank, waiting for Raff to continue. The captain remained silent for a few moments with a strange expression on his face.

"Perhaps you were right," said Raff.

"What do you mean?"

"Perhaps we should have fought for Sophie Delamere."

John studied him carefully. "Thank you for your help, but I want to think before I give the queen's letter to your leader."

"To think?" John nodded. "Alright," Raff replied, but he seemed puzzled. "I'll be staying on the Grand Island for several days. If you should want my help, you can find me at the Tide."

John smiled. He remembered the inn. It was one of his favourites on the island. He nodded curtly to Raff and hurried off the ship. The wind was strong, and John found it difficult to keep his eyes open. However, it was clear that nothing had changed since his last visit. Men were working all around, and several mountains loomed behind the harbour. The Grand Island was dry, and full of cliffs and huge rocks.

John's legs ached as he left the harbour as fast as he could, walking down a small alley near the shore. A tower came into sight. Begon's tower stood a few miles away from the harbour. John passed by a dozen stone inns with smoking chimneys; he turned left and found the place he was looking for. He'd decided to spend the day, as well as the night, in a brothel.

He opened the door and entered the small building. A handful of half-naked women looked at him lustfully, and he forgot the hardships of his journey.

"I knew I'd take care of a man like you today." A young woman with dark, curly hair and almond-shaped eyes approached him and opened her robe to show him her large breasts. He liked her strange accent.

"I've been anticipating seeing you for quite some days, my dear," John replied.

The woman put her hand into the crotch of his pants, and he was aroused at her touch.

"I like foreigners. I'm sick of locals." John laughed and stared greedily at her breasts. "Let's go and wash you, my lord," the woman said.

John followed her, eyeing the bodies of the other women around him. It was as if they were undressing him with their gazes—there were no other patrons in the brothel at this time. He decided he would sleep with all of them. He walked behind the dark-haired woman until they came to a small room with a tub of steaming water. It may not have resembled the beautiful buildings that housed the brothels of Iovbridge and Wirskworth, but he didn't care. He took off his clothes and got into the tub while the woman started caressing his body, her breasts brushing his neck.

Lust had taken charge of John until Elliot came to mind. John didn't know if he wanted to give the letter that Syrella had written on behalf of the queen to Begon. His only concern was to escape the war, and if the Leader of the Islands decided to throw himself into battle, there would no longer be a safe place for him in Knightdorn. John knew that he hadn't chosen to make this journey for Elliot, but for himself—the Ice Islands were his salvation from the war. However, he couldn't decide which path he really wanted to take. He remembered the moment he'd told Elliot he would be by his side.

Damn! He could no longer find peace, not even in brothels. The touch of the dark-haired woman drew him away from thoughts about Elliot as she gently began kissing his aching back.

The Invulnerable Arm

Elliot looked at the cloudy sky as he walked along the side of the mountain. He had received a new letter from Reynald the night before, and the words had made him anxious. When Hurwig arrived with a rolled parchment attached to his foot, Elliot had been surprised that Reynald would write again so soon.

He tried to tame his thoughts while his gaze wandered to dozens of elwyn sitting a few yards from him. They read from old books, lifting their gazes periodically to the view of the giant mountain before them. He wondered why the elwyn and the elves read so much and what was written in the books.

Elliot was bored that morning. Alaric and Alysia had gone hunting and so they hadn't practised. He'd been in the mountains for days, but he hadn't really achieved anything yet. Elliot touched the hilt of the sword in his belt. He'd become an even better swordsman over the last few days and had been trained in a new kind of battle. He'd decided that the training in the Mountains of the Forgotten World had been valuable, but he would have preferred to have achieved far more. Still, he continued to wonder why Althalos hadn't taught him these techniques when he had been training him.

Elliot silently approached an elwyn woman who had her head buried in a book. He stood beside her and tried to make out the letters on the pages out of the corner of his eye but couldn't understand a thing. Althalos had taught him to read, but the book was written in an unknown language.

"What are you doing?" came a female voice.

Elliot lifted his head and saw the woman looking at him. The rest of the elwyn stopped reading and turned their gaze towards him.

"I was just walking," he said, feeling awkward. He bet the woman had seen him trying to decipher the words in the book she was holding.

"Are you trying to see what I'm reading?"

"Excuse my prying. I was curious," Elliot apologised.

"Elliot," a second voice said. He turned and saw another elwyn woman. "Aleron wants to speak to you. Follow me."

What does Aleron want this time? he wondered,

Elliot obeyed and followed her. The rest of the elwyn returned to their books again, and he was thankful that he'd been saved from a tricky situation. He and the elwyn walked a while and a few drops fell on his head. Elliot had guessed that this day would be rainy.

A figure came into sight. It was Erin—the elwyn he'd seen attempting to leap off the cliff. Elliot looked away. He was afraid Erin had seen him that night before he'd moved away from the slope with Aleron.

"There, beside the tree," the woman said.

Elliot lifted his head and saw Aleron a few yards away wearing a white tunic. The man had his back to him, and his face was turned towards the sky. Elliot nodded to the woman and hastened towards him.

"How are you this cloudy morning?" Aleron asked.

Elliot hadn't expected Aleron to have been aware of his presence. "I saw Erin," he said.

Aleron turned slowly towards him. His starry-blue eyes had a contemplative sheen.

"If the curse is broken, will he die?" Elliot had found the courage to ask what had been tormenting him for days.

A soft smile drew itself on Aleron's lips. "I think so."

Elliot knew that if Erin died, he would be reunited with his soulmate. Nonetheless, he felt sorrowful.

"Why are you sad?"

Elliot lowered his head. He felt that his eyes had betrayed his feelings. "I would rather bring his beloved back to life...Death is an eternal nothingness."

Aleron smirked. "You have a pure soul, but no one can reverse death... Its existence is what gives meaning to life. Are you afraid of death?"

"Sometimes..." Elliot knew a knight shouldn't fear death, but he couldn't always shake the panic he felt when he thought about dying.

"I think that every being becomes one with the Light of Life after their death—becomes one with the infinite power of love. You needn't be afraid. The unknown is most times better than what we think."

"So will I meet my parents when I die?" The thought escaped his lips before he could restrain it.

"That doesn't matter," said the man. "Nobody knows exactly what happens after death. All that matters is that the memories of the dead we loved stay within us as long as we are alive," the elwyn spoke again.

Elliot felt a momentary warmth.

"I heard that a while ago you duelled against Walter Thorn," Aleron said and changed the subject.

Elliot was taken aback. He hadn't told him much about the events in Elmor, and he thought that Aleron didn't give a damn about what happened in the wars of humans. "It's true. How did you find out?" he asked.

"Many know that Walter was defeated for the first time on the soils of Elmor. Moreover, many know that he duelled against the son of Thomas Egercoll—the last apprentice of Althalos."

Elliot hadn't expected the elwyn to know all of this. "Is it important whether I duelled against him?"

"Yes."

"Why?"

"Did you notice anything strange?" Elliot didn't understand. "When you duelled against Walter," Aleron added.

"No..." Elliot remembered how fast and strong Walter was, but nothing had seemed strange.

"Anything that alarmed you?" Aleron insisted.

"The only thing that surprised me was the teeth of the tiger that tore my leg... It was a miracle that I managed to fight with the poison in my blood."

Aleron frowned. "Did you fight with Orhyn Shadow inside of you?" Elliot nodded. "You're stronger than you think... However, that's not what I meant."

Suddenly, a recollection popped into his thoughts. "There was a moment... I was sure my sword had cut Walter's hand."

"And?" Aleron seemed to be waiting for him to continue with great eagerness.

"His hand was unscathed," Elliot concluded.

The elwyn's eyes narrowed. "Strange," he responded, and he stared off into space for a few moments.

It was truly strange, Elliot thought.

"Walter has lived over three decades and yet he looks like he hasn't aged a day. Moreover, I've heard enough eye-witness accounts of his superhuman strength," the man said. "Something's going on with Walter... I've been trying to find out what for a long time, but I haven't been able to."

"Do you think he's found some way of getting stronger?" Elliot asked, a strange fear gripping him.

"I don't know," Aleron sighed.

One more thought crossed Elliot's mind—the thought that had kept him up the night before. "I'm exchanging letters with Reynald Karford," he said.

Aleron turned towards him, surprised. "With Reynald Karford?"

Elliot confided all he knew about the former Guardian Commander. "I swore not to divulge what he told me to anyone. You and Thorold are the only ones I've entrusted with these secrets."

"Many a time love hides in the most curious of places! Why did you share this with me now?" Aleron asked.

"Some of Reynald's words have worried me. He told me that Walter intends to ride with a few horsemen to the Mountains of Darkness. He wants to get branches from the Night Trees. At the same time, the rest of his men will march to Elmor, and they'll wait for him to get there before they attack Wirskworth. Walter wants to drench every spear and blade with Orhyn Shadow before the final battle with his enemies."

Aleron breathed out wearily. "The soul of that man is so steeped in darkness that I believe it will never see the light again… However, why do you think this is strange? Everyone knows Walter is ruthless."

Elliot frowned. "I wrote to Reynald and told him to constantly send news about their whereabouts. I didn't expect him to write for a few days, but I received another letter last night."

"You're lucky to have that hawk."

Elliot smiled. Aleron had seen Hurwig sitting on his shoulder before. "Reynald wrote me that Walter has one more goal he wants to accomplish in the Mountains of Darkness. He wants to tame the wyverns."

"That's impossible," Aleron exclaimed.

"That's what I thought, too. Alaric told me that wyverns can only be bonded with giants. Perhaps Walter doesn't know that."

Aleron rubbed his chin in thought. "I doubt it," the elwyn replied.

"Then why does he believe he can bond with a wyvern?"

"That is a very troubling question."

"Why do wyverns only obey giants?" Elliot asked.

"Because Orhyn Shadow is in their blood."

Elliot frowned. "You told me that the tigers of the north and the wyverns are the natural allies of giants. I'd therefore expect that the tigers would only follow giants just as wyverns do," he voiced his thoughts.

"The tigers of the north have shown their devotion to humans too through the passage of time. However, the wyverns have never been bonded with beings that don't have Orhyn Shadow in their blood. Nobody knows why," Aleron explained.

"Perhaps Walter believes a wyvern will obey Anrai and not himself,"

Elliot said.

"Nobody can bond with all the wyverns, only with one. As for Walter, I can't believe that this is what he's after. History has shown that he fears that someone might overthrow him. That's why he killed every Grand Master—why he tried to instil fear in every place he conquered. I find it hard to believe that he would want any man of his to have a wyvern by his side."

They remained silent for a few moments. "Reynald wrote me that Walter spends many hours with Leonhard Payne. A heal—"

"I know who he is," Aleron cut in. "Althalos believed for years that Leonhard was hiding in the ranks of Thorn. I'm sure that he and Walter have done things we don't know about. Nevertheless... I'm unable to discover what they might be."

"I thought you didn't care about Walter and the wars of humans," Elliot shot.

Aleron frowned. "Humans have been destroying the world for years. Nevertheless, I feel that Walter has taken it upon himself to do this more than anyone else has. I think he wants to change his very nature, and this is dangerous for any living creature. I hope he doesn't make such a mistake. The principles of nature are so profound that if they are disturbed, there will be dire consequences."

"So, you agree that Walter must be defeated, and every creature must contribute to that end?"

"No creature is obliged to help. They have the right to choose whether they want to do so."

"What's your choice?"

Aleron looked at him with eyes that sparkled. "I don't know yet. There's much to be done before I make my decision. Until then, forget about these thoughts," the elwyn said, his words filling Elliot with disappointment.

Elliot knew what he meant, though it didn't make him feel any better. "The centaur, Righor, wanted to fight Walter on my side, and the leader of the centaurs ordered him not to… I'd say that many are not free to choose."

"Centaurs paid dearly for their alliances with humans."

"I would expect them to want to take revenge on Walter for what he did to them!" Elliot countered.

"Then, the Elder Races should want to take revenge on Manhon Egercoll and his descendants."

Elliot remained silent for a few moments. "Perhaps the leader of the centaurs could have allowed Righor to fight with me, even if the rest of the centaurs did not."

"Have patience. It's hard to get over the anger and bitterness caused by what has happened… You must give Leghor time," Aleron responded.

Elliot glanced at the sky. "At least Righor gave me Hurwig. I'd never heard of centaurs being able to command animals."

Aleron's brow furrowed. "They don't order them. Some animals consider centaurs wise, and so they obey their wishes. These animals are not servants, but companions," he pointed out.

"Which animals consider centaurs wise?" Elliot asked.

"Hawks and horses—not all of them, though. Only some of them choose to accompany them and listen to them. Centaurs may have made mistakes in the past, but their race is steeped in wisdom and powerful magic."

"If the centaurs are so powerful, how did Reynald Karford and the Mercenaries manage to slaughter them?"

"They were attacked when they least expected it, and there were more of them," the elwyn explained.

Elliot's thoughts lingered on the centaurs. "You told me that centaurs don't have the Light of Life within them. Where does their power come from?"

Aleron took on a strange expression. "No one knows the true source of the magic of centaurs, just like that of the mermaids."

"Do centaurs and mermaids get burned from the Light of Life like humans?" Elliot asked. The elwyn nodded. "I'd never heard that mermaids have magic within them, too."

"Mermaids are a mysterious and unique species. They live for many years, and are invulnerable in water. Their skin only becomes vulnerable when they come out on land. Mermaids are so powerful in water that nothing except the Seven Swords can possibly wound them. In addition, they're the only intelligent species where there are no males, only females."

"And how do they reproduce?" Elliot asked.

"When they feel the need to procreate, their body creates eggs. In recent times, I feel more and more often that their powers..." Aleron stopped mid-sentence. "What you've told me about your duel with Walter is interesting. I have to think."

"Do you think Walter has found some way of acquiring the powers of mermaids?" The thought terrified Elliot.

"That would be impossible," Aleron said more to himself than Elliot. "Thank you for coming to speak with me. Now I wish to be left alone awhile."

Elliot remained where he was. "I don't have much time to free the Elder Races, Aleron. If Walter starts marching towards Elmor, I'll have to go. I've got to help my friends."

He expected an angry look from Aleron—he expected him to tell him that the life of the Elder Races was worth more than the wars of humans.

"I know. We've always known you might not be able to break the curse. If fate wants you to help us, we'll soon find out. Otherwise, your place is at the side of your race. The Elder Races will always remember that you tried," the old man said with a good-natured expression.

Elliot hadn't expected these words. He bowed slightly and walked away from Aleron. He felt grateful for his last remark—it was the first time in so long that he'd felt the weight of responsibility on his shoulders lighten. He continued walking and then, Walter came to the fore in his mind—had he found a way of acquiring special powers? He felt his palms sweat at the thought, until a question took root within him.

How many more unprecedented things will I have to face in order to defeat Walter Thorn?

The Training of the Ghosts

Reynald was searching for Walter's tent throughout the camp, feeling uneasy. He hadn't the faintest idea why the king had requested his presence. He searched for the largest tent on the site where they'd camped near the Yellow River—a fertile area, full of green meadows and joyful chirping. Men pitched makeshift tents while the neighing of horses pierced his eardrums. He'd never expected to find himself in the Vale of Flowers again. It had been almost three days since they'd left Iovbridge and already he felt exhausted. Walter had ordered them not to camp the previous night, and so they'd stopped in the afternoon. He hadn't travelled so much in quite some years.

The events of the past few days continued to play through his head. He was surprised that Walter had trusted him, asking him to ride with him on this trip. Walter had ordered Ricard Karford and Eric Stone to march on to Elmor with the rest of his soldiers. Reynald hadn't expected that he'd have more sway than his brother and the Governor of Tahryn since no other governor had travelled with Walter except Gereon Thorn.

Launus Eymor found his way into his thoughts. The Governor of Mynlands was the only one to have remained in his region's capital. Launus was very old, so he'd sent his men to be by Walter's side without journeying himself.

Reynald continued searching until at last he saw an enormous tent with a guard stationed at its entrance. He laughed momentarily upon seeing Short Death. It was strange that such a slight man was one of the most dangerous soldiers in the kingdom. He hastened his stride and stopped in front of him. Rolf was holding his helmet in his left hand, and he looked at him in a way that betrayed his anger.

"Walter asked to see me," Reynald said.

Rolf didn't step aside. "It's still unbelievable to me that you're here."

"Life is full of surprises."

"Did you study philosophy during the years you stayed in Stonegate?" Short Death asked.

Reynald laughed and took a step past Rolf, but Short Death was blocking his path.

"I don't trust you, Reynald. I don't know why Walter wants you by his side, but it's strange that you returned the moment a descendant of Thomas Egercoll made his appearance."

"Walter asked to see me. Step aside or unsheathe your sword."

Short Death remained where he was. "I won't fight you today," he said and moved aside, allowing Reynald to pass.

Reynald had grown irritated. He swept into the tent, then froze with an audible gasp. Berta Loers was naked on top of Walter. His gaze fixed on their wild coupling.

"Reynald!" Walter snapped.

"I'll come back later, Your Majesty," Reynald stammered and whirled around to leave.

"No!" Walter shouted.

Reynald stopped, terrified. Perhaps Walter would kill him because of what he'd just seen. He kept his eyes on his boots.

"I was waiting for you, and Berta found me before you did," Walter said out of breath.

"My humble apologies, Your Majesty."

"Look at me, Reynald."

He felt apprehensive. He slowly raised his head to see Walter sitting up straight, throwing a purple robe over himself. Berta had covered half of her body with a sheet, her breasts and shapely figure still visible. The woman didn't look embarrassed as she lounged on the bed. Reynald's gaze returned to Walter.

"Have you received any word from Elliot?" Walter asked.

Reynald was taken aback. "No, Your Majesty."

"Did you send him everything we agreed upon?"

"Of course."

"I would have expected him to have written to you by now. He must want to know more."

"I told him we would ride to the North beyond the North, to get Orhyn Shadow," Reynald told him.

"I don't suppose you disobeyed me and told him about the wyverns."

Reynald felt fearful and hoped his expression wouldn't betray him. "No... I didn't say a word about it. I showed you the letter I sent him, Your Majesty."

Walter appeared preoccupied. "I wonder if he managed to free the Elder Races."

"If such a thing had happened, I'm sure he would have written to me."

Walter frowned. "I've been pondering why he chose to go to that place... He'll have difficulty gaining allies in the Mountains of the Forgotten World. Those creatures won't easily ally themselves with an Egercoll, and if the legends are true, he also has to break the curse."

"I also wonder about all of that," Reynald said.

Walter strode towards him with his robe billowing behind him. "I think Althalos asked him to try to break the curse. The old man often spoke about the Elder Races... He said they'd endured the most unfair torture in the world."

"I wouldn't want to be imprisoned on a mountain forever," Reynald said.

"It's better than being dead!" snapped Walter.

"If he succeeds, do you think there is any chance the Elder Races will fight us?" asked Reynald.

Walter's face was inscrutable as he stopped in front of Reynald. "I'm sure the giants won't. As for the elwyn and the elves, I have no idea."

"Perhaps, I shouldn't have revealed our destination to Elliot, Your Majesty. If he succeeds in freeing the Elder Races, they will know where to attack us." Reynald tried to sound convincing.

Walter laughed. "The Elder Races have been decimated. Most of those creatures have put an end to their own lives after all these years. Moreover, the elwyn and the elves aren't as strong as you think they are. Their swords may be dangerous, but if they die, their mate dies too."

Many years ago, Reynald had heard about the light that infused the swords of the elwyn and the elves—the light that burned the hands of humans. However, he'd never heard about the elwyn and elves dying if their mates did. "What do you mean?"

"Althalos told me that their mating creates a strange bond between them. They only mate with one partner throughout their life and when that mate dies, so does their other half... Althalos would often say that that's what true love is." The blond man laughed again. "Now that I think about it, I think this is true only for the elwyn... The elves are short and nimble, like Rolf, while giants are the strongest of the Elder Races."

"All of that sounds pretty dangerous to me if we're attacked."

"They have neither armour nor horses. If a ground force of elwyn and elves attack my armies, they'll be slaughtered. Even with Elmor's army, it'll be impossible for them to win. As for us, we are a long way away from the Mountains of the Forgotten World. If Elliot succeeds, his concern will be to get these creatures to Wirskworth to help in the siege. It's his only hope."

"That's what he told me, too," Reynald responded.

"He told you the truth. However, the giants would be invincible in a battle," Walter said.

"That may be why it would be wiser to hide our whereabouts."

"Wherever we may be, giants mounted on wyverns would be able to destroy us. There's no point denying it."

"Why do you believe the giants wouldn't take Elliot's side?"

"I'm a man of the north, Reynald. A man with a giant and a tiger by his side. A giant raped Anrai's mother simply because she was Thomas Egercoll's servant. Do you think they'll fight for his son?"

Reynald could have sworn that Walter was furious that all of this hadn't occurred to him. He ought to watch what he said. "Forgive me, Your Majesty. I hadn't considered these truths."

"It's more likely that the giants will ally themselves with me to seek Elliot's destruction. The giants could become a mighty ally—an ally far stronger than the elwyn and the elves."

"I didn't know you wanted the giants on your side."

Walter gave him a thoughtful look. "It's better than having them against me. However, they may remain uninvolved in the battles of humans."

Something seemed to trouble Walter. However, Reynald didn't want to say more. The man opposite him used to mutilate those who asked too many questions. "We don't know whether the elwyn and the elves will ally themselves with Elliot. Perhaps they too will decide to stay away from hostilities. It's really foolish that the boy decided to go there... Even if he breaks the curse, he may not gain any new allies."

"Or there are things we don't know about..." Walter stood still a few yards away from him. "You said he sent his companions to Kerth?"

"Yes. After the death of Morys, he wanted to protect them," Reynald replied.

Silence spread between them. Elliot hadn't revealed to Reynald where the rest of his companions really were, and he'd instructed him to tell Walter that they'd travelled to the Western Empire. The boy had written to him that the fewer people who knew, the safer they would be, while he hoped that this information wouldn't reach the king's spy in Elmor.

"If you hear that he has freed the Elder Races, I want you to inform me immediately," Walter said, breaking the silence.

"Of course, Your Majesty." Reynald bowed slightly. "Is Gervin Gerber still under your command?" He'd been searching for an opportunity to get Walter to speak about his spies.

"Why do you ask?" The look in the blond man's eyes showed he was truly bewildered, but there was also a hint of menace.

"If he's in Sophie's guard, maybe he can send us information, or even get her out of the way."

"If I wanted him to kill Sophie, he would have done it a long time ago. My cousin will die by my hand. She will hang naked, without arms and legs, from the temple of Elmor."

Reynald looked into Walter's cold blue eyes. He knew he wanted to kill Sophie himself and show the entire kingdom the fate that awaited anyone who fought him again. He wouldn't kill his cousin treacherously—he would humiliate her in front of all of Knightdorn.

"Gervin is dead," Walter said suddenly.

Reynald frowned. "How?"

The man threw him a look. "I heard about it from some servants when I arrived in Iovbridge. I'd ordered a group of men to get old Borin out of the way before I attacked the palace. I wanted to create discord in the enemy ranks. Gervin and Sophie found themselves in the same chamber as Borin the night my men tried to assassinate him. Gervin saw the attack and stood idly by until my soldiers were surrounded by Elliot and Iovbridge's guards. Then, Gervin panicked and tried to help by killing Sophie, but Elliot killed him. He was foolish. He should have stayed in his place."

Reynald contemplated how he could find out what he really wanted to know.

"But don't worry. There's still one more man who can give us information about what's happening in Wirskworth."

"I thought William of the Sharp Swords was the only spy we had in Elmor." Reynald tried to appear surprised. The discussion had finally gone where he wanted it to go.

Walter smiled and strode towards Berta who'd been watching them in silence all this time. "It isn't time for you to find out about this."

Reynald swore under his breath. He'd thought that whoever the man might be, quite a few of Walter's soldiers would certainly have seen him when he came from Wirskworth to speak to his lord a few weeks ago. However, if he started asking questions, it could get him into trouble. He'd have to find out the truth in a clever way.

"Tell the Ghosts and the Trinity that I'll be training you this evening," Walter said.

Reynald was taken aback. "Will you train us?"

"You have to learn how to face the elwyn, elves, and giants. Giants are difficult to defeat, but I'll teach you all I know."

"This is the greatest of honours, Your Majesty," Reynald said.

"You're dismissed. I must first finish what I started with Berta."

Walter bent towards the woman who was looking at him with an expression of pure lust. The blond man pulled the sheet hard and cupped her breasts while she grabbed him between the legs. As Reynald hurried from the tent, he saw Walter force his way into her out of the corner of his eye.

He made it a few steps, trying to put his thoughts in order, when he heard Rolf's voice. "We've been waiting for you. Follow us."

He saw Short Death next to another member of the Trinity—Brian, the Sadist. He had no idea what they wanted. With a sigh, he followed them through the camp until they led him to a man lying on the ground by the remains of one of the campfires, chained and out of breath.

"I'm in a hurry, Rolf," Reynald said and was about to move away.

"I was looking for hares with some men, when we found a herd of sheep. I was about to slaughter one and then this bastard attacked me." Brian looked at the fallen man, whose eyes dripped with blood.

"He's not the first to attack those who kill their animals."

"He attacked the wrong man... The Trinity of Death only forgives with death!" Brian said with hatred.

"I have two daughters. Mercy! Mercy!" The man's words were drowned out by his sobs.

Brian kicked him in the nose. "Shut up!"

Blood poured down the captive's face. "You've had your revenge. Let him return to his daughters," Reynald said.

"A scoundrel attacked Brian, and he should spare his life?" Rolf shot Reynald a look of absolute fury.

"P-please, my lord," the captive stammered.

Brian kicked the fallen man again. "When you attacked me, you were brave. Have you become a coward now?"

Reynald didn't want to see what was about to follow. He knew that Brian liked to play with his food before eating it.

"Where are you off to?" Short Death asked him as he went to leave.

"As I said, I'm in a hurry."

"I need a favour from you, Reynald," Brian said, and Reynald looked him in the eyes. "I want you to punish him for what he did. I want his head."

Reynald felt enraged. "I'm not your servant."

He was about to leave again, and Short Death caught him by the shoulder. "Are you turning your back on the Trinity of Death?"

"Take your hand off me!"

"Have you forgotten who you're talking to, Reynald?"

Reynald knew he shouldn't overstep the mark. Nobody dared defy the members of the Trinity unless they wanted to meet with a martyr's death. "Forgive me, Rolf," he said in a mocking tone. He knew what they were trying to do. They suspected that he wasn't loyal to Walter and themselves and that he wouldn't want to follow their orders to kill. They wanted to expose him.

"Do as Brian told you," Short Death told him.

Reynald looked down at Rolf. Many soldiers around them were watching the scene. "I'm here to kill my king's enemies. Not to become an executioner of villagers."

"Do it." Brian's voice was brusque. It was an order.

"Will you kill me if I don't obey?"

Brian laughed. "Do you want our king to know that you objected to the Trinity of Death? That you refused to kill a villager who attacked his men when you have sworn allegiance?"

"Are you or are you not with us, Reynald?" Rolf touched the hilt of his sword.

Reynald glanced at the villager and walked towards him. He drew the Sword of Destiny from its sheath and met the teary irises of the fallen man who looked like he was praying. He'd vowed never to kill innocents again and had kept that vow for years.

The sword cut through the air and sank into his flesh with a chilling sound. The man's head was separated from his shoulders and fell to the ground.

"I may no longer belong to the Trinity, but I remember its men killing their own enemies." With those words, Reynald wiped the blood off on his cloak and marched towards his tent.

The Lord and the Thief

Aquarine felt like a place belonging to another, distant world—a world away from the war that had plagued Knightdorn. Eleanor looked around, feeling a strange joy. She had only been in Aquarine for a few days, but she had walked to every nook and cranny of the city. All she had seen were carefree people and children playing in the streets. She had never imagined that Aquarine would be so peaceful. She'd expected a ravaged city full of people fearful about the future, but she had found the opposite. Walter's attack on Felador's capital might have gone down in the annals of the history of Knightdorn, but the locals had managed to put it behind them.

Eleanor had heard about the Battle of Aquarine and the death of King Thomas countless times, but she'd never accounted for the fact that the city had remained without any cares for seventeen whole years. Lacking an army, Aquarine was rendered of no interest to the rest of the kingdom, so its people ran no risk of war.

Eleanor looked at the houses and blackened, smoking chimneys. The last few days, she'd often thought about her parents. The fact that she had found herself in her birthplace had given a strange boost to her memories, which grew stronger. Eleanor had never been able to remember her parents' faces. She had seen them in her imagination, but they looked like shapeless figures behind faint shadows. But, the previous night she was sure she had seen their faces in her dreams, and she had woken up with tears in her eyes. It was as if the air in Aquarine had some magic that brought her deepest memories to life.

She had now reached one of her favourite places in the city. The cobbled road leading to the Temple of the God of Wisdom was enchanting. Countless stalls with sundry goods and troubadours with old harps imparted a unique glamour to the atmosphere. She listened to the beautiful melodies until a familiar question took root within her.

What was Elliot's real reason for sending me to Felador? She didn't know, and she couldn't find any answers.

Eleanor had felt uncomfortable before the lords of Aquarine, but their refusal to give her the governance of the city had reassured her, much as she didn't want to admit it to herself. She didn't feel that she was capable of ruling.

Am I not able to or do I not want to rule? she asked herself and couldn't find an answer. She'd seen with her own eyes what it meant to rule. Eleanor preferred to die than to live a life like that of Sophie.

"I'd say you like walking in the city," came a voice.

Eleanor looked behind her. The aged figure of Andrian stood a few yards away dressed in white.

"I haven't walked around such a carefree city in years," she said.

The man smiled. "This city isn't plagued by the worries of war. If everyone understood that war only brings pain, Knightdorn would be a much more beautiful place," the high priest told her. "Walk with me."

Eleanor fell in step with him, wondering what he wanted from her. They headed towards the temple. "I've always wondered why Walter didn't hand over Felador to one of his lord-allies since it is so rich in crops," she said.

Andrian laughed. "Walter's attacks on Aquarine and on the City of Heavens were unduly destructive. Thorn wanted to destroy them and leave them to their fate, showing all in the kingdom the future that awaited anyone who got in his way. He wanted to make it known that the cities of his enemies would become ruined cemeteries. That's why he didn't offer these places to any of his lords."

Eleanor frowned. "But if he gave the rulership of these regions to some of his lord-allies, he would strengthen his power in the southern and central regions of Knightdorn."

"Not exactly. Walter's allies are mostly men from the north. The City of Heavens is a long way from their supply lines, and it's close to Wirskworth. Whoever took this city would be easy prey for attacks from southerners. Walter didn't want to waste a single one of his allies while he was fighting for the throne. As for Felador, it may be close to the north, but it has no army. Some of the queen's allies, such as Ballar, are a few miles away, and Walter would again have had to—"

"Waste men to guard it," Eleanor said, finishing his sentence.

Andrian glanced up at the sunny sky. "As for the crops, Walter doesn't need the rulership of Felador to get his hands on them. One of his most loyal lords—Aldus Morell—has been stealing most of our crops for years. Unfortunately, we can't stop him, not without risking an attack from the north. There are others, too—merchants, mercenaries, and a few other lords steal from our fields. These people are taking Felador's harvests from under Walter's nose. Those we catch on our land, we deal with. We might not have many men, but we try to guard the area as best we can. Fortunately, there are some merchants who are honest and pay for our crops. These merchants helped us rebuild Aquarine."

Eleanor mulled over his words as they continued walking in silence for a while. Ruling Felador would be harder than she thought. In reality, the wealth of the area was controlled by Walter's allies.

"I hope you bear no grudge against the lords of the city," said the high priest, breaking the silence.

"No." Her voice had come out brusquely.

"Respecting people's choices is one of the most important virtues of a leader."

Eleanor was taken aback. "Do you think I have the makings of a leader?"

"I think Elliot saw something in you and entrusted you with this mission."

Insecurity had surfaced before she could contain it. "Perhaps he really did just want to save my life."

"Perhaps... However, I'm sure he wouldn't have sent you here if he didn't think you'd make a prudent leader."

"I think he knew I wouldn't succeed... Why would Felador's people choose me?"

"Even if he thought it unlikely, if you succeeded, you would have had to rule. Elliot wouldn't have cast anyone in this role if he didn't believe in them."

"How do you know? You've never met Elliot."

"He grew up an orphan because of the war. He knows very well the pain that a bad ruler can bring, and he would never risk such a thing."

His words brought her momentary peace. She may not have wanted to rule, but she needed to feel that Elliot believed in her.

"Elliot sounds like a good lad," Andrian said again.

"Because he'd never risk the rise of a bad ruler?"

The man frowned. "He granted Reynald Karford his life and went to the City of Heavens to save Thorold. Few men forgive, and even fewer risk their lives to save an aged Grand Master."

Eleanor secretly admired the high priest, and agreed with the decision of the Felador lords to give him governance over the region. Andrian was undeniably wise. "Elliot was willing to sacrifice himself for me. He duelled against Walter to save me from certain death."

"Were you afraid of death?"

The question took her by surprise. "No... The only thing I was afraid of was losing more of the people I love. And here I am... I survived, having lost someone I loved once more." Eleanor's eyes filled with tears.

Andrian looked at her endearingly. "All the people you lost, all those who loved you, are still with you, Eleanor. They are in your soul, even if you can't see them anymore. Love is an invincible force. I'm certain that it remains in our world even after death."

She turned her tearful gaze away. The thought of the ill-fated people she loved who had died prematurely flooded every part of her body. "I don't want to lose anyone else. I can't take the pain anymore."

"Life is pain, Eleanor. Sometimes it's unbearable and at other times it makes you feel alive. A life without pain isn't a real life."

"You really are wise after all," Eleanor said, tears running down her cheeks.

"No. I've just lived longer than you," the man replied with a small grin.

"High Priest!" A young man with red hair ran up behind them, out of breath. "The lords have caught the traitor we've been looking for. You have to come to the great hall immediately."

Andrian headed to the Delameres' castle without saying a word.

Eleanor followed him, wiping away her tears. "The traitor?" she asked.

The high priest looked panic-stricken. "You'll see," he replied.

They advanced, hurrying to get to their destination, and after a few minutes the Castle of Knowledge came into view, the elaborate building standing out amongst all the others.

Eleanor felt that time was passing faster than usual—she, Andrian and the young man had already crossed the castle entrance, and soon they would reach the great hall. When they arrived in front of the entrance, the door was open. Eleanor hurried to keep pace with Andrian. The priest was taken aback by the sight of the crowd in the hall while a handful of men were on their knees in the centre. Ten armoured guards stood with raised swords around them.

"Governor Andrian, we got him at last!"

Eleanor saw Solor Balkwall with a smile on his face beside the rest of the lords of Felador who were standing behind the guards.

"Conrad!" Andrian's voice sounded shrill as he stared at the fallen man.

Eleanor turned her gaze to the place he was looking at and noticed one of the fallen men—his cheeks splattered with mud.

"He was the traitor!" Solor said again.

"Why?" Andrian asked.

Conrad stood and the guards aimed their swords at his neck. "Why not? Walter has been stealing our crops for years and no one is doing anything about it! I'm tired of giving them away! Am I a traitor because I wanted some gold, or are you the true traitors for refusing to fight all these years?" he said.

"TO FIGHT WHOM? WALTER THORN AND HIS ARMY?" Eleanor couldn't believe that the raging voice belonged to Andrian.

"Since you don't want to fight, you too are a traitor, Andrian..."

"You're free to fight on your own if you wish, Conrad," the priest told him.

"I once wanted to... but I've changed my mind. Now, I prefer Walter on the throne and my pockets full of gold," Conrad replied.

Eleanor looked closer at Conrad and remembered where she had met him. He was at the table with the lords just a few days ago. The traitor had big eyes, thick hair, and pimples on his face.

The priest looked again at the fallen men. "Why is Lord Morell here?" Andrian asked and looked in Solor's direction.

"We caught him giving gold to the traitor, and he asked our guards to let Conrad go north. The guards refused, and his soldiers attacked them. Our guards overpowered them, bringing everyone here without harming them or Lord Morell."

"We all know you will hurt neither me nor my men... If you do, Walter will destroy you," an old man among the captives said and stood up. "I would advise you to set us free, and we'll forget about this... disagreement."

Andrian turned to him. "You're right, Lord Morell. No one will touch you. Let them go," he said, looking at the guards.

"What will become of Conrad?" Lord Morell asked.

"He'll be hanged."

"I think you misinterpreted my words, Andrian. Lord Conrad Miller will follow me north," the aged man said again.

"This man belongs to Felador! He committed treason in this land and our law dictates we punish him" snapped the high priest.

"He belongs to me, and if you deny me him, I will see to it that you all die," Lord Morell said.

Eleanor didn't know what Andrian would do. While Aquarine seemed carefree to her eyes, in reality, it faced many problems that threatened its people.

Silence spread across the hall while Andrian's once peaceful face had become distorted with rage. "You've been stealing our crops for years, and now you think you can order me about, Aldus?"

Aldus Morell frowned. "I can do whatever I want, Andrian, and you will never be able to stop me. My king has the largest army in the kingdom. What do you have? A thousand men who have never fought in battle?"

"Your king is too far away to help you! I would advise you to watch your words if you want to keep your tongue and your head!" Solor shouted.

"Kill me then, Lord Balkwall, and I swear no one in this place will be left alive. Either I leave here with Lord Conrad, or you'll kill us and seal your own death warrants."

"What exactly has happened? What has Conrad done?" Eleanor couldn't believe she'd found the courage to speak.

"Be quiet, Lady Dilerion," Solor said, and Lord Morell turned to her.

"Lady Dilerion?" repeated the old man. "I'd heard you were on Sophie Delamere's side all these years. The fact that you are here means that Sophie has finally accepted her defeat and sent you to Felador to save you."

Eleanor felt afraid. She didn't want Walter to know where she was. However, it was too late now. "Why I am here is none of your business, Lord Morell." Eleanor turned to Andrian. "I want to understand what's going on. I'm a lady of Felador."

The high priest looked at her with an expression that didn't reveal his thoughts. Eleanor bet that every person in the room was outraged that a stranger had decided to speak, but she didn't care. She felt a strange strength in the place that was once her parents' home.

"Lord Morell has been stealing most of Felador's crops for years. He's one of the wealthiest nobles in Gaeldeath," Andrian said, looking her in the eye. "We tired of losing our crops to him, and so, we started farming different pieces of land in places no one knew about except for the men from Felador. In this way, we would be able to keep but also sell some crops to honest merchants.

"The plan worked for a while until Morell discovered several of the new pieces of land we were farming. His soldiers and carts always appeared on our land just before the harvest. We couldn't attack Morell, as that would have provoked Walter. However, we were sure there were traitors in Felador, and we had to find them. No one could have known so much about the fields we were cultivating and the harvest without there being an informant on our land. We'd been searching for a long time, and today we found out the truth. Lord Conrad Miller..."

"You're in luck, Andrian. Most of my men are by King Walter's side, so I had few to accompany me. If I had all my soldiers with me, your guards wouldn't have had the slightest hope of bringing me here. It was foolish of them to attack Conrad while he was with me. They should have waited for him to return to the city. As for your plan, sooner or later I would have found out," Lord Morell said.

"You're right... Nevertheless, Conrad will remain here."

"I've told you before. Conrad will follow me north. If you dismiss my words, you'll be bringing war to this city."

"Why do you want to save his life? He's of no use to you now. He'll never help you steal from Felador again," Solor said.

"He's both cunning and loyal to me. All he needs to serve me is gold and I have plenty of that. I can use him away from Felador and good informants are rare these days. You may think I'm not honest, but I protect those who make me richer, Lord Balkwall. That's why I am the richest lord in Gaeldeath."

"There is another solution," Eleanor said.

"Keep quiet, Lady Dilerion!" Solor shouted angrily.

Eleanor fixed her gaze on him with an angry look. "I'd advise you to remain silent, Lord Balkwall," she shot.

The lord gaped open-mouthed, but he didn't speak. Eleanor turned to Aldus Morell, and Andrian watched her with a strange look.

"What solution?" Lord Morell smiled.

"Conrad will remain in Aquarine, and he'll be imprisoned for his crimes. However, you'll have the opportunity to never again have to find an informant in Aquarine... You can take most of Felador's crops for free if you swear to leave a fair share of them to its people while protecting its land from the rest of the thieves."

"What jurisdiction do you have to strike deals on behalf of Felador?" Solor's face flushed with rage.

"I give her that jurisdiction," Andrian said.

Solor and the rest of the lords looked at the high priest in disbelief.

Eleanor felt courage awakening within her. "This man has been finding ways to take Felador's crops for years, and we can't stop him. However, I'm sure he's not the only one. The rest of the lords and mercenaries who steal crops from this land deprive Felador, as well as Lord Morell. This agreement will bring all of us more harvests," she said.

"If Conrad stays here, he won't stay to be imprisoned, but to die," Solor said.

"Then you won't be any different to Walter," Eleanor retorted.

Solor was about to speak, but Andrian's look silenced him.

"A generous offer," Lord Morell said. "However, why should I waste my men on guarding Felador's land? The crops that I steal are already quite profitable. I'm the only lord in the north whom Walter has granted the freedom to take crops from this place."

"I'm sure there are many merchants, mercenaries, and even lords from the north and central regions secretly stealing crops from Felador—crops that could become yours. Moreover, you will no longer have to waste men searching for the fertile parts of our land or for the harvest. The people of the city will gather the crops and deliver them to you whenever you wish."

"Interesting... However, I don't need to negotiate with you, my dearest lady. I can just use all my soldiers and take every crop on this land, even all of Aquarine, if I so wish."

"And why haven't you done so, my lord?"

Aldus Morell took on a strange expression. "I have more important thi—"

"That's a lie!" Eleanor snapped. "Your king needs your men to defeat his remaining enemies and he wouldn't waste soldiers, neither to attack Felador nor to keep it. There's war, and Walter has always wanted the regions of his enemies to remain headless and destroyed. If you ask for men to conquer Felador, your life will be in more danger than ours." Eleanor walked over to him.

"In exchange for a few dozen soldiers, you will get Knightdorn's most valuable crops. No more men will be needed since the city guards will also guard Felador's land. You'll get more crops than you did before, and you'll expend fewer soldiers than you would if you tried to rob our land. I'm handing you an offer that many lords from the north would want. I believe all of this is far more valuable than an informant."

Lord Morell studied her for a few moments. He appeared to be trying to come to a decision until he turned his gaze to Andrian. "If I accept this offer, it will never leave this hall—do I have your word?"

The high priest stood still for a few moments. Then he took a few steps towards the lord and held out his hand. Morell squeezed it.

"Escort Lord Morell and his men out of the city, and Conrad into the dungeons," Andrian said.

The guards lifted the captives to their feet and ushered them out of the great hall. Lord Morell walked away with a look of satisfaction on his face. Eleanor found Andrian staring at her strangely, as if he was seeing her and what she was truly capable of for the first time in his life.

The Glory of the Past

Elliot looked over his letter again. The night was rainy, and the parchment Aleron had given him had got wet in places. He carefully read the words he'd written, and then glanced at the smaller parchment—the one that contained his true message.

You must find out how Walter intends to tame the wyverns. These creatures have always only obeyed giants.

Try to find out more about the spy in Wirskworth.

Not much has happened in the Mountains of the Forgotten World these past few days.

I will be waiting to hear from you.

Elliot stared at the secret letter before his gaze returned to the large parchment. This one hardly contained any news since Walter himself would read it, so he had to be careful. Not much had happened over the last few days. Elliot had written that he'd tried in vain to free the Elder Races while at the same time, the elwyn and elves had been teaching him battle techniques. After his last conversation with Aleron, he'd decided to consult him about what he wrote to Reynald, and he hadn't regretted that decision.

Aleron had told him not to share what they'd discussed. If the letter fell into the hands of Walter's allies, it would be dangerous. The fact that something strange might be going on with Thorn wasn't to be spread. Aleron didn't want Walter to find out his thoughts about him, and this had astonished Elliot. He hadn't expected the aged elwyn to care so much about the new king of humans, but something about Walter scared Aleron. As he had told Elliot, he suspected that the new king might have tried to change his nature to gain power.

He read over both parchments one last time. He felt he ought to write more in the one that Walter would read. He knew Reynald had to give valuable information to his king to gain his trust again after seventeen years. A momentary thought crossed his mind, and he wondered if he should write it. A little later, he brought out the large parchment again.

I saw a wyvern for the first time a few days ago, and I wondered how anyone could fight the giants. There may be only two left in the world, but no one would dare to challenge them astride their winged monsters.

Elliot went over his sentences carefully. His words could arouse Walter's interest. He was sure that since he wanted to tame the wyverns, any information about their strength would satisfy him. A thought took root in his mind. He'd learned to deal with the elwyn and the elves, but he knew nothing about giants. They would be truly impossible for a human to defeat.

Thoughts about the wyverns and giants made him think about John, Eleanor and Selwyn. *Are they alright?* He wondered.

It was strange that he hadn't talked to them for so long when he was constantly hearing news of Reynald. He'd thought of sending letters to his companions, but couldn't. He had to keep sending Hurwig to Reynald. The news they exchanged was very important for the future of Knightdorn.

"I'd say you've spent quite enough time on those two letters."

Elliot turned to Aleron who'd appeared out of nowhere. "I have to be careful."

"Walk with me."

Elliot jumped to his feet and folded the parchments. "I have to tie the letters to Hurwig's leg."

"Later," the man said.

Elliot stuffed the parchments into his belt, and walked towards the hillside where they gathered at night. He glanced at the sky where countless stars danced across the expanse.

"It's the first time I've seen so many stars," Elliot said.

"You're right. It's a special night," Aleron replied.

"I've been wondering..." Elliot wasn't sure whether he should ask his question. "How might a person fight a giant? Only archers with innumerable arrows might perhaps be able to stop them."

"Why would humans fight against giants?" Aleron asked.

"Why would they fight against the elwyn and elves?" Elliot retorted.

"What do you mean?"

"I've been learning how to fight against an elwyn or an elf. I figured it wouldn't hurt to learn how to deal with a giant, too."

"I didn't train you to fight against us, Elliot. This training will simply make you an even better warrior against any opponent."

"I thought the elwyn didn't believe in war."

"You're right... However, it's impossible now to save humans without a war. There's no other solution as long as a man like Walter is alive."

Elliot sighed. "Then fight with me, Aleron. You know Walter must be—"

"You've been here for days, and you still don't understand..." the elwyn interjected. "The fact that Walter can destroy the human race doesn't mean that this war belongs to the Elder Races. I may not wish harm on humans, but the Elder Races have seen more than enough death because of them. Don't forget it was the humans who gave Walter power."

Elliot frowned. "I think quite a few have regretted that. Fear doesn't let them—"

"I agree," Aleron said. "If I believed that the majority of humans wanted him as a ruler, I wouldn't be helping you. Free will is the inalienable right of every race even if it leads to its destruction. Nonetheless, Walter has trampled on the free will of most people for a long time now."

They walked in silence for a few moments.

"The giants' weak points are their eyes and feet. Their feet are the only part where their skin isn't as thick. Of course, if they get hit by enough arrows, they might be killed, even if their weaker body parts aren't hit," Aleron told him.

"Why didn't you want to teach me how to fight against a giant? That might also make me a better warrior."

"There are only two giants left in this world. No other creature has their characteristics, and I hope you'll never need to fight against either Adur or Aiora."

"But I might have to fight against Anrai," Elliot said.

Aleron sighed sadly. "Maybe..." he admitted and stopped walking.

"Adur and Aiora would never help you in the same way as Alaric. An ancestor of yours is responsible for the destruction of their race. In their minds, if they showed you how to kill them, you might try to do so. They'd never help an Egercoll after what they've been through over the last three hundred years."

"They'd never help an Egercoll? I thought that if the elwyn and elves decided to fight against Walter, the giants would help, too."

Aleron frowned. "The best you can hope for is that the elwyn and elves help you, and that the giants remain uninvolved. The worst will be for no one to help you, and the giants to be on Walter's side."

Elliot couldn't believe his ears. "Would the giants fight against me?" Aleron looked blankly at the sky. "Egercoll blood runs through Walter's veins too!" Elliot snapped.

"Walter has spent his entire life trying to destroy the House of Egercoll—something that all giants wished they could have done. The fact that he fought really hard against this house, though his mother was an Egercoll, is admirable in the eyes of the giants," Aleron explained.

"So, they will fight *for* Walter?" Aleron didn't reply. "Then I have no hope! Humans don't have the Light of Life. If I free the Elder Races and the giants mount wyverns to attack me, we're doomed. Without the elwyn and elves on my side, there's no hope. I'm trying to help you! You can't allow my friends to be destroyed!"

"Remember your words...'*The Elder Races must be freed, regardless of the wars of humans'*."

"That's true... However, I had considered it possible that they wouldn't fight by my side... I didn't expect to find them against me on the battlefield!"

Aleron breathed out heavily. "Forget your ego, Elliot... Remember what the Elder Races have been through for three hundred years—the only question is whether you *want* to free them because you feel it's the right thing to do, not because of what they might do for you in return. You can't make your decision based on whether some tribe will fight you in the future. If you want to be sure that no one will ever turn against you, then sooner or later you will become like Walter."

Elliot looked at the ground. "You're right... I'm just scared. I already have too much to deal with, and I don't know if I can succeed—" He stopped mid-sentence. "Everyone's relying on me..."

"I know." The elwyn touched his shoulder. "However, I want you to be careful... I don't want you to make the mistakes most humans make."

Elliot stopped walking and looked into the man's starry-blue eyes.

"Adur and Aiora have their hopes resting on you. They hope more than ever that you will succeed. They have sworn to me that if you free them, they will stay out of the wars of humans. I hope they'll forget their hatred for the Egercolls and keep this oath if they're given the chance to choose," Aleron said.

Elliot nodded, feeling some small relief.

"If ever you come face to face with a giant, I'd advise you to run away. If you can't escape, stay away from them. As soon as you get a chance, drive your sword into their feet—giants never protect their feet," Aleron said.

"What if I'm faced with a giant on a wyvern?"

Aleron frowned. "The only giant that has a wyvern devoted to him is Adur. Aiora lost her wyvern in the Battle of Wirskworth and has never tried to bond with another since... I hope you never have to deal with something like that, Elliot. If necessary, your only hope will be to hit the wyvern's eye with an arrow."

"So, this is the only way… If Walter bonds with the wyverns, I'll have to—"

"I don't think he'll succeed," Aleron told him. "However, as I've told you before, no one can bond with all wyverns at once, only one at a time. Only if that one dies can another be tamed by the same rider. As for Walter, if you have to deal with him mounted on a wyvern, you'll find a way to defeat him when the time comes. You have more important things to do at the moment…" Aleron took on a strange expression. "We're late, and we must continue."

Elliot didn't know what he meant, but they started walking again without speaking until they reached their destination. Countless flames rose into the sky while thousands of creatures were seated along the mountainside. He would have expected most elwyn and elves to be asleep by then.

"Today is the Feast of the Glory of the Past," Aleron declared. "This day is very important to us."

"The Glory of the Past? What is this feast about?" Elliot asked.

"Since the time when the curse trapped us in these mountains, we've been searching for ways to alleviate the suffering. After years had gone by, we discovered that when all the elwyn and elves travel to pleasant memories, the Light within them strengthens, and the pain of the curse leaves their soul for a while."

Elliot didn't understand. "What do you mean? How do you travel to memories?"

"I think you know how."

Elliot swallowed hard.

"The Light of Life is a single force. When one of us travels to a happy memory, the Light within them grows stronger, and this gives hope to every creature of the Elder Races. When we all travel to a happy memory, the power of the Light becomes stronger and frees us from the torment of the curse for a while."

His words were strange to Elliot. "How often do you do that?" he asked.

"Whenever the sky is full of stars. The stars have always enchanted the elwyn and the elves. Without them, it's hard for all of us to be able to think of a happy memory."

"Rarely does the sky have so many stars."

"Unfortunately," Aleron replied.

They approached the slope, and Elliot saw two huge creatures by a fire. The two giants watched the elwyn and elves who held small spherical orbs in their hands.

"Unfortunately, giants cannot feel the warmth of the Light. However, they like to observe the celebration," Aleron said.

"Why do you want me here? I don't have the Light of Life within me."

Suddenly, something caught his attention. Elliot saw thousands of orbs flooded with blue and red light. They looked like huge fireflies next to the fires that warmed up the atmosphere. It was the most beautiful sight he'd ever seen.

"Do you remember telling me that no child should have been born in this place?" Elliot nodded. "I think you've met the only being that was ever born here."

The thought of Velhisya filled his soul with warmth. "Yes," he admitted.

"Velhisya was the only child conceived by an elwyn mother since the time Manhon unleashed the curse. When her father travelled here, he fell in love with Ellin. She was the only elwyn who ever fell in love with a human."

"Why did Ellin let Velhisya go? Why did she let her husband go?" Elliot asked.

"Ellin wanted her daughter to live happily, away from the pain found in these mountains... As for her husband, it was too difficult for a human to survive here. Arthur had to raise Velhisya in another place."

"She misses her mother..." The words came out of Elliot's mouth impulsively.

"I'm sure." Aleron said sadly.

"What happened to Ellin?"

Aleron stared at the stars for a few moments. "She died when Arthur died—her soul followed his."

Elliot was taken aback. "But the curse prevents the union of souls! Elwyn no longer die when their mate dies."

"No one knows how it happened," Aleron said "However, Ellin's soul followed Arthur as soon as he passed away. No other elwyn has been able to do the same for three hundred years."

"How did Ellin manage to fall pregnant? How did Velhisya manage to leave this place?"

Aleron frowned. "No one has any answers. It was as if the union of a human with an elwyn was so strong that the curse couldn't stop Velhisya's conception. Yet even then, Ellin couldn't leave the mountains. As for how the baby managed to leave is due to Velhisya's nature. Like that of Anrai, she is half-human, and the curse cannot imprison any being who's part human. I haven't seen Velhisya since she was a baby. I've no idea whether she looks more like us or her father's kind."

"She... She's unique," Elliot looked into the distance. He didn't want to betray how he felt.

"I'm sure of that. I want you to travel to a memory with me. I want you to see with your own eyes the power of love," the man said.

"But—"

"You've already managed once before." Aleron took out a small orb from a pouch hanging on his belt and held it in front of him. "Forget your pain and hardship. Forget your responsibilities. Forget it all."

With these words, Aleron closed his eyes and held the orb with both hands. Blue light flooded its surface, and Elliot's eyes darted to the giants. Adur and Aiora were looking at him and Aleron in bewilderment. He smiled at them and reached towards the orb. He was fearful of the pain, but something within him gave him strength; he wanted to see Aleron's memory. His hand touched the surface. The pain shook him, but he ignored it. Moments later, his body was lost in a wave of clouds—he swirled in their path until his feet landed on the ground.

He looked around—he was sure he was still on the mountainside, yet everything seemed different. There was more greenery, and the sky had no stars, only a full moon lit up half of the landscape. Elliot moved forward hesitantly, but the hillside seemed deserted. He turned back and then he was stunned. Thousands of creatures were sitting in a circular formation, and in front of them was a tent. The light from inside it created shadows against its fine material.

Elliot felt afraid. He remembered the villagers in the place he'd grown up in sacrificing animals in the name of the gods, and it looked like a sacrificial ceremony. He began to run, and his intangible body passed through several seated creatures. He had to reach the tent. Elliot continued going through elwyn, elves, even giants—hundreds of giants he knew were now dead. Soon after, he reached the centre of the circle and stumbled inside the tent.

Aleron was standing next to a woman who was lying down and weeping. Blankets covered her body while a man and another elwyn woman were seated by her side.

"Just a little more, my love. A little more," said the man.

"I don't know if I'll last."

"You'll make it, Ellin."

Elliot froze as he heard Aleron. Now he knew what he was seeing—the moment of Velhisya's birth. Elliot realised that the man beside the prostrate woman was human. He couldn't believe that every creature of the Elder Races was waiting for her arrival. He stood at the entrance to the tent and looked at the figures watching. Some faces were tearful, and others were whispering words that Elliot could have sworn were prayers—prayers for the baby to come into the world. Perhaps they believed it would break the curse.

A scream made him turn to Ellin.

"It's coming! It's coming!"

Arthur was stuck under the blankets, and the elwyn woman rushed to his aid as well. Elliot stared at the birth with bated breath. He felt the need to pray himself, and then a cry broke the silence.

"It's a girl!" Arthur poked his head out of the blankets holding an infant.

The baby cried in her father's hands, and tears rolled down Elliot's cheeks.

"Velhisya... Velhisya..." came Ellin's voice.

Syrella Endor's brother brought his daughter before her mother's eyes, and she took the baby in her arms. "I love you, Velhisya."

Elliot's tears streamed down his face and then he noticed Aleron's face. He too was crying. Elliot continued looking at the spectacle until loud screams pierced the air. He saw Aleron and Velhisya's parents turn to look out of the tent, and he rushed to see what had happened.

Elliot stepped out into the dark landscape, and it was then that he saw a strange sight. Beams of light shot out in every direction around those present. Elves and elwyn raised their swords and orbs flooded with light.

"I'm not doing it," came a voice.

He saw an elwyn holding a sword whose blade was encased in a blue glow, and then he understood. The objects made of Aznarin were flooded with light, and no elwyn or elf had tried to transfer their power into them. There was no red light anywhere, only blue. Another figure stepped out of the tent. It was Aleron looking dazed. Aleron pulled an orb out from a pouch on his belt—an orb that emitted light.

"That is the power of love, Elliot—the true power of Light."

Elliot felt a tap on his shoulder and turned his gaze to the right. The present-day Aleron was looking at his past self with tears in his eyes.

The Eternal Pirate

John felt happy as he gazed dreamily around the room. He reached out and cupped the breasts of the woman lying next to him. She raised her head and regarded him with a lustful look, which seemed phoney.

"What would you say to sleeping with me again, my lord?" she asked. Her black hair was tousled and clung to her pale shoulders.

John smiled. The women of the Islands called any man from Knightdorn "lord". "Give me a little time, my dear," he said and reached toward the floor.

His fingers gripped the cold surface of a cup, and he brought it slowly to his mouth. He tasted the wine and sighed, satisfied. He'd missed this life. He remembered spending whole days in the brothels of Iovbridge. However, everything had changed the moment he'd decided to help the boy.

You never wanted to help Elliot, you just wanted to get out of Iovbridge. John despised the voice of his conscience.

He tried to focus on the woman next to him, putting Elliot out of his mind. He enjoyed the brothels on the Grand Island, and he had more gold than he'd ever had in his life. He silently thanked Syrella Endor who had given him gold, thinking it would be useful on his journey, and in this place, Elmor's gold was of great value. To be exact, Elmor's gold was the most valuable in the kingdom.

Suddenly, the door of the room opened, and a young girl came in. "I thought you might want more company, my lord," she said. She had beautiful eyes, and she was wearing a red dress.

The woman next to him looked at the newcomer with a smile. He studied the young girl more closely, her green eyes, plump lips, and slim figure. As beautiful as she was, she wasn't attractive to him. She was terribly young, not more than fifteen years old.

"I think it's time for me to go..." John said.

"But why, my lord?" The young woman approached him and reached her hand between his legs.

John got up and pulled away from her. "I think I've spent enough time here." He might have liked prostitutes, but he felt disgusted every time he saw such young girls in brothels.

"Stay a little longer, my lord. I've been dreaming for a long time that a man like you would sleep with me." The girl moved closer, removing her tunic.

"Perhaps in a few years, my dear," he said, and with a low bow began to dress.

The young woman seemed disappointed. She put her tunic back on and left the room without looking back.

"Every man would want to lie with a girl like that," said the woman next to him.

John looked back at her. "I've never been like *every* man..."

He gave her a gold coin and left the room. Down the short corridor, he found himself in a room with a dozen women. There weren't many customers at that time. John smiled at them and walked out of the brothel, blinded by the daylight coming through the clouds. Hunger rumbled in his stomach. He had to find a tavern to eat at and get a room for the night. He needed a truly peaceful night.

He walked along the dirt streets of the Grand Island while men and women passed by. The people of the islands were tough, and it showed on their faces; he noticed two tall and muscular young men walking by. John knew the Ice Islands were renowned for their warriors. Their men were usually tall and bulky, but their battle tactics were primitive. He had heard thousands of times that they fought without armour, holding large swords and shields. There were no good armourers in this place, and steel was not readily available enough for plate armour to be made often.

Still, the warriors of the Ice Islands would be dangerous in a battle, he thought, looking at some men in his path. *Nonetheless, the lack of armour is a serious disadvantage.*

John was of the opinion that the Ice Islands could help Elliot more in a naval battle rather than in a land battle. Their skills at sea were indisputable, however, Walter wouldn't be attacking with a fleet in Elmor. John had suggested Elliot ask Begon to attack Tahos with his ships. That seemed more fitting for the men of this land. Nevertheless, the boy had refused.

"*The men of the Islands won't be much help on land. They have more skill at sea*," John had said.

"*I know they can take Tahos, but if we all die in Wirskworth, Tahos will be of no use to us*," Elliot had replied.

The words he had exchanged with Elliot whirled through his mind. The boy was right. John neared the port of the Grand Island and saw a dozen stalls selling their wares. The market was nothing like the ones in Iovbridge and Wirskworth. A woman with black hair and wrinkled skin held out some fruit in front of a stall selling cheese. The cheese merchant was looking at her with displeasure. Gold and silver were rare on the Islands and the exchange of food for goods was usual.

John passed a few more stalls and cast a look at the cloudy sky—it would rain soon. Dozens of birds flew low near the rocky crags of the island. John gazed at the green landscape and the thick bushes that sprouted across the stony hills. He may have felt carefree over the last few days, but he was guilt-ridden now. He hadn't decided what he would do, and Elliot's words were nagging at his conscience.

A building came into view. It was a little bigger than the others around the harbour and looked neat. *Finally, a nice inn*. John reached the door, but something made him turn his gaze towards Begon's tower. *Damn it.*

He needed to get rid of the guilt.

He pushed open the door and entered the inn, his stomach growling. He saw several figures eating and drinking and walked over to a man behind a tall, wooden counter.

"I want fish and wine," John said.

"I want silver for the fish. I won't trade it for anything else," replied the man.

John threw a gold coin onto the counter. "Add some cheese and bread. I also want a room for the night."

The man's eyes lit up as he looked at the coin, and nodded. John headed for an empty table at the back of the pub.

"At last! I've been waiting for days to find you here."

John turned in surprise to see Captain Raff smiling with a goblet in his hand. *What the hell*? His mind was so clouded, he'd forgotten the captain had told him that he was a patron of this inn.

"I thought you no longer liked the Tide," Raff said.

"I wanted to visit a few other places before I came here," John replied nonchalantly. He noticed another man next to Raff. He was quite old, with wrinkles and white hair; his face reminded him of someone.

"This is Sophie Delamere's messenger."

John froze. Many eyes turned his way as the old man stood.

"What might the Queen of Knightdorn want from me?"

John now knew who the man in front of him was. Begon, The Leader of the Ice Islands. The man looked at John with obvious interest. "Uh... The truth is that—"

"I thought you were here to talk to me, not to do the rounds of the whorehouses of the Grand Island, Long Arm," Begon cut him short.

Raff has told him everything. John remained silent, unsure what to say.

"Does the queen want to ask for my help before the last battle in Iovbridge?" Begon asked.

"Yes," John replied. *The news hasn't yet reached the Ice Islands.*

The man huffed. "I took an oath, and as much as I hate Walter, I will keep it."

"I know I'm only a messenger, my lord" —John bowed deeply— "but I think it would be wiser not to take part in the war. No one can stop Walter Thorn any longer." The words flowed effortlessly from his mouth, but inside of him, he felt shame.

Begon smiled. "I think the queen's decision to send you here was not the wisest. Envoys convey words and letters without giving their opinion."

"It's just that... I wanted to tell you the truth." Out of the corner of his eye, Raff looked at him in surprise.

"Do you have a letter for me?" Begon asked.

"I had, my lord... But I lost it in the storms of the Cold Sea." He had decided to lie. He wouldn't give this letter to Begon; if he learned about Elliot, he might decide to fight.

Begon turned to Raff. "I bet this scumbag tricked you into bringing him to the Grand Island for free. If there's anything more you want to tell me, you know where to find me, Long Arm." Begon nodded and left the inn.

"Did you lose the letter?" Raff asked John, raising an eyebrow. John nodded.

"I think you're hiding something, Long Arm... Did you travel all the way here just to say these words to Begon?"

John still felt that eyes were on him. "I may have come to the only place where I knew I would be safe."

He looked away and moved towards an empty table away from Raff's. A few moments later, the man behind the counter approached him with everything he'd requested, leaving a rusty key on his table. John began to eat hurriedly, eager to leave for his room.

"I knew you were a rascal... However, I didn't expect you to be a coward."

John looked at Raff as the captain approached him. "If you want to fight a losing battle, you're free to take your ship and set sail for

Knightdorn," he said angrily.

"Sophie Delamere could have sent many men to deliver this message and she chose you... She chose you, and you betrayed her. I don't know why they sent you, but it must seem strange to you to be counted on for something more than what you really are."

Raff turned and left the Tide while John stewed in his own thoughts. No matter how many regrets and how much shame he felt, he knew that he wanted to live. He was in a safe place and had decided that he shouldn't bring the Ice Islands into the war by talking about Elliot. Sooner or later the news about the boy would reach the Grand Island, but then it would be too late. Begon would no longer have time to help the only son of Thomas Egercoll even if he wanted to, so he wouldn't rush into battle. If Walter won the war, he would never take an interest in the Ice Islands, while if Elliot won, John knew he wouldn't blame him on account of his choices. He might have been consumed by remorse, but he preferred to save his life.

Suddenly, he remembered some of Elliot's words. The boy wanted as many soldiers as possible for the battle in Wirskworth, and had sent John to talk to Begon because he believed capable men could be found on the Ice Island.

"They don't have any horses in the Ice Islands. By the time they get to Wirskworth on foot through Stormy Bay, the battle will be over," John had told him.

"Tell them to sail to South Bay and to march from there to Wirskworth."

"Have you lost your mind? Do you know how far South Bay is from the Ice Islands? The storms in autumn—"

"The storms will help them get to South Bay quicker at this time of the year. The wind will be their ally."

"It's very dangerous with the autumnal waves."

"It's dangerous for every man, except those from the Ice Islands," Elliot had replied.

The boy was right, and Raff had proved this a few days ago by crossing the Cold Sea. The voyage to South Bay wouldn't be impossible for the men of this land. Moreover, Walter wouldn't easily breach the gates of Wirskworth, and the men of the Ice Islands would arrive at the right moment to attack him without him expecting it. All John needed was to convince Begon to fight. But, he wasn't going to.

John looked around the inn. A few people still glanced at him. *You're a coward*, his conscience told him, but he didn't care. He had made up his mind. Elliot would have to manage without him. As much as he wanted to change, he'd never be able to. He was just a selfish rascal—an eternal pirate.

The Mountains of Darkness

Many people said the Night Trees were ugly, but as Walter studied them, he believed they were simply different. Only a few people could admire their unique beauty and he was one of them. Walter and his men rode slowly up the lowest of the six mountains that made up the Mountains of Darkness. That mountain was the one with the most Night Trees, and legends said that wyverns lived on one of its slopes. The trees stood close to seventeen feet tall with knobby bark, adding to the gloomy atmosphere.

He glanced at the soldiers following him and sensed they were afraid. All of them knew that their purpose in that place was twofold. They had to collect branches full of Orhyn Shadow while searching for the wyverns. Walter was the only one who wasn't afraid of an encounter with the winged monsters. He swore his men wanted to rebel against him when it came to searching for them, but fear kept them in line.

Walter took note of the huge horse that bore Anrai as the man rode on his left side. He had frequently observed him over the last few days, and wondered about a lot of things each time he saw him.

Soon I'll know.

They continued riding through the trees. A few hours would be enough for them to gather the branches they needed. The horses' hooves were the only sound heard along the way, and they had yet to find the creatures he sought. Walter felt a twinge of despair.

The wyverns may not be here.

The possibility filled him with anger, but he kept trying to put it aside. His time was limited. They'd already ridden for seven days to reach the Mountains of Darkness, and they had to catch up with the rest of his armies and attack Wirskworth. He didn't want to exhaust his horsemen—a mistake he wouldn't make again. If he didn't find the wyverns soon, he'd be forced to abandon his plan, and he didn't want to contemplate such a possibility.

Walter began to lose faith as time passed. His fears had proven true—the wyverns weren't there. He cast a look at Annys following him by his horse. He may not have found the monsters he was looking for, but he knew he was lucky to have a tiger such as her as his most faithful companion.

"I think I see something."

Walter turned to Brian who was looking to the right. The trees seemed to thin out at that point. He pulled on the reins of his destrier and rode through the cloudy morning until he felt a flutter of excitement. A huge black wing rested on the ground a short distance away.

At last! My search hasn't been in vain.

Walter approached the giant creature lying on the ground, its eyes closed. He looked around and noticed more wyverns sleeping. They had to be careful. If his men spooked them, they would meet with a violent death.

He saw movement out of the corner of his eye, and his horse leaned back in alarm. A head lifted and a pair of yellow eyes landed on him. The wyvern opened its mouth, and a growl shook the air.

"Stay still!" Walter shouted as the rest of the wyverns raised their heads.

Walter dismounted and tied his horse's bridle to a rock. He moved towards the wyverns that were slowly pacing, forming a circle around him and his men.

"Perhaps you shouldn't go near them, Your Majesty," came Berta's voice.

"I think Lady Loers is right," Short Death said.

"Quiet!" Walter didn't mean to shout.

The yellow eyes of the nearest monster fixed on him. There weren't many wyverns—no more than twenty. Legend said that there had been thousands once, but Althalos had told him that after the battle between the giants and the elves, they had almost been wiped out.

The wyvern near him made a sudden move. Walter studied its legs and spiky wings as it approached. *Do you want to attack me?* Walter turned his gaze and looked for Leonhard, finding the old man's face. The healer nodded sharply, signalling him to continue. *I hope you're right, or your death will be the most harrowing in the history of the world.*

Walter took a few steps until he stood in front of the monster. The rest of the wyverns watched at a distance. Walter kept his gaze on the yellow eyes in front of him and gave a slight bow. He waited patiently, then straightened his body. The wyvern had frozen in place, but now it bared its teeth and growled. The rest of the wyverns started growling, too, and Walter prepared himself for an attack, remaining still. He'd decided to follow Leonhard's advice.

The monster moved its head, jaws nearing Walter slowly. Something inside Walter told him to draw his sword, but he didn't. *I'm not afraid of you*, he thought and looked at the big yellow irises drawing closer.

The wyvern stood watching, then it closed its eyes. Walter took a step back, and then, the creature lowered its head as if to bow.

What is it doing? Walter hesitated for a moment before moving to the side of the wyvern, and to his surprise, saw it lower its wing.

A fearful voice in his mind told him to stop and turn back to his men, but he didn't. He was the most powerful creature in the world, and nothing would make him cower. He stepped onto the rough hide of the wyvern and began to slowly climb up its back, leaning on its spikes.

This is why giants need to be immune to Orhyn Shadow, he thought as the spikes grazed his skin. He looked at his cuts for a moment, but the poison could no longer harm him. He struggled for a while until he reached the wyvern's back and sat between two spikes.

Walter felt a satisfaction he had never felt before. He knew he was destined to become the most invincible man who had ever lived. The wyvern had remained still while he had climbed onto its back, and he looked down at its hunched neck.

Get up, he thought, and the creature's body jerked. Walter held on to its horns as the wyvern lifted its head up with a sudden jolt. Immediately afterwards, the monster stretched its wings and took off, wind blasting around him.

His men grew smaller and smaller, and he realised that the wyvern's feet had left the ground. He felt powerful—so powerful that he might have to kill some of his soldiers to make a show of his strength. He looked down at them, and saw that they were watching him in awe.

Put me down, he ordered, and again cast a look at Leonhard who was watching him from afar. The old man had given him everything his soul desired.

The wyvern landed on the ground, and with a few nimble movements, Walter dismounted from its back. Then, he turned to the rest of the wyverns. Their yellow eyes followed him, but none of them moved. He tried to connect with them as he had done with the first, but nothing happened. Walter felt a hint of anger. Leonhard had been right once again. He had known deep down that this was what was going to happen, even if he didn't want to admit it.

"I think you should give your new companion a name," Leonhard said as he approached. "This wyvern has spines on its tail, body, and wings. I think only the males have spines on their tails... It looks bigger than the rest."

"Phobos[1]," Walter said. "That's its name."

Leonhard smiled. "I like it."

"You were right," Walter muttered, glancing at the rest of the wyverns. All of them were smaller, but some had larger wings than Phobos'. The colour of their bodies was black but two of them looked greener to him.

---

1. Greek for fear.

Leonhard seemed to understand what he meant, yet remained silent.

Annys looked at Walter as he headed for his destrier. He may now have had a new bloodthirsty creature as a loyal companion, but he loved his tiger more than anything else. The Trinity of Death and the rest of the soldiers dismounted from their horses. His men bowed before him—he could feel their awe radiating across his skin.

"Get up!" Walter shouted. "We don't have much time. The Night Trees await us—"

A cry stopped him mid-sentence. A wyvern had begun charging toward them.

"What's happening?" he asked Leonhard, feeling a trace of fear.

"I don't know."

Make it stop, Walter thought, looking at Phobos, but the beast stayed where it was. "Stay still," Walter spoke loudly, looking at his soldiers. "If you run, it'll attack you." The wyvern reached the men and then glanced down at one of them. Walter saw Anrai looking at it in surprise. "Don't bow!"

Anrai turned to Walter, not knowing what to do.

"Obey your king," came Leonhard's voice.

No, Walter thought angrily, and then Phobos let out a loud growl.

Anrai took a few steps back. The wyvern tilted its head, but the man continued to back away. Suddenly, the monster raised its neck and let out a loud noise. Anrai seemed dumbstruck, and the wyvern stood still for a few moments. After a while, it closed its eyes as if disappointed and returned to the rest of the monsters in its clan.

Damn. He had hoped that Anrai wouldn't have that power but what he feared had happened. "Do as I ask!" Walter shouted to his men.

Bewildered by what had happened, a few soldiers started to walk away fast, and the rest followed suit. Anrai hurried after them.

"Not you!" The giant man turned towards him, and Walter watched him. "We need to talk," he snapped and motioned for Anrai to follow him. *I have to put an end to this.*

Walter was preoccupied as Leonhard and Anrai walked by his side. Countless Night Trees surrounded them, obscuring the sky. Leonhard followed behind them while Anrai followed wordlessly, looking pensive. When they had moved far enough away from the wyverns and the soldiers, Water stopped.

"I have a mission for you," Walter said, turning to the giant man.

"As you wish, Your Majesty," Anrai said with a bow.

"I want you to go to the Mountains of the Forgotten World and kill the remaining giants."

"But... Why?" Anrai asked, eyes widening.

"I've been talking to Leonhard about this for a long time... They may decide to attack us, and it'll be impossible to defeat them."

"If the giants fight in the battles of humans, they will take your side, Your Majesty. You're a man from the north with a white tiger at your side. They would never side with Egercoll!"

"You may be right, my old friend, however, I can't be sure. Nobody may speak about it, but the blood of the Egercolls runs in my veins, too. I can deal with the elwyn and the elves, but if the giants break free and go against me, it will be very difficult for me to win... One day they may decide to attack me."

Anrai was speechless. "My father might be there..." he croaked.

"I know it's hard. I was also forced to kill my father to win the kingdom from those who stole it and destroyed it. Only I and my faithful men can bring prosperity to this land. Those who are capable of destroying us must die."

"I can convince him to take our side! I can convince all of them to take our side. I'm sure they would, even if I didn't ask them to," insisted the giant man.

"I can't take that risk, Anrai. Giants are aggressive creatures, and they hate humans. Only the elwyn and the elves can deal with them, and I know they would never fight for me."

"No one can beat you. You have a wyvern!"

"As you saw, there are others. If the remaining giants bond with the other wyverns, what hope will we have against them all? I don't know how many giants are still alive."

Anrai looked puzzled. "Why now? Why do you want to send me now to kill the giants?"

"I never expected that the son of Thomas Egercoll would try to free the Elder Races. In the unlikely event that he succeeds, I want to be prepared."

"You've known where Elliot is for days now... Why did you let me follow you here and not ask me to travel to the Mountains of the Forgotten World earlier?"

"I wanted to see with my own eyes how many wyverns were left. If I'd only found one or two of them, I wouldn't have needed to send you on this mission. You and I could each ride one and destroy our enemies. But, alas, there are more," Walter lied effortlessly.

"Wyverns tend to stick together when they aren't around their masters. Since the giants are imprisoned in the Mountains of the Forgotten World, I don't think there are more than what we saw. They are less than twenty. However, there are enough to destroy us if the giants break free and decide to attack us," Leonhard said.

"The giants are still imprisoned. You have a wyvern on your side... You can attack and kill them if you want," Anrai retorted.

"The giants are in the Mountains of the Forgotten World with the elwyn and elves. If I fly there alone, the elwyn might kill my wyvern and capture me. Only with my army can I defeat them, and I don't have time to march my men there."

"They could kill me, too! How am I going to kill all the giants myself?"

"You're one of them, Anrai. You can trick the Elder Races and quietly assassinate the giants. Then you'll run away and come back to be by my side. They'll never trust me, but you they'll trust."

Anrai looked solemn. "Why didn't you let the wyvern bond with me? If I became its master, I would be able to fly quickly to the south and kill the giants."

"It's dangerous! If the Elder Races see an unfamiliar giant astride a wyvern approaching, they might attack him. Moreover, if you mount the wyvern, it will then hear your thoughts. If there ever comes a time when you feel anger or fear, it'll rush to your side and may attack the Elder Races unnecessarily. Then the elwyn and elves will kill it and murder you, too. You have to travel there alone and find a way to quietly get the giants out of the way. As soon as you succeed, we'll be the only ones flying in the skies. No one will be able to stop us," Walter hoped he would agree. If he accepted this mission, he and the remaining giants would slaughter each other.

Anrai looked him in the eye. Walter couldn't read his thoughts.

"Alright. I'll set off immediately. I need several days to reach the mountains," the giant said.

Walter nodded brusquely. "Don't talk to anyone about this. I don't want my men to be scared. I want them to think that if ever the giants go to war, they'll be on our side. If you succeed, you'll be my most revered soldier forever."

Anrai remained silent as he bowed and walked away.

"I'd hoped this wouldn't be necessary. I wanted him in my ranks," Walter said. He knew that a man like Anrai was valuable in battle, but he couldn't keep him any longer—his power to bond with wyverns was too dangerous.

"It's the only way," Leonhard replied.

Walter watched Anrai leave and wondered if the old healer would turn out to be right once again.

The Lady of Flames

Reynald looked at Walter fearfully as the king read the letter carefully. Walter's blond hair looked like gold under the light of the candles. Reynald felt fear whenever he stood in front of Walter with the intention of spewing out lies to him.

"Interesting..." Walter's voice expressed a note of pleasure.

"As soon as I received it, I ran to find you, Your Majesty," Reynald told him.

Walter raised his head. "I didn't expect there to be only two giants left..."

"Nor did I," Reynald admitted. "However, if they should want to fight for you, you'll be all-powerful."

The man scratched his chin, pensive. "Elliot hasn't succeeded in freeing the Elder Races, but, if he does, I'm sure that the elwyn and elves will fight by his side."

"But you said that these creatures wouldn't easily fight for an Egercoll. How do you kno—"

"I thought you were clever..." Walter cut him short. "If they didn't care about him, they wouldn't have taught him fighting techniques."

"They may not want to fight. They may be doing it out of gratitude because he's trying to free them."

"Why do you think the giants aren't helping him as well? In the letter, he says he only practises with elwyn and elves."

"Because..."

"Because the giants hate him," Walter said pacing around the tent.

"I suspect Althalos had been talking to the elwyn and elves for years. He knew a lot about these creatures—more than any other man I've ever met. I'm now certain that it was him who sent Elliot to the Mountains of the Forgotten World. Althalos has always been one to hatch a plot and Elliot is his last hope. He wouldn't have sent him to such a place if he wasn't sure there was something to be gained," Walter continued.

"Perhaps... I don't have any answers, Your Majesty. Do you think Althalos came to an agreement with the elwyn and elves that if Elliot freed them, they would help him?" Reynald asked.

"He would be a fool to send his last apprentice there if he didn't hope for something... The old man knew that if the giants turned on Elliot, he would be doomed without the elwyn and elves."

Reynald took a step forward. He didn't know whether his thoughts would anger Walter, but he'd decided to voice them. "Do you think Althalos felt compassion for the Elder Races?"

Walter's blue eyes fixed on him. "What does it matter?"

"Althalos always tried to help the weak. If he felt compassion for these creatures, his heart may have got the better of his reason. He may have thought Elliot was the only one left to free them, so he decided to take the risk..."

"Do you think his pity for the Elder Races could have blinded him so much that he'd endanger the people he wanted to protect? Do you think Althalos would risk an alliance of giants with me because of compassion?"

Reynald nodded.

"Well then, you're not such a fool. The old man had compassion for every creature in this world. It wouldn't be difficult, after all, for his sensibility to affect his judgment. Maybe this is the answer I've been looking for..." Walter was lost in thought for a few moments. "Write a letter with what we agreed upon. Don't mention that a wyvern bonded with me," he said.

"Naturally."

"Now, I want to be alone."

Reynald bowed curtly and hurried out of the tent. Tucked into his belt was the secret letter Elliot had sent him. Fires smouldered through the camp and a few dozen men sat around them. They'd set up camp at the foot of the Mountains of Darkness. The night was cold and cloudy, the pale glow of the moon obscured by thick clouds, and Reynald's muscles ached from fatigue. The day had been exhausting, but they had managed to gather branches from the Night Trees while Walter had once again achieved what he desired—a wyvern devoted to him.

Reynald headed for his tent, lost in thought. He may not have known many things about wyverns, but everyone knew that those monsters would only bow down to giants, and he had no idea why. The fact that a wyvern had bonded with a human was unprecedented, and he was sure that it had never been done before. Reynald had expressed his surprise to many men, trying to find out if they knew anything more about it, but no one had the faintest idea or could explain what had happened that morning. He could have sworn that even the members of the Trinity seemed to be stumped upon seeing Walter on the back of one of the winged monsters.

A new thought came to his mind—the mystery of the giant was even stranger. Everyone had seen Anrai and the other wyvern. Reynald intended to speak to him since he was the only one who might have an explanation for everything that had happened, but Anrai had disappeared. Walter also hadn't mentioned anything about the giant man when they made camp, which seemed odd. The king used to praise the members of the Trinity for their exploits and the fact that a wyvern had hastened to bond with Anrai was certainly worthy of admiration.

Reynald was disappointed that he hadn't managed to find out any more information about the wyverns and Walter bonding with one. He passed by a deserted fire, his body warming momentarily as the flames crackled. Reynald eventually found his tent, eager to go to sleep at once. He hadn't expected to be given a tent, but he was grateful for it. He knew that several days of hardship awaited him along with a battle as soon as they reached Wirskworth. Nonetheless, he had to write to Elliot before going to sleep.

At the end of the tent, a candle burned on a small wooden board, its small flame flickering on the wick. It was surprising that it hadn't gone out yet. He sat on the ground next to the candle, sighing. He grabbed a quill, parchment, and a small pot of ink from beside the board. He quickly wrote down what Walter had instructed him to and tossed the parchment aside. Then, he grabbed a new one and cut it in half. Reynald carefully wrote down all that had happened that day—all that the king had forbidden him to share. When he finished, he carefully read the small parchment again. He felt satisfied and stood up.

Reynald left the tent and looked around the camp. There was silence except for the snores from the men who had fallen asleep. Several men were inside tents, but most of them were lying on the moss growing on the frozen ground.

Reynald headed for a copse of trees to send his letters away from prying eyes, even though Walter knew what he was doing. He made sure there was no one around him and looked up at the sky.

"Where are you?" he whispered. His eyes searched the branches, but he couldn't make out the white hawk. It always found him when he wanted to send a letter to Elliot, as if it could hear his thoughts. "Where are you, damned bird?"

"I was hoping to see that hawk," a voice said through the darkness.

Reynald clenched the parchments in his fist and turned. Berta Loers stood a few feet away from him. "What are you doing here?" he asked.

"I'm watching you," she said.

"On Walter's orders?"

The woman shook her head and moved closer to him. "Walter may trust you, but I don't."

Reynald breathed out angrily. "I know no one trusts me, but I have the king's faith."

Berta stepped toward him, and her black eyes pierced through him. Her face was youthful and beautiful. Despite her young age, her expression always radiated a raw cold-heartedness.

"Walter Thorn is the greatest man to have ever come into this world. He's managed to subdue an entire kingdom alone, tame a tiger from the north, even a wyvern..."

"He's indeed great..."

"If you betray him, you'll die so torturously that—"

"I know!" he snapped. "I'm not frightened by your threats, Berta. I'm loyal to my king and he knows it."

The woman sized him up, half closing her eyes. "Are you ready to send the letter to Elliot?" He nodded. "Show it to me."

Reynald closed his fingers even tighter around the parchments. *Damn. I should have put the secret letter somewhere else until I found Hurwig.* "Why? Walter didn't even ask me to show him the letter."

"Do you have anything to hide?"

His heart pounded against his ribcage. He half-opened his palm and let the secret letter fall to the ground before showing the larger parchment to Berta.

The woman pulled it from his fingers and began to read the words under the moonlight.

"Now, do you trust me?" Reynald said shortly after.

Berta looked up and returned the letter to him without speaking.

"After the battle in Wirskworth, you'll trust me. You'll see the reverence I feel for our king with your own eyes."

"If you felt reverence, you wouldn't have gone to Stonegate for seventeen years," Berta said.

"We all make mistakes... Nonetheless, I served Walter faithfully all the years I stayed in that castle and succeeded in cutting off the south from the palace. In Wirskworth I'll take my revenge for what happened in Stonegate and prove my loyalty to—"

Berta snorted contemptuously. "The king has a wyvern by his side. I don't think you can offer him much, Reynald."

"I think Walter disagrees. Still, I can't believe that a wyvern bonded with him," Reynald said, colouring his voice with awe. *Perhaps she'll let something slip about how he was able to do it.* Reynald hoped to find out more, but he knew the odds were slim. Berta Loers would rather drink poison than betray any of her lover's secrets.

"If you really believed in Walter, you'd know he can do anything."

"I wasn't the only one who couldn't believe it."

Berta looked at him with disdain. "Wyverns are wiser than humans. They can see true power and submit to it."

"You think this wyvern bonded with Walter because of his power? Legends say that—"

"I don't know any legend. I only know the power of my king... Since you enjoy legends and stories, have you heard the tales about my house—the House of Flames?"

Reynald looked at her in amazement. "House of Flames?" He'd never heard of that name before, and he knew nothing about the House of Loers.

"Many years ago, I travelled with my father on a hunting trip. I was just a little girl, but I really liked swords and bows."

And killing, Reynald thought.

"My father and a few other lords of Gaeldeath had set up tents in the forest for us to spend the night in. I still remember the screams that had woken me up in the dark. I stood up, startled, and felt smoke in my lungs..." She paused. "The men had lit fires to roast hares, and when they all fell asleep, the strong wind blew the fire into our tents. My father had also woken up; we could hear screaming around us... The screams of death."

"How did you survive?" For a moment, Reynald didn't think about the parchment that was on the ground.

"My father held me in his arms, crying. He whispered to me not to be afraid, but I knew he was afraid. Then, I pushed his hands away and approached the flames. I looked at them as if they were an old friend—a friend who wouldn't dare hurt me. I knew it wasn't my time to die, I knew I was special. I was sure the God of War had other plans for me..." she said as a smile formed on her lips. "I heard men breathing their last in the fire, and I stood before the fiery spirits and ordered them to stop. To leave me and my father unscathed. After a while, the screaming ceased and then, the fire went out."

Reynald listened carefully, shocked by the arrogance of Berta's youth. "How did it go out?"

"It went out because a part of the God of War lives within me. Even my own father couldn't believe what had happened, but I made it plain to him. I told him I was too special to die. Then he changed the emblem of our house. A torch full of flames became the new coat of arms of the Loers."

"Why are you telling me all this?"

"If you betray Walter, I'll make sure the flames that didn't take my life take yours. I'll burn you."

Berta turned and walked away, leaving Reynald lost in his own thoughts. *What the hell?* He knew Berta was paranoid, but he hadn't expected insanity. *This woman is more dangerous than any member of the Trinity of Death.*

Reynald bent down and picked up the letter on the ground with a feeling of relief. If Berta had seen his movement, he'd be dead. A crack snapped him out of his thoughts, and he looked back. Hurwig was on a branch right behind him.

He must have spotted Berta and was waiting for her to leave.

He stood up with the two parchments in his palm and approached the white bird. As soon as he got close to it, he looked deep into its black irises. It was strange how Elliot had managed to get such a companion from the centaurs. His thoughts lingered on the boy. He wondered if he'd be able to free the Elder Races—if he'd be able to defeat Walter and avenge himself for his parents' fate. For a moment, the image of Alice crossed his mind. He knew she wouldn't have wanted her son to waste his life seeking revenge.

The hawk raised its beak and trilled softly. Reynald tied the parchments to its leg and looked at its eyes again. They reminded him of Berta's. *If one day I make it out of Walter's camp alive, then a piece of the God of War lives in my soul, too.*

The Lone Ghost

Anrai couldn't sleep. Dawn approached, and the light of the sun shone faintly in the sky. He cast a look at Vaylor sleeping a few yards away. The brown horse was the only creature in the world he felt any affection for. Walter's men had been searching for a beast that could bear his weight for a long time, and the horse was the only one that had been able to. He remembered his joy when he'd first climbed into the saddle and decided to name it Vaylor. His grandmother had told him that this word meant "strong" in the language of the Elder Races. Anrai knew that Vaylor would have difficulty climbing up the Mountains of the Forgotten World, but in the end, he'd reasoned that it wouldn't be a problem since he'd never go there.

Frustration welled up within him again. It had been about a day since he'd left Walter, and it was as if an invisible hand was squeezing his guts. He remembered the feeling—the same he had felt when he found out the truth about his father and that his mother had been raped and fallen pregnant against her will. He'd wondered for years what had happened to his parents until his grandmother Orella told him everything—after learning the truth, he felt more alone than ever. His grandmother was the only person who had truly loved him. Orella always managed to shower him with the affection no one else gave him. She was the light of his life. She'd told him that his mother adored him, but he didn't believe it to be true. Anrai had robbed her of her life when he came into the world.

He continued thinking about his family. His mother was dead, and he didn't know about the fate of his father—whether he was dead or imprisoned by the curse. He didn't want to meet his father, and he didn't know if he had other living relatives in the Mountains of the Forgotten World. On his mother's side, he'd only ever known his grandmother, and she was gone forever, leaving him alone in the world.

Anrai let out a weary breath. The memory of Orella's death still shook him. His thoughts brought him nothing but anger and pain. He remembered his rage being rekindled the moment she died—anger at the Egercolls. They were to blame for everything—for imprisoning his father and forcing him to seek revenge on a human. He might have felt anger towards his father's actions, but he couldn't hate him the same way he hated the Egercolls. After Orella's death, Walter offered him what his soul yearned for—the chance to destroy the House of Pegasus once and for all.

I made a mistake, he thought.

Orella had told him countless times that he shouldn't blame any man for sins that weren't his. She reminded him that the descendants of the Egercolls weren't to blame for the deeds of their ancestors and that the one responsible for the curse of the Elder Races had been dead for hundreds of years. Nonetheless, he hadn't listened, the thought of revenge blinding him. Walter was the only leader who could give him what he desired. Moreover, he was the only man who had accepted Anrai for what he truly was. All his life, he'd been laughed at behind his back because of his huge build, and people had whispered malicious lies about his mother. Walter had included him in the Trinity of Death, and he'd taught him that his difference was a strength, not a weakness. Anrai was devoted to him with his life. Until a few hours ago... Until he'd discovered that, he was alone in the world.

How could he have asked me to do such a thing? As devoted as he was to the king, he would kill neither his father nor the last giants.

"*I know it's hard. I was also forced to kill my father to win the kingdom from those who stole it and destroyed it.*"

Walter's words whirled in his head. Giants hadn't stolen any kingdom.

They'd been decimated and imprisoned because of humans. Now, a Thorn was asking him to destroy their race once and for all. He'd admired Walter more than any other man, never realising how cowardly he was. *Coward*! he mused angrily. *Walter is a fool if he thinks he can convince me with that argument. Walter killed his father because he'd betrayed their house.*

The giants had never betrayed the House of Thorn, and Walter wanted to kill them out of fear. He feared that if they turned against him, they were the only ones who could destroy him. Even if they didn't do so, he didn't want to take the risk. Walter wanted to send a whole race to its death to be sure that no one would ever be able to overthrow him. He never trusted anyone and always used every weapon at his disposal to make sure he would achieve his goals.

Anrai had wanted to kill him with his own hands the moment he'd heard his words, but he hadn't found the courage to do so. He knew that even if he'd succeeded, it would have meant the end of him. So, he'd decided to lie that he would fulfil the mission while he'd lost all sense of devotion to his former king. He had no idea what he'd do, but he wanted to be alone.

I too am a coward. Fear of death had stood in the way of his attacking Walter.

He glanced at the sky that grew brighter as the sun rose timidly. The previous day replayed over and over in his mind. A wyvern had tried to bond with him. Orella had told him of the giants and their gifts.

"*Your mother asked me to tell you everything she knew about giants when you grew up.*"

"*Where did my mother learn so much about giants*?" Anrai had asked.

"*When your father...when your father lay with your mother, her belly began to swell a day later. No human had ever seen anything like it before, but the elwyn guessed the truth and told your mother what she needed to know—what you needed to know, too, once you were ready. Emy was afraid she wouldn't make it through the birth. She was afraid she'd die, so she asked me to tell you everything if she was no longer here. Your mother told me about the giants' strength, how many years they live, and that they grow faster than humans."*

Despite this, he wasn't sure whether her words were true. His grandmother had also told him why wyverns could only be bonded with giants and that the winged monsters chose only one rider with whom they'd never part until death. He remembered his grandmother saying that if a wyvern bonded with him, no other would—not until his wyvern passed away.

He recalled the monster that had approached him. If he'd bowed before it first, and it had imitated his movement, he would have become its master. But Walter didn't want Anrai to have the power he'd gained. That would make Anrai dangerous. Walter now feared him. That was why he hadn't allowed him to bow to the wyvern, and had driven him away from his ranks.

Anrai felt desperately lonely. *The man I swore to protect my whole life, has driven me far away.* He thought about all the things the king might be scared of. He knew he feared that Anrai would return to the wyverns, intending to bond with one of them in secret. So, Walter had sent him to kill the giants, driving him away from the Mountains of Darkness... Anrai believed that the king expected him to fail the mission. It would be almost impossible to kill the giants right under the nose of the Elder Races. He'd sent him there to die because he was now dangerous. However, in the unlikely event that Anrai succeeded, Walter would kill him afterwards, having easily got all the remaining giants out of the way.

Anrai had asked himself why Walter hadn't just killed him outright as soon as the wyvern had run to him. Walter was cunning. The king knew he could still use him, and killing him without reason in front of his men would have caused turmoil and raised questions just before the battle in Wirskworth. It was better to send him to the Mountains of the Forgotten World to get him killed or have him kill the remaining giants. Either way, Walter would win and would only have to deal with whoever remained. Anrai was also certain that Walter had ordered his wyvern to devour anyone who came near the rest of the winged monsters.

Giants had been taming wyverns, ruling the skies with them for centuries, and Walter wanted this power for himself alone, he thought angrily.

"I wanted to see with my own eyes how many wyverns were left... If I'd only found one or two of them, I wouldn't have needed to send you on this mission. You and I could each ride one and destroy our enemies, but, alas, there are more."

Walter's words poisoned his mind. Anrai knew that he'd lied to him—he knew that he would have kept him near him only in the event he'd found *one* wyvern. Only then would he and the rest of the giants no longer be a threat to him.

Anrai never expected a wyvern to want to bond with him. Orella had told him that Orhyn Shadow was in the blood of giants and that this is what bound wyverns to them. He didn't know whether it was true for himself. Nobody knew, since he was the only being with a giant for a father and a human for a mother. Anrai was certain he didn't have Orhyn Shadow in his blood, feeling that his human nature was stronger than his giant one. Deep down he knew that he was hiding the truth even from himself. Anrai actually felt anger and sorrow for his father's actions and hoped that he was different. He hoped that if his nature was more human, it would keep him away from the mistakes his father had made.

Anrai looked at the sky. There was a simple way of finding out if the poison was in his blood, but he hadn't ever wanted to try—never wanted to know the truth. Perhaps Walter knew... Perhaps he was aware that giants are immune to Orhyn Shadow. Anrai frowned and scratched his chin. He wasn't sure whether Walter knew, but most likely Leonhard did—that man knew everything.

Why did he never ask me to try? A few drops of Orhyn Shadow in his blood would have proven whether he was immune to the poison. Walter would have known the truth, and he could have chased him away years ago or even killed him. *He wanted to see how many wyverns were left... If there was only one, he could have kept me in his ranks.*

Walter didn't have a clue about how much Anrai knew about the race of giants. Perhaps he feared that if he asked Anrai to put Orhyn Shadow in his blood, he would ask questions. If Leonhard and the king believed he didn't know a thing, they wouldn't have wanted him to get suspicious. The truth may have made Anrai leave and search for a wyvern years ago.

Anrai laughed for a moment. If he was right about what scared Walter, this was funny. Anrai hoped that the giant's nature was powerless within him, and Thorn feared that he would seek out a wyvern. He saw in his mind's eye the winged monster running towards him. After the wyvern approached him, there was no doubt that Orhyn Shadow was in his blood, and it made him feel dirty. He didn't want to be like his father; he couldn't stand the thought.

How many rapes did you witness in the years you fought alongside Walter? If you hate such men so much, why did you fight by their side? his conscience asked. He had no answers.

He often told himself that he was fighting with this army for an ultimate purpose—a purpose that was more important than anything else. The fall of the Egercolls would bring an end to the misery in the kingdom, possibly releasing the giants from their suffering. All of it would bring a catharsis. No giant would take revenge on humans like his mother again, and Walter's men would no longer have any enemies—killing, raping, and pillaging in the kingdom would stop. He'd turned a blind eye to all that he didn't like in the army ranks that he served. How wrong he'd been...

Even if your deepest nature is like that of the giants, that doesn't mean you're like your father. Perhaps the rest of his kind are better than him. Anrai knew that was logical, but he didn't believe it. He was a Ghost Soldier, a member of the Trinity of Death, and he had committed many crimes during his short lifetime.

Anrai heard a sound and turned to the right. He saw his horse getting up. *About time.* He stood up and moved towards Vaylor. *How had Walter managed to bond with a wyvern without Orhyn Shadow in his blood?*

That was both the strangest and the most worrying of all that had happened the previous day. Orella had told him that it was impossible for a human to do this, and Walter was probably the only one who had succeeded in doing so. If nothing else, Walter astride a wyvern was a terrifying combination. Only the Elder Races may have known why something like that could have happened, but he had no intention of meeting them. He wanted to be alone. He had to go someplace where the land would be rich but deserted—somewhere where no one would look for him.

Anrai stroked Vaylor's back gently. He was ready to saddle him when he heard a voice. "I didn't expect to find a soldier from the north alone here."

He turned and saw a short, ugly man on a horse. "Who are you?"

"Don't you remember me? You and the rest of the king's soldiers found me on your way to the north and bought many of my goods a few days ago. I could never forget such a big man...You must be Anrai, the Ghost of the Trinity of Death," he said, watching him.

Anrai remembered. He was the only merchant they had come across so far north, so they had bought hares and spices from him.

"It was the highest of honours that the king paid for my goods," the merchant said again.

Anrai adjusted the saddle across his horse and tightened the straps around Vaylor's girth. "Walter wouldn't steal from the men of the north. What are you doing here?"

"I'm searching for new wares, my lord. As soon as I find some, I'll return to Tyverdawn. Are you alone?"

"Yes," Anrai replied and mounted Vaylor. "Goodbye." He was about to pull on the reins when an idea crossed his mind. "Do you know the roads in the kingdom well?"

"Where are you going, my lord?"

"To Felador," Anrai responded.

"If you cross this valley, you'll find yourself on the Path of the Wise. From there, continue east. In a few days, you'll find yourself at your destination."

Anrai nodded curtly and kicked his horse, his mind made up about where he would go.

The Past and the Future

Eleanor reached over to the wooden table and grabbed a fig from a large platter as she lounged in her chamber. She brought the fruit to her lips and bit into it. It had a gratifying taste, but it didn't succeed in sweetening her bitter thoughts. Days had passed, but she still couldn't stop thinking about everything that had happened in the great hall. She'd dared to speak before the nobles of the city—dared to propose an agreement on Felador's behalf. She couldn't explain how she'd found the courage to do all this. Andrian had even sided with her, which was even stranger. She was afraid that sooner or later the lords of the city would ask her to leave to avoid her getting in their way any longer. Andrian may have taken her side, but the priest wouldn't go against the nobles.

Eleanor hadn't left her private chambers much over the past few days except to take walks around the city early in the morning or after dark. That way it would be difficult for her to bump into Andrian or any of the lords. She didn't know why, but her courage in the great hall made her feel a strange shame.

I should have stayed in Wirskworth.

It would take years to acquire loyalty and respect in Aquarine. If nothing else, in Wirskworth she would be with Sophie. Now it was too late—Walter would arrive in Elmor soon, and if she travelled there, it'd be impossible for her to enter the capital. She had nowhere else to go.

Elliot believed in you. This thought was comforting, but she wasn't sure that it was true. Selwyn and Long Arm had travelled to places with an army while she had gone to Felador—to a region that couldn't offer a thing towards winning the war. She couldn't decide whether Elliot believed in her or whether he just wanted to save her.

She let out a weary breath and wondered whether he'd made it to the Mountains of the Forgotten World. If the curse was broken and the Elder Races fought on their side, Elliot would build the strongest alliance they'd ever had. Eleanor had heard of quite a few legends of the past about the Elder Races being superior to humans, and she believed that some of them were true. She stared into space. Eleanor hadn't told anyone about where her companions were. Elliot had told her it was dangerous to reveal such secrets.

My friends can really help the war while I came here to fail.

No matter how hard she tried, she couldn't get that thought out of her mind. It was the bitter truth. She had to accept that she couldn't offer anyone anything useful while great men and women had died for her. A tear rolled down her cheek. She didn't want to be flooded again with thoughts of everyone who had sacrificed themselves for her.

There was a knock at her chamber door, snapping her out of her thoughts. Eleanor wiped her eyes, got up, and opened it.

Andrian was looking at her with a good-natured expression. "May I enter?" he asked.

Eleanor had no idea what he was doing at her chamber. Perhaps he'd finally decided to speak to her about everything that happened in the great hall. She stepped aside, and the high priest entered the room.

"I wanted to talk to you."

"I'm sorry," Eleanor apologised. The man looked at her questioningly. "I shouldn't have pursued an agreement with Lord Morell. That was your responsibility."

Andrian smiled. "Your thinking was right. That deal was the best we could have hoped for."

Eleanor was taken aback. "But... Are you sure?"

"No matter how many years I remain in this world, I'll never be able to come to terms with this truth!"

She didn't understand. "Which truth?"

"The people who make the right decisions—the ones who can help our world—have no self-confidence at all. On the contrary, those who are dangerous and foolish, are always extremely sure of themselves!" Andrian hadn't lost his smile. "It's impossible for us to fight against any enemy without condemning whoever is left in Aquarine to death. A deal with a lord of Gaeldeath who will grant us protection in exchange for crops is the best we can hope for. I should have come to this agreement years ago."

Eleanor hadn't expected those words. "I hope it doesn't reach Walter's ears...Neither the deal, nor my presence here," she said shortly afterwards.

"I don't think Walter will care about you, my dear."

"I don't think he would... Walter only cares about Sophie and the throne," Eleanor said.

"Exactly," Andrian replied.

"Nevertheless, the new king won't be happy if he finds out that one of his lords has men protecting Aquarine. You told me that he wanted to leave the regions he destroyed headless, to show his enemies the fate that awaited them. I think Morell's head will decorate a spike if word gets round that he made a deal with us."

Andrian scratched his chin. "You're right... But Lord Morell will do everything in his power to keep the truth hidden. This deal will save him from searching for new informants in Felador, and it will give him more gold while using the least number of soldiers."

"Perhaps one day he'll decide that it's wiser to kill us all and take everything... Then he'll attack us, and no one will ever know about this deal," Eleanor exclaimed.

"The majority of his men are on Walter's side. As you said in the great hall, he cannot call for his soldiers while there is war. Moreover, Lord Morell is a man of the north. Men like him would never leave Gaeldeath for Felador. If they were to attack us, our people would resist. He knows that if he were to kill us, he would have to travel here frequently to oversee the rulership of the region, and he'd waste a good many men on farming and guarding the land. I'm sure he prefers us to be secretly subordinated to him," Andrian said confidently.

"Nonetheless, we must be careful. Someone may find out that some of Morell's men are guarding Felador. The agreement must not reach Walter's ears," Eleanor told him.

Andrian frowned. "You don't know Aldus Morell. He's one of the most cunning lords I've ever met. I'm sure his soldiers will patrol our land carefully. They'll be disguised as merchants and kill the thieves and anyone they consider unreliable and dangerous. He's used this trick before, trying to spy on us. As for us, we'll see to it that word of this agreement doesn't spread in Felador."

Eleanor listened to his words carefully.

"Even if Walter finds out the truth, he'll kill Morell and send other lords to steal our crops—lords who will swear not to make deals with us. We'll deal with it, as we have done for many years..." Andrian added.

"Perhaps Thorn will kill us all."

"You know he doesn't want to waste men on that."

"Not while there's a war... But if he destroys all his enemies, he may change his mind."

"Then, either with this agreement or without, we're doomed," Andrian said.

That is a fact, Eleanor mused.

"I want to ask you something else..." the priest said. "If Morell hadn't accepted the deal and had insisted on taking the traitor to the north, what would you have done?"

"It wasn't for me to decide. I just tried to help."

"Let's just say it was for you to decide."

Eleanor thought for a moment. "I would have ordered the guards to take him and his soldiers to the land near Yellow River. There they would have abandoned them, tied up."

Andrian looked surprised. "Why?"

"That place is full of wolves—they would have eaten them alive. Then, I'd see to it that word got out that they were attacked in their sleep. They'd deserve such a death, and no one would blame Felador... Come to think of it, maybe that's a good solution if Lord Morell goes back on our agreement..."

Andrian remained speechless for a few moments. "Well, I never... You're wiser than I'd dared to hope," he said.

Eleanor felt momentary pride. "Thank you... However, I'm not sure why you're here. Have you come to congratulate me on the deal?"

The man looked at the ceiling of the chamber for a moment. "Not only because of that. You see... I'm quite old and for years I've been looking to see who could succeed me." Eleanor froze. "I belong to the past of this land, and I think you're its future."

"But..." It was so unexpected that she didn't know what to say.

"Now I can see all that Elliot saw in you. You can really help this place. I don't think he sent you here just to save you."

Eleanor's mouth was dry. She was about to say something, but choked.

"You care about people, and seek out the best solution, without putting them in danger. Moreover, you have compassion. You asked for Conrad's life to be spared when every lord asked for his death. You're a wise and considerate leader, though you know when you should show might," Andrian continued.

"I don't know whether I want to rule..." Her fear had made itself apparent before she managed to contain it. She feared she would go through everything that Sophie had been through.

"All good leaders are afraid to rule. It's because they understand the weight of the responsibility they have to bear. However, you have a gift, and it's your duty to use it to help those who need you. You must be brave."

Eleanor was bewildered.

"I want you appointed Governor of Felador, and I'll be your adviser to the end of my days," Andrian said firmly.

"I don't understand... You're the governor! Governors and kings can lose their office only upon death. After your death, the lords will choo—"

"As you already understand, we don't follow the decrees of Thomas with reverence in this land."

"The lords of the city don't want me as their ruler. They are Felador's council, and I don't want to rule in a place where my councillors will hate me," Eleanor told him.

"The truth is that I had difficulty convincing them. Youth and stubbornness are often fellow travellers in life. However, they trust my judgment."

Eleanor couldn't believe it. "Even if they do agree, they might change their minds when you're gone. I don't want to be found murdered in my sleep."

"I know you heard about a lord-traitor, but most nobles in the city are honest. They've suffered under Walter and have learned to tell the truth, whatever that truth may be. They'll disagree with many of your decisions, but if they swear allegiance to you, they'll keep their oath."

"Do you believe that only Lord Conrad was dishonest?" Eleanor asked.

The man nodded. "Conrad was overcome with greed. He'd gotten tired of having his land robbed. However, I don't think he'd have agreed to something that would have put either the city or me in danger. I also believe the rest of the lords won't betray you... Nevertheless, all rulers have to be careful."

"I don't think the lords will swear allegiance to me..."

Andrian smiled and moved towards the door. He opened it and looked out as if searching for something. Eleanor couldn't understand what he was doing and then a dozen figures approached the entrance. Soon, the lords of Felador stood outside her chamber.

"Felador belongs to you, Lady Dilerion," said Andrian.

With this phrase, the priest knelt, and the lords did the same without speaking. A tingle spread down Eleanor's spine. It was the first time she'd accomplished something alone—the first time she felt that the sacrifices of her loved ones had had a real purpose. A tear rolled down her cheek and she took a silent oath. She vowed that she'd make them all proud and that she would sacrifice her life to repay Felador for the honour she'd been given.

The Battle of the Gods

Syrella was lost in thought as she sat on the edge of her bed, wondering whether she was about to accomplish her greatest victory or whether her House would be destroyed once and for all. The days were going by, and she knew that Walter would soon reach her city once again. The coming battle would be the hardest of her life, and she didn't hold out any hope for help from elsewhere. Syrella had never believed that Elliot and his companions would succeed in bringing new allies to Elmor. As if that weren't enough, Velhisya's mission brought her anguish. She felt vulnerable now that her niece was away from Wirskworth for the first time in all these years.

A hand caressed her right shoulder. She turned and found Jahon's face close to hers. "You shouldn't be here," she said.

"I know. But we may soon die... I want to spend what time I have left with you."

Syrella smiled and her eyes fell upon his naked body lying beside her. The sight of him filled her with love. She moved closer to him and took his hand. His face was peaceful and calm as he shut his eyes. A few days ago, she'd told him that Sophie and Peter had presumed that the gossip about their illicit affair was true and that she had confirmed their suspicions.

"Have you lost your mind? If they reveal our secret, there'll be great discord in Elmor," Jahon had said fearfully.

"I've thought about it a lot. Elmor is devoted to me... Nothing will happen as long as I'm governor," she had told him. *"However, if the secret*

is made known, our daughters will pay for our sins after my death. No one will believe they are the daughters of Sermor Burns any longer."

"Many lords may rise up against you."

"I condemned thousands of souls to death at the Forked River, and Elmor is still devoted to me. Do you think they'll turn their back on me because I wasn't faithful to my husband?"

Jahon had sighed. "*Sadon Burns will do anything to take revenge on you if he finds out you dishonoured his son."*

"Sadon's power is trifling compared to mine and that of my House. Don't fear for me but for our daughters... What we've done will create untold friction around Linaria and Merhya. They may have Endor blood flowing in their veins, but I don't know whether the council will give one of them the rulership of Elmor after my death. My adultery will tarnish their name. Moreover, they'll hear whispers about their real father their whole lives. If the secret gets out and I pass away before you, you might also be attacked in Wirskworth."

"*Perhaps we should kill Sophie and Peter.*" Jahon disagreed with her decision to confirm their relationship.

"*No... Every alliance in the kingdom was built on lies. If my time has come, I want to leave trying to change something in this world. I want to build a true alliance and finally be able to truly trust in it, even if I'm making a mistake.*"

"*They may never betray the secret...*" Jahon had mumbled wearily.

"*Then, I'll know that I've succeeded... I'll know that I've brought to my city not only allies, but friends. Friends who, instead of betraying me, stand by my side. My whole life has been lived amid lies... I don't want my end to be like that too. Sophie and Peter will fight with me knowing who I really am, whether that destroys my House or not.*"

Syrella blinked and looked back at Jahon again. She was sure Sophie wouldn't betray her before the battle. They had to remain united, otherwise they'd have no hope against Walter and such information would bring turmoil to Elmor. However, if they won the battle, the queen could sow discord in her city whenever she wanted. Syrella didn't believe that Sophie or Peter would do such a thing. They had proven themselves to be honest, and however many misgivings she felt about her decision, she knew she couldn't have entrusted the secret to anyone better than them.

Suddenly, she felt a pang of guilt. She'd never told her daughters the truth. She didn't want to burden them with that load—the load of her own sins. She knew it would be better if they heard it from her, but she had hoped they would never have to know the truth. She wanted to save them that pain.

Jahon's hand caressed her back for a moment, and Sadon Burns came to mind. Sadon was devoted to her, but he'd loved his son more than anything. If he found out the truth, it would become his life's purpose to avenge Sermor, and she'd seen how cruel he could be. Syrella wasn't afraid of him, but she often wondered why he'd never asked her about the rumours. If the whispers of her affair had reached Peter and Sophie's ears, they must have reached Sadon's as well.

He didn't believe it. Sadon never believed that I would have betrayed his son so brutally. Sadon may also have feared that if he'd uttered such a thing in her presence, she would have condemned him to death.

Syrella kept thinking about Sadon until Velhisya intruded in her thoughts. She and Giren had left the city some days ago. She felt fearful for the fate of her niece. Syrella and Sophie had decided to burn the Liher messenger's body and try to free Selwyn with Giren's plan. However, the plan had a low chance of succeeding, and she prayed for her niece to return alive.

"What are you most afraid of?" she asked Jahon suddenly.

The man raised his head with a look that didn't reveal his thoughts. "That I'll die on the battlefield and not near you..."

Syrella closed her eyes and kissed him, shutting out the rest of her thoughts. No matter what, Jahon was the love of her life—the love she could never spurn.

A sound came from outside the chamber and their lips parted. Surprise crossed Jahon's face. "I didn't expect anyone to be here at such a late hour."

"Whoever it is, it's easy for them to knock on the door since my only guard is in my bed!" Syrella said under her breath.

"Lady Syrella, may I speak with you?"

Sophie's voice echoed round the room. Jahon got up quicky and began to dress. Syrella did the same. She had no idea what Sophie wanted in the middle of the night. A heartbeat later, Syrella was wearing a purple robe, and Jahon a silk jerkin and some leather trousers—he had hung a sword on his belt.

Syrella walked over to the door and cracked it open. Sophie stood dressed in a night robe, her blue eyes looked troubled. Seeing that the queen was alone, Syrella opened the door wider to let Sophie into her chamber. Sophie glanced at Jahon who nodded curtly to her and stepped outside, closing the door behind him.

"I'd swear he knows that I know," Sophie said.

"That would be a fair assumption," Syrella replied. They hadn't found themselves alone since the death of Liher's messenger.

"I understand that it's impossible for there to be other guards when he visits you, but it's dangerous for your chamber to be unguarded at these times."

"Don't worry about me..." Syrella said, and silence spread between them. "Why are you here?"

Sophie appeared hesitant. "I..." She stopped mid-sentence. "I feel so alone. I've spent many years alone, but now, just before the end..." The words came out of her mouth with difficulty.

Syrella moved to her side and embraced her tightly. Sophie returned the embrace, apparently trying to hold back her tears.

"I have no one left in this world," Sophie stammered as soon as they parted. "My family is dead, Bert is dead, and Eleanor is far away... I've gotten used to loneliness, but now I don't want to die alone..."

"You aren't alone. Peter and I will be by your side," Syrella insisted.

Sophie smiled for a moment. "Peter is a great man. However, he doesn't know... He doesn't know how it feels when your leadership has led so many people to their deaths," she whispered.

Syrella felt sympathy for the queen and hugged her again. Sophie hadn't stayed awake only because she feared she'd leave this world alone—she felt guilty about everyone who had died and would die for her. She felt guilty about all her decisions over the years. Syrella knew the feeling. She'd felt it countless times in conjunction with what had happened at the Forked River. Sophie was looking for someone who bore the same burden she did—the burden of power.

The two women broke apart again, and Syrella smiled mirthlessly. "We may die, but I'm happy about what we've accomplished."

Sophie sighed wearily. "I'm not sure I've accomplished anything whatsoever..."

"You're wrong. We're the only women to have ever ruled in Knightdorn. We're two women who've fought for their land, despite how many mistakes we've made. Remember the stories about the old kings we learned when we were little. All of them only sought gold and power. We're different—we both gave what we could and wished we could have done better. Maybe, if there are more rulers like us, men like Walter will cease to exist. Perhaps one day the world will become a better place."

A real smile painted itself on Sophie's lips. "I often wish my uncle had marched his armies to Gaeldeath and killed Walter as soon as he took over from his father as the region's ruler."

"Many a time I wish I'd attacked Reynald Karford, kicked him out of Stonegate, and united Iovbridge with Elmor earlier," Syrella said.

Sophie seemed thoughtful about Syrella's words. "I hope the Guardians of the South will help us..."

"I thought that you met them on your way to Elmor, and they swore to you that they would fight."

The queen frowned. "I met them. Elliot hadn't revealed to them that I'd be travelling with my people to Elmor. When I met the Guardian

Commander, he told me he would remain in the castle. He was certain that Walter wouldn't march through the Land of Fire and waste men to take Stonegate. However, Jarin didn't want to take the risk. He confided to me that he would stay guarding the castle while he sent some horsemen to watch over the Road of Elves in Elmor. If the Guardians see Walter's army approaching, Jarin will rush to Wirskworth to help us."

Syrella nodded sharply. "I've never understood how the Guardians of the South managed not to owe allegiance to Elmor! Stonegate is the only independent place in its land."

Sophie smiled grimly. "I hope we make it, with or without the Guardians."

They remained silent for a few moments, and it was then that Syrella made a strange connection. "My father used to tell me that the God of War and the God of Souls are twin brothers—the two sons of the God of Death who always fought in search of supremacy. My father believed that in the Battle of the Gods, the God of War won and so his brother has sought revenge for thousands of years. I think that soon the two gods will face each other again. The protector of Elmor and the protector of Gaeldeath cannot be absent from a battle between Walter and I."

"I've never heard of the Battle of the Gods," Sophie said.

"The children of the first two gods fought for dominance of their world in this battle. The battles between the God of War and the God of Souls are legendary."

"Let's hope the God of Souls gets his revenge, this time."

"I hope so, too... This will be his best chance," Syrella stammered and prayed that the battle would come to a better end than the one at Forked River.

The Lord-Slave

Velhisya couldn't see well in the dark as she rode her mare slowly behind the men ahead of her. They'd been travelling for nine days, and they'd tried to reach Vylor unseen. A forest close to the city was the best way to achieve that, and they had used the path that crossed it to arrive quietly in Goldtown. Riding a short distance ahead, Giren scanned the darkened cold landscape. Velhisya secretly admired him for his courage in undertaking this mission. She wanted to express her admiration, but nevertheless, they hadn't exchanged many words on their journey. Their company was taciturn, their only goal was to free Selwyn and return to Elmor alive.

Goldtown would appear along their route at any moment. Velhisya often thought about the Governor of Vylor. Syrella had said that Liher Hale was a hard and brutal man, and that he had taken over the rulership of Vylor by promising to ally with Walter—the very man who had condemned his older brother to death. The council of Vylor had accepted Liher as their new governor immediately after the death of his brother. The men of the Black Vale may have adopted Thomas' decrees, but their choices were always based on the traditional male line of succession.

Velhisya was certain that Walter would soon change several of King Egercoll's decrees, but not all of them. Rumours in the kingdom abounded that Walter had promised many lords that he'd once again let them have hundreds of soldiers under their command without taxes. That would allow them to return to their castles. Furthermore, he'd promised them that he'd reinstate the traditional male line of succession for positions of office in Knightdorn. Syrella and Velhisya were certain that all of that would never happen. Walter would keep the soldiers subservient to him and the governors since he'd be able to control them more easily that way. Moreover, the trade in the cities was very strong now and the lords would decide not to return to their old castles, even if they had enough soldiers under their command.

Walter knew the truth. He'd made promises about things that would now hurt the lords, and they would reject them in the end. Velhisya believed that Walter would only restore the male line of succession for the king's office. The governors would continue to be elected after the death of their predecessors. If any governor betrayed Thorn, he and his house would lose every right to power once and for all.

For a moment, she thought about how ruthless Walter was. He had violated Thomas' laws even against his own father when he'd taken the rulership of Gaeldeath from him and then killed Robert Thorn in the Battle of Aquarine. Robert had gone to his son's troops requesting a truce and Walter had murdered him.

Many times, human cruelty had nauseated Velhisya. She thought she was different. It was as if her soul couldn't bear the malice and hatred she saw around her. Torture, beatings, and rape repulsed her. She couldn't ever imagine causing so much pain to another being.

My nature must be different, she'd thought countless times as she observed other humans.

Velhisya looked at the moon in the sky. Her father had told her that the elwyn race was much purer than the human race. It was the only race that was created from within the Light of Life. She felt this purity existed in her soul. However, though she felt different, she didn't find any of the other powers of the elwyn within herself. It was as if *purity* was the only thing she had inherited from her mother's race.

As her gaze shifted, she caught sight of a flicker—a flicker different than that of the stars. She squinted, and then saw the outline of the city they were looking for in the distance. The torches in the turrets on the wall of Goldtown gave off a soft light into the black veil of night.

"We'd better rest here. We mustn't get any closer to the city," came a low voice. Ivar was the best warrior amongst the twenty soldiers in the company, and he knew every region in the kingdom.

"Alright," she said and dismounted her mare under the trees. They'd agreed that they shouldn't get near the wall of Goldtown any sooner than they had to. If the guards spotted them, they would all die.

She and the rest of the men looked for a place to tie their horses. A little further off, Giren was doing the same. Velhisya wondered if the man was afraid. His role in their plan was both the most pivotal and the most dangerous. She often felt panic at the thought of what they planned to do. It was the first time she had ventured far from the safety of Wirskworth or tried to carry out such a daring plan.

She tied the reins of her mare to a tree and spread a woollen blanket on the frozen ground. Soon after, she grabbed a piece of bread from her leather bag. She ate ravenously as she watched the soldiers throw their swords and armour to the ground. She wasn't armoured, and she wasn't skilled with a sword, so her role on this journey was different. Velhisya had never imagined herself in the position of commander, yet things had gone well so far. Now she felt more confident that they might succeed in freeing Selwyn.

Giren quietly approached her. "Would you like some fruit, my lady?"

Velhisya gave him a fleeting glance and held out her hand. The young man offered her an apple and some grapes.

"Thank you," she said.

"I hope we'll be successful and get back to Elmor as soon as possible," Giren said.

Velhisya studied him in the dark. "Are you afraid?" she asked.

Giren was expressionless. He sat down slowly by her side and ate a grape. "Yes... However, I won't let that stop me."

"Because you're brave."

The young man smiled. "I've been called many things in my life, but *brave* has never been one of them."

Velhisya felt a tinge of sorrow—she knew his story. "I'm sorry about all you've been through, Giren. You didn't deserve any of this."

"Thank you, my lady."

"Do you remember your parents?" Velhisya asked, but immediately regretted it. Giren's face had darkened.

"Yes... I was a child the last time I saw them, but I remember them. I remember my mother's eyes and my father's smile. I even remember my sister's cries. She was just a baby the last time I saw her. These are some of my fondest memories. Unfortunately..." His voice broke. "I recall other things, too... I remember my mother running with my sister in her arms towards a fishing boat, trying to get away from Tahos. I remember her being panic-stricken as she pulled me by the hand."

Velhisya didn't know this. "Your mother tried to sneak you away?"

"Yes," Giren said.

"And what happened?"

The lad seemed stupefied. "We were running towards a small ship that was to take us to the Ice Islands. Just before we reached the port, I slipped out of my mother's hand and ran back to the city. I wanted to find my father and convince him to leave, too... He'd told my mother to sail away from Tahos and save our lives. However, his place was with his people. My mom was screaming my name, but I ran away, trying to find my father. Tahos was burning to the ground, and I could hear screaming and cries everywhere. I ran through the city, seeing blood and death, until I found him..." His eyes welled up with tears. "He was kneeling in front of Walter, who cut his head off. Then, Thorn's men hung the headless body on a spike and left it outside the castle of my House."

Velhisya couldn't imagine the pain that a child had felt faced with this sight. She felt her eyes growing wet.

"I tried to run away, but Walter's soldiers caught me, and with the help of a few men of Tahos, they found out who I was. Eric Stone became Governor of Tahryn, and I became the *lord-slave*—that's what I was called all these years."

"You're more of a lord than all of them, Giren. You're braver... You're a better person."

The young man raised his eyebrows. "I heard that you also lost your father a few years ago. Is your mother alive?" he asked.

Velhisya felt an emptiness within her as she thought of her parents. "No... The only time I saw her was when I was a baby. My father took me from the place where she lived. Her land was unfit for a baby. My father raised me in Elmor until he passed away. Many hated him for what he'd done—hated him for loving a woman different to humans."

"So, it's true... Your mother was an elwyn."

Velhisya nodded. "My father... a lord of the House of Endor lay with an elwyn, a creature that was cursed by fate and the gods."

"That's all nonsense... I'm sure your mother was an honest and courageous woman, just like you."

"I don't know that I'm courageous," Velhisya said.

"You're trying to save Selwyn instead of staying hidden in your city. You are braver than most in the kingdom. Don't let anyone make you forget who you really are."

She lifted her head and looked him in the eyes. "I hope that one day you'll take Tahryn back from those who stole it. But, even if you never accomplish that, you must know that you're always welcome in Elmor, Lord Barlow."

Giren's face shone as he got up and bowed slightly. "You must know that I will always be by your side, Lady Endor."

He moved away and lay on a small blanket a few feet away. Velhisya watched him thoughtfully. *Why did the good people of this world have to suffer so much?*

Pain and Freedom

Elliot stared at the golden flames as they danced before his eyes. The cold of the night was biting, and he drew as close to the fire as he could. There were other fires along the hillside, and he could make out thousands of elves trying to warm themselves near them. Elliot was jealous of the elwyn—they were lucky they couldn't feel the chill of the night. It was the coldest night he remembered on the mountain.

He looked at the two elves by his side. Alaric and Alysia were shivering, even though they were dressed in wolf furs—Alysia moved towards Alaric and clasped him tightly, trying to warm him up. He returned the embrace. Elliot wanted to help, but he didn't know how.

"I can give you my cloak," Elliot said, looking at them. He was freezing too, but he felt responsible for these creatures imprisoned on the mountain.

The two elves turned to him. "We thank you, but we want you to stay alive...The cold will kill you. You must go to the cave to stay warm," Alaric said.

"And you?"

"We're used to the cold," came Alysia's voice.

Elliot wanted to insist, but he knew that he wouldn't convince Alaric or Alysia. The elves may have been small-bodied, but they were some of the strongest creatures he'd ever met.

Elliot was aware of how tired he was. He'd trained with Alaric for hours that day. He thought of taking a few sticks and lighting a small fire in his cave to make his sleep more comfortable, but he felt guilty.

The Elder Races had granted him a cave, while the giants and elves had endured the torture of the cold for centuries. Elliot had hoped he could help them carve new caves, but he had been told it was dangerous. Aleron and Alaric had explained that every time they had tried it in the past, landslides had occurred. Thus, the Elder Races had decided to sleep in the open air of the mountain, while the four kids in their settlement used the only two caves that were hospitable. In the last few days, the children had been squeezed into one, so Elliot could sleep in the other. Something within him demanded that he remain out in the open and face the cold—that he face the torture his ancestors were responsible for.

"Why are you here?" came a familiar voice.

Elliot turned to the right and saw Aleron approaching. "I'm keeping Alaric and Alysia company."

"I'm sure their company is pleasant, but they are more resilient against the cold than you are."

Elliot glanced at the elves. "I'm not sure that's true."

Aleron sat next to the fire. "Humans and elves have the same tolerance to frost. However, Alaric and Alysia are used to the cold. You, on the other hand, grew up in a village in the southern part of the continent."

"I'm a trained knight... I can endure the frost."

"Naturally... However, it would be a great waste to lose your life to it."

Elliot didn't answer. He turned his gaze away from Aleron and two large figures came into his field of vision. The giants, Adur and Aiora, were sitting by a large fire trying to keep warm. They seemed to be suffering from the cold.

"I thought giants always lived in the North beyond the North... I expected them to be able to tolerate the frost," Elliot said.

"They can brave the cold, but when they're hungry they become weak. It's the hunger combined with the cold that's making them suffer!" Alaric snapped.

"The centaurs will be bringing supplies soon," Aleron spoke.

As time passed, Elliot felt guiltier. However, there was nothing he could do to help, and soon he would have to leave to return to Elmor and fight alongside his friends. Elliot wouldn't forget the Elder Races. If he managed to defeat Walter, he'd return to the mountains and try to free them again. A strange sound brought him out of his reverie. For a moment he thought he heard the whistle of the wind, but the sound was different.

"Hurwig!" Aleron said, and Elliot turned to his right.

The white hawk was flying towards them, its wings flapping in the wind. Hurwig landed awkwardly on the ground and took small steps. Elliot reached out and stroked his little head. The hawk closed its eyes at his touch. His feathers were frozen. Elliot was sure it had really struggled to reach the mountain in the freezing cold.

Hurwig must have been trying for days. A scroll was wrapped around his left leg.

Elliot took the letter. He unrolled the scroll, and it was then that a smaller one fell into his fist. He read the large letter as fast as he could and then he opened the smaller one. A cry of surprise escaped his lips before he could hold it back.

"What has happened?" Aleron asked.

"It's Walter... a wyvern has bonded with him," He felt scared uttering these words.

Many eyes fixed on him. Aleron looked bewildered while Alaric and Alysia momentarily forgot about the cold.

"That's impossible... Perhaps Reynald is lying. Perhaps he's loyal to his old lord and wants to mislead you," Alaric said.

"No. Why would he write something like that if it wasn't true? This news would result in Elliot and his allies being better prepared. Walter wouldn't want the news to reach their ears... He'd want to mount an attack on the back of a wyvern without anyone knowing," Aleron said.

Elliot agreed with him. "Reynald wrote nothing about that on the large scroll," he told them. "He only said all of this in the secret letter. Walter didn't want me to know about it."

"How can it be possible?" Alysia asked.

"My suspicions were correct. Walter has challenged some of the most profound laws of nature. I don't know how... but something has changed in his body," Aleron said with an expressionless tone.

"That's very dangerous," Alaric said.

"I know," the aged elwyn said, looking at the elf.

"How will I stop Walter with a wyvern by his side?" Elliot asked, terrified.

"I don't know." Aleron's forehead furrowed.

"We are doomed, my people and I." Elliot felt himself panic—a panic he hadn't felt since he was a child.

"Does Reynald know how he succeeded?" Aleron asked.

"No... He hasn't managed to find out anything more. In addition, a wyvern hastened to bond with Anrai, but Walter ordered him to distance himself from it. Soon after, Anrai went missing from the camp. No one knows where he is. That's what it says in the letter."

Aleron covered his face with his palms.

"Anrai? The son of Ador and Emy?" Alaric seemed puzzled.

"He's on Walter's side—one of the men of the Trinity of Death," Elliot said.

The two elves looked stunned. "Did you know that?" Alaric asked, looking at Aleron.

The elwyn lowered his gaze and nodded.

"Why didn't you tell u—"

Aleron's expression was guilt-ridden. "Because it doesn't make any difference, Alaric! The Elder Races already have so many cares of our own—many more than Anrai's fate. None of us could help that child... No one could protect him. I'm sure he grew up angry at what his father did to his mother and hating the Egercolls. Most children can't hate their parents, so I assume he blamed the curse for Ador's deeds and took Walter's side by trying to destroy the Egercolls once and for all. He followed the path of revenge and hatred, and no one could protect him from it!"

"Why didn't Walter let Anrai bond with a wyvern?" Alysia asked.

"Because he's afraid of him. He knows Anrai would be dangerous astride a wyvern. Thorn may have killed him as soon as he saw that he was able to bond with one of those creatures. Maybe that's why Anrai went missing from the camp," Aleron said.

Alysia frowned. "Then why did Walter keep him by his side all these years? He's a giant. They were always able to—"

"He didn't know," Aleron said, cutting her off. "He's half-human... The only half-human and half-giant ever to exist. Walter may have hoped that the wyverns wouldn't bond with someone like Anrai. Then, he could keep him in his ranks; Anrai is undoubtedly a mighty soldier. However, now he knows that Orhyn Shadow runs through Anrai's veins. If Walter killed him once he found out the truth, he wouldn't want news of his assassination going around in his camp just before the battle in Wirskworth. He would have had to explain why he killed such a powerful soldier. Such incidents bring discord, and Walter doesn't want his men distracted."

"Walter bonded with a wyvern... That means that Orhyn Shadow flows in his veins, too," Elliot said, the words heavy. He trembled from more than just the cold.

"That's impossible," Alaric said.

Aleron sighed. It was obvious he had no answers. That scared Elliot as much as Reynald's letter did.

"We have to do something, Aleron. This is mighty power for a human to have. It's very dangerous," Alaric went on, raising his voice. A few elwyn and elves sitting close to them turned their faces in their direction.

"Aremor believed the same thing about the Egercolls and pegasi, and look where that got us," Alysia told her beloved.

"The bond between the Egercolls and the pegasi was a bond of nature itself. Walter tamed a wyvern and that's against every law of nature," Aleron countered. "I can't understand how he managed to do something like that..."

"It doesn't matter how. What matters is that he's now unstoppable. He has a huge army and a wyvern. No human can stop him. We don't have the powers of the elwyn and the elves," Elliot said. "He could be in Wirskworth riding his wyvern even as we speak. Right now, he could be attacking my people."

"Walter won't attack alone. Even on the back of a wyvern, an arrow would be enough to kill him—it would be too dangerous for him to attack alone."

"You don't know Walter..." Elliot said with some irritation.

"I know more than you think," Aleron responded.

"Walter is like Magor the Terrible! His thirst to kill anyone who opposes him is great, and it wouldn't be impossible for him to take advantage of the element of surprise and attack Wirskworth on the back of a wyvern in the middle of the night. He's vicious and reckless," Elliot told them.

Alaric laughed. "I don't know whether Aleron knows Walter, but you don't know Magor at all. That giant may have spread death everywhere, but he wanted what was best for his race. His dream was for giants to rule the world. He may have been cruel and made some bad decisions, but he never killed the giants who opposed him. He was never like Walter."

"Walter never cared for anyone, human or otherwise. Magor would have given his all for his race," Alysia added.

"Perhaps then you should have shown mercy and taken him hostage instead of killing him!" Elliot snapped.

"He may have deserved to die, but the elves never killed him!" Alaric cried. "That was just a myth the giants spread around. None of us know what truly happened to Magor. If we had killed him, we would never have hidden his body. We would have given it to the giants to be purified by fire."

Elliot wasn't sure whether he believed him.

"Magor was reckless. It wouldn't have been unlikely for him to attack a city alone in the dead of night on the back of his wyvern. However,

Walter has never been reckless. On the contrary, he has always been Althalos' most cunning yet careful apprentice," Aleron said.

"Even so, it doesn't matter. My people are doomed! I'm doomed!" Elliot said, crumpling the letter in his fist.

Aleron looked troubled. He opened his mouth to say something when a cry shook the air. Elliot turned in fright as more cries reached his ears. Aleron jumped to his feet and took off running toward the cliffs with Alaric and Alysia following close behind. Other elwyn and elves stood and looked around. Elliot chased after Aleron, and heard the raised voices more clearly.

"AIORA! AIORA!" Elliot heard Adur's voice booming in the distance.

Elliot searched for the giants by the fire where he had seen them earlier, but they weren't there. He continued to run after Aleron and the elves until they reached a cliff.

"AIORA!"

He looked around, and spotted Adur was on the edge of the cliff, screaming. Aleron spoke in an unknown language and the giant turned to him. Elliot could see the tears in his eyes.

"SHE JUMPED. SHE COULDN'T STAND IT ANY LONGER. I TRIED TO HOLD HER BACK! I TRIED!"

Adur's voice was heavy and full of pain. Elliot had never heard the giants speak the Human Tongue before. Tears streamed from Elliot's eyes, as Aleron, Alaric, and Alysia cried as well.

"SHE'S DEAD. GONE FOREVER. SHE LEFT WITH SO MUCH PAIN."

"She's free now, Adur... She's free now—she'll never feel pain again," Aleron said.

Adur let out another cry as thousands of elwyn and elves began to gather around them. "SHE LEFT ME. SHE COULDN'T TAKE IT ANY LONGER!" his words were choked by his tears.

"She'll be by your side forever," Aleron said again, his voice full of sorrow.

Adur glared at Elliot and pointed a shaking finger at him. "HE'S TO BLAME. HE AND HIS ANCESTORS ARE TO BLAME FOR OUR FATE. YOU'LL DIE. YOU'LL DIE FOR WHAT THE EGERCOLLS DID!"

Elliot knew he was speaking Human Tongue for him. He knew Adur wanted him to understand every word he said.

"Elliot isn't responsible for any of that! He didn't unleash the curse!" Aleron shouted.

"I DON'T CARE! STEP ASIDE!"

"No!" came Alaric's voice as he raised his sword, its blade flooded with a red light.

"IF YOU DON'T GIVE HIM TO ME, I'LL KILL YOU ALL. SOMEONE HAS TO PAY FOR MY RACE BEING DECIMATED! SOMEONE HAS TO PAY FOR AIORA!"

"Elliot isn't the one who has to pay!" Aleron said.

"Why not? The centaurs have tried to help us all these years. What have humans done? What have the Egercolls done? They only came here to ask for help when they needed us! This Egercoll said that *we* betrayed his House when he arrived here. He came to the place where my whole race died, demanding help. He wanted to free us only for his benefit while he dared to accuse us of treason! It's time for you to learn the taste of treason!" screamed the giant.

Adur made a run for Elliot, and it was then that dozens of swords were raised before him, their blades filled with light.

Agonising pain surged through Elliot. He felt responsible for everything. He couldn't bear this torture any longer. From the moment he was born, he had had to bear the responsibility for everything that had happened in the world, and the weight had become too much.

"You're right, Adur. I deserve to die," he said, looking at the giant. Elliot pushed past the few elwyn behind him and started running.

"Elliot!"

Aleron's voice had a tinge of terror to it, but he didn't care. He didn't care about anything any longer. Elliot barrelled through the crowd standing in his way. He wanted to die, unable to find any meaning in his life. His friends were doomed, and he had failed. He'd failed to help them; he'd failed to accomplish anything. And now he was responsible for the death of a giant—a giant that had fallen into the void. He should have found a way to free them, but he wasn't worthy. He was the same as his ancestors. Elliot had travelled to this place only for his own selfish purposes without ever having understood what Manhon Egercoll had done to the Elder Races. He'd dared to speak about treason to creatures that had been imprisoned because of his House.

Elliot now knew that his House had to be destroyed. Perhaps this was the only way—perhaps if every human with Egercoll blood in his veins died, the curse would break. The Egercolls had to be destroyed. and he was ready to help with this purpose.

Elliot's lungs burned with every breath of cold air, wishing to get as far away from the Elder Races as he could. He wanted to be alone until he found the strength to put an end to his miserable and worthless life. Adur's gaze twisted his guts. He imagined himself on a mountain alone with the woman he loved—on a mountain where all the humans had put an end to their lives. And then, his beloved also jumping into the void, leaving him alone in the world to embrace death.

Tears froze along his cheeks as he ran. Elliot's foot caught on something, and he lost his balance. His face hit the cold ground, and his hand tore on something sharp. He lifted himself up slowly, feeling dizzy. He turned to his right and saw a big branch—the object he'd tripped over. His hand had got torn on its pointed edge.

Elliot tried to move and noticed something strange gleaming a few feet away. He advanced slowly and his gaze fell upon the grave of Aremor. He didn't know how he'd gotten there. Elliot hadn't been back to the tomb since his visit with Aleron; the gravestone shone under the moonlight.

He stumbled towards the resting place of Aremor, and his eyes fell upon the letters that had been engraved in the centre of the grave—the letters he was unable to read. *May you one day be freed*, he said to himself, remembering Aleron's words.

Elliot walked around the grave, and he tripped again on something hard. He managed to keep his balance, and he looked down. His mouth half-opened. He'd stumbled on the Sword of Light.

Why did Aleron leave it here again? Elliot took hold of the hilt and raised it high. The blade gleamed as the light of the moon fell on it.

Elliot looked at his father's old sword with mixed feelings. This weapon was responsible for everything that the Elder Races had been through. It was the only object that belonged to Thomas Egercoll—the only thing of his father's that he'd ever held. A screech caught his attention, and he looked up high. Hurwig was flying over his head.

"Go away—you're free," he told the hawk.

Hurwig landed on the ground and looked at him with its black eyes. It was as if it could feel his pain and didn't want to leave him alone at that moment.

Elliot looked at the sword again and knew what he had to do. *This is the most fitting way.*

"Put the sword down, my lad."

Elliot hadn't expected to hear Aleron's voice. He turned and met the elwyn's stare. "No."

"Elliot... You must list—"

Fresh tears stung his eyes. "It's over, Aleron. I've failed."

"You're making a mistake."

"You won't change my mind. I failed to save Morys, failed to help the queen, and failed to help all those who had faith in me. Even when I came to the Mountains of the Forgotten World, I failed from the very start. I came here just to find allies. I came thinking that the Elder Races may have deserved their fate. I didn't think of the pain that existed in this place—I never thought of anything else but myself."

"It doesn't matter, Elliot."

"It doesn't?" Elliot muttered.

"No one was born wise... The only thing that matters is that you've changed—that you've managed to understand. As long as you can change and become better, there'll always be hope," Aleron told him.

"It makes no difference now," Elliot said.

"It does... You're our only hope."

"I'm the reason Adur is the last giant in the world. I'm the reason that Aiora died consumed by pain!"

"No... You didn't unleash the curse. As for Aiora, she's now free, and you did everything you could to help her."

"I think I now know how to break the curse, Aleron." Elliot swallowed as he looked back at the sword. "If the blood of the Egercolls vanishes from this world, the curse will be broken. I can't take the lives of those who are left with this blood, but I can take mine."

"You're mistaken."

"It's the only way... Soon Sophie will die, and if one day Walter dies too, you'll be free once and for all."

"That's not the way, Elliot," Aleron said, desperation entering his voice.

"I think it is, but, even if I'm wrong, I don't want to live anymore. I can't do it! I can't carry the burden I've had on my shoulders since I was born, and I can't live knowing I've failed."

"Elliot..."

"I may not be responsible for the curse, but it's my blood. My blood is responsible for the fact that a giant lost the love of his life. I can't live with this blood in my veins, Aleron. You were right," Elliot said. "If I felt the pain of what the Elder Races went through, it would kill me. You were right from the very start."

"Lower the sword," the elwyn told him.

Elliot looked at the blade with courage. "No... This is the most fitting way to end things. This sword symbolises the suffering of the Elder Races, but at the same time it is the only thing left to me by my father."

"Don't do it, Elliot." Aleron's voice was full of grief. "Your death will bring us nothing but more pain."

"Perhaps the centaurs misread the stars... Perhaps the male Egercoll that would be born during an alignment of the moon and the sun had to be sacrificed so that the Elder Races could be freed."

Tears streamed from Aleron's starry-blue eyes. "No... You don't have to sacrifice yourself."

"Goodbye, my friend..."

Elliot lifted the sword and turned its point towards his belly. He closed his eyes and prepared to thrust his sword downward when another scream pierced his ears. His eyelids flew open. A white creature streaked across the heavens, large wings brushing the clouds.

"What's that?" he asked.

Aleron didn't speak. He looked at the sky with a strange look. A look of awe.

The creature approached at great speed, and Elliot backed away from the grave. Thindor looked like he was about to land with force, but his steps were light as his hooves touched the ground. He lifted his head and his golden eyes looked Elliot over. The pegasus trotted towards him and stopped in front of him. Elliot didn't know what to do and remained frozen in place, unable to believe what he was seeing.

"Bring the sword before his eyes," came Aleron's voice.

Elliot raised the Sword of Light in front of the creature's irises. Thindor took one more look at him, then bowed before the blade. Elliot's heart had stopped as a small tear fell on the metal. The blade of the Sword of Light filled with blue light, and Elliot nearly lost his footing. He brought the sword in front of his face and looked at the light that shone on its blade. A few moments later, it went out, and the hilt of the weapon took on a peculiar warmth.

"I-impossible," he stammered and turned to Thindor.

Thindor met his gaze and turned his body, his wings opening with a powerful gust of wind. Elliot moved aside, trying to avoid the pegasus as he rose into the sky.

Elliot was stunned. "What happened?" he asked. "Have I become the rider of Thindor?"

Aleron seemed lost, too.

"I don't know... However, I'm sure of one thing. You're the master of the Sword of Light. Now, you can put an end to the curse."

Elliot swallowed and turned to the grave. He lifted the sword, and then a mighty power rose within him—a power more intense than anything he'd ever experienced in his life. Elliot felt the aura of thousands of spirits in his body, and a million souls flooded his with love. It washed over the agony that had been eating him alive for days like a soothing current. He brought the weapon before his eyes and stared at the grave for a few moments before bringing the sword down with all his might.

The blade struck it, and a light poured out from the cracks in the centre of the stone, nearly blinding him. Elliot stepped back, covering his face. He heard a strange sound that seemed like a long, deep breath. He peered through his fingers and saw a disembodied figure hovering over the grave with arms open wide. Aremor's soul hovered in the air for a few moments and vanished.

Elliot searched for Aleron and saw him a few yards away, his expression baffled. "What happened? Did I succeed?" he asked.

Aleron stared at the spot where his brother's spirit had been, and then he started running away from the tomb. Elliot took off after him, trying to catch up with him. Aleron ran with an unexpected speed for his age, and Elliot had difficulty in keeping up.

Did I succeed? Are the Elder Races free?

They went on for some time until the familiar slope came into view. The fires were still burning, but now something had changed. Countless figures were embracing each other. Elves and elwyn wept, shedding tears of joy. They ran around while a few howls reached his ears; Elliot could have sworn they were howls of delight. They continued for a while until an elwyn found Aleron.

"Aleron! We're free! We're free! I feel it, everyone feels it!"

The elwyn hugged Aleron, and a moment later they stepped towards the centre of the slope. Elliot followed them, looking around.

"Aleron!" came another voice. "Erin's gone."

Elliot instantly remembered the night he'd seen an elwyn trying to find the courage to jump off the cliff. A limp figure was lying before them. Elliot recognised him immediately, and tears rolled down his cheeks. Finally, he had succeeded in sending Erin into his beloved's arms.

"His Light went to find that of Eshina."

Aleron leaned over Erin and caressed his face while tears ran down his face. Elliot watched the sight, touched, until a roar shattered the celebrations. Several figures turned their gazes to the sky, and Elliot saw a monster above them—a monster with Adur on its back.

"Protect Elliot!" Aleron shouted, jumping in front of him.

Adur brought the wyvern near them. "I don't care whether he broke the curse. He's mine!" the giant shouted.

"No!" Aleron yelled.

Elliot raised the Sword of Light as the wyvern opened its jaws and made a sudden move in his direction. He tried to run to the right when a beam of blue light hit the wyvern in the face. The monster flew away, letting out a cry of pain. He turned his gaze and saw a dozen elwyn raise their swords. The light from their blades had become one, aiming at the wyvern. The monster swayed in the air as another beam of light hit its body. This beam was red. The wyvern roared and flapped its wings mightily to try and escape the assaults. Countless beams of light struck it again and again, forcing it to turn and flee until Elliot could no longer discern it in the sky.

The Oath of Truth

The sun rose in the sky next to a long, strange-looking cloud. Elliot squinted at it, the shape reminding him of a goat. He rubbed his eyes, feeling tired; he hadn't been able to sleep the previous night. He remembered himself trembling by the fire with Alaric and Alysia. That seemed to be from another life—a life when the Elder Races were enslaved by the curse and he was feeling guilt-ridden.

Elliot sighed wearily. No matter what he'd achieved, Aiora's visage still haunted him. Breaking the curse should have eased his guilt, but he couldn't get her and Adur out of his mind. He remembered the helpless look on Adur's face after the loss of his beloved, his howls and cries still echoing in Elliot's ears. Elliot wasn't angry with the giant for attacking him. He knew he deserved it. Even though he'd freed the Elder Races, he deserved to die. He'd failed to save Aiora.

Elliot believed that Adur would rush to find Walter. *Maybe he'll take Thorn's side, but I can't be sure of that, since Walter's mother was an Egercoll,* Elliot thought. Such a thing would normally have terrified him, but all he felt was numb.

His gaze wandered to the sky again. He suspected that Adur probably didn't care about Walter's mother. Walter Thorn had renounced whatever connected him to the Egercolls throughout his life. He was only a Thorn, ready to destroy the house of pegasus once and for all. Adur wanted revenge, and Walter—the only man with a tiger from the north and a wyvern at his side—could give it to him.

How am I going to face Walter and a giant riding wyverns? The thought swirled around his mind, but the events of the previous night stopped him from panicking.

Thindor had torn the heavens and wept upon the Sword of Light Elliot had been holding, and thus, he'd broken Manhon's curse. Elliot wondered whether he had become Thindor's rider since the pegasus hadn't appeared again. Moreover, he hadn't the faintest idea whether the elves and the elwyn would choose to help him. He'd thought of speaking to Aleron, but after all that had happened, he and his tribe deserved some peace.

Body stiff, Elliot stood and cast a look around the deserted slope. He'd felt the need to be alone and had left the elwyn and the elves who were celebrating their freedom. Elliot headed to his cave, thinking that as soon as he woke up, he'd have to set off on his return journey to Elmor. Walter would soon attack, and he had to return to his friends. His mission to the Mountains of the Forgotten World was complete.

As he neared the cave, Elliot noticed two figures walking towards him. He tried to make out their faces more clearly, but his sight was blurred from weariness. They got closer, and he recognized Aleron and Alaric.

"We've been looking for you for some time now," Alaric told him.

"I wanted to be alone," Elliot replied.

"You're looking the worse for wear," Aleron said.

"I need some sleep... I'll be leaving for Wirskworth before nightfall."

"You won't leave alone," Aleron said curtly.

"What do you mean?" Elliot asked, thinking he had misheard the elwyn.

Aleron smiled. "You know what I mean."

Deep down Elliot knew the answer. However, even now, he found it hard to believe. "Will the elwyn fight?"

"Not just the elwyn," Alaric said, his red eyes bright. "The elves trust Aleron, but they trust me too. I told them it was our duty to fight a man like Walter Thorn beside the humans."

"It'll be an honour to fight beside you, Alaric." Elliot bowed, and

Alaric smiled.

"I believe Adur will look for Walter and will ally with him," Aleron said.

Elliot looked at the aged elwyn and wondered if he could fight at such an advanced age. "I know," he replied.

"Unfortunately, Adur's soul was consumed by hatred, and Walter can help him get what he wants," Aleron told him.

"If Aiora were alive, it may not have been like this... Perhaps she and Adur would have stayed out of the war," Alaric added.

"Perhaps... But we'll never know."

"I'm responsible for what happened to Aiora," Elliot said, sadness washing over him.

"No. The sins of one Egercoll don't weigh upon every man of his House," Aleron said.

"I should have succeeded sooner. If I'd felt the pain..."

"No one is born wise, Elliot. What matters is that you changed while Adur, after hundreds of years in this world, can see nothing apart from his hatred."

None of them spoke for a few moments. The distant sounds of the celebrations felt strange against the solemn tension around Elliot.

"I don't know whether we can win. Walter has a wyvern and a huge army... If Anrai and Adur fight beside him, he'll be unbeatable," Elliot said.

"Leave the giants and the wyverns to us," Alaric told him.

"Adur and Anrai are the last giants of the world. I don't want them to lose their lives unless there's no other way," Aleron looked at Alaric and the elf nodded sharply.

Elliot remembered everything they'd said about him. "Anrai may no longer be alive."

"True," Aleron agreed. "It wouldn't surprise me if Walter secretly assassinated him when he realised he could bond with a wyvern."

"If that's so, he might kill Adur too..." Alaric pointed out.

"Walter knows nothing about what has happened here. If Adur finds him, he'll tell him everything. Walter will assume that the elwyn and the elves will fight him. I believe he'll decide to use Adur until he finishes off his enemies, then perhaps kill him."

Alaric looked at Aleron. "He could do the same to Anrai."

"Walter didn't know whether the Elder Races would be freed when he saw a wyvern running to bond with Anrai... Nevertheless, that may be his plan. We can't be sure that Anrai is dead. He may have disappeared from Walter's camp on a mission that hasn't reached Reynald's ears."

"We must be prepared for the worst!" Elliot said. "Reynald will inform me if Adur finds Walter or if he sees Anrai again. I need to talk to him about what has happened here."

"It may be better if he doesn't know. It would be best if Walter didn't expect our involvement in the battle. If the letter falls into Thorn's hands, he'll be prepared," Alaric told Elliot.

"As I said, I am sure Adur will find Walter and tell him everything," Aleron insisted.

"If I don't send Hurwig to Reynald, I won't hear from him. He may be able to tell me how Walter intends to attack and if Adur has allied with him. Any information would be useful," Elliot replied.

Aleron closed his eyes for a moment, sighing through his nose. "Send Reynald a letter and tell him what happened here. Tell him that the Elder Races will fight by your side. However, write that we may not get to the battle in time. Without horses, we need about twenty days to go down the mountain and march to Wirskworth. Even if Walter reads the letter, he'll assume that we'll miss the battle."

Aleron's words knocked Elliot sideways. *How could I have forgotten something so important? Without horses, it'll take too long.* "We won't be in time for the battle. My people are doomed." Elliot began to panic.

"Don't worry. We'll make it," Aleron said.

"How?" Elliot asked.

"Trust me. An alliance is built on trust."

Elliot was tired of secrets and wanted to press Aleron for a clearer answer, but he decided not to quarrel with him.

"If Adur finds Walter, he'll tell him what you would have written to Reynald. So even if your letter falls into Thorn's hands, he won't find out much more. On the other hand, we might find out something important from Karford," Aleron said more to himself.

"I have to send a letter to Wirskworth, too. They know nothing about what has happened. They're only expecting Walter's men to attack. They have no idea about the giant and the wyverns, nor do they know that we'll help them." For a moment Elliot's mind wandered to his companions. *Have they also managed to find new allies?*

"If Adur wants to find Walter, he'll do so quickly. We need to hear from Thorn's camp as soon as possible. Send Hurwig to Reynald, and when he returns, send another letter to Wirskworth," Aleron said firmly.

Elliot nodded. Hurwig was a quick hawk. "How many of the elwyn and elves are able to fight?" he asked.

"There are about ten thousand of us left. Only half of us are able to fight," Aleron said. "However, there's one detail you must remember. There are three thousand elwyn who will fight. Amongst the warriors there are men and women, and many of them are couples."

Elliot half-opened his mouth, perplexed. "If the mate of an elwyn dies, their other-half dies, too."

"Exactly," Aleron said.

"I'll do whatever I can to protect the elwyn and the elves in battle. I'd like to thank you for fighting for humans who betrayed you in the past..." Elliot said and lowered his gaze.

"As for that, it's time you swore an oath."

Elliot met his gaze. "An oath?"

"An oath of truth. We'll help humans, but you and all those who are devoted to you will come to our aid if we ever need you."

Elliot held out his arm to Aleron. "I swear on my parents' memory." Aleron squeezed his hand and nodded with a smile. "Have I now become

Thindor's rider?" the question that had been tormenting him all night slipped from his lips.

Aleron studied him for a moment. "Do you feel any different?"

"What do you mean?"

"Do you feel some strange power within you? Like you can feel more things, hear more, see more? Pegasus riders could see something before it even happened."

"I felt a power. A few moments after Thindor shed a tear onto the blade of the sword, I felt different... However, that power left after a while."

"Interesting. I think when Thindor unlocked the power of the sword, you felt a fragment of his power. Thindor transferred a piece of himself to the blade, so it shone with his light for a few moments. Nevertheless, I don't think you became his rider. He entrusted you with the sword, but nothing more."

"You told me that if Thindor sheds a tear on the sword when it's in my grasp, I'll become his master!" Elliot was irritated. He had hoped he had become the rider of Thindor.

Aleron frowned. "If Thindor sheds a tear on the sword, that makes a being the master of the sword, not his rider."

Elliot's mouth dropped open. "Why would Thindor give the Sword of Light to someone he doesn't want as his rider?"

"I don't know... I didn't think such a thing could happen," Aleron replied. "Perhaps he did it because he wasn't sure you were ready yet to be his rider—it's the only explanation that makes sense. Maybe he felt that for now you should only take the power of the sword. I have no answers, Elliot. Manhon—the only man who became the master of this sword—was Thindor's rider, before this sword was even created..."

"That is unbelievable!" Elliot exclaimed annoyed.

"In theory, it's possible for Thindor to choose someone who isn't and may never become his rider as master of the sword. Nonetheless, I'd bet that as long as the master of the sword lived, Thindor would be without a rider. It would be impossible for him to choose a rider other than the master of the Sword of Light. Pegasi don't bestow anything on more than one being in each of their lifetimes," Aleron said.

"So, I may never get to be Thindor's rider," Elliot said sadly.

"Greed has haunted your soul! Thindor has entrusted you with the Sword of Light. It was the first time he's done that in nearly three hundred years." Anger entered Aleron's voice.

"If I had Thindor, I may have been able to beat Walter," Elliot mumbled disheartened.

"If you're destined to have the last pegasus of the world bond with you, it will be when the time comes," Aleron insisted. "Now, Thindor is in greater danger than ever."

"Why?" Elliot wondered.

"If Adur rushes to Walter's side, he'll reveal that a pegasus is alive... There are seven swords that can take Thindor's life. If humans find out about his powers, they will seek him out, and when they realise that he won't bond with them, they'll attempt to kill him. Moreover, Walter and many others will try to prevent the union of an Egercoll with a pegasus."

"I thought Thindor was powerful. What hope will humans have against him?"

Aleron's gaze was sharp. "The pegasi are not warmongering beings. They follow the orders of their riders, but aren't quick to attack if you approach them. Their nature makes them trusting and friendly. I think that's why Thindor didn't bond with anyone all these years. He wanted to be sure that no one would make him do anything against his nature again."

Elliot sighed wearily. He gripped the hilt of the Sword of Light hanging from his belt. "You told me this sword can't wound its master, and that its blade can light up with Thindor's light."

Alaric scratched his chin and Aleron nodded. "It's true."

Elliot unsheathed the sword and held it up high. He brought the blade close to his left forearm and tried to cut into his flesh. To his surprise, the steel disappeared. It looked like it had entered his hand, leaving his skin intact.

He glanced at Aleron who looked thoughtful. "What's wrong?"

"It's possible that while you've become the master of the sword, it cannot yet absorb the Light of Thindor for you, so it won't light up," said the man.

Elliot didn't understand. "But you said that—"

"I think the Light of Thindor will illuminate the blade for a creature that isn't only the sword's master but also Thindor's rider," Aleron interjected.

"Are you sure?"

"No. But it stands to reason. It would be impossible for Thindor to allow you to taste the power of the Light that lives within him without first bonding with you. This power can't be unlocked with the Sword of Light alone. You need him, too."

Elliot heaved a sigh, wearily. He stared at the sword's hilt for a few moments. "Thindor may have made me master of the sword but that changes nothing. This sword belongs to your race, Aleron. The Egercolls owe it to the elwyn after all that Manhon did."

Elliot flipped the hilt around toward the elwyn. Aleron and Alaric looked at each other in surprise. The aged elwyn studied Elliot, his expression softening.

"You've changed so much..." Aleron murmured. "This sword belongs to you, and you're the only person who has proved worthy of winning it."

Pride enveloped Elliot's soul. For a moment he could have sworn that he saw Althalos' figure among the clouds, smiling down on him.

The Power of Gold

Giren lowered his goblet onto the wooden table, the taste of beer coating his lips.

"I've always said that Goldtown has the best beer in the kingdom," said Eric—a guardsman—laughing.

Giren returned the man's smile and raised his goblet again. It was a wonder how everything had gone so well. He'd ridden to the gate of Goldtown with some wares that same morning under the guise of selling them in the city, and the guards had let him in. Soon after, he'd found out which was the most famous tavern and had rushed to spend the rest of his day there. He'd treated various men to beer and wine, managing to find out the identity of the guards in the dungeons of Goldtown Castle. Luck favoured him when he discovered that a dungeon guard was in the same tavern and he'd struck up a conversation with the man, Euric, treating him to countless beers at the same time.

"You said you're leaving Goldtown for Tahos tomorrow?" Euric asked. Giren nodded emphatically. "I'd never leave a city like this one for the north!"

"Undoubtedly, the brothels and the ale are better in Vylor, but the homeland is the homeland. I also have a son back in Tahos," Giren said.

Euric smiled. He was young and stocky with a broad back, thick hair and light-coloured eyes. He wore a black cloak and leather jerkin, and Giren had seen a long sword hanging from his belt.

"I've never seen you in the city before. When did you start trading in Goldtown?"

"A few months ago. I used to sell my goods in the north, but a friend suggested I come to the Black Vale, and I haven't regretted it! I sold everything for a good price, and I can gather some herbs that aren't available up north on the return trip," Giren told him. "My trip was so profitable, I'll treat you to another beer."

Euric raised his goblet, and Giren clinked it hard. He got up and headed towards a wooden bar.

"Two more beers," Giren tossed a coin at the old man standing behind the counter.

The man took it and hurried to fill two wooden goblets. He placed the foaming cups down, and Giren grabbed them. He felt courage surge through him, and headed back to his table.

"You're very generous, Tom," said Euric as Giren returned.

Giren was afraid that at some point he'd forget the false name with which he'd introduced himself to the guard. "The Goldtown guards let me sell my goods and spend the night in the city. I think it's worth being generous."

"I've never been to Tahos. Is it nicer than Goldtown?" Euric asked.

"It's different..." Giren heard himself say.

"Do you think it would fall more easily in a siege?"

Giren wasn't sure. "The geographical location of Tahos is strange. It can be attacked both from land and from the sea. Nevertheless, the tide would make an attack from land difficult."

"The tide?" Euric didn't seem to understand.

"The tide cuts Tahos off from the land every few hours. So, if an army doesn't succeed in getting past its wall, there's a risk they'll find themselves at the bottom of the sea." Giren's thoughts travelled to Walter; he remembered how he'd managed to subdue Tahos. However, this was of no importance—he had to remain focused on his goal.

"I've never heard of that before," Euric admitted.

Giren smiled. "I think Goldtown is safer. I'd say it has a stronger wall than Tahos."

"I don't think Goldtown's wall is particularly strong," Euric said, drinking a little of his beer.

"I was never taught much about walls and sieges. My brother has always been a soldier and a warrior, not me," Giren continued.

"Is he in Iovbridge now? Word has spread throughout the kingdom that Walter has taken the throne and that the men of the north are marching with him."

"No, he stayed in Tahos. My brother is a stonemason and a warrior. The Governor of Tahryn assigned him a mission, so he didn't travel to Iovbridge. Speaking of which, perhaps you can give me some useful information." Giren held his breath. This was the opportunity he'd been looking for.

Euric sneered. "I wouldn't deny such a generous man anything... What information are you looking for?"

"I've heard that most cities in the kingdom have secret tunnels—tunnels that lead outside their walls. Tahos has no secret passages. Should it one day be sieged, and its army defeated, our governor won't manage to get away."

"He could leave by sea," countered Euric.

"It's difficult to escape silently by sea. Moreover, Tahos may be under threat from both an army on land and from a fleet. A secret tunnel that leads to the land of Knightdorn would be useful."

"You said that the tide cuts Tahos off from the land. It'd be impossible to make a tunnel."

"There's a cave under the water—a cave which nature itself has made. My brother, along with a few more men, has been trying to convert it into a tunnel, but the stone is very hard."

"And how can I be of help?"

"Well... I've heard that there's a secret passage in Goldtown. A tunnel that starts from the Castle of Goldtown and ends outside the city. The ground in Vylor is of the hardest in the kingdom. You may be able to tell me how the stonemasons managed to quarry the stone and make that passage."

Euric lowered his goblet and looked at him thoughtfully. Giren wondered whether he'd given himself away, but he hoped the man opposite him couldn't think straight after drinking so much.

"Very few know about this tunnel. How did you find out about it?"

"The Governor of Tahryn found out from Liher Hale years ago. Eric Stone told my brother that the men of Vylor had discovered a way to quarry such hard rock." Giren hoped he seemed persuasive.

"Liher betrays more secrets than his own men do!" Euric said and started laughing. "I'm not a stonemason, so I haven't the slightest clue about any of that."

Giren chuckled, feeling momentary relief. "Have you ever seen the tunnel? Does it have a high ceiling? I still wonder whether the stone roof is stable or whether there are frequent landslides."

Euric looked at him hesitantly, as if he was trying to decide whether he should say what he was thinking. "I've never been inside it. However, it is in the place I guard," he said.

Giren felt his heart race. He had to keep treating the guard to beer. If Euric was sober, he wouldn't be willing to talk.

"I wish I could see it. Perhaps then, I'd be able to give my brother some valuable information and help my city," Giren said.

"You're not a stonemason. I don't think you'd understand much."

"I've learned quite a bit about quarrying stone. If I saw it, I might understand how the tunnel was dug."

"I'm sorry, Tom, but I can't take you there, especially at this time."

"At this time?"

Euric set his cup down with a scowl. "I shouldn't be talking about it, but so be it..." he mumbled, his words slurring. "This passage is in the dungeons of the castle where the prisoners of the city are kept."

"Have you got any important prisoners?"

The man hesitated. "Everyone in the city knows... Syrella Endor and Sophie Delamere sent an emissary to Goldtown. The son of Peter Brau."

"Peter Brau?" Giren tried to look puzzled.

"He's one of Delamere's most important officers."

"Why did Delamere send an emissary to Vylor?" Giren asked.

Euric shrugged. "I don't know. Guards rarely find out such information."

"What bad luck! Perhaps, if there wasn't an important captive at this time, you could have shown me that tunnel."

The guard looked torn. "Maybe... The cells in the dungeons are usually empty, so perhaps I could have taken you, but now that's impossible. There's only one guard at each watch, but it would be reckless to take you there even if there weren't any prisoners."

"You're right. I'd give you half of my gold if you took me to this tunnel, but you're right to refuse, Euric. You're a man of honour, and honour is more important than gold."

"Half your gold?" The guard's gaze became more focused.

Giren motioned as if trying to shoo away an annoying fly. "It doesn't matter."

"How much gold do you have?"

Giren looked around before he lifted a pouch onto the wooden table and showed Euric its contents.

"Hell's Teeth!" exclaimed the man. Euric brought his goblet to his mouth and gulped down its contents. He pursed his lips and leaned forward, lowering his voice. "You're in luck, Tom... I may have never opened the entrance to this tunnel, but I'm one of the few men in this city who knows where it is. Moreover, I'm one of the few men who has a key to it and can take you there."

"Will you do this for me?" Giren whispered.

Euric glanced around and brought his face close to that of Giren. "My watch starts soon. I'll take you with me and tell the guard I'm replacing that you attacked me and that I've decided to imprison you. Once he's gone, I'll show you the passage and then quickly get you out of the castle."

"Whenever I'm in Vylor, you'll drink for free, Euric," Giren said, grinning. He'd known that a man from Vylor would never say *no* to so much gold. The power of gold was even stronger than the gods in this land.

"Are guards in the habit of imprisoning men there?" Giren asked.

"No... Most of us kill anyone who bothers us. However, it's not unheard of to imprison someone who causes trouble in the city," Euric replied.

"You'll say nothing to anyone about this. You need to be quiet in the dungeons. Delamere's man is the only prisoner, but I don't want him to hear a single thing," added the guard.

"You have my word."

"Give me the gold."

"I'll give it to you in the dungeons. You have nothing to fear. If I don't give it to you, you can imprison me and take it all," said Giren and pulled the pouch of gold back toward him.

Euric pulled away and looked at him, rubbing his chin. "Alright. But you can buy me one more beer."

"Of course!" Giren said, smiling.

He stood and headed back to the wooden counter. He motioned to the old man, and he went to fetch two beers. Giren couldn't believe his luck. He'd managed to get into the city and had exchanged Elmor's gold for Vylor's so as not to arouse suspicion when he showed his pouch. Furthermore, he'd managed to convince the guard to take him to the dungeons. Now, all that was left was to get Euric out of the way as soon as they reached the secret tunnel.

The old man placed two goblets on the wooden counter. When Giren turned to return to the table, he saw Euric talking to a stranger. He hesitantly stepped forward until the guard noticed him. Euric gestured brusquely and the stranger left just as Giren reached the table. Euric smiled, took the beer from Giren's hand, and drank it in one gulp.

"Do you have many friends here?" Giren asked.

"Friends? That scumbag owes me gold, and if he doesn't give it to me, I'll have his head," Euric said. "You bought me so many drinks that I lost track of time. We have to go before I miss my shift."

Giren left his beer on the table without taking a sip—he was already feeling a bit drunk and needed to stay focused. Euric staggered to his feet, swaying, and Giren followed him out of the tavern, praying that luck would continue to be on his side.

Giren followed Euric down the winding staircase beneath Goldtown Castle. His breath clouded in the air and the guard's torch threw orange shadows against the walls. Only a short amount of time had passed since they'd entered the castle, and the deeper they went, the more anxious Giren got. The guards at the gate had looked at Giren with indifference when Euric had claimed that he'd attacked him in a tavern in the city.

They walked a little further until they came to an open door. Euric passed its threshold and Giren caught sight of steel cells in the chamber beyond. For a moment he wondered if Euric would decide to just imprison him and take the gold. Then the rescue mission would fall apart.

"You're late," a voice said as another guard appeared. "Who's this?"

"That's why I'm late." Euric gave Giren a smack across his head. "This bastard attacked me while I was drinking my beer. I decided that he deserved to stay here for a while." The guard didn't seem drunk anymore.

"Well, aren't you kind-hearted, Euric? I would've expected you to kill anyone who dared to attack you." The guard yawned and left.

Giren cast a look at Euric who motioned for him to remain silent. He tried to look at the cells for any sign of Selwyn, but the shadows were too thick to discern what lay behind the bars. A few moments later, Euric leaned the torch against a wall and walked to a place a few feet away from the cells on the right. Giren followed.

"There it is," the guard whispered and stared at the wall.

Giren didn't understand until he saw a hole that looked like a keyhole in the stonework. *Unbelievable. The tunnel entrance is as one with the wall.* It would be impossible for anyone to discern this passage if they didn't know what to look for.

Euric pulled a ring from his belt with a dozen keys on it and selected a rusty one. He stuck it into the keyhole and opened the door, which let out a long hissing sound.

"Look quickly."

Giren walked inside the passage, trying to look intrigued while he studied the tunnel. *Selwyn is only a few yards away*, he thought as he touched the walls of the tunnel and pretended to measure its height.

"Is there another door at the end of the tunnel that leads out of the city?" Giren asked, his voice reverberating off the stones.

"Yes," Euric said.

"Do guards here hold keys to both tunnel doors?"

"The same key opens both doors. You ask too many questions." Euric's whisper sounded like an accusation.

"Many people tell me I'm curious," Giren said quietly.

"Are you done in there?"

"Yes. This has been very insightful," Giren said and walked back to Euric.

The guard closed the door behind Giren and locked it.

"Thank you," Giren said and held out the pouch of gold to the guard. "Here's your payment."

Euric put his hand into the pouch, took a fistful of coins, and stuck them into a small bag on his belt. Giren swore he took more than half, but he didn't care.

"It's time you left," Euric told him and looked around nervously.

"Of course. I don't know how to thank you, Euric."

"By leaving."

"Alright." Giren pulled a small flask from his belt. "One more beer before I go."

Euric's eyes lit up. "I brought you here and you're going to drink this last drink by yourself?"

The ploy had worked. A drunk man who adored ale could never say no to one more drink.

"I've got two flasks with me," Giren said, smiling and pulled out a second flask strapped to his belt.

Euric returned the smile and took the flask. "You're the most generous man I've ever met, Tom."

Drink up, Giren thought. They raised the flasks and brought them to their lips. Giren was about to empty the contents of his when he felt a sharp pain, and then everything went dark.

Velhisya sat up straighter in her saddle and looked at the mounted soldiers surrounding her. She was anxious. They were near the west tower of the wall, hidden from sight under the cover of night. None of them knew exactly where the secret passage was, so they waited in silence. Luckily, Goldtown didn't have many men guarding the corridors behind the battlements of the walls.

The stars danced in the sky, and she hadn't the faintest idea whether Giren had made it. If all had gone well, the man would be appearing soon. *Will we be successful?* The question echoed in her mind.

She kept imagining returning to Wirskworth with Selwyn. If she succeeded, no one would ever look down on her again. However, time was passing, and they'd agreed that they wouldn't wait long. The plan was clear. If Giren didn't show up with Selwyn by the light of dawn, they would make their way back to avoid being caught.

A strange sound brought Velhisya out of her reverie. She turned to the left and heard a thump.

"Archers! Run!" shouted one of the men in her company.

Velhisya pulled the reins of her mare, terrified. She could make out the outline of a man on the ground a few yards away from her. He'd fallen off his horse, an arrow protruding from his skull.

"RUN!" came another voice.

Velhisya saw horses galloping past her, and she kicked her mare into a gallop. She lowered herself against the horse, and it was then that she discerned hundreds of arrows coming towards her. Her mare squealed and lost its footing in the confusion, crushing her left leg as it landed on top of her. She screamed against the pain and tried to free herself. Dozens of voices could be heard around her. Everywhere Velhisya looked, men fell from their horses as arrows struck them. She made another attempt to free herself, as her horse thrashed on top of her, mangling her leg even more. Velhisya couldn't bear the pain and felt a dark vortex enveloping her. She fought with all her might to stay conscious until darkness engulfed her.

The Honourable Hale

Selwyn prodded the man crumpled on the ground again. He didn't move. *What the hell*? He bent over him and pinched him hard on his right arm. The man gasped, and opened his eyes.

"Who are you?" Selwyn asked.

The man seemed scared. He tried to get up, but couldn't; then, he rolled onto his side and vomited.

"They hit you on the head. Try to calm down," Selwyn said.

The man wiped his mouth with his hand. "Where am I?"

"In the dungeons of the Castle of Goldtown."

"Damn! He caught on to me. He took my pouch..." The man searched for something at his waist. "Are you Selwyn?" he asked.

Selwyn was confused. "How come you know my name?"

"Your father, Sophie Delamere, and Syrella Endor sent me to get you out of here and take you to Wirskworth... I thought the plan had worked, but Euric must have suspected me."

Selwyn could hardly believe his ears. He felt compassion for the Queen and Syrella who had tried to save him, but the plan had failed. Death was his only future. "I heard you, but I didn't realise what was happening. At some point I heard a loud sound and a moment later, Euric threw you into the cell. What's your name?"

"Giren... Giren Barlow."

Selwyn couldn't believe his ears. "How did you get here? I know you've been Walther's slave for decades!"

"Your father freed me when he attacked Ramerstorm. Where's the guard?" Giren asked and made another attempt to stand up.

"He left a short while ago after he threw you in here."

Giren managed to stand. "He must have run off to inform the governor. I believe Liher Hale will be here soon. I hope the others are safe."

"Others?"

"I didn't make this journey alone. I was accompanied by twenty men as well as Syrella Endor's niece."

"Velhisya?" Giren nodded. Selwyn never expected the Governor of Elmor to risk her niece's life for him. "Did Syrella send Velhisya to free me?"

"Yes, Velhisya led the mission."

"Where is she?"

"I'm not sure. There's a secret tunnel in these dungeons that leads outside the city wall, near the west tower. Velhisya and the rest of the men were to wait for us there, but we agreed that they'd leave if we didn't meet them soon..." Giren slumped against the wall. "Damn! I thought that the guard had gotten drunk and that he'd slug one last drink and pass out. Then, I'd take the keys and get us out through the tunnel."

"The fact that you're here, trying to get me free, means that Syrella didn't agree to Liher's terms," Selwyn muttered.

"Liher demanded all of Elmor's gold to free you..."

Selwyn cursed softly. "That damned bastard will die one day!"

"Why did he put me in the same cell as you?" Giren seemed puzzled. "All the other cells are empty."

"I've no idea," Selwyn admitted.

Giren stopped short, looking at something through the dim light. His eyes landed on the chair that was nailed to the floor. "What's this?"

Selwyn avoided looking at the chair, his throat suddenly feeling tight. "They've been tying me to this chair every day since I got here. I don't know how much time I've spent in this place..."

"About twenty days," Giren told him, and Selwyn's chest tightened. "Do they leave you strapped to this thing?"

Selwyn swallowed hard. "They strap me down and wrap a fork around my neck... The Heretic's Fork..."

"What?"

"Perhaps, that's why the guard put you in this cell. Liher Hale probably wants to subject you to this torture, too and they need you here with this chair."

"Damned Hales! Filthy sadists!" Giren shouted.

"Liher's brother is a man of honour. He spoke to me the first few days I was brought here. He told me he'd try to swap my guard with his men so that I'd be subjected to this torture as little as possible," Selwyn was glad for that. He still felt pain in his chest and chin from the torture, but he could cope. He hadn't seen Lothar since their last visit, but the man had tried to help him.

"And did he?" Giren asked.

"Yes... However, Euric is the only guard who isn't loyal to Lothar. He always puts on the damned fork. Fortunately, the rest of the guards are devoted to Liher's brother and don't subject me to torture. Otherwise, I might not be alive."

Giren sighed heavily. "Do you have any idea how we can escape?" he asked.

"I don't think we can escape, Giren. Euric will be back soon, and you must be ready for what awaits you," Selwyn said.

Giren approached the bars of the cell door and looked around. "I was Walter's slave for a long time. I've stopped being afraid of torture and death," he said, his voice unwavering.

Selwyn observed Giren's back. "I'm sorry about all you've been through," he said.

Giren turned to him. He was about to say something when footsteps echoed through the dungeon. A shadow loomed on the wall until a man stood in front of the cell.

"You've woken up." Euric's eyes narrowed as he looked at Giren. "Did you think you'd fooled me? Did you think I didn't realise what you were after when you started asking me about the city's secret tunnel?"

Giren remained silent.

"Nevertheless, I was wondering how you intended to get me out of the way... I didn't expect a slender man like you to think he could kill me. Once I saw this, I understood." Euric raised his hand and waved a small flask. "Does it have poison in it?" asked the guard.

Giren didn't answer.

"It doesn't matter. I was sure you weren't on your own. I figured that whoever sent you had ordered others to accompany you to free the son of Peter Brau. Since you knew about the tunnel, I was sure that your companions would be waiting for you near the exit, so I informed the City Guard when we were at the tavern. Vylor's soldiers killed your men, and Lord Hale will soon come here to kill you both. Syrella Endor will pay for her choices!"

"What? Our men are dead? Velhisya is dead?" Giren seemed panicked.

"I will kill you, you fucking cunt!" Selwyn touched the bars of the cell.

The guard smiled.

"One day you too will die, Euric, and that day will come soon!" Giren shouted.

Euric laughed. "If nothing else, you do have imagination. I knew it when you tried to convince me to bring you to the tunnel, pretending to be interested in its architecture. Only a fool would think of such an excuse. You'll soon be dead—you, Syrella Endor, Sophie Delamere, and every other enemy of Walter."

"You are also Walter's enemies!" Selwyn snapped.

"We, however, will survive. We won't fight the new king. The men of this land have always been clever without being foolish rebels!" Euric said.

Footsteps drew closer and Selwyn felt that the end was near. Liher and his men must have arrived. The time had come when he would finally be reunited with his brothers. He was no longer afraid. The days spent in the cell had made him accept that death was a part of life and sooner or later every human would cross its threshold.

"What are you doing here?" Euric's tone revealed his annoyance as he looked to the right.

Selwyn tried to discern who the newcomer was. "When you speak to me, you'll address me as *Lord Hale*." Lothar came into view and stood in front of Euric; Selwyn felt hope rising within him. "The Governor of Vylor requests your presence."

The guard looked puzzled. "My presence?"

Lothar weighed him up. "You know my brother doesn't like to wait."

"But I have to guard the prisoners."

"I'll wait here until you come back."

"But—"

"No talking back at me."

Euric stopped short before he let out an angry huff. For a moment, he looked like he wasn't going to leave, but then he started walking away. His footfalls echoed through the dungeons until they faded.

"We don't have much time," Lothar said and glanced at them. He took a key from his belt and opened the cell door. "You must leave as soon as possible."

Giren had frozen in his place. "What do you mean?" Selwyn asked.

"My brother now knows that the emissary he sent to Elmor is dead or being held captive... Otherwise, Syrella wouldn't have tried to free you by sending him," Lothar said, pointing to Giren. "If you don't leave now, my brother will soon have your heads."

"What has happened to Velhisya?" Giren's voice betrayed his fear. "Is she dead?"

"I heard that Syrella's niece is being held hostage—I don't know anything else. My brother will interrogate her soon."

"We must take her with us!" Giren raised his voice.

"That's impossible. You must leave!"

"No. We won't leave without Velhisya!" Giren insisted. Selwyn admired his courage.

"I can't free her right now, but I'll try to. Nonetheless, you two must leave *now*."

"Your brother will find out that you let us go. He might decide to kill you, and you won't be able to help Velhisya," Selwyn said.

"My brother won't dare touch me!" Lothar replied angrily, his face reddening. "Many in Vylor whisper behind his back about his decision to fight by Walter's side. Walter killed Lain, the first heir to Vylor, and immediately after his death, Liher fought for Thorn. He fought for the man who killed his own brother!"

"I never understood why a man like Lain Hale went against Walter instead of fighting by his side," Giren said.

"Lain hated the Thorns... The First King sent Captain Richard Lamont to slaughter his soldiers who were looting the castle of one of the lords of Oldlands. So, Lain vowed never to fight on the side of a Thorn. What matters is that my brother won't dare to harm me—not after what happened to Lain. That would enrage all of Vylor. You have to trust me!"

"Promise me that no harm will come to Velhisya," Selwyn said.

"I'll try to protect her, but you must also promise me something. You must tell Sophie that not all Hales are like my brother. If ever she should get the chance to avenge Liher's deeds, you have to promise that she won't wipe out the whole of Vylor, that she'll show mercy..."

Selwyn nodded sharply.

"We don't have any more time," Lothar said hurriedly.

Selwyn strode out of the cell, and Giren followed him. They followed Lothar until they came to a wall. The man looked carefully at the dead-end and stuck a key into a hole. Selwyn couldn't believe his eyes. There was a door that was indistinguishable from the stone that made up the wall.

Lothar placed a key in Selwyn's palm. "Take this key and open the door at the other end of the tunnel."

"Thank you." Selwyn knew that without Lothar he would have been dead.

"Hurry!" hissed the man.

Selwyn and Giren started running. A loud noise shook the atmosphere. Lothar had closed the secret door behind them. The tunnel was pitch black, and they continued walking blindly until they came to a dead-end.

"Here it is. We have to find the keyhole," Giren said.

Selwyn groped around the wall, and his fingers found a hole. He put the key inside and turned it. The secret door opened, and Selwyn saw the night sky for the first time in days. He stepped out of the tunnel and felt fresh air fill his lungs. Selwyn locked the tunnel door and was about to run when Giren's hand pulled him by the shoulder.

"What?" he asked, surprised.

Giren motioned to him, and Selwyn turned to the right. A grim-looking man stood a few yards away. He was looking around while a black horse was tied to a stone at his side.

"This is where Elmor's men must have been caught. They've left him on guard in case anyone escaped. They want to guard the passage now that they know we know about it..." Giren whispered.

Selwyn moved silently towards the man.

"What are you doing?" Giren asked in a whisper.

Selwyn motioned for him to be silent and continued walking as quietly as he could. A while later, he grabbed a stone from the ground and held his breath. Selwyn charged at the guard and before the man could turn, he hit him on the head. The man fell to the ground unconscious, a river of blood pouring from his battered skull. He drew the sword hanging from his belt and untied the horse. Selwyn felt pain in every bone and muscle from his torture in the cell, but he managed to climb into the saddle.

"Get up quickly," he said to Giren, who was staring at him in surprise a few yards away.

The lad ran and jumped onto the horse. Selwyn pulled hard on the reins, and the horse tore across the field as the night air whipped his face.

The Last Decision

John stared out at the open sea. The Cold Sea had a strange serenity to it, and he always liked looking at water under the light of the stars. He stood on a small shore, not far from the port of the Grand Island. He fingered an oddly shaped stone and threw it into the sea with all his might. The stone bounced six times before disappearing.

Damn it. Still not enough. He'd never been able to beat the time he'd made a stone bounce ten times before it sank into the water as a child. *Did Elliot make it to the Mountains of the Forgotten World and find allies?*

As much as he tried to forget the boy, the thought of him kept coming back. *Stop thinking of Elliot. You're old now and deserve a quiet life filled with pleasures*, he thought.

Half of him wanted to live a restful life now, complete with whores and wine, but those delights depended on the gold he'd taken from Syrella Endor. He knew his gold would eventually run out, but he didn't care. Elmor's gold was priceless in the Ice Islands and would last a long time. However, a part of him kept reminding him that he had a chance to help someone who might be the only hope Knightdorn had for freedom.

John carried on looking at the sea, trying to empty his mind of all thoughts. Something whizzed past his head out of the water, and he saw the water foaming in one spot in the distance. He glanced around, and his mouth dropped open. The stone he'd thrown earlier on was now a few yards away from him on the shore.

His head snapped back towards the sea. *Who could possibly be out there?*

John hadn't seen anyone swimming near the shore.

He squinted at the patch of frothing water, but he couldn't discern anything. He took off his boots and moved towards the waterline. The water froze the bare soles of his feet as he walked.

"Who's there?" he shouted.

No one answered. John took one more step until something leapt out of the water at him. He stepped back and fell. The freezing water soaked his clothes and the cold seeped down into his bones. He looked up, and the sight astonished him. A mermaid was raising herself up on her thick tail. The human part of her was beautiful, and her body looked as if it were made of silver sapphires.

The mermaid dragged herself across the shore toward him, and he noticed that the scales on the lower part of her body were blue-green with a tinge of purple. He hadn't seen a mermaid for over two decades; only a few from afar in the Sea of Shadows years ago, but he'd never met one of them up close.

"Why are you here?" The mermaid studied him and produced a strange sound as if trying to speak. John realised how foolish his question was. Mermaids didn't speak Human Tongue. "I don't know your language. I don't understand!"

"Heeelp..."

John wasn't sure, but he swore that was the word he'd heard. "Help?"

"They tok our sasters—humns tok our sasters. I've searched for tem for yeers."

"Humans took your sisters? Humans caught mermaids?" John asked, brow furrowed. The mermaid nodded her head, wet locks of hair clinging to her cheeks. "Who?"

The creature clasped its hands, then opened them as if to say it didn't know.

"I don't know how to help you... I don't know who took your sisters." The mermaid produced a strange sound again. "What did you say?"

"Humns will pay!"

"I don't know who took your sisters, but not all humans are to blame! Only those who deserve to should pay!"

The mermaid looked at him with rage, crawled back towards the ocean, and dived back into the water, disappearing from sight.

What the hell?! What just happened? John was baffled. He stood, put on his shoes, and walked away from the water. *Who had dared to attack mermaids and hold them hostage? And I didn't know they spoke the Human Tongue. Mermaids are terribly powerful creatures, so why would anyone want to kill or capture them? Only northerners could have done such a thing.*

Mermaids had lived in the Sea of Shadows and the northern part of the Sea of Men for centuries, and those places were far from the southern regions of Knightdorn. It had to be the work of Walter or his allies. The mermaids didn't know who'd attacked their race, and if they began to flood the seas and attack ships, they would kill an untold number of humans.

I'm now convinced about my decision to stay here and be safe, he thought, shivering.

John knew that the war would end with great suffering, and countless creatures would die in its wake. Something inside him urged him to be on Elliot's side, but he was too old for all that. He wouldn't speak to Begon, and he wouldn't tell anyone that a mermaid had appeared before him. He would remain on the Grand Island, putting everything behind him while living a life filled with joy, women, and wine—a life away from pain and death.

The Yellow River

Valyor snorted and Anrai stroked his head gently as the horse lay next to him. They had been travelling for five days and had made only a few stops to rest up. Anrai was more resilient than his horse and most humans. He might have often hated the nature of the giant that dwelled within him, but he knew that it gave him several advantages.

His eyes fell upon the Yellow River, which had proven to be a valuable source of water since he'd arrived in Felador. He had decided to continue his journey until he reached East Bay. He remembered the merchants of Tyverdawn saying that it was usually deserted here. Thus, it was a good spot to stay while he decided what he wanted to do.

A sigh escaped him. He didn't have the faintest idea what he was going to do. He hated Walter, he hated the Egercolls, and at the same time he didn't want to travel to the Mountains of the Forgotten World. The sun was slowly sinking, giving way to the moon, and he was overcome by a familiar feeling of loneliness. He wished his grandmother were still alive. That would have made him feel so much better. He would have known that he wasn't alone in this world.

A strange sound caught his attention. He turned his gaze and saw nothing but trees. Anrai swore the sound was a figment of his imagination, yet he felt something wasn't right. He got up slowly and grabbed the large sword resting at his side.

He quietly took a few steps, and there was complete silence until a hiss made him start and fall to the ground. An arrow sunk into the trunk of a tree in front of him. Anrai straightened and raised his sword. It was then that he saw another arrow coming towards him. He dodged it quickly and ran for cover behind the trunk of a tree, his horse screaming.

"Who are you?" an unseen voice shouted.

"Nobody!" Anrai replied. "Go away, before you regret it."

"There are twenty of us and only one of you."

"YOU'LL REGRET THIS!" Anrai was furious. There was nowhere he could find peace.

"Kill his horse and surround the tree."

"NO!" Anrai jumped out from behind the trunk.

"Stay where you are!" A soldier with a steel breastplate and a green cloak was standing by the treeline. A dozen men had their bows drawn, their arrows pointed at him while a few more had their swords raised.

"Don't touch my horse."

The soldier approached him slowly. He was tall for a human with a thick beard and blond hair. "What are you?" the man asked.

"What do you mean?"

"I've never seen a man as tall as you."

"I'm half human and half giant."

"You're Anrai! The man from the Trinity of Death!" shouted a young soldier on the right.

The soldiers seemed terrified upon hearing his words and, Anrai felt that many arrows would soon be freed in his direction. "Not anymore," he said.

"Not anymore?" the blond soldier repeated.

"I'm Anrai, but I no longer belong to the Trinity of Death."

"Did Walter kick you out?" the man asked.

"Yes... and I want you to let me continue my journey."

The soldier brought his hand to his chin, clearly troubled. "We can't let him go... He's too dangerous. He may be lying or spying for Walter!" a man on the left spoke for the first time.

"Walter will soon attack Wirskworth. I see no reason for a member of the Trinity of Death to be here," the blond man said.

"Will you let him go? Think about it carefully, Ronald," said another soldier.

Ronald walked over to Anrai. "I'll take you to the governor. She'll decide your fate. Follow us."

Anrai took a closer look at Ronald whose blond hair reminded him of that of Walter. After a moment, he glanced at the rest of the soldiers. He knew he could kill several of them, but he and his horse could die, too. "Alright," he said.

"March forward!"

Anrai sized Ronald up and then a strange thought flashed through his mind. "*She?* Does Felador have a governor, and a woman at that?"

"March on, I said."

Anrai decided to obey. He went to Vaylor and tugged gently on his reins. He was led along by the soldiers with only one question going through his mind. *How do I always manage to get into trouble?*

Eleanor paced the great hall in agitation. One of Thorn's men—one of the men of the Trinity of Death—had been caught in Felador. She thought it was a joke made in bad taste when two guards had knocked on her chamber door with the news. Eleanor had practically run to the great hall when she realised the guards were telling the truth.

She glanced at Andrian who stood a few yards away with a stern expression on his face. "Perhaps we should wake the lords of Felador," she said. She'd thought of informing the high priest the moment the guards had told her what had happened. However, in her panic, she'd neglected to send word to the lords.

Andrian looked at her. "It's not necessary. You're the governor. You can decide his fate."

Eleanor remained silent. The sound of footsteps approaching made her turn towards the entrance of the hall. A dozen guards escorted a huge man whose hands were bound with thick chains. The guards and the giant prisoner stopped short a few yards away from her.

"That's him!" Eleanor exclaimed. "I remember him... I remember him hitting Elliot." She'd seen Anrai's face when he'd momentarily lifted his mask outside Wirskworth.

The captive looked at her in bewilderment. "What are you doing here?" Anrai asked.

"I ask the questions!" Eleanor snapped and took a step forward. "Why is a man of the Trinity of Death in Felador?"

"Why does a companion of Elliot Egercoll answer to the title of *governor* in this land?"

"I told you I'm the one asking the questions."

"And if I don't obey, will you kill me? Do it! I no longer care."

Eleanor watched him carefully. Sophie had mentioned Anrai's name many times before in the past, her voice full of pain. The man had killed countless soldiers of Iovbridge, yet his story was a sad one. Eleanor had heard the rumours about his father and what he'd done to his mother. She'd often doubted whether the gossip was true.

Perhaps his father was just a giant of a man, she thought. However, Anrai's size was such that it seemed impossible for him to have come from humans.

"Did Walter send you to spy on Felador?"

Anrai huffed angrily. "Walter intends to attack Wirskworth and kill Elliot Egercoll, Sophie Delamere, and whatever enemies remain in Knightdorn. Do you believe that just before the battle, he'd send a soldier like me to Felador?"

Eleanor thought the very same, but she couldn't find any answers. "Then, why are you here?"

"Walter sent me on a mission, and I chose to defy him. I chose to leave him once and for all."

Eleanor didn't believe a word he said. "Perhaps I can keep you imprisoned until you decide to tell the truth."

"What other reason could there be for my presence here?" Anrai asked.

Eleanor turned to Andrian. He looked thoughtful. "What mission?" the high priest asked.

Anrai swallowed hard. "He asked me to travel to the Mountains of the Forgotten World and kill the remaining giants," he said.

She couldn't believe her ears. Andrian seemed puzzled. "Why did Walter ask you to do such a thing?" the high priest asked.

Anrai didn't reply. He seemed to be deciding whether he wanted to say more. "He fears that soon the giants will be freed from the curse... He fears that if they're freed, they could destroy him with the help of the wyverns." His voice was tinged with rage and sorrow.

Andrian took a step towards him. "The giants haven't been seen for hundreds of years. Why does Walter believe they'll appear again in the kingdom?"

Anrai turned to Eleanor. "Walter knows about Elliot."

Eleanor's mouth fell open in horror. "Does he know where Elliot is?" The giant man nodded. "How?"

"He had an idea of Elliot's whereabouts, and it was confirmed by Reynald Karford."

"Reynald Karford?"

The prisoner lowered his head. Eleanor never understood why Elliot had chosen to free the former Guardian Commander of Stonegate. Nevertheless, whatever the reason, she didn't think Elliot would have confided his journey's destination to Reynald.

"Where is Elliot? I thought he was in Wirskworth," Andrian said.

Eleanor shot him a look. She hadn't told anyone about Elliot's or her companions' whereabouts.

"Elliot has no chance... Walter is now invincible," Anrai said, ignoring Andrian. "He managed to bond with a wyvern, and he has the largest army in the kingdom. He knows that only the giants might be able to stop him, so he gave me this mission."

Eleanor shuddered. "A wyvern?" she asked, and Anrai nodded. "Leave us."

"Lady Dilerion... This man is very dangerous," one of the guards said.

"He's chained, and you'll be outside the door. If the slightest thing happens, you'll hear my cries and run into the hall," Eleanor said, looking at the guards.

The guards bowed and moved towards the exit. Once they closed the door behind them, Eleanor turned her gaze to Andrian. "Elliot is in the Mountains of the Forgotten World. He wants to free the Elder Races."

The high priest's eyes widened. "What? Who advised him to go there?"

"I think it was Althalos' wish, and Thorold agreed," Eleanor replied.

"If that is true, Althalos had too much faith in this young man. No one has ever been able to break the ancient curse that haunts the Elder Races," the priest said a moment later.

Eleanor didn't know what to say and turned to Anrai. "The information you just shared with us is very important! Will Walter attack Wirskworth on a wyvern?"

"Yes," Anrai said.

"We must send an emissary. We must warn them."

"Walter will be in Elmor before your emissary," the giant told her.

Andrian looked troubled. "How did he manage to bond with a wyvern? Wyverns can only bond with giants."

"I don't know," Anrai said and sighed deeply.

The high priest looked thoughtful for a few moments. "I wonder, did a wyvern try to bond with you...?" he said.

Anrai frowned and began to speak in a voice that reflected his sorrow. Eleanor felt more terrified listening to his words. Andrian hid his face in his fists.

"So, once Walter realised you could tame a wyvern, he sent you on this mission?" the old man asked.

Anrai nodded. "I think he doesn't want anyone left in the world with the power to bond with a wyvern but him. He sent me there to slay or be slain by the remaining giants. Then, Thorn would have murdered whoever stayed alive."

"I'm truly sorry, Anrai," said Andrian.

"So am I," the giant responded.

"You may not have seen the light before, but I think you have now realised that Walter is a man without honour—a man who must die," Eleanor said.

"There's no one who is honourable... Neither Walter, nor Elliot, or anyone else."

"You're mistaken," Eleanor insisted.

Anrai frowned. "Why are you here?"

"Elliot sent me to help this land."

The giant was visibly disconcerted. "And the people of Felador accepted you as their ruler? You're a stranger to them!"

"I'm Eleanor Dilerion! Nevertheless, I wasn't chosen because of that..."

"Why did they choose you?"

"Because of who I am."

Anrai studied her for a few moments. "You're the sister of Bert Dilerion—Sophie's lover. I would never have expected Sophie to send you on a mission with Elliot... It's a miracle you're alive after what happened in Wirskworth."

"The queen didn't send me on this mission," Eleanor said. "Elliot asked me to travel with him, and I chose to follow him. I also chose to listen to him and ride to Felador to help its people."

"And here we are. What are you going to do with me?" Anrai asked.

"Where are you planning to go?"

"I don't know... I'd thought about spending a few days in East Bay. It's pretty deserted, so I'd have time to think."

"I'll give you a choice, Anrai. I could order that you be killed for all the things you did while at Walter's side, but that would make me the same as the new king... I think you're telling the truth. I think you're remorseful of your deeds. So, I'll let you go to East Bay if you wish. However, you can stay in Felador if you want."

Anrai frowned. "If I stay here, you'll ask me to fight for Elliot, and I'll never fight for an Egercoll! I won't fight for the House that condemned the race of giants to eternal torment—the torment that led to my father doing what he did to my mother. The Egercolls are the ones who ought to be damned." His face had gone red.

"I'm sorry about all that the giants have suffered. However, I've heard about your father's deeds and no Egercoll is responsible for those," Andrian said.

Anrai's face contorted with rage. "Had the giants not been imprisoned, my father wouldn't have sought to avenge himself on humans! He wouldn't have raped my mother, and I wouldn't have been born. I'm responsible for her death. The Egercolls have to pay for—"

"You're mistaken!" Eleanor's voice echoed through the hall. "Do you think the Egercolls haven't paid the price? Their House was destroyed, the City of Heavens was filled with pain and death, and Elliot, the last to bear their name, grew up orphaned in a village. As for you, you may feel guilty about your mother's death, but you're not to blame for it. Nonetheless, you *are* responsible for everything you did while you were at Walter's side. Now you have a chance to redeem yourself and help the weak instead of wasting your life seeking revenge."

"I'll never fight for Elliot!"

"You don't have to fight. Elliot sent me here to help the people of this land, and you can help me. Elliot has never forced anyone to fight for him. 'Only a tyrant forces others to fight for him. A true leader doesn't ask anyone to fight for him, but everyone wants to follow him to their death.'" Aleron's words flowed effortlessly from her lips.

"The only way to get over your hatred is to forgive..." Andrian said.

"The Egercolls?" Anrai asked.

"No... your father and yourself. Only then will you find peace for all that you've been through. Remember that your nature isn't only that of a giant. I can see your mother in your face..."

"What do you mean?"

Andrian smiled. "Your appearance is more that of a human than of any other giant I've ever seen."

"You've seen giants?" Anrai asked with a frown.

The high priest nodded, and Eleanor looked at him with curiosity. She'd underestimated him. He'd seen more than she imagined.

"Would you really let me go?" Anrai asked, looking at Eleanor.

"Even if you choose to stay, you'll be free to leave whenever you wish. However, if you betray me, I'll see to it that you suffer a torturous death," she told him.

Anrai smiled. "And if I stay, are you sure you won't force me to fight for Elliot?"

"I'll never make you fight for anyone unless you want to."

The man looked at her closely, curiosity clearly visible in his gaze. "If Walter finds out I'm here, he might become enraged... He might mount his wyvern and hasten to destroy Aquarine."

Andrian scratched his chin. "When you decided to leave Walter once and for all, didn't you want to sneak back to the Mountains of Darkness and bond with a wyvern?"

The giant lowered his eyes. "No... I know wyverns have always been the giants' most loyal companions, but I didn't want to bond with one. I'm also certain Walter had ordered his wyvern to watch over the Mountains of Darkness. If it had seen me approaching, it would have killed me. Thorn is cunning; he must have suspected I might do something like that."

"If you decide to stay here, we'll make sure it doesn't reach Walter's ears," Eleanor told him. "If he finds out the truth, we'll do everything in our power to prevent him from destroying the city. If you help me, I won't desert you. I'll never leave a man devoted to me defenceless."

Anrai looked at her strangely as he furrowed his brow. "Now I understand why the people of Felador chose you as their ruler."

Eleanor remained silent, expecting to hear what he'd decided. The giant man continued staring at her for a few moments before he knelt on the stone ground and bowed his head before her.

A Man Without Honour

Velhisya tried to breathe, but the cloth in her mouth made her nauseous. Her hands and feet were torn, and she felt pain all over her body. She took a brief glance at her limbs—they were tied with thick ropes to the ends of a wooden bed. She felt that the leg her horse had fallen on wasn't broken, but it hurt a lot. She had only been awake for a few minutes and had no idea where she was. She looked around; the room was lit with dozens of candles, and colourful tapestries hung from the walls. She wondered why they hadn't thrown her into a prison cell, and the only answer that came to mind made her want to take her own life, but she couldn't do it since she was tied up.

Giren must be dead. Everyone who had left Elmor to free Selwyn was dead. She knew her end was soon approaching, too. Nevertheless, she feared that the torment she'd be subjected to until that time came would be harrowing.

The chamber door slammed open, and Velhisya tensed. "We tied her to your bed as you requested, Lord Liher."

A man of medium height with curly hair was looking at her, smiling. His eyes were small and fierce, and his beard was bushy. He looked younger than Syrella, and from his belt hung a long sword. Velhisya looked at Liher Hale with hatred.

"I can't believe it... Look how beautiful she is," Liher said, throwing a glance at his men." They nodded in agreement. "The rumours may have been true after all. The brother of Endor may have lain with an elwyn."

"Perhaps she's simply beautiful," a guard replied.

"No. I've never seen such beauty before. Legends say that elwyn-women looked like fairies," Liher said with a laugh that to Velhisya seemed paranoid. "The whole castle has heard that we're holding Syrella Endor's niece. Did she tell you that she's her niece?" Liher looked at the guards again, and they nodded.

"She asked to speak with the Governor of Vylor. I asked her what she'd done with the soldiers outside the city, and she refused to answer," said one of the men.

"We know what she did. She sent that cunt to free Peter Brau's son. The rest waited for them outside the secret tunnel to escort them to Elmor. I can't believe that bastard and Selwyn managed to get away!" Liher's cheeks were flushed with rage.

Velhisya's eyes widened, and his words lifted the sorrow she felt just a little. Liher looked at her and bowed his head.

"I know you didn't expect this. Selwyn got away with one of Syrella's men. But you will never leave Goldtown. Syrella Endor will pay for her choices. She sent a woman of such beauty into the lion's den. I'm furious about what happened tonight, but this will be a good reward for all my woes."

Liher approached Velhisya and she wished her revulsion for him was enough to kill him. Liher reached out, and she felt his fingers brush against her breasts. Velhisya jerked away and the bed's wooden slabs creaked loudly.

"If you dare move again, I'll kill you."

Do it. I would prefer to die than this, she thought.

Liher touched Velhisya's right thigh and reached between her legs. She jolted again and the bed groaned so loudly that it felt as if it was about to break. Liher struck her with the palm of his hand and the cloth flew out of her mouth.

"If you touch me again, you'll die!" Velhisya shrieked, despite the pain in her jaw.

Liher laughed loudly. "You're the only one who will die, Velhisya

Endor. But before you do, you'll keep me company for many nights."

Velhisya spat in his face, and as he raised his hand about to hit her again, the door to the chamber flung open with force.

"What is going on here?" A man entered the room with two soldiers behind him. He was younger than Liher, and his face was red with anger.

"I didn't expect you'd have the audacity to come uninvited into my chamber, Lothar." Liher looked as though he was about to lunge at him.

Lothar. Velhisya remembered that name. Syrella had told her that Liher's younger brother was the most sensible of the Hales.

"What do you intend to do with this woman?" Lothar asked.

"I don't owe you any answers!" Liher snapped. "You freed my prisoners and still dare to come into my chamber?"

"That's not true. They managed to open the cell door and attack me. It was then that they stole the keys to the tunnel. If anyone's to blame, it's Euric, who showed the intruder where the secret passage was, and didn't lock the cell properly. He was also stupid enough to put both prisoners into the same cell."

"Do you take me for a fool, brother?" Lothar didn't speak. "You'll pay for what you did," screamed Liher.

"What do you intend to do with this woman?"

"Whatever I please."

"Syrella Endor sent men to our doorstep to free the son of Peter Brau. What do you think she'll do if she finds out you're holding her niece?"

"Nothing! Walter will be on her land in a few days."

"Walter may not make it there. He may be forced to retreat again and then, Syrella will kill every man in Vylor."

"Syrella Endor won't manage to do anything, even if she attacks my land one day, but you will pay for what you did."

Lothar didn't back down. "Will you kill me, Liher?" he asked.

"I'll think about it!" Liher shouted.

"You may be the Governor of Vylor and bear the Golden Sword of our House, but you won't dare shed the blood of a Hale!"

Velhisya looked at the hilt of the sword hanging from Liher's belt. She hadn't realised that it was one of the Seven Swords.

"If you betray me again, I'll spill your blood. I couldn't care less that you're my brother. Now leave my chamber."

"No... You may be a man without honour, but I'm not. I won't let you rape this woman," Lothar said and took a step forward, his big sword hanging from his belt.

"How dare you talk to me likc that!" Liher yelled.

"If you do, you'll condemn the whole of Vylor to death. I won't allow it," Lothar drew his sword and the men who had accompanied him did the same.

Liher's guards drew their swords, too. The governor looked at his brother with eyes full of rage. Velhisya didn't know whether she'd escaped danger. Her heart pounded so loudly that she swore everyone could hear it.

"If you kill me, civil war will break out in Goldtown. Then again, if you don't kill me and still rape this woman, I'll rise up against you," Lothar said.

"Lower your swords," Liher told the guards.

The men slowly lowered their weapons, and Lothar watched his brother carefully. A moment later, he sheathed his sword in a swift motion.

"Take her to the dungeons." Liher said and turned his gaze to Lothar. "As for you, brother, we're not finished speaking about this."

Velhisya looked Lothar in the eyes. *Even if my aunt burns this city to the ground, I'll remember what you did*. She wished Lothar could hear her thoughts.

The Power of the Thorns

Walter glanced at the people around him as he walked past them through the camp. Several men rose and bowed as he passed by, nodding curtly. The crescent moon and campfires cast a soft glow over the evening landscape. He and his men were now on the Road of Steel and would soon reach the Road of Elves. In less than seven days, they'd meet his allies who were ahead of them, and then, they'd attack Wirskworth and destroy it once and for all. Fate had given him all that he needed to succeed and soon his wyvern would be tearing down the towers of the old elven city.

The last battle was approaching—the battle for supremacy over Knightdorn—and Walter wanted to be alone. Soon, he would succeed in killing his sworn enemies. Sophie Delamere, Syrella Endor, and the only son of Thomas Egercoll would soon meet with a violent death. He wondered if he'd find Elliot in the upcoming battle. He wasn't sure whether the boy had decided to stay in the Mountains of the Forgotten World until he succeeded in freeing the Elder Races. However, something told him that Elliot wouldn't miss the last battle for Knightdorn.

Walter continued walking until he was far enough away from their encampment. His gaze wandered over the trees behind which the moon was hiding. A strange branch caught his attention. It looked like a human hand. He stared at it, lost in thought, until a growl made him turn to the right. He saw Annys padding towards him, and his hand loosened its grip on the hilt of the Blade of Power. The tiger was the only creature he could tolerate when he wished to be alone.

Annys walked over to him, and he stroked her white fur. He remembered the moment he'd seen her for the first time. He was just a boy, and Annys was a cub. She'd approached him one night when he was roasting rabbits, and he'd hastened to pet her. Althalos had told him that the tigers of the north were dangerous, but he had ignored the Master. He knew he was a Thorn and as such, that a creature of the north wouldn't harm him. Annys had sat next to him, and they'd eaten together. Since then, she'd never left his side. He was the only man from the north who had tamed a white tiger in decades. Even Althalos himself couldn't believe his eyes when Walter had appeared with Annys at his side.

A roar brought him out of his reverie. Walter glanced at the sky. The trees obscured his vision, but he was sure he'd seen something flying in the skies—a wyvern with a strange figure on its back.

He started running with Annys close behind. *Who could have mounted a wyvern?! Anrai*? The giant had fled the Mountains of Darkness. *He might have ignored my order and returned to the wyverns*. However, his scouts hadn't caught sight of him anywhere in Gaeldeath.

A soldier stopped when he spotted Walter racing to the camp. "Your Majesty, we saw a wyvern in the sk—"

"I saw it, too," Walter said and brushed past the man.

He looked at the sky and saw the winged creature descending. He got a better glimpse of the figure on its back—a huge man. Walter pushed aside anyone in his path. His men looked bewildered, and he saw some raising their bows at the monster speeding towards the ground. His tent came into view, and Phobos rose from where he had been lying next to it, spotting the other wyvern. Walter stood beside his wyvern and drew his sword while Annys bared her teeth. The second wyvern landed with a loud thud and the dust on the ground scattered. A giant was on its back—one that Walter had never seen before.

"Who are you?" Walter shouted.

The newcomer looked at Walter next to Phobos. He lowered himself to the ground without a word.

Walter tightened his grip on his sword. "Who are you?" he asked again as the giant set foot on the ground. He wasn't going to ask a third time.

"My name is Adur," the giant said in a strange accent.

"How did you find your way here?"

"The curse of the Egercolls has been broken. The Elder Races are free now."

Walter lowered his blade a few inches and looked at the giant in surprise. His men had gathered around them, listening silently.

"Did Elliot break the curse?"

Adur nodded. His words filled Walter with a strange feeling. He wasn't often pessimistic. Walter remembered his mother saying that only a special Egercoll could break Manhon's curse.

So, was Elliot special? "How?" Walter asked.

"How?" Adur repeated.

"How did he break the curse?"

"Thindor made him master of the Sword of Light."

Walter didn't know what he meant by "master of the sword", but something else scared him more. "Thindor? The pegasus of Manhon Egercoll? It's still alive?"

"Yes" the giant told him.

Walter wasn't sure he believed him. It was as if all the legends he'd heard as a child had come to life. "How do I know you're telling the truth?"

Adur took a step forward and thousands of arrows were aimed at him. "I know you're a great man, Walter Thorn. A man with a power that no human has ever had a taste of until today. However, you must broaden your mind if you want to win the last battle against your enemies."

"Legend says that the pegasi were slaughtered with the Seven Swords by the First Kings, and Thindor disappeared when Manhon died. I've heard many say that the pegasi died when their riders passed away," Walter said.

"When pegasi die, they are born again, ready to bond with a new master. Only the Seven Swords can truly kill them. Thindor is the last of the pegasi and has been searching for a new rider for centuries."

Walter frowned. "I've never heard about this. No one alive today has ever seen a pegasus."

"Thindor was in hiding. Althalos knew about him. He's known about all this for a very long time."

Blazing rage rose within Walter. "And did Elliot become Thindor's rider?"

Adur didn't speak for a moment. "I don't think so."

"You said the pegasus made him master of the Sword of Light."

"I wasn't present. In the three hundred years I was in those mountains, I'd heard many times that only when Thindor made a man master of that sword could the curse be broken, and the curse broke."

"Master of the Sword? I always thought the Seven Swords were the deadliest weapons ever made. However, I didn't know one could become their master."

"This is only true of the Sword of Light, which was made from the tear—"

"The tear of Thindor. Yes, I know that story," Walter snapped.

"The seventh sword has more powers than the rest," the giant said.

Walter watched him closely. "What powers?"

Adur frowned. "It cannot kill its master. Its blade becomes intangible when it is about to pierce their body. Moreover, the sword can absorb Thindor's Light. Nonetheless, Aleron used to say that this power might not be unlocked for the master of the sword. Perhaps, one needed to become Thindor's rider in order to use it."

Walter approached the giant. He'd guessed years ago that his old Master had taken the Sword of Light from Thomas Egercoll before his death. Althalos always said that the sword was unique. Walter wanted to steal it from Thomas but had failed. Memories were awakened in his mind—an old legend said that the Sword of Light was the only object that could set the Elder Races free. He'd never believed those stories, and he was probably wrong not to have done so.

He looked at the giant again. "How did Thindor make Elliot master of the sword without the boy becoming his rider?" he asked.

"Aleron told me that if Thindor wept on the blade while it was in Elliot's hands, the boy would become master of the sword," Adur said. "However, this wouldn't make him the rider of the pegasus. No one knew for sure whether Thindor would give the boy that power."

"Who is Aleron?"

"The wisest of all the elwyn."

"Why do you think the boy didn't become Thindor's rider?" Walter wondered.

"As soon as the curse was broken, I tried to attack him. I rode my wyvern and was about to kill him, but the elwyn and elves protected him. Thindor didn't go to his aid. If Elliot had become his rider, he would have protected him."

"How does one become the rider of a pegasus?" Walter never expected to be asking such a question.

"I'm not sure. Aleron believed that a pegasus had to choose you as its rider and then you would feel its powers within you."

"Which are?" Walter remembered hearing the legends about the pegasus many years ago, but he could no longer recall them.

"The Egercolls who rode the pegasi used to say that their senses were heightened and that they could see things before they even happened."

Walter returned the Blade of Power to its sheath and eyed the giant. "I wonder why you're here, Adur. Elliot Egercoll broke his ancestors' curse and freed the Elder Races. I would have expected you to be devoted to him, not to want to kill him."

The giant glanced at Phobos, and the wyvern lowered its gaze. "My race was destroyed because of the Egercolls. The giants couldn't stand the torture of the curse and have been killing themselves over the years. All of them. Even..." He stopped abruptly. "I'm the only one left."

Only you and Anrai.

"I don't care if he broke the curse. I want every human with Egercoll blood running through their veins to die. I want that House to pay for the death of my race, and nothing will save Elliot from my wrath."

Walter brought his hand to his chin. *He doesn't know about my parents.*

"I know your mother was an Egercoll," Adur said, as if reading his thoughts.

"Have you come here to kill me, too?" Walter's hand remained by his sword, and Phobos shifted, sensing his master's worry.

"No. I respect you. You've spent your whole life trying to destroy this House, even though your mother belonged to it. You're the only man I can trust who won't stop until he destroys the Egercolls, and I want to help you. I want Elliot Egercoll and Sophie Delamere dead."

"And if we succeed, then I'll be the last with the blood of the Egercolls in my veins."

"No..." said Adur, and Walter frowned. "The Egercolls always feared power. When they saw that the Elder Races had betrayed them and could make weapons to kill the pegasi, they tried to destroy them. They were afraid because they felt the Elder Races were more powerful than them. The elwyn and elves feared power too; that's why they gave six of the Seven Swords to the Egercolls' enemies despite the giants' insistence that they shouldn't. The elwyn and elves wanted to kill the pegasi—they wanted to have their power dispelled.

"You aren't afraid of power. That's why you never tried to kill the wyverns and why one of them is standing next to you. The Thorns are like the giants. The power of the Thorns lies in their constant desire to attain more power rather than banish it. The only blood that runs in your veins is that of the Thorns."

Silence followed Adur's words, and Walter smiled. The respect the giant had showed him filled him with strength; he had not thought that a giant would think of him in such a way. However, he couldn't let Adur find out about the mission he'd sent Anrai on. There were other things Walter had to consider carefully, too.

This time there is no room for mistakes. "Will the elwyn and the elves take my enemies' side?" Walter asked.

Adur frowned. "I think they will, but they had not sworn to help Elliot before I left them."

"Can I defeat them in battle?"

The giant smirked. "Even if they decide to fight, I doubt they'll succeed. They have no horses. They won't make it to the battle in Wirskworth in time unless you delay the attack."

"They may manage, and if they do, I want to know whether they can defeat me."

Adur looked Phobos in the eyes. "You have a wyvern and a huge army. I'm sure we can win."

"And if Elliot becomes Thindor's rider, can I defeat him with a wyvern on my side?"

Adur's smirk vanished, and he seemed troubled for the first time. "Wyverns are afraid of pegasi. However, you don't need a wyvern to kill Thindor and Elliot. The First Kings killed six pegasi without a single wyvern. All they had were six of the Seven Swords, and I'm sure you're more capable than they were."

Walter looked at his men who were watching the scene in silence. He could feel their awe. A giant had sought him out to fight for him and to tell him he was the strongest man ever to be born.

"I've heard that another man with giant blood is on your side—the only man with giant-blood who wasn't trapped in the Mountains of the Forgotten World. Is he here?" Adur asked.

"No. Anrai is on a mission."

"What mission? I expected him to come to the mountains one day. I expected that he would want to meet his tribe. But he never did. Does he have a wyvern too?" asked the giant.

"Not yet. However, if you'd remained in the Mountains of the Forgotten World, you would have met him soon enough. I ordered him to travel there and seek an alliance with the giants in case the curse was broken. I wanted this to remain a secret, but now it no longer matters."

"Forgive me, Your Majesty, but Anrai didn't ride towards the Mountains of the Forgotten World," came a voice.

Walter turned to see a short, wizened man he'd never seen before looking at him from behind his soldiers. "Who are you?"

"I'm just a merchant," the man bowed. "I sold goods to your men when you were travelling north. A few days later, I saw your horsemen returning southward, and they asked me to sell them the rest of my wares. I was also offered a position as a servant in your army. I had a horse and so I accepted. I'm a man of the north, and I wanted to help my king!"

"What do you know about Anrai?" Walter asked.

"I saw him a few days before I saw your men leaving for the south. He asked me whether I knew in which direction Felador was."

"Felador?" Walter didn't understand.

"Yes." The man lowered his head.

"Perhaps he didn't want to tell you his true destination."

"I don't think so. He could have asked me about the road west of Isisdor without divulging where he was going. I saw him riding towards Felador with my own eyes."

"Are you sure it was Anrai that you saw?"

"He's a man with giant blood in his veins. Wherever he goes, he can't go unnoticed."

Walter remained silent. The merchant had no reason to lie. He'd believed that Anrai was blindly devoted to him, yet something seemed to have changed over the past few days. The giant man's expression was troubled when he'd ordered him to go to the Mountain of the Forgotten World. He tried organizing his thoughts to decide what to do now that he knew everything. Walter didn't realise how quiet the camp had become until Adur broke the silence.

"Since you sent Anrai to request an alliance with the giants, I know you'll let me fight by your side," the giant said.

Walter was silent for a moment before he smiled. He'd found the answer, and now he'd kill off all his enemies once and for all.

Reynald was panic-stricken. He raced hurriedly through the trees under the moonlight, holding a scroll. He wanted to inform Elliot as fast as he could. When he was far enough away from the camp, he stopped and looked around him. No one was there.

"Where are you, damned bird!" he hissed.

A screech made him turn. The white hawk was perched on a branch a few yards away. He wondered how it found him every time he called, and it always managed to appear so quietly.

"So, this is Elliot's famous hawk," came a voice, and Reynald whirled around in horror.

Walter stood a few yards away with a smile on his lips.

"Yes, Your Majesty." Reynald bowed.

"You didn't tell me Elliot had written to you."

Sweat rolled down Reynald's forehead. "I saw the hawk in the sky while you were talking to the giant. I waited to hear what Adur had to say and then hurried to the forest to get the letter."

"Did you get it?"

Reynald nodded. He couldn't lie. There was no letter on the bird's feet.

"Give it to me."

Reynald swallowed hard. He drove his hand into his belt, pulled out Elliot's letter, and slipped the parchment he'd written a moment earlier in its place. Then, he walked towards Walter and handed him the letter. Walter took it and read it while Reynald stood waiting, hoping the king wouldn't suspect anything.

"Interesting," Walter said after a while.

"I would have sought you out to bring you the news. Nonetheless, everything the letter says is what Adur already confided to you."

"Not exactly." Walter said in a low voice. "The giant wasn't sure whether the elwyn and elves would fight for Elliot. However, this letter confirms that they will."

Reynald nodded in agreement. "Be that as it may, they can't stop you."

Walter began to walk round Reynald before he stopped, his eyes going to a point between the trees. "You're right. But if the elwyn and the elves get to the battle on time, they may make it difficult for us. You're aware of the light that floods their blades and their advantages in battle" the king said.

"They have no horses. Even if they get to the battlefield, they'll be exhausted. Set up some archers around the men who will be besieging Wirskworth, and if these creatures come near, they will be killed before they can get to use their swords."

Walter turned to him. "Wise words," he said with a look of appreciation.

Reynald felt his spirit's lift. Walter couldn't possibly know that he'd received Elliot's letter the day before. The boy had sent only one parchment without a secret letter, so Reynald had decided to keep everything he'd found out hidden from Thorn. Reynald had only thought of a reply when he'd seen Adur. Then, he had hastily decided to write only one letter to Elliot.

"What will you write to the boy?" Walter asked.

"Whatever you order me to," Reynald replied and looked down.

Walter stepped towards him. "You've always been a clever and devoted man. I've been lucky to have a soldier like you by my side."

Reynald bowed slightly. "You honour me, Your Majesty."

Walter drew his sword so quickly that Reynald didn't see the blade that tore through his leg. Reynald fell to the ground, bellowing in pain. Walter turned and hurled a dagger toward the trees. A loud screech cut through the air. Reynald saw Hurwig flying away to gain height, his right wing appearing red. Walter hurled one more dagger towards the hawk, but it managed to avoid being hit.

"So be it. That bird won't get far," Walter said, watching Hurwig struggle to fly away. "As I said, you've always been a devoted man, Reynald. Until I killed Alice Asselin."

"What do you mean, Your Majesty?" The pain clouded Reynald's mind.

"You know what I mean... I've always suspected that was why you asked to take Stonegate and leave the Trinity. However, I wasn't completely certain. From time to time, I would send you information that almost no one knew about." Walter looked up at the sky.

"Very few, apart from you, knew that William of the Sharp Swords was spying for me, though you were the only one I didn't trust. I expected you would make a mistake—that you'd tell someone my secrets. If such a thing reached my ears, I'd have proof that you were no longer faithful. I also expected that you would confide your own secret to someone. However, you were careful. I had no proof until I heard that you'd killed William and saved Elliot Egercoll's life."

"Your Majesty..." Reynald tried to find a way to escape. He wasn't afraid of death, but it wasn't yet his time.

"Once I found out that Elliot is Alice's son, I knew, and the moment I saw you in my palace I realised what you were going to say. You were going to claim that you killed William to gain the boy's trust and save your life. In fact, you'd come to spy on me." Walter didn't take his gaze off the sky.

"The day you arrived before me, you said, '*I was curious... I knew that if I saved his life, he would tell me the truth. I wanted to know who'd trained such a skilled warrior, I wanted to know if he was the son of Alice Asselin and Thomas Egercoll*'. No one else would give a damn whether Elliot was Alice Asselin's son. The only thing that mattered was whether he was Thomas' son. I was ready to kill you, but then your words changed my mind. I'd been carried away by my rage and had ignored my logic."

Walter turned to him. "I asked you how you intended to send the boy information. I wanted to know how you would send letters to the

Mountains of the Forgotten World. It was then that you told me about the hawk and gave me an idea. You told me that you were going to give Elliot misleading information to lure him into some kind of trap and take advantage of his trust." The king smiled, and the hilt of the Blade of Power seemed to glow in his hand.

"Your idea was wonderful. All it took was for me to give you false information as well, and then I would be able to lure Elliot into a trap. At the same time, you'd inform me about everything he was doing. I knew that you'd hide the important pieces from me, but you wouldn't be able to only mouth lies. You and Elliot knew that for you to keep your head, you'd need to divulge some truths as well, otherwise sooner or later I'd realise your intentions. My plan was flawless. I would keep you until the last minute and so trick Elliot into doing exactly what I wanted.

"I know what you're thinking. That I may have lost the element of surprise. I could attack Wirskworth with a wyvern without anyone expecting it. However, news spreads quickly through the kingdom, and the enemy's scouts might find out about the wyvern before my attack. So, I chose to keep you close and entrust you with *information* about the tactics I plan to follow in the battle—information that would send Elliot to his death. In addition, I wanted to know whether the Elder Races would fight against me. I believed that if the boy freed them, you'd find out and tell me. As I said, you had to also tell truths to keep my trust."

"You're mistaken." Reynald's words came out in a whisper as he tried to stop the blood that soaked through his trousers. He had to find a way to survive and avenge himself.

"You were always a brave man, Reynald. Don't become a coward in the face of death."

Reynald let go of the wound and looked into Walter's cold eyes. Anger burned in him—anger so strong that it made him forget everything.

"I didn't want to die before I was sure there was someone who could take your life. Now I'm not afraid anymore, because I *know* Elliot will defeat you," Reynald told him.

Walter didn't lose his smile as he stood over Reynald. "Too bad you won't be here to see what will happen to the boy."

"You said that you intended to keep me until the end—to use me. Why did you decide to kill me now?"

"I could tell you... I know you won't talk to anyone. However, I prefer you to die without knowing."

"I'll die knowing you'll be defeated!" Reynald spat out his words in hatred.

Walter frowned. "The giant was wrong. The Thorns' strength was never their thirst for power. The Thorns' greatest merit is that they can see their opponents' weak spots, no matter how well-hidden."

Reynald saw the blade glinting under the light of the stars and felt the cold pain. Blood spewed from his throat as he struggled to breathe. Everything began to go dark until he saw a woman smiling at him in the distance. He knew that smile. Alice Asselin was ready to welcome him into her arms.

Glorified Murderers

Eleanor entered the Castle of Knowledge's great hall in a hurry. She knew that the anticipated meeting with the lords wouldn't be pleasant as she drew closer to the entrance. One of the guards pushed open one of its doors. Eleanor walked inside hesitantly and was taken aback by the sight that awaited her. Anrai's hands were tied behind his back with large chains while the Felador lords and a dozen soldiers stood around him.

"What's going on here?" she asked.

"That's the exact question I have, Lady Dilerion!" Solor snapped.

"Who ordered that this man be chained?"

The other lords seemed embarrassed, but there was a defiant determination in Solor's face. "I did!" he said.

"Release him immediately!" Eleanor shouted, looking at the soldiers.

The men shifted, glancing at each other. None of them moved and they seemed torn.

"Are you sure about this order?" Solor spoke out again.

Eleanor was enraged to see the hesitation on the soldiers' faces. She assumed they were Solor's men. "You and the rest of the lords of Felador gave me the leadership of the region. You swore allegiance to me. Do you deny your oath, Lord Balkwall?" Solor looked like he was about to say something, but decided against it. "If these men don't obey me immediately, they'll be punished."

The soldiers seemed frightened and removed the chains from Anrai's limbs. The giant man brought his hands to his face with an expression of relief.

"We gave you Felador, and you welcomed a member of the Trinity of Death onto our land!" Solor shouted at her.

There was a sound and Eleanor turned towards the door to the hall. Andrian had entered the room, looking dignified in his priestly robes. He glanced at the soldiers around Anrai and then at the lords. "What's going on here?" he asked.

"Lord Balkwall didn't find my decision to allow Anrai to remain in the city wise and decided to chain him."

"Solor!" Andrian's voice was irate as he walked towards the lord. "Lady Dilerion is the Governor of Felador!"

"You went to such great lengths to convince us to give her Felador, and she allowed a man of the Trinity on our land!" Solor protested.

"You've no right to imprison men she lets remain in the city," said the high priest.

"Perhaps it was a mistake to have given her the rulership. You should have remained the Governor of Felador!" Solor spat out his words.

"In every region of Knightdorn your words would be punishable by death. If I'd remained governor, I would have made the exact same decision as Eleanor," Andrian said angrily.

Solor seemed surprised. "This man is responsible—"

"This man abandoned Walter!"

"That doesn't absolve him of his sins. He must die for what he has done!"

"If you can't forgive, Lord Balkwall, take your horse and ride to Thorn's camp," Eleanor said.

Solor stared at her, mouth agape. "Can't forgive? Forgive a murderer who slaughtered an untold number of men by Walter's side? He and the Ghosts wiped out the people of Felador."

"I hadn't been born when Walter attacked Aquarine. I didn't fight in the battle where the men of Felador died!" Anrai shouted.

"You may not have fought in that battle, but you're still a murderer!"

Solor told him.

"All warriors are murderers! All soldiers who fight by the side of any king are murderers. Throughout the Age of Men, men and women have glorified the heroes of war. Nonetheless, all great warriors are nothing more than glorified murderers. I don't want to fight for any king again—neither a Thorn nor an Egercoll. Only if Aquarine is attacked will I fight. I'll fight for the governor who gave me a new home when I had nowhere else to go and who trusted me when she had every reason to have me killed."

Silence followed Anrai's words, while Solor had his eyes fixed on the giant.

"I don't believe a word," came a woman's voice belonging to Lady Iris Alarie. She stepped forward. "A man of the Trinity of Death just decided to leave Walter Thorn one day and live in Felador. Nobody would ever believe such a thing."

"I agree," Solor said approvingly.

Naturally, Solor and Iris would agree... After so many days in the city, Eleanor had discovered that they were a couple. She had to be prepared to argue with them over most of her decisions in the future.

"Walter ordered me to hunt down my own kind. He ordered me to kill the remaining giants in the world," Anrai said. "After that, I decided to get away from him once and for all."

"Walter wants to kill the remaining giants? But there are no more giants in the kingdom!" Iris responded.

"A man with giant blood stands before you, Lady Alarie, and no one knows how many more remain in the Mountains of the Forgotten World," Andrian told her.

"Do you believe the legend about the curse and the Elder Races?" Solor looked at the high priest.

"Leave us." Eleanor looked at the guards circling Anrai.

They nodded and left the hall. Eleanor heard the door close and turned to Solor.

"The legend of the curse is true, and Walter fears that if the giants are set free, they may be the only ones who can overthrow him. So, he sent Anrai to kill them, and that was when he decided to leave Thorn once and for all."

Solor frowned. "Even if all of this is true, why is Walter now afraid of giants? If the legends are true, the giants would have been imprisoned in these mountains for centuries."

"There's a possibility that the Elder Races will be set free soon," Eleanor told him. "Walter knows about this and wants the giants out of the way before they are able to oppose him."

"How will they be freed and who will set them free?" Solor asked.

Eleanor remained silent. She knew that whatever else she said would bring about more questions. She wouldn't say a thing and had asked Andrian and Anrai to keep their mouths shut too.

"You ask us to trust you, but you refuse to tell us what you know," Iris said.

Eleanor looked at her with what she hoped was a pointed expression. "I have nothing else to share with you."

"If Walter finds out he's here, he might get angry and decide to kill us all. Thorn punishes those who betray him," Solor said, pointing to the giant.

"We'll keep it a secret," Eleanor said.

Solor burst out laughing. "I'd say it's not easy for him to go unnoticed when Aldus Morell and his men guard Felador. If they find out about him, the news will reach Walter."

"Neither Lord Morell nor his men will find their way to Aquarine. Felador's harvests are outside the city," Eleanor replied.

"Does Morell guard Felador?" Anrai asked.

"I swore to him that if he does, I'll give him most of the crops in the region. That way, he doesn't have to look for them on my land," Eleanor said.

The giant snorted. "He was always cunning and greedy."

"Do you think no man of Morell's will find out the truth about a man of the Trinity hiding in Felador?"

Eleanor looked Solor in the eye. She knew it was risky, but she was sure she would find a way to hide the news.

"If Walter attacks the city because of me, I'll leave. I'll make sure he finds out I left," Anrai said.

"I don't trust you," Solor countered.

"Naturally. However, you have to trust your ruler. You shouldn't disobey her orders again. Something tells me that next time, she won't spare your life."

Solor glared at Anrai and turned to Eleanor.

"Anrai will remain in the city. If Walter finds out and decides to attack us, we'll deal with it when the time comes. This matter is considered closed," Eleanor told the lord.

Solor was enraged at her decision, but he didn't speak and began leaving the great hall. The rest of the lords did the same.

"Lord Balkwall." Solor stopped and turned to look at Eleanor. "Don't take a man I've decided to host in the city captive ever again." The threat was blatant in her voice.

Solor reddened but nodded curtly and left the room with the rest of the lords behind him.

"I think the lords will soon rise against me." Eleanor looked at Andrian. They were the only three left in the room.

The high priest frowned. "They won't. I'll talk to Solor... If he wasn't so hotheaded, he might have taken over the rulership of this place years ago," he said.

"And now you'll forgive me, Lady Dilerion. Some matters demand my attention in the city temple." With these words, the high priest bowed curtly and left the hall.

"I wonder why you want me in Aquarine. I expected that you would have wanted to kill me, too," Anrai said suddenly.

Eleanor sighed. "I've told you before that I'm not like Walter. A true leader should know how to forgive. If only all the men fighting for Thorn could see the truth about him, just like you have."

Anrai smiled. "You have hope in your soul, Eleanor. Nonetheless, as long as men crave power, there will be those willing to destroy everything to attain it. Most of the soldiers fighting for Walter don't want to see the truth. All they would ever want is his power, and if they had it, they might have carried out worse deeds than him."

"I don't believe that. I'd like to believe that there aren't, nor will there be, many men like Walter. I'd like to have faith in people."

The giant carried on smiling. He probably thought she was naive.

"The nobles are right... If Walter finds out that I'm here, he might destroy the city. We'll have to quickly spread the word that I've gone before he attacks, but even then, his rage may be unstoppable."

"With a little luck, the news won't reach his ears. He might take no notice of us even if he finds out," Eleanor said.

Anrai looked thoughtful. "I think that once Walter destroys the last of his enemies, he'll hasten to attack Felador, whether he finds out that I'm here or not. The reason he left this region ungoverned and ravaged all these years was to sow fear. When he no longer has enemies, he'll want to give this land to some man who is loyal to him, and whoever opposes him will die. However, I believe that if you hand Felador over to him peacefully, you'll save your lives. Even if he finds out I was here, he may not hurt you if he takes the city without a fight," he said.

Eleanor closed her eyes wearily. "Walter could even destroy the city out of sheer boredom. If he decides to attack, you're free to leave."

"I'll leave only if he takes Felador without a fight. If you choose to fight, my sword will be yours."

"Will you truly fight for me?" Eleanor hadn't believed him when he'd blurted it out the first time.

"You're the only person who reminds me of my grandmother. Perhaps, if you stay alive, I will find hope again, too."

Eleanor regarded him with bewilderment, feeling a momentary affection for him. "I want you to do something for me," she said. "Few soldiers have remained in this land. I want you to teach our young lads how to fight."

"I thought you wanted a better world without battles and death."

"I don't want soldiers to siege and destroy cities but to protect my land and my people if Walter attacks Felador."

"Aren't you afraid of what he could do to you if he besieges the city? I'd have expected you to want to run away if—"

"I'm no coward! I'm the Governor of Felador, and my place will always be next to my people!" Eleanor said, back straight and gaze unwavering.

Anrai smirked. "My grandmother would have adored you."

His voice softened whenever he spoke of his grandmother. "What happened to her?"

"She died." Sadness coloured Anrai's tone.

"I hope you get a chance to pay tribute to her memory by my side."

Anrai watched her for a few moments. After a while, he bowed and walked away without saying a word. Eleanor could have sworn she'd seen a tear rolling down his face.

The Secret Ally

The morning sun was strong, and Elliot's woollen clothes made him feel hot under its bright rays. He couldn't remember such a hot day since he'd travelled to the Mountains of the Forgotten World. He walked cautiously as he went down the mountain, his blue cloak billowing behind him. The gentle breeze felt like nature's medicine as it cooled his face.

Elliot stopped and looked around. Thousands of elves and elwyn were descending the mountain with him. The heat may have made his mouth feel dry, but he was glad that the rain and freezing wind hadn't accompanied them over the last few days. The cold didn't affect the elwyn, but he and the elves would have had difficulty going down the mountain in wintry weather.

How are we going to get to the damned battle in time without horses? Elliot thought with a huff.

The elves and the elwyn had had little sleep over the last few days, trying to descend the mountain as fast as they could. He knew they were in a hurry to get to the battle. Aleron had sworn that he'd help him, and Elliot knew that the old elwyn took his oath seriously.

"Don't stop. We're almost there," said a female voice.

Elliot turned to his right and saw Alysia. Her cheeks had taken on the same red colour of her eyes. Alaric smiled beside her.

"I was thinking..." He stopped mid-sentence, unable to find the courage to say everything that plagued his mind.

"This is no time for discussion. We have to get down the mountain!

Do you want us to lose the battle in Wirskworth?" Alaric winked at him and continued the descent with Alysia following close behind.

The sun was getting lower in the sky. The wind grew stronger, and Elliot's knees hurt the longer they walked. He stopped to catch his breath, and he caught sight of Alaric and Alysia a few yards ahead of him. For a moment, he wondered where Aleron was. He hadn't seen him over the last two days. It was as if he'd disappeared. Elliot wanted to talk to him about everything that was weighing on him. However, even if he did see the elwyn, he didn't know whether he'd find the courage to do so. His friends needed him, and if he returned alone, he wouldn't be able to help them. Walter had a wyvern and an enormous army. If Adur had joined Thorn, they'd have to fight against two winged monsters.

Aleron won't change his mind, no matter what I may say. Elliot believed in Aleron's honour, but something inside him was afraid. He wiped the sweat off his forehead and started walking again.

Twilight made its appearance, and Elliot's eyes blurred from exhaustion. Suddenly, he felt the ground flatten. He raised his head and looked around, trying to take in where he was. The landscape was still rocky, but he was in the foothills of the mountain.

"We did it!" Alysia shouted. Nearby, Alaric seemed happy.

Elliot looked back and saw streams of Elder Races reaching the foot of the mountain.

"Soon we'll be ready to set off for Elmor," Alysia said.

"Where's Aleron?" Elliot asked.

"I don't know, but I'm sure he's here somewhere. I know he was ahead of us," Alaric said, and his red eyes bored into him. "Is everything alright, Elliot?"

"I have to talk to him."

"I'll help you find him," Alaric said sharply.

Elliot nodded and they started moving through the throngs with Alysia close behind. It was crowded at the foot of the mountain as the elwyn and elves that descended waited for the remaining tribes to arrive before they began their journey to Elmor.

"Aleron must be ahead of the crowd. Perhaps, he wants to speak to his people before we set off for Wirskworth," Alaric said as they searched through the crowds.

Elliot couldn't see Aleron anywhere.

"Look! There!" Alaric said, pointing ahead.

He followed Alaric's finger and saw a gaunt old figure. Aleron was watching the crowd coming down the mountain, looking pensive. Elliot strode towards him.

"I've been looking everywhere for you," he said.

The aged elwyn turned slowly. "Are you afraid we won't get to the battle in time?"

Elliot frowned. "Yes," he admitted. "But that isn't all I fear."

Aleron watched him closely, waiting for him to continue.

Elliot hesitated. "You have no armour. Walter's men will be armed, ready to lay siege to the most powerful city in the world. Even if we reach the battle in time, I fear the elwyn and elves will get slaughtered. With no horses and no armour, Walter's men will butcher you."

"I thought you wanted us to help your friends," Aleron told him.

"I don't want your demise. I didn't set you free so that you'd all die," Elliot said, paying no heed to the consequences of his words.

Aleron scoffed. "I've told you this before, Elliot. You've changed." His starry blue eyes showed hints of affection and admiration.

"Don't worry about us," Alaric said brusquely.

"You're a great warrior, Alaric, but if a group of archers attacks us, we won't have time to even reach Walter's men."

"Remember what I told you. You have to trust me." Aleron winked at him and looked up at the mountain.

Elliot followed his gaze, and something caught his attention. Along one of the mountain paths, hundreds of elwyn and elves were pulling great big carts. He hadn't seen them before since he had been ahead of the group every day of their journey.

"What are they carrying?" Elliot asked.

"Armour. Breastplates, mostly," Aleron replied.

"Armour?" Elliot couldn't believe his ears. "Made of Aznarin?"

"Aznarin is extremely valuable and hard to come by. We only use it to make swords—our armour is made of plain steel," Aleron explained.

"I didn't expect the elwyn and elves to have any armour!"

"Elwyn never made armour until a few centuries ago. Nevertheless, the elves forged some great plate armour just before they fought against the giants," Alysia said as she stood next to Aleron.

"And did they carry them to the Mountains of the Forgotten World?" Elliot didn't even want to contemplate climbing those mountains armoured.

"No. The elves left their armour in Iovbridge before they set off for the mountains. George Thorn destroyed it since elves are shorter than most humans and it would be of no use to him," Aleron said.

"And so how did this armour get here?" Elliot asked.

"We've lived in these mountains for three centuries. There were forges and mines full of steel before the big earthquake, which destroyed them. Many years ago, we decided to make new armour. Trust me, it's better than those humans have," Alysia said.

"One could say you were preparing for war," Elliot replied.

"For years we feared that the curse wouldn't be enough to quench Manhon's hatred. We feared he would attack us again. While trapped by the curse, the elwyn made armour for the first time with help from the elves," Aleron told him.

"And the giants? Did they make armour, too?" Elliot asked.

"Giants don't need armour. Their hide is adequately thick. However, thanks to our generosity, Adur is the only giant with a blade made of Aznarin. With this sword, on the back of a wyvern, he'll be truly dangerous." Aleron looked across at the mountain again. "The descent would have been difficult if the elwyn and the elves were armoured, so we decided that the strongest amongst us should pull carts laden with armour to the foot of the mountain."

"I agree. Nevertheless, the armour won't be enough if the archers attack us. We won't easily manage to reach Walter's soldiers without horses," Elliot said.

"I told you that you have to trust m—"

"I do trust you, Aleron! However, my faith in you doesn't..." A strange noise made Elliot fall silent. He turned and looked towards the plains stretching beyond the Mountains of the Forgotten World. He could have sworn he heard horses' hooves thudding against the ground.

"What's that sound?" he asked.

Aleron's eyes sparked. "Hope."

Countless creatures appeared on the horizon. Elliot could have sworn his eyes were deceiving him. Thousands of horses were running towards them, with a cloud of dust being kicked up behind them.

"But how?"

"Do you remember what I told you about the centaurs?"

"About the centaurs?" Aleron was smiling, and a sudden realisation hit Elliot. "Some horses and hawks obey them!"

Aleron nodded approvingly. "I'm sure that even Adur has forgotten this truth."

Elliot understood what he meant. Walter wouldn't find out about this. "Do the centaurs know what's happened? Will they fight for me?"

"The centaurs know a lot more than you think. Whether they'll fight or not, I have no idea. However, they don't need to be on the battlefield to help you. Many times, the help we're looking for is different than the help we need."

Elliot was moved. Countless creatures had chosen to help him while deep down he felt he didn't deserve it. Not yet.

Suddenly, Aleron took him by the shoulder. "Whatever happens, don't ever forget to hope, Elliot. Hope is the cradle of life."

The Insanity of Power

Syrella sat by the fire in her chambers, the flames warming her and filling her with a sense of optimism. She threw a glance at Sophie sitting on her right as the woman sipped a goblet of wine. She had never expected to be spending her nights with Sophie Delamere, but now she felt that she'd found a true friend in the queen. Syrella couldn't remember having any other friends in her life.

"What do you think Walter will do to us if he takes the city?" Sophie asked.

"He'll have his men rape us, and he'll have our heads on spikes outside the Temple of the God of Souls," Syrella replied, frowning.

Sophie scoffed. "What would you do to him if we managed to win?"

Syrella hadn't expected this question. "I've never liked torture. All I want is his death. Then, I'd sleep peacefully for the first time in decades."

Sophie looked troubled. "I've always wondered why powerful men chase power. Walter lives for the battlefield. If he destroys all his enemies and sits on the throne, he'll kill himself out of sheer boredom. I can't imagine him ruling and listening to the requests of the people."

"Men like Walter don't know what to do with power. All they care about is getting it," Syrella told her with a smile. "Once Walter has no other enemies, he'll start making new ones, until he even kills the Trinity of Death itself. Power drives most people crazy, particularly those who are as powerful as he is..."

A knock came from her chamber door. "Damn," Syrella muttered and got up to answer it.

"Your Majesty, a scout wants to talk to you. He says it's urgent," said one of the Sharp Swords out in the hall.

When she opened the door, her eyes landed on a flushed young man behind the Sharp Swords. Syrella wondered how a scout had worked up the courage to come to her chamber at such a late hour. She nodded sharply and the lad entered the room as she closed the door behind her.

"What's wrong?" she asked.

"Your Majesty... I've been watching Walter's armies from afar. In about four days, they'll be in the city," he said.

"Have you come to my chamber in the middle of the night to tell me things I already know?" Syrella was irritated.

"Your Majesty, I saw something else too—something that couldn't wait until morning."

"What did you see?"

"A monster arrived at Walter's camp, and on its back was another huge creature."

Syrella's brow furrowed as she tried to process the scout's words. "A monster? A huge creature? What do y—"

"A wyvern and a giant are in Walter's camp."

Her goblet fell to the floor, and Sophie's voice was strained. "What?"

The young man swallowed hard. "I think they'll attack the city with Walter's forces."

Eleanor had stood in front of the fountain for a long time. Its deep waters were blue-green under the light of the moon, and the sky was filled with stars that night. Two people could stand on each other's shoulders in the fountain, and their heads would barely break the surface. Her brother used to talk about the huge fountain in their homeland, but she'd never imagined that she'd see it up close. Now, she couldn't take her eyes off it. She remembered feeling like a small child the first time she'd seen it. At its centre was an elaborate statue of the First King of Felador. She looked around at the gardens that stretched out ahead only a short distance from the Castle of Knowledge. It was her favourite part of the city.

"I've never seen a bigger fountain," said a voice.

Eleanor saw Anrai heading towards her. "Me neither," she admitted.

"I may have admired the gardens around the Palace of the Dawn when I was in Iovbridge, but Aquarine has a unique beauty."

Eleanor nodded. "Why are you herc?" she asked.

"I couldn't sleep, so I decided to take a walk. I like the sound of water—it fills me with a sense of peace."

She frowned. "I never expected that the sound of water could bring a sense of peace to someone like you."

Anrai seemed puzzled. "Why?"

"You were a member of the Trinity of Death... Only murders bring a sense of calm to those kind of men."

The giant's jaw tightened, and his nostrils flared, but he didn't respond.

"I'm sorry, but the rumours about the Trinity are so terrifying that I'd expect nothing could pacify any of their members, apart from killing," she added.

Anrai let out a weary sigh. "I can't say that the rumours are unfair. Short Death is one of the most bloodthirsty and dangerous men in the kingdom, and it's no accident that Brian, the Sadist, has that nickname."

"And yet you stayed by their side for years."

"Don't judge me."

Eleanor felt it was a plea. "Did your grandmother ever find out you had become a member of the Trinity?" she asked.

Anrai's face darkened. "No. The grief would have killed her if she'd found out. My grandmother would always tell me that the path of hate and revenge only brings pain," he said.

"And she was right."

The man let out a weary breath. "I was never able to follow her words.

I always felt she wanted to hold me back because she was afraid—she was afraid of what I might do."

"Few people get a second chance. Don't waste it."

The man didn't answer, but only nodded curtly. "I know your parents died in the Battle of Aquarine. Do you remember them at all?" Anrai asked.

Eleanor felt sad. "Sometimes I dream of their faces," she said in a low voice.

"And that man whom Short Death crippled? Was he your friend? He tried to protect you when you were caught by Walter's men."

The thought of Morys filled her with pain and rage. She remembered Anrai standing outside Wirskworth when she'd been stripped.

The giant watched her face. "I'm sorry, Eleanor. I'm sorry about what happened that day."

"Walter's men stripped me, and Walter himself was about to cut off my breasts. Morys tried to help me and you... and you..."

"I can't change the past... I've done terrible things that will haunt me for the rest of my days. All I wanted was to destroy the House of Egercoll and I didn't care what I or Walter's men did to achieve that. I was wrong..." he muttered and lowered his gaze.

Eleanor looked away from him. She may have tried to be fair, but his face roused a venomous hatred within her.

"I've never met a ruler like you in all my life," the giant suddenly said.

"Someone as weak?" she asked.

"Someone with compassion. No leader I've caused pain to would have accepted me into his ranks. I've hurt people you love, and you accepted me without my giving you the slightest thing. You accepted me without asking me to fight for you. Even now, when I see the hatred in your eyes, you won't ask your men to kill me. Any other ruler I've met would have had my head on a spike days ago."

"Unfortunately, rulers like myself don't survive long," Eleanor told him.

"Rulers like you are the ones we need," Anrai said. "Most people go mad when they come into power, but not you. You're one of the few who can lead."

Eleanor turned to him again.

Anrai's tone was sincere. "No one really trusted me my entire life. I wasn't lying when I said that I'll fight for you and if needed, I'll even give my life. Not for Elliot Egercoll, not for Sophie Delamere—for you."

Eleanor's eyes watered and glanced up at the sky. "I feel that Felador is full of fear for the first time in many years. Many suspect what you've told me. They know that Walter will soon attack Wirskworth, and he'll destroy his enemies once and for all. They're afraid that once this battle is over, Thorn will send tyrants to plunder and rule places like Aquarine. The people of this land have put the worries of war behind them for years and now... now they're more afraid than ever. I want to do something for my people. We can't move forward living in fear," she said.

"Feasts have always been a good distraction for the people. I've heard that when Ricard Karford took Oldlands and sided with Walter, there were riots. Walter wanted to impose order by punishment and death, but Ricard suggested a feast—a feast to inaugurate the new governor. The banquet was so rich that it caught the attention of the common people. They were convinced that their land would become the richest in the kingdom and so, most chose to put everything behind them."

Brilliant. "This would be the perfect place for something like that," Eleanor said, staring at the fountain and its surroundings.

"The perfect place?" repeated the giant.

"Ricard's idea was smart. A feast to inaugurate the new governor will be a perfect distraction."

Anrai nodded with a smile, and Eleanor felt a familiar unease while looking at the giant man.

Is my decision to trust him wise?

The Army of the Cursed

A sea of red banners with white tigers in the centre rippled outside the city, held by the slaves standing amongst Walter's soldiers. The enemy army was out of arrow range, but too close for comfort. Thorn's men had drawn up massive siege towers, and they also had the largest battering ram Sophie had ever seen. She wondered if they'd survive the siege. Syrella had long believed that even if Walter managed to enter the city, it would take days for him to conquer them. However, now things had changed. If the news that the scout had brought was true, Walter's men would quickly invade Wirskworth. They had tried to fortify the city as best they could, but she wasn't sure if it would be enough.

Sophie thought over everything that had been tormenting her over the past few days. If a giant riding a wyvern was in Elmor, it meant that Elliot had set the Elder Races free. Nevertheless, no news of Elliot or his companions had arrived in the city, and no one knew what had become of Velhisya. They weren't expecting help from anywhere, and even the Guardians of the South hadn't appeared on the battlefield.

The giant that the scout saw may have been Anrai, and the Elder Races may still be imprisoned, she thought.

Sophie looked at Syrella standing nearby. The governor's face was determined. She'd ordered multiple groups of archers to man the tall towers that rose along Wirskworth's wall. They would be the first line of defence if they were attacked by a wyvern.

Sophie glanced at those who were standing around the majestic statue in the centre of the elevated portico of the Temple of the God of Souls;

they were at the middle layer of the city and the view outside the walls was clear. The Sharp Swords were frowning, and the lords who stood a little further off looked scared. The nobles of Iovbridge also looked pale and afraid of what was to follow. Only two faces seemed ready to fight. Linaria and Merhya were born for the battlefield.

"There are fewer of Thorn's men than there should be," came a whisper in her ear.

Sophie turned to Peter who had crept up quietly behind her. "What do you mean?" she asked.

"There aren't sixty thousand men down there. I spoke to all the captains. They agree with me. Even the high priest of Iovbridge told me it doesn't look like there are that many of the enemy's men!"

"Did you meet Jahon?" Sophie asked in a low voice.

The Lord of the Knights nodded. "He also told me that the enemy soldiers are fewer than he expected. Moreover, no one has seen either a wyvern, or a giant."

Sophie glanced at Syrella. The governor had spoken about what the scout had discussed with her during their councils. However, no other reports corroborated his words. Most of the officers and lords believed that the young scout was a foolish drunk who was trying to get attention.

"There's something I don't like about this," Peter whispered again. "The movements of Walter's men have been very strange over the last few days."

"How many times are you going to tell me this, Peter?"

The man looked distressed. "The scouts have been giving us detailed reports for some time until suddenly Thorn's men set up perimeters around the places they camped at. We haven't been able to verify a single piece of information for days! Some say they saw Walter's men travelling north, and then one scout speaks of a giant astride a wyvern."

"I know all of that already! The only thing that matters is that we come out of the siege alive."

"Walter is very clever. I'm sure this is all a tactic to somehow trick us...Where are the rest of his men? Why are there archers in his army? Where is Walter himself? I haven't seen his golden chariot yet!" Peter went on.

"I don't know!" Sophie snapped. "Do you want us to win the battle or to try and solve the mystery?"

Peter's face grew red. Syrella turned in Sophie's direction and walked briskly towards her.

"Thorn's men are too few," the governor said.

Sophie sighed. "Peter was telling me the very same thing a moment ago."

Syrella glanced at the Lord of the Knights. "Something's up," Peter told them.

"I wonder what they're waiting for," Sophie said. "Why don't they attack?"

A wrinkle formed on Peter's forehead. "They're waiting for the signal—a war horn."

Sophie looked at Walter's men beyond the wall who were about to lay siege to the ancient elven city. She felt that something wasn't quite right either. A humming noise reached her ears that she could have sworn was the wind, but the sound was slightly different. She searched for the source when a scream shook the air. Sophie looked up, and her heart stopped. A black monster tore through the air, flying directly at her.

"RUN!"

A hand pushed her. She fell to the ground as a wing full of thorns knocked down the statue of the God of Souls.

"RUN TO MOONSTONE!" Syrella's scream echoed as the wyvern flew at her again.

Peter pulled Sophie back, and the monster's tail severed one of Elmor's lords in half. On the wyvern's back was a giant shouting in an unknown language.

"Sophie, run!" Peter grabbed her hand, and they ran through the mayhem.

Thousands of war horns sounded battle, and pain shot up Sophie's leg as she fled. Peter pushed aside anyone he could, pulling her towards the stairs. They made it through the portico and hurried down the stairs. A roar pierced her ears. Sophie turned round and saw the wyvern beating the entrance to the temple with its clawed feet, tearing it apart, while men and women ran for their lives.

"Syrella!" Sophie's voice was drowned out in all the commotion. Out of the corner of her eye she saw the governor running as her daughters supported her between them.

Peter yanked her forward, and they continued away from the wyvern amid screams and shrieks of terror. The man hurried through the labyrinthine, narrow streets of the city until a stone staircase filled with soldiers stood in front of them. Sophie followed the steps upwards to the wall.

"We have to go to Moonstone! We'll be safe there," Sophie said.

Peter looked north, and she followed his gaze. The wyvern was near the road leading to the castle.

"We can't turn back. We have to climb up onto the wall. We can hide in that tower." Peter pointed to a stone building on their right.

"Take cover!" a voice suddenly screamed before Sophie had a chance to make a decision.

Sophie saw a black tail coming towards her. A heartbeat later, Peter pulled her close, and the monster destroyed a part of the stairwell, dismembering dozens of men.

"We need guards. We need help!" Peter's voice was overtaken by fear.

"What can they do against a wyvern?" Sophie asked, trying to get up.

"Keep running!" Syrella appeared behind them out of nowhere with her daughters.

"Quick!" Linaria screamed.

Sophie grabbed Peter's hand again and started running. They moved down the stairs quickly, heading for the lower levels of Wirskworth. Sophie looked behind her. She felt panic—the wyvern was pursuing them while countless people fled around them. They had to run as fast as they could, or they'd be swept away by the crowd. A few arrows streaked above their heads as a handful of archers tried to wound the monster.

"Archers! Loose!"

Another shower of arrows flew through the air, and she heard the wyvern roar. She continued running alongside Peter, pushing through the pain in her leg. A shadow fell over her, and she and Peter fell to the ground. The wyvern was about to attack when an arrow hit its rider in the left foot. The giant screamed, and the monster rose up into the sky.

"Don't stop!" Syrella got ahead of her.

Sophie scrambled to her feet and followed with Peter by her side. Cries and voices rang out all around them as they tried to escape. Suddenly, Sophie slipped on the smooth ground, but Peter caught her elbow and held her upright. They continued for a while until a crowd of countless people appeared before them.

"What's happening?"

"We're at the lowest level of the city near the gate." Peter's voice was muffled.

Sophie was overcome with terror—hundreds of soldiers stood in front of them. People jostled her and pushed against her. The crowd shoved them forward while the soldiers behind the gate kept up their resistance against Walter's men.

"Make room for the governor!" Linaria and Merhya screamed.

"MAKE ROOM FOR THE QUEEN" Blood rushed through Peter's face as he tried to be heard.

A roar covered the voices, and the wyvern charged at the crowd. A dozen swords tried to strike it but in vain.

"Take cover!"

Sophie crouched on the ground and hordes of people scattered in all directions. The monster flipped through the air and lashed out with its tail, dismembering men and women. A dozen soldiers aimed their bows at the wyvern from a tower on the wall. The arrows hit the monster's torso and it turned with a roar, ready to strike again. The wyvern's wings beat against the air as it rose up and then another flurry of arrows shot towards its body.

"Stop, idiots! You're going to hit your governor!" Merhya shouted and then the wyvern let out a howl of pain.

Sophie saw an arrow protruding from its eye socket. The monster rose into the air in a circular motion until it disappeared from her sight. Then, a sound like thunder shook the air.

"What was that?" Sophie asked.

"Walter's men are ramming the gate! We have to get back to Moonstone!" Peter cried.

"No! It's too dangerous. The monster will kill us before we get there!" Syrella shouted.

"If we stay here, it'll definitely kill us!" Peter protested.

Syrella looked at the gate to Wirskworth. "We must climb up the wall and hide in a tower."

"No! Not on the wall above the gate! The siege towers will soon bring Walter's men up there." Peter's face had gone red again.

"If we stay here, we'll be trampled by the hordes. The crowd in front of us is smaller than that behind us. We can't go anywhere else!" the governor retorted.

Sophie looked behind her. "Syrella's right."

"It's too dangerous," said Peter.

"It's impossible to make it back to Moonstone with so many people behind us. Even if we could, I'd rather climb up to a tower on the wall than run to the castle with a wyvern chasing me!"

"If Walter's siege towers get close to the city wall above the gate, we'll run down the corridor behind the ramparts. From there, we'll be able to get back down into the city again and find cover," Syrella said.

Peter cursed but nodded sharply.

"MAKE ROOM FOR THE GOVERNOR AND THE QUEEN. MAKE ROOM!" Linaria's voice drowned out the screams of the soldiers and the crowd who began to create a small opening.

"My lady! Why are you here?" asked a soldier standing next to Syrella.

"It doesn't ... matter, I ... have to ... climb up ... onto the wall," Syrella panted through her gasping breaths.

The man nodded and shouted orders. The crowd parted, and Sophie and Peter hurried after Syrella. A moment later, they reached an undamaged stone staircase. They started climbing quickly, and Sophie felt a pain in her right knee. She was sure she'd been wounded, and the hundreds of steps tired her. Sweat dripped from her forehead as she walked behind Linaria. Syrella and Merhya led the way, and Peter was just behind her. Sophie was out of breath but managed to make it to the corridor behind the wall's ramparts. Men rushed around, barking orders while outside the city, three siege towers were closing in on them.

"Take aim at the men who are dragging the towers! Loose!"

Sophie saw a dozen arrows find their targets, and a few of Walter's men fell to the ground. A handful of enemy soldiers ran behind the towers, grabbed the ropes, and began dragging the massive structures again. Sophie heard a loud sound and looked to the west. Thousands of soldiers were outside the gate, holding the battering ram. Peter tugged Sophie's arm, and she followed him.

"MAKE ROOM, THE GOVERNOR IS PASSING!"

The archers stepped aside, and Sophie walked up behind Syrella. Soon after, she found herself in a stone tower full of arrows and swords resting here and there.

"DROP THE OIL," came an unknown voice.

Sophie saw Syrella and her daughters watching from the windows of the tower, and she hastened to their side. She may have been high up, but she could hear the screams of the enemy's men as hot oil seared their flesh. A few yards away from the wall outside of Wirskworth, thousands of the enemy's soldiers waited for the gate to fall so that they could attack inside the city walls.

"We can hold them back," Linaria said.

"If the wyvern attacks again, we've no hope," Peter told her.

"That scout wasn't foolish after all," Syrella said.

"Why are you here?" someone yelled.

Sophie saw Jahon standing at the entrance to the tower.

"The wyvern attacked us in the temple and the crowd drove us to the gate," Syrella said.

"I told you to stay in Moonstone! Why did you want to go to the damn temple?" Jahon shot, worry and anger warring on his face.

"My city is under attack! From the temple I could get a clear view over every part of Wirsk—"

"We knew a wyvern might attack the city!"

"Up until yesterday, you kept on saying the scout was a fool!"

"Enough!" cried Peter. "If this monster attacks again, the gate will fall."

"Then, I will die beside my men!" Syrella walked towards the entrance of the tower, pushed Jahon aside, and yelled, "POUR THE OIL! BURN THEM ALIVE!"

Sophie saw the golden snakes adorning the wall ooze a thick liquid and death screams reached her ears.

"TAKE COVER!"

Peter's voice was drowned out by the loudest sound she'd ever heard. The wall shook, and Sophie hit the ground, her head nearly hitting the stones.

"Run to the gate! Help the guards to keep the enemy out of the city!"

Sophie heard cries through the ringing in her ears, but she couldn't understand what had happened. Someone lifted her to her feet, and she saw Linaria's face in front of her.

"What happened?" Sophie asked.

"The wyvern... It came out of nowhere and pounded the gate."

Sophie started coughing and stumbled out of the tower. The huge gate had been breached and the wyvern was rising into the sky from within the city. Enemy soldiers were trying to enter Wirskworth while Elmor's men attempted to stop them. She turned to the right and looked out over the wall. Walter's men were leaving the siege towers and running towards the battered gate. A dozen archers were taking aim at the wyvern.

"You'll hit our men!" Sophie saw Jahon yelling orders.

Somebody grabbed her shoulder. "We have to run along the length of the wall. If we stay here, we'll die!" Peter shouted.

"We're already dead," Merhya said as she stood next to Linaria, blood streaming from her forehead.

"Watch out!" came a voice and Sophie saw the wyvern rising in front of her as it opened its huge wings.

"COME HERE, YOU FUCKING MONSTER!" Horrified, she saw Syrella, bow in hand, taking aim at the wyvern.

The monster roared. An arrow still protruded from its left eye socket. If Syrella managed to hit its other eye as well, they might win.

"SYRELLA, RUN!"

Jahon ran towards the governor as the wyvern opened its huge jaws, ready to attack. Syrella screamed as death prepared to embrace her, and a blue light hit the monster in the face. The wyvern shrieked as another beam of light hit its body. The monster took off into the sky, and Sophie searched for the source of the light. Thousands of armoured horsemen stood arrayed in never-ending lines along the rocky hillsides to the east of the city, their horses prancing impatiently and the light seemed to emanate from objects in their hands. Hope had at long last arrived and Sophie felt her spirits rise.

"Soldiers to the west!" yelled a man.

"There are more to the east!"

Sophie looked to the left, but she couldn't see them.

"Who are they?" Syrella stumbled to Sophie's side, out of breath.

"They're holding the banner of the sun. They're the Guardians of Stonegate!" Jahon shouted, looking west.

"If the Guardians of Stonegate are in the west, who is in the east?" Syrella asked.

Sophie was filled with unexpected courage—a courage she didn't remember ever having before. "It's Elliot, and at his side is the army of the cursed."

Elliot raised the Sword of Light and threw a look at Alaric and Alysia at his left. Their red and blue blades seemed to shine under the light of the sun. "It will be an honour to die by your side," Elliot told them.

"We will not die today!" screamed Aleron, and with a cry, Elliot flicked his horse's reins.

They charged at Thorn's men as dozens of arrows headed their way. Elliot bent forward as he heard shouts coming from the enemy soldiers. They weren't expecting them to be on horseback. He raised his head and saw Walter's men trying to line up alongside the archers while the riders of Stonegate joined the fray along with a thousand elves. Elliot neared a group of spearmen. He smiled as he snapped his horse's reins. The destrier threw its head down and streaked past Walter's men like a tornado, knocking them down before they could raise their spears at his horse. Dirt filled the air, but Elliot saw a sword aimed at his right foot.

The Sword of Light flashed, and the enemy's head was detached from his shoulders. He turned and struck two more soldiers in one go. His sword tore through the air, striking anyone within range. A man on horseback sidled up to him. Elliot ducked and dodged the sword while his horse whinnied. The enemy readied for another attack, and Elliot slid his sword into his mouth. Then, a horse fell onto his with force and knocked him off the saddle.

Elliot stood up in a sweeping motion, his horse darting away, and saw a spear coming his way. He jumped out of range, and found a sword aimed for his neck. He raised the Sword of Light, but a red blade tore through his enemy's throat. Alaric winked at him and charged back into the thick of the fray, severing the legs of countless soldiers with masterful moves.

Suddenly, a sword sped towards his chest, but he blocked it, and struck down the swordsman.

Returning to the fighting around him, Elliot let out a cry and raced across the battlefield, striking down Walter's men. Dirt and blood coated his face as he swung and sliced through a man's neck before he could raise his weapon. A horse thundered towards him, and he cut off its front legs with a bellow. The horse fell to the ground screaming, and with a thrust of his sword, he impaled its rider in the neck.

Panting, Elliot scanned the roiling mass of combat around him. Elwyn and elves fought anyone in their path while Walter's men shouted orders trying to line up. He caught sight of a huge man clad in black running towards a short figure. He ran towards Alysia as The Ghost brought his sword down towards her head. Elliot managed to pull her out of its way, and the sword hit the ground. The man raised his sword again with a yell, and Elliot was preparing to defend himself when Alysia darted behind the Ghost and stuck her sword into the back of his right leg. The Ghost howled, and Elliot rammed his sword into his armpit between the plates of his armour.

Someone shoved him to the side, and he fell to the ground. He got to his feet quickly and saw another Ghost in black armour covering his entire body. Elliot dodged a thrust of his enemy's blade and tried to find weak spots in his armour. The Ghost attacked again, and Elliot parried it. He was about to strike his enemy in the back of the legs, but his opponent made a quick strike. Elliot dodged the sword and hit the Ghost in the chest, trying to push him away. His sword pierced through the steel breastplate and blood poured down the black armour. He couldn't believe his eyes—*Aznarin and Thindor's tears.*

"Retreat! Retreat!" The voice made him turn, and he saw the enemy horde riding away from the battlefield.

He looked to the right. A man on horseback rode towards him. He prepared to defend himself when he noticed a red-and-black sun on the cloak. The Guardian raised his sword and stopped his horse.

It was Jarin, the Guardian Commander. "We've hammered them," he said.

"We must help with the battle at the gate," Elliot said. He saw a Ghost on a horse charge at them. Jarin made a sudden move, swung his sword around, and struck his helmet. The Ghost fell from his horse, and Elliot brought his sword down onto his chest. The tip pierced the steel breastplate, and the Ghost let out a death rattle. Elliot mounted the Ghost's horse, and Jarin yelled. A few dozen men followed his signal.

Elliot rode past elves and elwyn killing Walter's soldiers across the battlefield. He searched for the gate, and he saw the battle at the entrance to Wirskworth. His horse galloped behind Jarin and a few more Guardians when a huge creature attacked them from the side. Elliot ducked to avoid the wyvern's tail, and he saw Adur in the distance.

"YOU'RE GOING TO DIE, EGERCOLL!" The giant's scream was so loud, it echoed across the battlefield.

The wyvern swooped at him when a red light hit it in the face. Changing course, the monster prepared to attack again when blue and red light hit it in the chest. The wyvern roared and Adur screamed as he tried to control it. Elliot neared the gate, and the wyvern followed, trying to bite him. He turned his horse away from the Guardians and charged towards the city wall.

Come and get me!

He pulled on the reins with his left hand and raised his sword in the air. He could feel the monster's giant jaws at his back as the wall came ever closer. He heard Adur's voice and braced himself for the clash when a blue light blinded him. Elliot fell from his horse, and a thunderous sound shook everything. He spat out the dirt that had entered his mouth and rubbed his eyes. His vision came back into focus, and he saw the Sword of Light by his foot. A little further away, his horse was slumped against the wall dead. A roar made him turn to the right. The wyvern writhed on the ground while a huge form lay a few yards away from it.

Elliot grabbed his sword and started running towards Adur until he was by his side. He knew that the giant might kill him, but he didn't care. Adur's face was covered in dirt and blood, his wide eyes looking at the sky. His body twitched as he struggled to breathe. Elliot wanted to help him. He didn't want him to die. He flung his sword aside and tried to raise Adur's heavy head. The giant's convulsions became more intense. Colliding with the wall must have shattered many of his and his wyvern's bones. Elliot looked at the city wall; it was intact. He knew that any other city wall should have been destroyed by that hit, but Wirskworth had one of the strongest and thickest walls in the world.

"You can't save him."

Elliot turned and saw Aleron dismounting his horse. The elwyn approached Adur, and the giant looked into his starry-blue eyes.

"Aiora... Aiora..." The words came out in a whisper.

Aleron leaned over him and stroked his face with tears in his eyes. "You'll meet her now and nothing will ever come between you ever again."

The giant closed his eyes, and his body convulsed one last time. Elliot heard his breathing trail off, and Adur's eyes stared into space, unable to see anymore. A bellow made him turn, and the wyvern raised its head towards the sky. Then, it fell to the ground with a loud thud.

Elliot looked at Adur's lifeless body and the dead wyvern, and a tear rolled down his cheek. He knew they'd won the battle, but that wasn't enough to alleviate his pain.

Elliot walked with Aleron while elwyn, elves, and Guardians followed them. Several areas around the Wirskworth gate had been destroyed. Men and women ran in different directions, trying to help the wounded. Elliot looked around, praying that Sophie and Syrella were alive. Most of Walter's men were dead while only a few of them had retreated.

"Elliot!"

He saw Sophie standing next to Peter Brau. A little further off was Syrella, her daughters, and General Jahon.

"I can't believe you did it! You set the Elder Races free!" Sophie was out of breath.

Elliot walked over and hugged her tightly, and her arms tightened around him.

"How did you get to Wirskworth without anyone noticing?" Syrella asked.

"We rode behind the mountain range the city is built on. There we found the Guardians of the South hidden among the trees. We arrived last night. Had we come any closer to Wirskworth you would have known we were here. However, Walter's men would have seen us, and the Guardians insisted that we not lose the element of surprise. We also expected that the giant and wyvern had sided with Thorn, and we didn't know whether they'd be patrolling Elmor. We had to remain hidden," Elliot explained.

"What took you so long to attack?" Syrella asked.

"We were waiting for the right moment. We wanted the enemy soldiers to be distracted."

"None of this matters. Where is Walter? Why wasn't he on the battlefield? Where are the rest of his men?" Peter asked.

"I was wondering about that, too. That wasn't sixty thousand men," Aleron said.

Elliot had no answers and he looked at Aleron. A strange sense of foreboding overwhelmed him. Something wasn't right, but he couldn't figure out what it was. His instinct told him something terrible had happened.

The Scarlet Feast

Joy filled Eleanor as she looked at the crowd that had gathered together in the gardens of Aquarine. The common people of Felador had tried to spruce themselves up as best they could. Countless stalls had been set up along the length of the gardens, and soon food and wine would be served. The majestic fountain seemed to sparkle in the sunlight.

"Your dress is magnificent, Lady Alarie," Eleanor said looking at the red silk outfit draping the lady's body.

Iris Alarie turned towards her, startled. "Thank you," she replied.

"Will Solor not honour us with his presence?" Eleanor asked.

The lady frowned. "He told me he'd be late. He's gone with some men to inspect his crops," she said.

Eleanor scoffed. "I know he thinks Anrai is a spy. I'm sure he's looking for Walter's soldiers on our land..."

Iris wasn't expecting that measure of honesty. "These are dangerous times. We must be careful."

"I agree. Nevertheless, you ought to have more trust in my judgment since you chose me as governor." The woman didn't answer. "I hope you enjoy the feast, Lady Alarie."

Iris curtsied sharply and walked away. Eleanor looked at her back in dismay. Now, she could sympathise with Sophie—ruling was undoubtedly hard work.

"You look beautiful, Lady Dilerion." She turned and found Andrian standing next to her, smiling. "I would never have expected you to arrange for a feast in such times."

"I told you before, Andrian. People need distractions; otherwise, they remain steeped in fear about everything going on in the kingdom."

"I agree. Yours was an excellent idea. Now, I have to find some of that delicious beef I tasted earlier." The high priest bowed and left hastily.

Eleanor wandered towards the fountain, her spirits lighter than they had been since becoming governor. As time went by, the more convinced she became that the feast was truly what Felador needed. The lords had mentioned it had been decades since there had been a banquet in Aquarine. She had made sure that all the people of Felador were informed of the event, even the villagers outside the city. Most happily agreed to attend and thus, Aquarine was buzzing with life. She looked intently at the waters of the fountain and the statue of the First King of Felador. It was built on a flat plinth surrounded by ornate lion heads with jets of water shooting out. Eleanor looked closer at the streams spewing from the beasts' mouths, the sun's rays turning them a crimson hue.

"The idea of having a feast was not a bad one after all. The people of Felador seem happy."

Anrai came towards her dressed in woollen clothes and a huge green cloak. "Perhaps you could give me more ideas in the future," said Eleanor.

The giant laughed. Eleanor took one more look at the fountain. Despite her happiness, a slew of uneasy thoughts clouded her mind. Walter would attack Wirskworth soon, if he hadn't done so already, and everyone she loved might die in that battle. She thought of Sophie, Elliot, Selwyn, and John.

Eleanor stared at the waters, the sounds of the celebration growing distant. *Are they alright? Did they accomplish their missions?* she thought.

"You look troubled," Anrai said. "I know what you're thinking... Walter is going to attack Elmor soon, and he may kill your friends."

Eleanor sighed, hands clasped together in front of her.

"I hope your friends survive."

She was about to glare at him and rebuke him, but she didn't. Deep inside of her she knew that Anrai had changed, and that his life hadn't been easy. He was trying his best to be better.

A thunderous sound shattered her thoughts, and Eleanor almost fell to the ground. "What was that?" she asked, heart pounding.

The giant looked scared, turning his gaze towards the Castle of Knowledge. "I don't know."

The laughter of the feast's guests stopped and worried conversations circulated around them. A new sound echoed through the gardens, and Eleanor headed towards the castle quickly. The third sound was the loudest, and screams reached Eleanor's ears, causing her to break out into a sprint.

"WE'RE UNDER ATTACK! WE'RE UNDER ATTACK. RUN!"

A soldier ran towards the gardens, out of breath as he shouted.

"We've got to leave. We've got to get out of the city," Anrai said.

"Do you know who's attacking us?" she asked.

Anrai's face had turned white. "No, but I've seen the extent of the guard of Aquarine. Anyone could take over this city without much trouble. I won't let you die."

"I have to stay with the peop—" A scream cut her off.

A black monster flew through the sky and descended towards the ground with a roar. Everyone was screaming. Anrai grabbed her by the hand, and they started running in the opposite direction. The wyvern bellowed, and Eleanor reached the wall surrounding the huge fountain. She thought of jumping into the water but decided to turn back—her eyes swept over the scene before her and she was confronted with her worst nightmare.

Thousands of soldiers had entered the city, killing anyone they encountered while the wyvern tore through human flesh with its teeth. She saw people running and screaming while the gardens next to the fountain had turned red.

"THE GATE HAS FALLEN. THE GATE HAS FALLEN. THE MONSTER HAS DESTROYED IT. RUN!"

Panicked voices pierced the air, and Eleanor turned to Anrai. She desperately searched for ideas of what she could do, but nothing came to her mind.

The giant's face was determined. "We must find a way out."

"How?" Eleanor asked.

A roar caused them to whirl around, and they saw the wyvern flying a few yards above their heads. Eleanor noticed the man sitting on its back for the first time. Walter Thorn was looking down on them with obvious hatred.

"I never expected you would betray me, Anrai," Walter shouted.

"YOU BETRAYED ME! YOU ORDERED ME TO KILL THE LAST OF MY RACE. MY OWN FLESH AND BLOOD!" Anrai roared.

"I didn't know you were a coward! I killed my own father to save the kingdom!"

"The giants did no harm, not to you nor to the kingdom. You wanted to kill them because you were afraid of them. YOU'RE A COWARD!"

"TRAITOR!"

Eleanor's rage blazed within her. "YOU'RE THE TRAITOR! ONE DAY YOU'LL DIE AND ELLIOT WILL SIT ON THE THRONE. ONE DAY ELLIOT WILL TAKE EVERYTHING AWAY FROM YOU!"

The wyvern turned so quickly that Eleanor barely had time to see its tail coming towards her. She was flung back, and her flesh tore as she fell into the water. She tried to take a breath, but couldn't. Pain ripped through her insides like knives as she tried to swim to the surface. The spikes in the wyvern's tail had ripped through her chest and stomach, and Orhyn Shadow had begun to take effect. She knew she would die quickly. Her wounds were too deep. Water filled her lungs, and her eyes began to close. The vortex embraced her, enveloping her in endless darkness, and then she felt something touching her hand.

She mustered all her strength to open her eyelids one last time. The bottom of the fountain drew closer, and then she saw Anrai holding her hand, his chest spurting blood. She squeezed it with all the strength she had left and smiled. She was glad she wasn't alone as she let the darkness envelop her—glad she'd have company on her journey to the kingdoms of the dead.

Walter didn't know how long he'd been in the air. Aquarine was burning to the ground below, and the flames filled him with satisfaction. He had no idea what had happened in Wirskworth, but something told him that he'd achieved his goal. *All the giants must be dead by now*, he thought.

Anrai had breathed his last, and his enemies might have killed Adur. He glanced up at the night sky, lit up by the fiery spirits. If Adur was dead, that meant Walter was now the only sentient being with Orhyn Shadow—the power of Zhilor—in his blood.

Time passed and Phobos flapped his wings. Leonhard's words echoed in Walter's mind. He was undoubtedly the most valuable man he had by his side.

Was Leonhard right this time? Was the forgotten legend true?

Walter had decided to wait in the air above the ruined city. He knew that his men might have been defeated in Elmor, but he didn't care. The sacrifice of thirty thousand soldiers was insignificant considering what he'd set out to achieve, and he felt that his plan hadn't failed. He carried on watching the flames consuming the city until a roar brought him out of his reverie.

He raised his head and saw black masses approaching quickly. Phobos' wings beat the air as two dozen wyverns surrounded them. The black monsters flew around Walter, and he felt invincible, as if nothing could stand in his way. He was the strongest man in existence endowed with the power of the gods.

"The only person who can bond with *all* the wyverns is the last one to be left in the world with the power of Zhilor in his blood," he whispered, the words of the forgotten legend Leonhard believed in so strongly. Adur and Anrai were dead. He might have sacrificed half of his soldiers but he had succeeded in killing the last giants and now the whole clan of wyverns would submit to his will forever.

Destroy everything.

The thought flooded his mind, and the wyverns roared through the air. They turned towards Aquarine and descended upon the city.

Walter stroked Phobos' hide. *How fitting that the last being with the power of the God of Death should be me and not a giant.*

From Gregory Kontaxis

If you enjoyed this story, please consider leaving a review on Amazon. It would mean so much to me. And if you are on Goodreads, would you share your thoughts with friends and followers?

You can also find all of my latest writing news, a free novella of the Dance of Light series, interactive maps, and much more on my website at www.gregorykontaxis.com.

About the Author

Gregory Kontaxis was born in Athens. He studied Informatics and Finance in Greece and the United Kingdom, and he has worked as a Financial Analyst in Vienna and London. He currently resides in London, where he busies himself with investment risk management and writing. *The Return of the Knights* is the first book of his pentalogy, *The Dance of Light*.